SIMON ...

PAPER TRAIL

Imprimata

Published by **Imprimata**

A CIP Catalogue record for this book is available
from the British Library

ISBN 978-1-906192-17-4

Set in 10.5pt Adobe Caslon Pro with InDCS3

Printed in Great Britain

Imprimata

Imprimata Publishers Limited
50 Albemarle Street, London W1S 4BD.

To Jeanette.

Contents

Ulysses,

"…Prerogative of age, crowns, sceptres, laurels,
But by degree, stand in authentic place?
Take but degree away, untune that string,
And, hark, what discord follows!….'

Troilus and Cressida, 1,3.

William Shakespeare.

Acknowledgments

Being a complete novice in the novel writing business, I felt it necessary to ask several friends and relations to look over draft attempts of what follows so that I might gain some reassurance that all was not in vain. They have been most generous, and without exception have been positive and encouraging. I would like to take this opportunity to express my gratitude to them.

It was Sue Campbell who first pointed me in the 'right' direction, warning me about the dangers of evangelising, and advising me to make sure the story stood up on its own, regardless of the 'authorship' issue. My friend and one-time teaching colleague, Alan Geary, proof-read one of the earliest drafts, and made constructive suggestions which I haven't forgotten. Elizabeth Imlay, chair of the De Vere Society, has been most generous in proof reading what became, virtually, the final draft, and I'm indebted to her for the patience she showed as I slaved over half a dozen alternative openings - The one between these covers definitely works!

My four step-sons have given me unstinting encouragement, and their insights and incisive comments boosted my confidence after refusal letters from agents and publishers started to flutter down onto my doormat. So to Ian and Mark, but, even more so, John and Peter, whom I dragged in from very early on, many, many thanks. Finally to my wife, Jeanette, who can now have her husband back. She had complete faith in me from the start, and, several times when I was prepared to throw in the towel, assured me that it was a good story to tell, and that I owed it to myself to see it through. We were both surprised how quickly the tale resolved itself, and the right characters seemed to take up their roles so effortlessly, but, as I suspected, the devil turned out to be in the detail, and she had to watch me, hunched over my computer for another twelve months sorting out the glitches. I am not the giving-in type, she knows it, and my gratitude to her speaks for itself.

Simon Fry, Ebrington, 2008

Author's note:

Please note the following variation in spelling takes place at various times throughout the novel: William Shakspere refers to the businessman from Stratford-upon-Avon. William Shakespeare refers to the playwright and poet active in London.

Prologue

LOSS

Helena,

'…What power is it which mounts my love so high,
That makes me see, and cannot feed mine eye?….'

All's Well That Ends Well, 1,1.

William Shakespeare.

'….Two…three…four…'

'Oh! My lord, you strike *le ore con il campanile grande di* Sant' Eduard!' Squealed Virginia in sheer delight.

Oxford gripped her even more fervently '…five…six… seven…' he chimed.

Suddenly, she struggled to raise her face and head from the pillow. '*La porta,* my lord, *la porta. Qualcuno bussa.* Somebody is at the door!'

'God in heaven, woman! - would you have me moderate the spirit of Apollo - pah!…Eight…nine…'

'Shh! Shh! There. *Ancora,* Eduard. Again, I hear it.'

The unmistakable sound of knuckles rapping on the apartment door grew louder and more urgent. 'My lord. My lord.' Came an impotent wail from the other side.

'Who in God's name?' shouted the Earl. 'Declare yourself.'

'It is I. Your obedient servant Nathaniel, my lord.'

'Away man, away. The *Bucintoro* ploughs majestically up the Grand Canal, and its journey will not be interrupted!'

'But, but - forgive me, my lord, for our gentle hosts do dispose of all your goods; they are being cast down as I speak, and are strewn all about the courtyard.'

A dishevelled, sweaty, and hastily dressed Edward de Vere, the Seventeenth Earl of Oxford, still fighting to stuff himself into his codpiece, tore open the door. A startled and embarrassed Nathaniel Baxter, the Earl's manservant, bowed quickly, and stood aside as his master charged out like a bull onto the landing.

He stopped and spun round. Back through the open doorway, he blew a kiss to the naked Virginia Padoana, his personal courtesan. From her bed, half kneeling, half spread-eagled, she poked her tongue out at him and grinned. He continued to lace-up his hose. 'These girls of Italy, Nathaniel,' he panted, 'take heed of them!'

He flew down the dark, narrow flight of steps from her first floor apartment, and out into the already sun-drenched Campo di San Geremia. Nathaniel struggled to keep up as Oxford rudely barged his way through the early morning crowds in his eagerness to get to the Palazzo Magretti-Bellini half a mile away, and hopefully, avert a disaster.

Despite the apparently dissolute life he had been living during his ten month stay in Italy, Oxford kept himself supremely fit, and looked younger than his twenty-five years. So, in less than ten minutes after he had been lapping up Virginia Padoana's favours, he was able to reach the palazzo, just past the Ca' d'Oro, on the north bank of the Grand Canal.

He had spent with a profligacy that beggared belief as he toured Italy, lavishing a small fortune on his greatest passion: Italian *alta moda*. But now he stared in horror through the ornate courtyard doorway as his precious silks and brocades were tossed from the first floor balcony. His extensive collection of dresses, hats, doublets and hose, capes, gloves, underwear and the rest were all of the finest quality, but now they lay with the rest of his personal belongings in an untidy heap, or were strewn about the high-walled *cortile*.

He felt violated, and was apoplectic with rage. From the balcony, Lorenzo di Magretti-Bellini, the head of the family, poured down a torrent of scorn and insults at Oxford, who gave back as good as he got. However, Lorenzo's armed guards were not allowing him to set as much as a toe on the stairs that led up to the first floor entrance; he wasn't being allowed entry to either the palazzo, or the private apartment which had been his temporary home during his stay in Venice.

The Earl's increasingly extravagant behaviour had pushed

tolerance of him to the limit. His wayward sexual habits, continued absences, and refusal to pay his rent - now a monstrous debt - proved to be three last straws. They were finally kicking him out.

Preparations for a carnival ball to be held the following day, March the sixth, and last day of Carnivale, were almost complete. As Oxford got down on his hands and knees to start gathering up his beloved garments, a group of artists trampled over them to get to the stairs: it was Giovanni Battista Zelotti and his crew. They were taking a day off from working on the *Palazzo Ducale*, to deliver several huge cartoons for a new series of frescoes, commissioned by Lorenzo. The coloured drawings, which to the untutored eye appeared to be finished paintings, would take pride of place among the decorations. Eventually they would become the crowning glory of the portego on the secundo piano nobile. But there was no place in the celebrations, no 'ticket to the ball' for the *'Inglese Italianato'* - Lorenzo and his family didn't want Oxford showing off at their annual do.

Nathaniel got down on his hands and knees to assist Oxford in gathering up, and then separating and folding the mass of ostentatious and brightly coloured garments. A small crowd, made up of the family and their domestic staff, gathered on the balcony. They laughed and jeered at the sight of England's second most premier earl down on all fours like a dog, and yapped and barked at him. William Lewin, another of Oxford's servants, who had previously been busy organising the small flotilla of gondolas necessary to get them and their baggage over to the mainland, came along to help - but Oxford had another important job for him to do.

'Go quickly and fetch Orazio, Will,' said Oxford, 'I can't possibly leave without him. You know the house?'

'Aye my lord, but what of his parents, will they not disapprove?'

'They have given their blessing, Will. They are certain the experience of England will add greatly to his improvement. I spoke with them only yesterday; they said there is rumour of plague again, and believe he will be safer in England too. He is a dutiful boy and sings sweetly - he will make good company on our journey - mark my words. Hurry now!'

'My lord,' he said, bowed, and left up the short fondamenta to the Strada Nuova, the main thoroughfare through the *sestiere* of Cannaregio. The Cuoco family lived about a mile away in Castello, close to the Greek Church where Oxford had worshipped. William knew that his master's desire was for rather more than just listening to the fifteen year old's sweet singing, but he felt pretty sure that the choirboy was mature enough to take care of himself. Time would tell.

Six of the gondolas had already left, and now the last two eased away from the short flight of steps opposite the courtyard door. They made off sedately along the palazzo-walled corridor of the Rio di Magretti that led to the Grand Canal. The gentle splash and splosh of the oars yielded to the haughty tones of Oxford, as he went through an inventory of his goods.

'Which boat has my writing-box and papers, Nathaniel?' he said.

'I haven't seen them, my lord,' he answered, and called across to the other gondola. 'Will, do you have my lord's writings and his document-box?'

'We have only boxes of my lord's garments, and our own belongings, Nat. I've not seen my lord's stationery, or his box.'

Oxford looked up at the palazzo and the jeering and gesticulating gentry leaning out of every window. 'Damn it, Nathaniel - it's all still in there,' he said. As soon as they were on the Grand Canal, he ordered the gondolier to turn left across the façade of the Palazzo, and called up to the group waving out of the first floor loggia. 'My writings. My poetries,' he implored.

'Non li capisco, inglese!' Came the mocking response.

'Le mie scritture, la mia poesia, e la mia scatola di scrittura,' he shouted.

The glare from the palazzo's elaborate Gothic façade, combined with the flickering light that skipped off the water, was blinding in its intensity. He looked over to Orazio. Like an indolent Adonis posing for a masterwork in oil or marble, he lay sprawled across his seat to the rear of the boat. He too shielded his eyes from the midday sun. A few moments later, a shower of paper fluttered down like oversized confetti, to settle on the murky green water.

'*Qui*, il mio signore, *nuotate per le vostre carte!*' They sneered.

'Swim for them yourselves!' he said; but he knew arguing was not going to get him anywhere, and told the gondolier to turn about. 'The Brenta, and make good speed,' he said, 'I want to be at the Villa Foscari before nightfall'.

Part One

Goneril ,

"…Beyond what can be valued, rich or rare,
No less than life, with grace, health, beauty, honour,
As much as child e'er loved, or father found,
A love that makes breath poor, and speech unable,…"

King Lear, 1,1.

William Shakespeare.

1

'If I hear someone say - "Well don't start something you can't finish" just one more time...'

'Leave it out Randy, you love every second of it; and I bet you've got your next talent show planned for the poor suckers already - am I right, or am I right?'

'I'm not saying it can't be a lot of fun, Eddie, but you want to try sitting through hours and hours of wannabes and nevergonnabes day in day out, week after...'

'Quick, pass me one of those napkins would you pal?' said Eddie, pulling open his jacket, 'look - my heart's bleeding already!' With the self-congratulatory laugh of someone who can never get enough of their own jokes, he downed a good half of his third G and T. 'And I'd bet my pension - if I had one - that your accountant isn't mopping up many of *your* tears.'

Randy picked up his Bourbon and Dry, but before it reached his lips he was alerted by a call on his mobile. He checked the screen and smiled, welcoming the interruption. 'Hi! Pumpkin,' he said.

'Hi! Daddy.' It was his daughter, Bianca, updating him on her travels from somewhere in Europe.

'Where are you, Darling?'

'We're on a TGV heading south. Jess says we have just gone past Lyons! Daddy, Jess had a call from Tony a few minutes ago and he says he can't make it.'

'That's bit of a god damn nuisance. Did he say why?'

There was a short delay while Jessica told Bianca why her

boyfriend would be missing the trip to the Venice Carnivale. 'He's got to go to a trade fair in Manchester. Things are going belly-up with his suppliers in China or something. We'll be OK, Daddy.'

'I'll ring the Cowells and get them to pick you up from the station. Nice crawls with paps and I don't want to see you splashed all over *Hello* or anything else if we can help it.' He took a welcome drink from the heavy squat tumbler. 'Tony can't even make it just for the weekend then?'

Bianca looked at her friend, who shook her head and shrugged her shoulders. 'Doesn't look like it,' she said.

'I'd prefer someone else to be there. I would be much happier.'

'Oh, Daddy. You're fussing too much. I've got Jess, and Angelo is living in isn't he? We'll be OK.'

'Give me a ring as soon as you arrive, Pumpkin. Yeah?'

'Of course, Daddy. Love you lots - Jess sends hugs!' She hung up.

'Kids, Eddie. Kids!'

'Don't start,' replied Eddie, 'Don't start. The older they get, the more you worry.' He drained his glass and motioned to get up. 'You're getting old pal. Same again?' Randy wagged his head. The celebrity had no intention of trying to keep up with his old college friend.

They were in 'Madge's Big Bar,' their favourite haunt off Great Audley St. in London's Mayfair. Randy looked rather resignedly around the club's main lounge. A young Billie Holiday bluesed away in the background, and the four original Vettrianos complemented the retro Art Deco ambience perfectly. A former boy band lead singer, Randy Middleton had made his fortune from music production and reality TV shows. Born and brought up in the US, his father had emigrated from England in the late sixties to follow the silicon trail, eventually being snapped up by Bill Gates. He settled in Kirkland, just outside Seattle, where, twenty years later, his eldest son Randy formed a rock group. After only a couple of years, they were successful enough to embark on a tour of Europe, and it was in the UK on that tour, that he found he had an intuitive gift for spotting the potential in would-be singing stars. He saw a gap in the market begging to be exploited, quit his group, and never looked back.

Now in his late forties, with a beautiful wife and daughter, enviable good looks, and a great screen presence, he was adored by the media as someone who had everything - just the right stuff for filling magazine pages, and sofas on chat shows. The self-made multi-millionaire was undaunted by all the attention that came with public exposure, and would often use the media to his advantage whenever it suited him. But he was fiercely protective of his wife and daughter. 'B' to friends and family, Bianca was in her last year at Cambridge, and had a promising career in film and TV waiting for her. Randy didn't want anything to spoil it.

'You'd think it would be simple, wouldn't you Eddie?' he said, 'getting together with Helena on Valentine's Day used to be a sacred ritual - but now, she's in one country, I'm in another, 'B's in another, and I don't think we've even got rid of all the Christmas decorations yet!'

Eddie, now out of his seat, nodded, acknowledging how he too was often having to play catch-up games with time. He made for the bar.

The two had met ostensibly to discuss where Eddie's latest project was going. Having an excellent track-record producing short films and television documentaries, Eddie Gascoigne had got way behind with what he had always hoped would be his greatest production to date. He had borrowed heavily on the back of an earlier, critically acclaimed period drama to finance what he called 'The Big One!' Unfortunately, he wasn't the only film producer, or director, to jump on the historical bandwagon. Every twenty years or so, history movies had a resurgence, but, day by day, his chance of being in on this one was disappearing into history itself.

He had a lot on his mind. Now hugely in debt, his life wasn't made any easier by his predilection for drink, horses and women

- in that order - and although nobody else knew it, it was Randy's money paying for the next round. He was hoping to go over ideas for foreign locations with Randy before finalising and costing the CGI content for his film. He was also very keen to see the inside of Randy's recently acquired Venetian palazzo, hoping it would be an ideal - and cheap - solution to at least one of his problems.

Their conversation was interrupted by another call: this time from Venice. It was Angelo, Randy's live-in security man.

'Hi, Angelo, what's the problem?'

'Mr. Middleton, I think you must come as soon as you can. There is a terrible accident!'

'Calm down, Angelo. Calm down. Now, speak a bit more slowly, and tell me precisely *what* has happened that is *so* terrible.'

'Signore, we have a terrible flood.'

'For heaven's sake, Angelo! We dealt with the acqua alta more than a dozen times during the winter. There's no need to ring me every time…'

'No, no, Mr. Middleton, is a flood from above - from the roof. There is water everywhere, and there is no acqua alta.'

'Switch off the electricity, immediately,' he said. 'Now tell me - is there any serious damage - and I mean *serious* Angelo?'

'Si Signore, on the secundo piano, in the portego, a piece of one of the frescoes has fallen on the floor.'

'How big a piece?'

'About two or three square metres, sir.'

'Get on to Sr. Benedetti from the conservation department straight away, and be sure to tell him I'm on my way - do it immediately Angelo, OK? I'll get there as soon as I can.'

'Si, Signore,' he replied, and rang off.

'Got your passport Eddie? How do you fancy a trip to Venice? You've been dropping hints about seeing inside the 'Magretti' for months.'

As part of his business dealings, Randy leased his HondaJet to other media celebrities, sports stars and the like, on a fairly regular basis; fortunately it was currently at Northolt Airport in west London, barely half an hour away. He called the flight staff agency, who immediately set about finding if his regular pilot was available. They also logged the flight to Venice, while he and Eddie made their way through the lunchtime traffic to the A40, and the airport.

Forty minutes later, their passports had been checked, and they were off through the small lobby, and onto the apron where the jet was waiting. As they boarded, Randy checked his watch. 'With a tailwind it'll take about an hour and a half to get to Venice,' he thought, 'which would make it around five local time when we arrive - it'll be getting dark.' By the time they had fastened their seatbelts, the plane was already taxiing towards runway one.

2

When the water-taxi emerged from under the Rialto Bridge, Randy got his first sight of the stricken palazzo. It may have stopped raining, but it was still blowing something of a gale. He looked up at the roof from the bobbing and rolling boat to where all the problems had originated. Everything appeared to be in place; so he called Angelo, who had sent some rather dramatic pictures to his phone. 'I'm on the opposite side of the canal right now, Angelo,' he shouted over the noise of the wind, 'looking up at the front, and nothing seems to be flapping around. So - che problema?'

'Ah, Mr. Middleton, Signor Zenobi himself came earlier this afternoon. He has only just gone. His men, they secure the protection on the roof. He seemed very angry and impatient.'

'That's only a taster of the emotions he's going to feel by the time I've finished with him,' snorted an equally angry and impatient Randy. 'Anyway, thanks for sorting things out so quickly, Angelo. We're just entering the rio; see you in a minute.'

The Rio di Magretti ran up the west side of the palazzo to the Ponti di Magretti carrying the Strada Nuova, the Cannaregio's main street. On their right ran a fondamenta, or quay, which led down from the main road past the courtyard's high wall, to an ornate doorway. The huge carved and panelled doors had once been blue, their faded and peeling paintwork having last seen a brush more than a century earlier. Opposite the doorway, a short flight of steps led to the water.

Only a short distance from the Ca' d'Oro on the Grand Canal, the 15th century Ca' Magretti-Bellini, an exquisite four storey Gothic palazzo, had been owned by the same family for over five hundred years. Since the 18th century, it had remained almost completely unaltered, and stories abounded about its hidden treasures. It sported at least two, if not three, Tiepolo ceilings, and it was known that both the Tintoretto and Zelotti families had done oil paintings and frescoes in there. Hardly anybody but the previous owner's family and their friends had seen its interior for two hundred years. But those centuries of jealous ownership had also been centuries of neglect, and both its interior and exterior were now looking distinctly sad. Even back in the nineteenth century when Ruskin sketched it, he described it as '..one of the best.' Even though - '..neglect has brought it to a near ruinous state..'

The Magretti-Bellinis, once rich and influential, their huge fortune having dwindled away, remained proud to the end. Last of her line, the redoubtable old Contessa had shared the decaying pile with her cats and her housekeeper for the past twenty years. She finally succumbed to putting practicality before pride, and was off to join her nephews and nieces in Viareggio. Eighty Venetian winters had taken their toll on her, and she deserved a gentler and more caressing climate. To the last, she could be seen on most days, strolling alone along the Strada Nuova which, she insisted, was the liveliest street in all of Venice. "There is only one, and it is Venezia; there is no second." She would cry; but, long before this winter had set in, she had already said her last arrivadercis, to her Venezia, her Cannaregio and her palazzo, consigning them to memory for ever.

Following her father's example, she had constantly rejected the overtures of art and architecture book writers, television programme makers, and latterly, the very lucrative fields of holiday and business rental. But now that the *casa* had finally changed hands, everyone was hoping to get their cameras inside.

Randy's decision to buy came through a combination of patience, love and luck. Never having had a desire to put his major property investment into a stately pile in a grand estate in England, his dream had always been to own a palazzo on the Grand Canal. His friends and family thought he was being over-romantic, but, for a businessman like him, it was a very practical decision: only two hours from his work in London - not too near and not too far - and the Venetian topography gave it the added advantage of a unique natural security.

It was extremely rare for an old property on the Grand Canal to come up for sale, as nearly all of them were already in corporate or municipal hands. But Randy was a member of that elite who were kept informed of what might become available. It was a waiting game and fraught with problems. But, when stories emerged that offers were being invited for the 'Magretti', he determined that, if he had to, he would move heaven and earth to acquire it. The old Contessa, so reluctant to put it on the market, didn't want to see her 'palazzo bello' become another office or apartment block - or worse still a hotel - and it took all Randy's negotiating skills to convince her that it would remain a family home.

But, buying an 'unaltered' palazzo doesn't count for much in Venice - unless you have extraordinary resilience and bottomless pockets. 'Unmaintained' would have been more accurate. Inside, the stucco was so thick with dust that it looked as though it was illuminated from below, and the re-gilding was going to take months, and cost a small fortune. Essentially, it was a glorious shell, which looked deceptively perfect, and could benefit hugely by just having a breath of fresh air through it.

One part that certainly wasn't perfect was the roof. Because it was in need of such urgent attention, and Randy was so often away in England, it was the repercussions of this repair, that would give rise to so much animosity in the Venetian press. The *Gazzettino* - having an absolute field day with the affair - would be quicker to lay the blame at the feet of an absent foreign owner than to question too closely the quality of their own craftsmen's work.

Contractors had queued round the block for the opportunity to work on the prestigious building, and secure several months of steady work from a foreign client, with the profits that that could mean. The Zenobis turned out not to be the best choice. Their promise of getting the new joists and rafters up, and the tiles back on, by the end of January, proved hopelessly overoptimistic. Weeks behind schedule, one of their workmen had been careless when he attached a length of temporary plastic sheeting to cover the exposed timbers. It was part of this covering which had come adrift, when a sudden storm of high winds and torrential rain blew in from the Adriatic. It lashed Venice and the palazzo incessantly for twelve hours, resulting in what Angelo had so aptly called - "A flood from above."

The water-taxi slipped quietly past the scaffolded side of the building, and Randy and Eddie disembarked at the short flight of steps opposite the doorway. A flustered Angelo greeted them, and, without a moment's delay, the three of them scampered across the courtyard and up the two flights of marble steps to the first floor balcony. Its doors opened into a small lobby, which in turn opened into the portego, which ran the length of the building. In the gloom, they could make out the floodwater reflecting the glazed doors to the loggia at the far end, but, before Randy could comment on the apparently minimal damage, a breathless Angelo said, 'The secundo piano, Signor, in the portego - it is terrible.'

They went straight on up to the second floor, and, from the top of the baroque staircase where the invading water had already created a mini-waterfall, they could see the worst of the effects of the disaster. Across the unlit portego, on the wall opposite, four or five square metres of fresco, plaster and stucco, had parted company with the bricks. It was now lying face down on the pink speckled terrazzo in a couple of centimetres of rainwater .

Randy dashed up to the top floor, originally the servant's quarters, to assess the extent of the problem. It didn't appear too bad. The rain had penetrated only one room, and its shrunken boards had allowed the deluge to escape along one wall. Hence the ceilings had avoided the worst of the damage. He came back down.

'Angelo, switch on the portego lights, and then go down to the main switchboard and throw the trip-switch for the second floor lights - and make sure your hands are dry!' After a short, but pensive, wait, the opulent portego, the size of a small ballroom, was bathed with light.

'Good,' said a relieved Randy, who then called down. 'Bring up three brooms, Angelo, and bring a couple of pairs of gumboots - as quick as you can.' Within a few minutes they were all hard at work.

'You certainly know how to make a guest feel welcome, I'll give you that!' chirped Eddie, for whom labour had replaced worry - at least for the moment.

'Shut up and keep sweeping!' replied Randy.

The three of them worked like slaves, but it still took nearly an hour to sweep out all the storm water via the only practical outfalls, the second floor balcony, and the first floor loggia.

Randy phoned Venice Buildings and Monuments again. Sr. Benedetti was on his way, they said, and was only two minutes away. As the Veneto's foremost expert on the conservation and preservation of frescoes, he was in the best position to advise on how to deal with the fallen masterpiece. Randy returned to look at what he assumed was a lost fresco. Could it be retrieved, he wondered, and if so, do I keep it wet, or do I leave it to dry out where it is and run the risk of it sticking to the floor? What magic could Sr. Benedetti work? He looked up at the exquisite ceiling by Jacopo Guarana, its angels searching in vain for the lost world of decadence that created them. 'Thank God you lot are still OK,' he thought.

Stepping around the plaster and stucco fragments with the greatest of care, he began to realise how lucky he was. Obviously the rainwater, having found a route down from the floor's edge upstairs, had soaked into the plaster here on the wall below. Getting heavier by the minute as the water continued to penetrate, eventually it gave way under the added weight. It was fortunate that there was so much rainwater already on the floor, because, when it fell, it allowed the fresco to stay more or less in one piece.

'Do not touch her, Sr. Middleton, please, do not touch her,' affirmed the fastidious and protective expert, 'allow her to dry out in her own time, just where she is signore, and we will put her back, piece by piece, so very, very gently.' He sounded so concerned and so passionate, you would have thought that he was talking about repairing his favourite granddaughter, whose arms and legs had just fallen off! The dapper, late middle-aged man, with his swept back, dyed-black hair, and half-moons, had the appearance of those ubiquitous, anonymous men who scurry about their city centres, all alone, making you wonder whether they are all on secret missions to save their country's national treasures.

He walked up to the fallen fresco, and, with his hands clasped behind his back, tiptoed around the fall, stopping jerkily every now and again for a closer inspection, rather like a chicken searching for grain. 'She mustn't be rushed, Sr. Middleton,' he said, 'Venezia and the world can wait.'

He expressed his gratitude to Randy for contacting his department so promptly, and apologised for not getting to the palazzo sooner. He also thanked him for the care the three of them had exercised in sweeping out the water, and for not disturbing the precious fragments, as though they were arranged for an art installation, which he would be back later to finish off. He laid a striped plastic tape very delicately around the upside down picture, and left, adding that he would be in touch very soon.

As Angelo showed him out, Eddie pointed to the exposed brickwork. 'What do you make of that?' He asked. Randy, who had been more preoccupied with getting on to his lawyers in order to instigate proceedings against Sr. Zenobi for his negligence than in checking out the freshly exposed bricks, looked at the wall. What had attracted Eddie's attention was unmistakable. There, in the right hand side of the newly exposed space, was a bricked-up doorway.

'Well, I'll be damned,' said Randy.

'More than likely!' Replied Eddie.

Randy went into the bedroom behind and to the left of the fresco, but there was no evidence of any door on the reverse of the damaged wall. The same was the case to the right, where there was also a servants' staircase. On close inspection, it appeared that the distances somehow didn't match up. A missing distance between the various walls couldn't be explained.

'Some of the old plans and architect's drawings are in the dresser in my office downstairs.' said Randy. 'C'mon Eddie, let's check 'em out.'

They went downstairs to Randy's makeshift office next to the kitchen, and soon had the sheets unrolled and spread all over the floor. Eddie was quick to identify the location of the mysterious missing space. 'Look Randy, there, above that section of the second staircase, there's a small ante-room or store room of some kind.'

'You're right, there is. Now, somewhere around here I've got a laser-measure - ah! - here we are. Bring that plan with you, Eddie, and let's see what those Venetian 'brickies' were up to.'

When they completed their check, they were amazed to find that the void above the servants' staircase, about three metres by four, was completely sealed up. No doors, no windows, no staircases. The two men looked at each other. 'Shall we?' asked Randy.

'It's your house, pal,' came the reply, and as Angelo continued to sweep out the last of the water, Randy went down to the ground floor to get some tools. The piantereno, originally the trading floor of the classic casa fondaco, joined the courtyard to the Grand Canal and had storerooms on either side, as well as a mezzanine. It was on this mezzanine that all maintenance equipment was kept. It was also where Angelo had his rooms.

Back upstairs, they stepped over Sr. Benedetti's tape as though they were naughty schoolboys and he was still there, keeping an eye them. With some trepidation, they tiptoed around the plaster fragments, and then laid a dustsheet over the part nearest the wall. On closer inspection, the hasty in-fill brickwork in the doorway, differed considerably from equally shoddy work in the rest of the wall. This meant that it was probably inserted later, but as Randy was aware, having studied the history of his new home thoroughly, no later than 1578, as that was the year when the painter of the fresco, Giovanni Battista Zelotti, had died.

Randy began to scrape away at the soft, wet mortar. Handing the first brick to Eddie he was soon at work on the second, the third and the fourth. The unique excitement of imminent discovery gripped him, as it might an archaeologist, expecting to find fabulous treasures in an ancient tomb. When a dozen bricks or so had been removed, he couldn't wait to shine his torch into the long-abandoned room.

He peered into the space, the first eyes to do so for over four hundred years. His optimism evaporated. His heart sank lower than when his last protégée, 'the greatest act since Madonna,' quit the music business to settle down and start a family in Nuneaton - "Nuneaton for God's sake!" he would cry in sheer bewilderment. The room revealed almost nothing. There were just a few old clothes, a small decorated box, and a few pieces of paper scattered about. 'Can't see any gold,' he said.

'Any skeletons?' enquired Eddie.

'Not even a dead mouse. Someone used this as a junk room.' Randy removed a few more bricks, and squeezed in his head and shoulders. 'It's pretty musty, and some of our floodwater has got in by the look of it. I want to get all this jumble out before it's ruined. There are a couple of books here too.'

Once the opening was large enough, Randy climbed through, and handed all the objects carefully back through the hole to Eddie. 'Fifty euros for the lot, and that's my final offer!' He joked.

'You may well laugh, Eddie, but these could have been lost for ever if we hadn't got here in time, and you hadn't spotted this doorway. They might not be worth a fortune, but historically they could be priceless. Make no mistake, this decorated box was owned by someone very rich, and if we had a bit more time I'd like to find out who our "Venetian Millionaire" was.'

Randy called down to Angelo, who assured him that the front

drawing room on the first floor was completely dry. 'We'll spread them out down there Eddie; I'll take the box and clothes - can you bring the books and manuscripts?'

As he gathered the manuscripts together, Eddie took a moment to study the top few sheets. 'They're written in English, Randy. This lot must have been written by an English aristo' doing his Grand Tour.'

Downstairs in the Baroque room overlooking the Grand Canal, they spread the three dozen or so handwritten pages in a neat rectangle near the window. They placed the three books on the only table in the room, indeed, the only piece of furniture in the room. Eddie's voice echoed round the dusty uncared-for space 'It's mainly poems and letters by the look of it,' he said, 'and a few jottings about travel.' While he continued to read through the pages, Randy picked up one of the books. It was a copy of Arthur Golding's translation of Ovid's *Metamorphoses*. He opened the slightly damp book with extreme care.

'He must have liked this one, Eddie,' he said, 'the pages are littered with annotations and underlinings.' An engraved coat of arms in silver on the front, matched the one on what was clearly a writing or document box. The wooden box was covered with embossed and gilded leather in red and yellow, and had silver hinges and re-enforced corners. About sixty centimetres long by thirty deep and forty high, it had a gabled top, and its drop-down front revealed four drawers. The top compartment contained some writing instruments: ink bottles, quills, sealing wax, and a few other odds and ends. The dense renaissance ornament, tooled into the leather, was of the highest quality, and both men felt that the box must have belonged to either a rich merchant, or a member of the high aristocracy.

Randy was now on the phone gleaning anything he could, from anyone who would take his calls. As the evening wore on, he found it harder to conceal his impatience. Avoidable delays made him hopping mad, and he made life a misery for anyone who was careless, negative or lazy in their dealings with him. As a result he gave the impression of a no-nonsense man on the make. But he was no philistine; he was erudite and articulate on both Italian renaissance art and architecture, regarding himself as a man of taste. This love of Italy and its culture, compounded his feeling of guilt that a prize piece of Venetian history like the Zelotti fresco should suffer so badly whilst in his care.

'The press are going to just love this' said Eddie.

Randy, stood over the modest find, with the small leather-bound volume still in his hand. 'Stuff the press,' he said, 'Italian rags are like any other, and they'll print what they're going to print, no matter what.'

'I was just thinking: this could be worth a fair bit you know. I'd get it catalogued, get an expert in or whatever.' Eddie had noticed that quite a few of the sheets contained drafts for plays, and it didn't take a university professor to spot that they were Shakespeare's. An undelivered letter to Lord Burghley was signed 'Oxenford', and other pages contained travel itineraries including Verona, Padua, and Florence, not to mention Palermo and Messina in Sicily.   It was difficult for him to take in the full significance of what he was looking at. If this evidence was verified, and he could see no reason why it shouldn't be, then the whole world of theatre and drama history might be turned on its head. He would have liked more time to study the find, but was denied it.

'Well, will it make the perfect location?

'What? Oh, perfect Randy, perfect.'

'You'll have to be quick if you want some shots, but promise me Eddie, no-one else sees them without my say-so, and strictly no pictures of the damage!' He went down to make arrangements with Angelo for the builders, conservators, insurers and the rest. He then went into his office, and popped the Ovid into a drawer in his desk. This was the room that the Contessa had lived in, for her last twenty years. He knew she'd be in tears when the press got hold of what had befallen her 'palazzo bello.' He called to Eddie to get a move on. The feeling of guilt made him unusually irritable. 'Eddie, come on,' he snapped, 'the taxi's here.'

Within two minutes, the two men were leaving the Rio di Magretti and turning left onto the Grand Canal, bound for the airport and London.

3

The lumbering vaporetto swung left under the huge, white marble span of the Rialto Bridge and on past the Pescheria towards the Ca' d'Oro bus stop. To the right, the Ca' Magretti-Bellini was probably more noticeable now than it had ever been in its entire history. Usually, its perfectly proportioned gothic frontage took its place in the architectural frieze of the snaking Grand Canal with consummate ease. Today, however, it rudely interrupted that harmony by hiding away behind Sr. Zenobi's blue plastic cladding. But, if you looked closely, you could still see some of its delicate features peeping out at you, like a courtesan from behind her carnival mask.

As they prepared to disembark, the two final-year students shuffled their way towards the exit. Breaking the silence, Bianca, the fairer, and arguably, the prettier of the two, chirped 'My daddy's got a palazzo!' Having gained the attention of most of the passengers, she addressed them again in mock apology, adding 'It's not a *big* one!' The pair looked at each other and burst into fits of giggles. They quit the vaporetto with a bound, skipped across the wooden staging, and disappeared up the side of the Ca' d'Oro to the Strada Nuova. As they turned right, Bianca slipped her arm through Jessica's. 'It's only just along here,' she said 'You'll simply die when you see it. The outside's an awful mess, but the inside's a-mazing.'

The two students, far too attractive for their own good, dazzled in the late morning sunlight. Bianca boasted an enviable head of dark blonde, almost titian hair, which framed her tanned, and what would have been a classically proportioned face but for a slightly short nose, making her look younger than her twenty-two years. Jessica, taller and more lithe, wore her darker hair full too, but, perhaps, slightly too long. In contrast to Bianca's fresh and impudent appearance, her strikingly aquamarine eyes, modest lips and high cheekbones gave her an almost aristocratic look. Even here in late February, it was mild enough for them to wear low-rise jeans and crop-tops, unlike the Venetians who were all very well wrapped. With seven 'A's at 'A' level between them, and 2.1s waiting for them both at the end of the year - provided they didn't mess things up - these best of friends were all too aware of how brief the luxury of university life was going to be. So, as Venice geared herself up for Carnivale, now a vulgar, tourist-dominated monstrosity, these girls were determined to have fun.

Fifty metres from the Ca' d'Oro, they crossed the Rio di Magretti bridge, and turned down the fondamenta leading to the palazzo's courtyard door.

'Angelo!' Shrieked Bianca, as she hammered on the huge doors after ringing the bell a second time. 'Are you there?'

'Doesn't Randy trust you with a key?'

'There's only two, Jess, Daddy's got one and Angelo the other.' She stepped back and peered up at the pediment in desperation, as though she expected him to emanate from its richly carved entablature. 'He's supposed to be living in,' she shouted, 'so where is he?'

No sooner had she spoken, than a clunking and sliding of bolts was followed by the turning of a key in the lock. The slowly opening door revealed the smiling face of the twenty-eight-year-old security man. 'Ah, Signorina Bianca, buon giorno, and you friend. Aah, two such beautiful English girls….'

'Yes, all right Angelo, thanks for that. Now, can you show us to our rooms so that we can dump these bags?'

'Si, si, signorinas this way per favore, allow me please.' And with that he took their bags, leaving the girls to lead the way up the marble stairs to the first floor balcony. After passing through a small lobby, they walked across the end of the mysterious and exotically decorated portego, to the room they were to share, accompanied by no more than the soft sound of their trainers, and the odd '*wow*' from Jessica.

'Thanks Angelo,' said Bianca, rather curtly. 'Can you put them down there?' As soon as Angelo had left, the pair started to unpack.

'That was all a bit offhand 'B', what was all that about?'

'Oh, nothing.'

'Come on 'B', there was history behind that - dish the dirt, I want all the grubby details.'

'Honestly it was nothing, he just made a bit of a nuisance of himself back at home, that's all.'

'And, *and*?'

'And, he made a pass at me - OK? Well, several times actually, when I was about sixteen or seventeen. He got a bit obsessed - as men do.'

'That is *so* the biggest secret you've ever kept from me! How could you do that? And don't tell me *you* weren't tempted either. God, 'B' - he's a hunk, and what's more he's a Latin hunk!' She looked straight at Bianca. 'You did didn't you? - Come on 'B', you couldn't resist could you?'

'No, yes, well - OK, just the once,' admitted Bianca, 'but it was only a snog, honestly, nothing more,' she added, with an ever reddening face and broadening smile.

'Your pants are on fire!'

'No they aren't, and they stayed on. All right.'

'Really - cough, cough!'

'Yes, really - and it *was* only the one time. You must know how much Daddy trusts him, Jess, and I wasn't going to fuck things up for him was I? He finds Angelo *so* reliable, he'll never sack him, and you know what Daddy can be like? I wasn't going to tell him was I? Anyway, he's originally from Venice, so - here he is: bit drop dead gorgeous though isn't he?'

'I wouldn't kick him out of bed!' laughed Jessica.

'Shhhh,' said Bianca, 'you can hear everything someone says in this place, it echoes like anything, and he might be listening. And 'don't let your darling Tony hear you talking like that.'

'Yes, well, Tony isn't here is he, and you're only young - twice, or is it three times - no four!'

'Ah, spoken like a girl with a real sense of commitment.' said Bianca. 'Go on then Jess, tell me, if there was absolutely no chance of anyone else ever finding out, and he made a move on you - would you?'

Jessica carried on unpacking in silence, and then looked across at her best friend. 'Bitch,' she said. 'I do love Tony you know, but he's deeper than any other man I've met, and he doesn't make knowing him particularly easy. Maybe it's the unknowable bits that are so attractive.'

'I take it that's a pass then?'

'Pass.'

They had a quick wash and freshen up, and Bianca took Jessica on a guided tour. At the far end of the portego, a beautifully engraved pair of glazed doors opened onto the loggia. The eerie blueness caused by the plastic sheeting gave the whole scene a movie special-effects quality. With almost no view of the Grand Canal to speak of, not to mention an unwelcome cold wind, they came back in, and hurried up to the second floor to inspect the damage. The portegos on the first and second floors, ran all the way from front to back of the palazzo, with three or four rooms on each side. The eighteenth-century main staircase was halfway along on the left, or east side of the building. From the lobby at the top of the ornate marble flight they could see the damage clearly.

'My God!' exclaimed a surprised Bianca, 'I didn't think it would be that bad. Daddy just said that a bit of fresco had come down in the rain.'

'Can it be restored do you think?' asked Jessica.

'Daddy's got one of the best restorers in the business on the case and he reckons it's doable, but where the hell would you start?' They stepped gingerly round the fallen fragments, avoiding Sr. Benedetti's tape.

'So this is what all the brouhaha in the media has been about?'

said Jessica. 'It is bad though 'B', isn't it?'

'Certainly is,' answered Bianca, 'and it'll take forever and cost a small fortune. It would probably be quicker and cheaper to raise the original artist from the dead, and get him to redo it, than to call in some modern outfit of consultants and arty-farties. It doesn't bear thinking about does it? Come on, come and have a peek at what used to be the Magrettis' private apartments.'

Although she had never been to Venice before, Jessica, apart from being overawed by the quality and quantity of the craftsmanship around her, was rapidly getting to appreciate what a sophisticated society this had been. Travellers from England, seeing how prosperous traders lived in Venice, even before the time of Henry VIII, must have marvelled at this city and its culture, and trembled at these overt expressions of its wealth and power.

'It's only when you're here, surrounded by so many examples of the Italian arts, that you begin to see why, back in Tudor times, the English wanted a slice of their action,' commented Jessica.

'And not just their painting, sculpture and architecture either,' Bianca replied, as they recrossed the portego to look at the remaining rooms, 'it was their literature, music, drama, and fashion as well.' She stopped in front of a Tintoretto. They were now in the principal bedroom which overlooked the courtyard. 'Remember what we found out in English Lit.,' she continued, 'not counting the histories, three quarters of Shakespeare's plays are set in and around the Mediterranean, and mainly in Italy - and the Elizabethan audiences just lapped it up.'

Back on the first floor, Bianca took Jessica straight to the front drawing room. She remembered from her only other visit in the Christmas holidays that there was a fabulous ceiling. It was by Tiepolo at his best - a breathtaking example of virtuoso illusionistic painting. The sort of picture that you would have thought took months of patient brushwork, but actually he was probably in and out in a couple of weeks.

'Watch where you're walking 'B',' called Jessica.

'What?'

'Look, all over the floor, what's all this?'

She was staring down at the rectangle of drying pages that Randy and Eddie had so carefully laid out four days earlier. The early-afternoon sun was squeezing its way through the leaded glass, in a half-hearted attempt to place some dappled light across them and the soft pink terrazzo.

'I haven't a clue, Jess, Daddy didn't say anything as far as I can remember - hey, there are some books as well, here on the table - and a note.'

'What do you make of this, Pumpkin? Be careful won't you as it's pretty old and it may turn out to be historically valuable. I found it in a 'secret' room behind where the fresco fell from. It looks more like your field than mine – all poetry and plays and stuff. Let me know what you think of it. I'm afraid we're in a bit of a hurry, have lots of fun at the carnival – give my love to Jess ,
take care,
love dad   xxx

'I'm seriously intrigued, Jess,' added Bianca, and the two of them soon found themselves squatting on the cold bare floor. Both of the girls were reading English at Cambridge, and Elizabethan and Jacobean drama and literature were still very fresh in their minds. To their surprise and delight, they were now studying what appeared to be the pages of an English renaissance notebook that had come unbound. A closer inspection revealed that this was not the case. The pages showed no signs of ever having been bound, and differed very slightly in shape and size. There were sheets containing sonnets, poems of differing length and structure, and what seemed to be whole scenes for plays, probably comedies. There was also an unmailed letter and other assorted jottings.

'It's all in English, 'B'; none of it is in Italian, French, Latin or anything else, and it all looks like the same handwriting, doesn't it?'

'I think it's the work of an English toff on his Grand Tour,

38

Jess. Here, look, he's making plans to visit Palermo in Sicily, and notes it's better to sail from Genoa than to go from Naples.' Bianca started to rearrange the pages, and put them in some sort of order. She was interrupted in her filing by Jessica, who was suddenly conscious of how their day had changed, and how absurd their situation must seem.

'Now this is what I call living it up - let's go to Venice, sit on an ice-cold floor, and do some English Lit.!' But she in turn was cut off by Bianca.

'Oh, my God!' She declared, 'if this stuff is all genuine, then we've got dynamite here.' She handed a sheet over to Jessica. 'Take a look at this.'

Jessica took the beautifully written page, and read. As she did so, her jaw visibly dropped, and she looked up at Bianca.

'Are you thinking what I'm thinking?' She said.

'I don't know *what* I'm thinking,' replied Bianca.

The page they were studying was headed 'The Jew', and the dialogue clearly included Portia's 'the quality of mercy is not strained' soliloquy. It wasn't verbatim the speech we all know now, and Portia had a 'z' in her name, but Bassanio was the same, and 'Shylock' was referred to simply as 'The Jew.'

'Don't let's get carried away girls,' said Bianca, as she fumbled for her mobile phone. She went over to the window to get a stronger signal. 'Daddy, hi, can you talk?'

Randy was in a meeting, but would always find a way to give his 'darling girl' a couple of minutes. 'We're in the palazzo and looking at the pages of writing yeah, and we were wondering, did it all come out of the 'secret room' as you put it?'

'Yes, Pumpkin, up on the second floor - what do you think of them?'

'Great Daddy, really, *really* interesting, but was the room actually a secret room?'

'It must have been sealed up before the fresco was painted, Darling. As there is no other entrance to it but the bricked up doorway - it's like a time capsule. Eddie and I both checked it out - there was never any other way in. You'll have to do a little homework if you want to find out precisely when it was done.'

'Thanks, Daddy, love you lots, byee.' She hung up. 'We have to find out exactly who painted that fresco and when.' They looked at each other.

'The *Gazzettino*,' said Bianca. 'Daddy said the local rag has been having a field day at our expense, so it's bound to have all the details.'

They rushed off to find Angelo, figuring he was just the sort of man to buy the paper, if for the football reports alone. They headed for his apartment on the mezzanine in the pianereno. His low ceilinged rooms were still safely above the infuriatingly regular visits of the aqua alta. Climate change, that uninvited guest, was grabbing Venice by her feet and toes, and dragging her under the tide. For the time being, a pair of wellingtons at the ready, had to be sufficient protection for the irrepressible and adaptable Angelo.

Their visit to the damp, dark underbelly of the palazzo was postponed though, as they found Angelo in the courtyard wrestling with a rampant vine which clearly had the intention of having the palazzo for itself. The plant, a gift to the Contessa from her great grandchildren a few years earlier, had flourished unchecked in the mistaken belief that because its distant fruity cousins gave rise to the drink of the gods, it had a divine right to an unbridled existence here.

'Have you got the last issues of the *Gazzettino*, Angelo?' called Bianca from the balcony. He stopped pulling on the resistant stems, turned his head slowly, and looked up. 'Please.' She added, with a tilt of the head.

'Si, signorina, si. A moment please.'

They went down to the courtyard, not only to save time in making progress in their quest to solve the mystery of the pages, but to get a glimpse into the private world of this enigmatic man to whom Bianca's father had entrusted the safety of both the palazzo and them. As Bianca mounted the bottom step that led up to his apartment, Angelo came out with an armful of newspapers. What could have been an embarrassing silence was cut short by Angelo, who came down the steps with a macho positiveness.

'Here,' he said, 'the last three or four days, Miss Bianca. You must sort them for yourself as I am rather busy, OK?' He looked her straight in the eye, and with a kind and knowing hint of a smile, brushed past her to get on with his work. He had defused the charged moment admirably, put the students in their place, and refused Bianca's invitation to join in any games, all in one go.

'Oops!' whispered Jessica, breaking the silence. They walked briskly across the marble flagstones, and hurried up the long flights of steps to the balcony. As they entered the lobby, Bianca turned to her friend.

'Sorry, girl!'

'Don't start getting defensive 'B', let's put it down to experience and a long day, OK? Now, come on, I want to get on with solving the riddle of those pages.' But before following Bianca inside, she took a moment to watch Angelo resume his struggle with the vine.

They spread the papers on the kitchen table, and searched them for all the articles about the palazzo. Jessica made a cup of coffee, while Bianca scoured the tabloids for evidence. Once the sheets were in order it made life much easier, and quite quickly Bianca found what they were searching for.

'Here, listen to this Jess…Palazzo Magretti-Bellini…blah, blah, blah, look at this photo of Daddy! Heavens I wish I knew Italian better…here's a name…Giovanni Battista Zelotti, 1532 – 1578, and something about the Palazzo Ducale. So, he was good enough to be employed at the Doge's Palace, he must have been good then. It goes on a bit…blah, blah, blah, 'secundo piano nobile'…'frescoes,' so there we are, he must be our man. I reckon the door was blocked up so that the great man could do the fresco.'

'And I guess the intention would have been to open up an alternative door one day…'

'….Which they never got round to doing,' said Bianca.

'It still doesn't explain why our English toff left all his stuff behind.'

'Perhaps he had to get out in a hurry - who knows?'

Spilling coffee as they went, the pair dashed back to have another look at the find. As they sat cross-legged on the floor for a second time, Jessica asked Bianca. 'How old would Will Shakespeare have been in 1578?'

'I don't know. When was he born? Oh, I see what you mean, er...'

'He was born in 1564, 'B'; he would have been fourteen in 1578, and Zelotti must have painted this before then. Will couldn't have been here to write any of this. Whoever this aristocrat was, Shakespeare must have got it from him.'

'Fourteen!' Said a wide-eyed Bianca, 'not even swotting for his GCSE's! Then if we're right, Shakespeare didn't write Shakespeare after all, or at the very least, he must have got a load of it from this guy.' She studied the pages again and again. 'I can't take it in Jess. There is a page here on which I know is a plot line from *The Taming of the Shrew*, and another here from *Much Ado*. It just can't be what it is!'

"B', do you remember that supply teacher we had in year twelve, who told us that there was an anonymous play called '*The Jew*', and it was registered and played in London in the late 1570's?'

'Yes, and the *Merchant of Venice* is always dated to the 1590's. He told us all sorts of stuff, didn't he? What was his line – "The glover's son didn't do it"? He reckoned some aristocrat in the Court of Elizabeth I was behind it, didn't he? We had a stand up row with him because he said the *Tempest* was years earlier than everyone claimed, do you remember?'

'I do, he said that if you look at the Strachey Letter, which is used to date the play, it was probably spiced up by the author, because he'd seen the play, or perhaps even the manuscript. What if he was right all along? Bloody hell 'B', we could end up being world famous, do you realise?'

'If we're right with this, all the history books are going to have to be rewritten, because of us - and Daddy of course. Can you believe it? I've got to take a closer look at some of these Jess, I'm hanging onto these two, and that one of '*The Jew*"

The excited pair jumped up, and started to dance a sort of impromptu jig, round and round, until Jessica caught her ankle on the lid of the open writing box, which neither of them had noticed. 'Oh, shit!' She exclaimed petulantly, and bent down to slam it shut. In doing so, she couldn't help but recognise, prominent in the decoration, a coat-of-arms which barely one in a thousand people would know. 'Oh my God! - It's the Earl of Oxford's! 'B', I've got to ring Tony. He's not going to believe this.

4

An habitual early riser, whether at work or on holiday, today being no exception, Mark Dryden had a big breakfast to set himself up for the unpredictable day ahead. A coffee-lover, he winced as he downed his second cup of the hotel's stewed offering. Realising that it was only just after six in the UK, he stepped outside into Campo Santa Maria Formosa, and went for a short stroll around Castello to soak up the early-morning atmosphere, before phoning John Fletcher. When he did, the reply was immediate and assured.

'Go straight upstairs to the Consulate,' he said, 'and ask for Bill Harvey, or, better still, just go past reception and along the corridor; his office should be the first door on your right. I've told him you're on your way.'

John Fletcher's years in the Foreign Office had equipped him with an enviable social ease, and a string of friendships and contacts all over the world, especially in Western Europe. It was unusual for him to call in a favour, but this looked like one of those occasions when a little help was going to be essential.

'Thanks John, I'll give you any news as soon as I've got something.'

'Best of luck Mark,' replied John. 'You're still sure you don't want that second pair of hands?'

'If I do, you'll be the first to know. I'll speak to you later.' With no further comment, Mark hung up.

Those last moments made John Fletcher feel uneasy.

He had been a friend and colleague of Mark's for years, and picked-up on the tension in his voice. They had met at

Marlborough and gone through St. Johns, Cambridge together, cementing a deep friendship as well as developing an enduring love of Elizabethan and Jacobean Theatre. Eventually, their relationship became unique and unbreakable, and, although they had gone their very different ways on graduating, they remained in close touch.

It was more than five years since any really serious matter had troubled them, but they had both been taken aback at seeing the name 'Ca' Magretti-Bellini' appear in an article, tucked away on page seven, in the previous day's *Telegraph*.

'AQUA ALTA' CAUSES FLOOD OF PROTEST FOR BRIT-POP IMPRESARIO : MUSIC producer and media darling Randy Middleton, 48, was at the centre of a storm of protest in Venice yesterday, over damage to his 15th Cent. Palazzo.

He bought the Ca' Magretti-Bellini six months ago from right under the noses of some very angry Italian shipping and media tycoons, who wanted to keep ownership at home.

A real storm blew up last weekend, however, which opened up the roof to let in rather more than just a flood of rainwater. A deluge of criticism in the popular Italian press descended on our celebrity owner over his allegedly cavalier attitude towards 'their' Gothic masterpiece on the Grand Canal, etc., etc..

Venetian palazzos rarely made the British press, but any news concerning this one was of particular interest to both men; Mark Dryden had made a detailed study of the history of the palazzo some years earlier.

The Magretti's, he discovered, had owned it for over a century before marrying into the Bellinis in the mid-sixteenth century. Their shrewdness as merchants led them to own three palazzos in Venice, but only one on the Grand Canal. Like many of their fellow Venetians, the Magretti-Bellini's would rent out apartments in their palazzos to anyone who could afford them - Ambassadors, foreign dignitaries, royalty, or aristocrats doing the

'Grand Tour'. As long as they had the cash, they were welcome.

Both Mark Dryden and John Fletcher knew that certain English aristocrats back in Tudor times had stayed there. Of special interest amongst them was Edward de Vere, the Seventeenth Earl of Oxford, to be rumoured publicly since the early twentieth century as the real author of the Shakespeare canon. Oxford spent a fortune on his accommodation and lifestyle during his stay in Venice, 'building himself a house', as reports at the time put it, but had left in some haste. The two friends had to be sure that, at this, the first time the palazzo had changed hands in over four centuries, nothing would identify it as the temporary home of the great dramatist.

Mark Dryden was quite well known in literary and dramatic circles back in England, and, with no wish to have his journey abroad made known, travelled under a false identity and carried a false passport. For the journey he was Tom Underhill, a glass product buyer from Oldham; for the business in hand, he was George Drummond of the FCO. He also travelled with a false appearance. As something of a success on the amateur stage, he enjoyed role-play and kept a small kit of make-up handy for times when he didn't want to be recognised - particularly by CCTV cameras.

He had spent the two hours of his flight memorising all the routes he would be using. There would be crowds of tourists and visitors milling about in all the main calles, so he familiarised himself with alternatives, lesser used streets and fondamentas, to rid himself of their inconvenience. He was prepared for the whole trip to be a wasted one, but this was likely to be his only opportunity, *ever*, to get inside the building that had once been the centre for the Earl's Italian travels. Whatever the hazards, he had to take it, and so, now, his next and most important task was to secure a convincing 'official' means of entry.

Less than twenty minutes after dropping his key into reception, his vaporetto was approaching the Piazzale Roma. From there he boarded one of the frequent buses to Mestre that crossed the Lagoon using the Ponte di Liberta. From the bus terminus in Mestre centre, a three minute walk along Via Carducci brought him to Piazzale Donatore di Sangue, and the well concealed British Consulate housed on the first floor of a block of flats.

He skipped lightly up the stairs and strode quickly and confidently into reception. It may as well have been an English dentist's waiting room. He timed his arrival to a few minutes after they opened at 10.00 am, hoping that the staff would still be busy preparing themselves for the day. He excused himself to the receptionist, and, being careful to sustain his best public school accent, explained that he was in a bit of a hurry and had an appointment with Mr. Harvey. As John had rightly informed him, the office he was looking for was along the corridor and first on the right. He knocked and entered.

'George Drummond, FCO,' he said, offering his hand.

'Bill Harvey,' came the reply, acknowledging the greeting with a fraternal handshake.

Working in a wide range of appointments in northern Italy over many years, Bill Harvey's ambition had always been to get a position in Venice. Stocky, and a little below average height, now in his late fifties, he sported a healthy and alert appearance, a carry-over from his years of athletic success at Radley and Oxford. But for his thinning silver-grey hair, he would have passed for late forties. As Deputy Consul, he was head of security, and had proved himself a dependable member of the consular staff, with fourteen years of loyal service.

Dryden closed the door. The cramped office, half-filled with filing cabinets, and piled high with box-files and lever-arch binders, looked as though little had been touched since they moved the Consulate from the exquisite Palazzo Querini on the Grand Canal twelve years earlier.

'This is an unusual request, George. May I call you George ?'

'Of course, Bill, of course, and yes, it is irregular, I know. We wouldn't impose on you unless we felt it was important. Did John give you some of the details?'

'He wasn't that clear, which was unusual for him, so perhaps you could be a bit more explicit.'

'Certainly, though I'm not able to go into the finer points of the operation for security reasons you understand. I'm afraid we've been a little slow off the mark where the Ca' Magretti-Bellini is concerned. As you must already be aware, the old Contessa sold up last autumn, and now it's owned by one of ours - some media chappie or other. The old dear was living with her aged housekeeper and a dozen cats as a virtual recluse for decades. I daren't imagine what the place must have smelt like! Did you know that she was a copious diarist?'

'No I didn't,' replied Bill, whose days were normally filled with bureaucratic tedium, and endless rounds of drinks parties. He welcomed eagerly any new anecdotes to spice things up. He was ready for anything.

Dryden obliged by plying him with imaginary tales of the Contessa's wartime liaisons. Gossip had come down the grapevine, he said, that there was a strong likelihood that she may well have left some of those 'very personal' diaries in the palazzo when she sold up. It was of the FCO's opinion, that the contents of those diaries, should any of them be there, could still be most embarrassing to HMG.

'Mustn't let them get into the wrong hands, eh? 'Red-tops' and all that?'

'I couldn't have put it better myself, Bill. Which is why the fewer people who know anything about my being here, the better. He nodded in the direction of the CCTV camera in the corner of the room. I'm sure we will find a way to show you our gratitude.'

'It's no trouble, George, none at all,' said Bill, who now caught a glimpse of a CBE glittering brightly on the not so distant horizon. 'Well, you'll want to get into the crumbling pile then, and to be sure of a trouble-free access, *you* need an official pass. Come with me old chap, and I'll get you kitted out.'

On the opposite side of the corridor from Bill's security office was a reprographics suite.

'First of all, I need a passport-sized photograph for your identity card.'

'Certainly. Nothing will be stored of course?'

'Of course,' answered Bill, removing a compact digital camera from a drawer under the printer. He took Dryden's photograph, and slotted the camera into the top of the printer, put in a blank ID card, and ten seconds later, out it came with his photograph on it. 'Sign it across the bottom of the picture please, George.' Dryden did as he was told, and Bill then put it through a laminator to seal it. 'This old printer has no memory,' he added.

'No, but that camera has. May I?' He took the camera from Bill, and erased all traces of his image.

'Just one last thing, old boy,' said Bill, holding out the card, but not yet handing it over. Dryden's heart missed a beat. 'I must, and I mean must, have this card back before you leave Venice. A terrorist group would kill to get hold of one of our IDs. Oh!, and don't show it to anyone you don't have to, will you?'

'Goes without saying. You'll probably have it by tomorrow. What sort of time do you get away?'

'Fivish.'

'If I don't see you Bill, it'll be in the post - only be another day or so, is that alright?'

'Of course, George. Of course.'

After another fraternal and cordial handshake, they parted, and Dryden made his way downstairs and out into the garden in the middle of the Piazza. He pulled up his collar to fend off the stiff breeze blowing in from the Adriatic, and slipped the security-pass into a windowed pocket in his wallet. He then struck out for the bus-stand, Venice, and the Palazzo.

From Piazzale Roma, he stood for the short journey along the Grand Canal to the Ca' d'Oro bus stop. His vaporetto struggled along like a complaining hippopotamus, wallowing in a narrow and crowded stream; as he passed the campanile of San Geremia at the entrance to the Cannaregio Canal, he phoned the Palazzo using the number Bill Harvey had given him.

If no-one was in, he thought, he should have plenty of time

to look the place over from the outside. If the builders were still around, they should all be busy; but, even if they weren't, their guard could well be down and he might be able to slip in and do his search there and then. Middleton's family was the problem. If any of them were there, they would have little time to prepare for his impromptu visit. This might leave them on the defensive, and hopefully make them quite open and talkative.

As the vaporetto pulled away from the San Marcuola stop, the last one before Ca' d'Oro, his call was answered.

5

Angelo answered the phone.

Mark Dryden introduced himself, and asked if the owner or someone else in authority was available to speak to him.

'Signorina Bianca,' called Angelo. 'Signorina Bianca.' He entered the portego, went across to the girls' bedroom and knocked on the door. 'Is a phone call for you Signorina. It sounds very official.'

'Do you know what time it is Angelo? It's *carnival* time Angelo - that's what time it is! Tell them to ring back.'

'A man from the consulate is coming,' he persisted.

She came to the door. 'OK, OK, give it to me….hello?'

'Who am I addressing please?'

'This is Bianca Middleton, who are you?'

'I'm sorry to trouble you, Miss Middleton,' said Dryden, maintaining his best public school manner, 'George Drummond, from the consulate. I'm here in response to the absolute field-day the press and everyone else in Venice seems to be having at your expense. We were wondering if we could be of any assistance, hope we're not too late to help and all that.'

Bianca thought for a moment. She ambled up the portego wearing nothing but a T-shirt and a pair of socks. She went into the loggia, leaving the doors wide open, leant over the marble rail, and checked her watch.

'When would you like to come up?'

'Well, my vaporetto is approaching the Ca' d'Oro as we speak, but if this morning isn't convenient?'

'Give me fifteen minutes Mr. Drummond,' she said, and hung

up. She ran back down the portego. 'Come on Jess - we've got some sport.'

'Go away,' she groaned from under the duvet.

'Come on you lazy cow - he sounds really dishy.'

Dryden stood on the landing-stage in the glare of the sun-bleached marble cliff of Gothic decoration that was the Ca' d'Oro. Looking along the canal to the sharp blue tower of the stricken Palazzo, he reflected on this place from two very different perspectives. Over four centuries earlier, not fifty metres from where he was standing, Edward de Vere, the Seventeenth Earl of Oxford, had fled the city owing a mass of debts. The day before Carnivale, he and his entourage - and a Venetian choirboy - quit the palazzo under a cloud. Amongst other things, the 'Italianate Earl', as he became known, was keen to get his extensive wardrobe of Italian fashions back to England, and Dryden had a document in his secret file, hinting that he didn't get away with all his belongings. This was why he was here; it was vital to find out whether anything that might be of value had survived. Even though the Middletons had acquired the property six months earlier, and had had plenty of time to go through it, this was a building full of hidden corners, and who knows what treasures may lie unfound or unrecognised? He studied very closely the scaffolding and its boarded walkways, some of which could just be made out behind the offensively blue cladding. If he was unable execute a thorough enough search in the presence of the owner's daughter, and whoever else might be there, then for a second visit, the scaffolding might afford him a very convenient and 'unofficial' means of entry.

The shrill sound of the electric door bell announced the arrival of the self-invited guest. Angelo admitted him, and showed him up to the first floor balcony. Dryden got quite a surprise as he stepped into the entrance lobby. He was greeted by what could only be described as two models ready for a fashion shoot. Their minimal make-up and long, loosely tousled hair, was evidence of a well-practised display of their looks. Daringly low-rise jeans, cut-down tops and an assortment of underwear, overwear, belts and whatever, gave them all the allure of pop-video chic.

'Bianca Middleton,' said 'B' offering her hand and a multi-braceletted wrist.

'Jessica Marston,' said the more elegant and self-assured Jessica, offering her hand and looking him straight in the eye.

'George Drummond, and call me George please.' It would be difficult for any man not to be at least a little on the defensive at this youthful full-frontal assault. The friends loved to play games with the male ego, and no-one was safe from the unrestrained exercise of their charm-offensive when they were in top gear. Old or young, rich or poor, they took no prisoners. When the duo were really on form, it was a pretty tough man who could walk away without the feeling that a bit of him hadn't been stolen, and he wouldn't be getting it back. The six-foot one, athletically built Dryden, was quick to assess their opening move and calmly made his. Now in his mid-forties, experience was very much on his side.

'My, my. You're quite a brace of girlies and that's for sure - but I was hoping to see Mr. Middleton.' He took out the ID card and showed it to Bianca. 'Is he in?'

She took it from him and looked it over. 'No. He's at work in England. Can I help?' Handing his wallet back to him, she deliberately kept him waiting in the lobby to assert her possession of the building and the situation. She had an intuitive mistrust of presumptuous people and needed a few moments to assess their suave visitor.

Dryden immediately realised that the owner's daughter, for all her show of confidence, was on the defensive. She had no need to volunteer the fact that the palazzo owner was out of the country, whether he was her father or not. He knew that she would be the next to speak.

'Please come in Mr. Drummond.'

'Thank you.' He said, and followed the girls into the unlit portego. 'So, this is the Magretti. Well now, this is pretty fancy isn't it?'

'Yes it's lovely isn't it? Daddy says nearly everything's original and it's hardly been touched for hundreds of years.'

As the three of them moved slowly along the portego, Angelo suddenly called out. 'I'll have the rest of the vine out by lunchtime signorina.'

'Thank you Angelo,' Bianca replied. She appreciated his reassuring comment. He wasn't going to leave them entirely alone with a stranger in the building. The children of several celebrities had been kidnapped in recent years, and Angelo knew you could never be too careful with any unknown visitor, no matter how plausible they might appear. Not only would he be not far away, they would know exactly where he would be. She felt more at ease, and switched on the portego lights. The room seemed to laugh and dance at its release from darkness.

Bianca broke the silence, her voice taking on a gymnasium-like echo. 'Of course it all needs a jolly good clean; but you have to get experts in to do it,' she said, 'Oh, and no photos Mr. Drummond. Daddy was most insistent.'

'Your word is my command', he said, 'and it's George, remember?'

'Well, George, perhaps you can tell me a bit more about why you're here?'

He saw that Bianca was quite astute and not to be underestimated. He continued with his friendly easy-going air in response to her directness.

'Er, just a courtesy call really. To let you know you're not alone. We are well-aware of the tough time the Itie press and TV have been giving you, and what with Venetian bureaucracy, lazy builders and winter storms well, we know that one can begin to feel rather alone in a foreign clime.'

'Thanks, that's very considerate of you, but it's Daddy you really ought to speak to. He's a busy man though and not at all easy to get hold of - some people say it's easier to get an audience with God!'

They were standing beneath one of the two huge and fussy

Murano-glass chandeliers, in which a third of the bulbs were blown or missing. She looked up. 'Over the top - or over the top?'

'Like you I think, Miss Middleton, I have little time for this sort of ostentation. But the portego would be a sadly deprived place without it would it not?'

Dryden was determined to remove any sense of threat from his presence. Engaging in a discourse on the qualities and merits of the ornament that surrounded them, and inviting a response from his host was, he felt, a sound starting point - even if she was only just out of her teens.

'Hello! What's that?' he said, and pointed to a dark patch of stucco on the cornice near the doors to the loggia.

'I think it must be some of the water damage,' Bianca answered, 'but it's far worse upstairs. Do you want to see what all the fuss has been about?'

'Lead on,' he said.

The girls were getting more and more relaxed, and Dryden's confident, easy-going, upper class way, was clearly winning them over. By the time they had escorted him up the main stairs to the second floor, they were talking to him more as though he were a family friend than a bureaucrat.

'The top floor is always kept locked and anyway there's nothing to see but bare boards and flaking paint. This is the interesting bit,' said Bianca, pointing to the rain damaged wall and the collapsed fresco. As he followed his beautiful guides to the scene of all their problems, he was keeping a mental note of everything in case he needed to return; the number of steps on each staircase; the floor surfaces; whether or not doors were kept locked, and if any of their hinges squeaked. Also, where all the furniture was situated, particularly if they contained drawers or cupboards.

'What happened there?' he asked indicating the hole in the bricked up doorway.

'It's a small storeroom or something. It was bricked up centuries ago apparently.'

'A bit creepy, isn't it? You could write a short story based on that, couldn't you?' added Jessica.

'You're so right,' he smiled, 'Anything interesting?'

'Just a few bits and bobs,' Bianca said, 'but it's quite empty now.'

Dryden couldn't resist walking round by the balcony to have a closer look for himself. In doing, so he noticed the key still in the lock in the ornamental glazed doors. After a cursory look into the empty room he went over to take in the view from the balcony.

'You won't see much, I'm afraid - Sr. Zenobi's plastic sheeting.'

'Ah,' he said, and came straight back in, closing the door. Unseen, he deftly turned, and then extracted, the key, slipping it into his pocket.

They continued the tour through the remaining rooms of what were once, not only the private apartments of the Magretti-Bellini's, but also the accommodation rented out to the Earl of Oxford during his stay in 1575-76. They went on down to the first floor and the only rooms their visitor hadn't yet seen. Jessica asked if anyone would like a coffee, and all agreed that it was good idea. She went along to the kitchen while Bianca showed Mark the front drawing room. They walked up the portego towards the loggia and turned left into the baroque room.

Suddenly, Bianca felt ill-at-ease. She whipped an elasticated bangle off her wrist, and in a moment had her hair in a ponytail. Avoiding what was about to become an uncomfortable silence, she said. 'These are the odds and ends Daddy found in the 'secret' room upstairs. See, no ghosts.' She walked over to them. 'They got a bit wet when the rain came in. Isn't that sad after all those years?' She was doing her best to play down their importance, and knew her father would be furious if he found that she had drawn too much attention to them.

Mark Dryden's relaxed air was brought to an immediate halt. He had become increasingly convinced that this had indeed been an abortive trip, and that, if anything had been left behind by Edward de Vere, it must have disappeared long ago. Crouching down for a closer inspection of the carefully arranged pages, he, too, didn't want it to look as though he had much interest in them. It would be neither natural nor wise, however, to dismiss them with no more than a couple of casual comments.

'He had a highly disciplined hand whoever he was,' he ventured. 'There are few corrections, and it is all so formal and regular - though not like a clerk's hand if you understand me.'

Bianca did understand him. 'Yes I do. I suppose he would have been highly educated as well. The vocabulary is so broad and knowing.' She was in danger of drawing him in too far, and proffered the first escape route that sprang to mind. 'We reckon he was an aristo' doing the Grand Tour,' she continued as she sidled towards the window, 'because it's all in English.'

Dryden carefully picked up one of the small parchment-coloured sheets of hand-made paper. He had handled many sheets just like this before, as he was something of an expert on 16th and 17th century handwriting and documents. He recognised this handwriting immediately. The verse structure and the content left him in no doubt as to what the Middletons had stumbled upon. As he read the lines, he felt catastrophe looming. All manner of actions and scenarios fought for dominance in his mind. Out of the confusion, he was certain of only one thing - that those sheets mustn't remain there for one more night. He glanced up at the figure of Bianca, silhouetted against the stained glass. She wouldn't take her eyes off him. He was in danger of drawing suspicion on himself, but was desperate to delay leaving the room, if only for a couple of minutes.

'These could be quite valuable, you realise. Someone like the British Library would simply adore to have a whole set of jottings by an Englishman abroad, especially a Tudor Englishman. Has your father contacted any experts to cast an eye over them yet?'

'I don't know, I don't think so. He only found them a few days ago, and as I said, he's very busy.'

He stood up still holding one of the pages. He didn't let on that he knew it was covered in verses from Shakespeare's extended narrative poem Venus and Adonis.

'Look after them won't you, and, seriously, the British Library, or possibly the British Museum might make you a handsome offer if you're not interested in hanging onto them. In fact…'

Dryden was interrupted by Jessica at the door with a tray of coffee. 'It's instant I'm afraid. We've run out of real. Is that OK?'

He took the nearest mug. 'Oh, that's fine, Jessica, thank you.' He took a sip. 'Mm, just how I like it.'

'What do you make of the English Lit., Mr. Drummond? We don't seem to be able to get away from it. It's all pretty cool, don't you think?'

'Yes, as you so rightly say, Jessica - pretty cool.' He was about to put the page back where he found it, when he glanced back at Bianca. She had moved towards him. She quickly took the sheet off him, and after replacing it, found herself checking that they were all there. It was an inexplicably loaded moment. Why, she wondered, did he look across at her, instead of just putting it back? Had he come here with another agenda? He could have put it back, and carried on discussing the Baroque ornament that surrounded them - but that impassive glance, did it conceal an ulterior motive for his presence or was she just being paranoid?

'And the two books, were they in your 'secret room' too?' he asked.

'Yes they were,' interposed Jessica, 'but I don't think they're completely dry yet.'

'Then I won't touch them.' He moved to leave the room, but not before stopping at the door to comment on the interior. 'The decorative artists who executed all this trompe l'oeil must have been amongst the best,' he said. 'If all this marbling had been damaged, or even destroyed, in your 'flood from above', it would have proved almost impossible to find artists with comparable skills to repaint it, would it not?'

The girls offered no opinion, but looked at the ornament surrounding them in a new light.

'How knowledgeable they were, how sensitive and how patient. You have to touch these architraves to know whether they're marble or paint.'

'How do you tell?' asked Jessica.

'The marble is always colder,' he replied.

As they moved on quickly to the last rooms - the one's once occupied by the aging Contessa, Bianca added, though in no way critical of their guest 'Our art teacher told us that the decorative painters who did all these effects, worked really quickly. In fact, he said, if they went slowly it looked laboured and therefore false.'

There was no reply from Dryden whose mind was now elsewhere. He had become a man consumed by the urgency of his mission; it was imperative that he remove the manuscripts at his earliest opportunity. He had overheard the girls talking about going to a masked ball at the Palazzo Zanardi that evening, to join in the 'Casanova Games.' He shuddered to think what *they* were, but at least it should leave the coast clear for when he returned, and hopefully, he would only have Angelo to worry about.

'There must have been loads of decorative artists all over Italy for simply centuries, don't you think?' she added.

'Yes, loads, as you so rightly say. Well, I must take my leave. Thank you so much for your generosity, and at such short notice too.' He took Bianca's hand and kissed the back. 'You have been the perfect hostess and guide.'

'Prego,' she said. 'I'll tell Daddy you called, and if he needs the consulate for anything, I'm sure he'll give you a ring.'

He stepped into the kitchen and placed his mug on the worktop by the dishwasher, at the same time thanking Jessica for her kindness. He bade them farewell, and, as he went down the steps called back. 'I do hope the fresco goes up without too much fuss, good-bye.'

'Go on then; what was all that about?' asked Jessica.

'Search me - girly!'

They giggled at their guest's sexist put-down.

'And one minute he's wandering around with all the time in the world,' added Jessica, 'and the next he can't wait to get away. Is that what consular officials do all day, swan around and get to see the inside of everyone's houses?'

'No idea.'

'Mind you, as a PR exercise I thought he did a pretty good job. I mean, he could charm the birds out of the sky couldn't he?'

'Maybe, maybe, but I'm going to ring Daddy anyway, and see what he says.'

6

Mark Dryden strode up the fondamenta towards the Strada Nuova with all the relaxed ease of a local resident, turned right at the bridge, and made for the Rialto. Having memorised his most likely journeys through the Cannaregio and Castello sestieres, he reached the Fondaco de Tedeschi, now the main post office, without so much as a second glance. He bought a pack of envelopes and addressed one of them to Bill Harvey at the British Consulate. After heading the envelope – 'Riservato e Confidenziale', he put in the ID card and stamped and posted it. Back outside, he tossed the remainder of the envelopes into a waste bin, but before setting off for his hotel, stopped to update John Fletcher.

'Hi, John. There's some material there. Not a lot, and it's small, so it shouldn't be a problem either acquiring it, or getting it back to the UK.'

'What do you mean – shouldn't?'

'Well, Middleton's in England, but there's a live-in security guard and a couple of teen-and-twenty girls. One of them is Middleton's daughter.'

'I can arrange some back-up. It's not a problem.'

'No, I'll be fine, honestly. The kids are going out to a carnival ball tonight, and I've found an easy way in and out.'

'You mean through the open roof on the top floor?'

'No - it's far too messy up there. I'm going to use the balcony on the second floor. It's cleaner and far quicker.'

'Just how much stuff is there?'

'About three dozen pages - Oh! and a couple of books.'

'OK. Now you're sure you don't need that second pair of hands?'

'I'll ring you if I need you. Bye, John.'

'Cheers Mark.'

Before returning to his hotel he had a bit of shopping to do. He went to Rigini's, the general store a couple of streets away, to buy a small back-pack and a camper's headlight. Next, he went to a busy mask shop to buy one of the most generic masks he could find. He then made his leisurely way back to the hotel. Using the phone in the lobby he checked with Marco Polo Airport for any late flights to the UK. There were only two: one to Bristol and one to Stanstead. Fortunately there was seat availability on both, so he booked a water taxi for each of them.

————

8.00 pm.

But for a pair of white shirts, Dryden's wardrobe was entirely black, including his gloves and the trainers brought especially for the occasion. He now packed everything he didn't need into his overnight bag, and took it down to reception. After settling up in cash, he went out to join the revellers.

Working back from the Easyjet departure time, he knew that there wouldn't be a moment to waste later that evening. If events did slow him down, it could mean having to leave from Verona or even Milan. He wouldn't remain in Venice in case Angelo discovered the robbery quickly whilst doing his rounds, and alerted the police. He hoped that the theft, committed so soon after his visit, would seem too ridiculous a plan for even the most calculating burglar. He felt certain that the police, whenever and if ever they got involved, would put it down to sheer coincidence, and anyway, by then he should be back in England.

Traffic jams of visitors and tourists blocked the main roads well into the evening, and so he used the minor calles to get to Campo dei Santi Apostili, two minutes from the Palazzo. At the

Ristorante Apostili, he enjoyed a light meal of seafood pasta and a glass of Prosecco, before making his approach.

Halfway down the dark and deserted Fondamenta Magretti, his heart quickened as he approached the courtyard door. 'It would be just my luck for those girls to come out now,' he thought, and even though he was wearing trainers, he found himself rather illogically tip-toeing past the door. Suddenly there was a sound of scraping metal, and voices talking and laughing on the other side of the door. His luck held long enough for him to climb to the first level of builder's planks on the scaffolding. Light suddenly blasted out of the doorway. The sharp white light sparkled across the girls' silk costumes as they stepped through the doorway to enjoy their night of merrymaking. The door banged shut. Dryden breathed a sigh of relief, and continued on his way to the front along the unsteady boards.

Within moments he was on the second floor balcony. A gust of wind made the plastic cladding flutter as he approached the door. He put on his surgeon's gloves, took out the key, inserted it into the lock, and turned it - 'please don't be bolted,' he prayed. Fortunately it wasn't. The door swung open silently and he slipped in, closing it behind him. His trainers were as quiet as a cat's paws on the now dry terrazzo, and he made his way quickly and stealthily along the edge of the portego and down the stairs. The only sounds to break the eerie silence were those of distant motorboats, far off bursts of laughter and shouting, and the faint tinny sound of a soccer match on television. 'Enjoy the game, Angelo', he whispered, and crept into the front drawing room. Staying alert for the slightest new sound, he opened his small black bag, removed the headlight, strapped it to his forehead, and switched it on. Its ghostly violet-white light lent to the ornate eighteenth century interior, the air of a scene from a black and white horror movie.

Once the books and pages were gathered up, it was time for him to leave - but not before checking that all the drawers in the Earl of Oxford's writing box were completely empty, and that he had the writing materials stowed safely in his bag. He removed the headlight and put it in his pocket, replaced his mask, and left the room. Moments later, he was half way down the portego and entering the stair lobby, but before he could mount the first step of the marble flight, the noise of the soccer match was suddenly louder. The portego lights flooded the lobby and stairs. He dashed to the second floor landing and entered the portego. The sound of Angelo's brisk footsteps were soon followed by the sudden brilliance of the second floor lights being switched on. Carefully avoiding the fallen fresco, he headed for the glazed screen of the balcony doors, fed the key into the lock, opened the door, and slipped through, closing it silently behind him. Before he even reached the balcony rail, the massive shadow of Angelo appeared silhouetted on the decorated panes. It grew smaller and sharper as he neared the unlocked door. Angelo rattled it and turned the key in the lock 'Ragazze stupido inglesi,' he said, walking away.

Dryden climbed over the marble rail onto the boards, and was soon on his way back down the side of the building. Hidden behind Signor Zenobi's plastic cladding, he stopped for a moment to readjust his mask, before dropping down to the fondamenta, and making his way back up to the main road and its boisterous merrymakers.

Out of the night, two revellers came round the corner onto the paved quayside. It was so dark that they didn't see him at first, black on black, but as they neared the stone architrave of the courtyard door - there he was.

They stopped dead in their tracks.

'Who the hell are you, and what are you doing here?' demanded Bianca. Almost no-one ever used the fondamenta but themselves, so to all intents and purposes it was their own private quay, leading only to their door. The masked figure remained still and silent. Was it guilt or because he didn't speak any English? Either way, the girls blocked his way. 'And what's that?' she added, pointing at his bag. She reached for the doorbell.

It was a cue for action. He struck out at her, knocking her hard against the stonework. 'Get away Jess, *run, run!*' she shouted, and grabbed at her assailant's arm; but her struggle with the strong man was cut short by another blow. This time he knocked her across the fondamenta and against the iron handrail at the top of the steps. As she fell, he turned and chased after the terrified and fleeing Jessica.

Entering the crowd on the Strada Nuova, noisy with carnival excitement, Jessica ran for her life, pushing her way through the sea of costumes. She slowed, wondering whether to go back and help Bianca, but when she looked over her shoulder, all she saw was a black and masked figure getting ever closer. She ran on as fast as her costume would allow, pushing wildly at the crowd as she searched desperately for any means of escape. She rushed on through the mass of masked faces; they all seemed to be chasing her now, hunting her down. She caught her heel and stumbled, letting out a piercing scream. A crowd of cloaked figures quickly gathered round, like vultures swooping on fresh and unexpected carrion. She leapt up, pushing her would-be helpers aside. The only thing in her mind was to rid herself of the black figure who was bringing down all the terrors of the night to devour her. Frightened to the core, she ran on past the post office and entered the Campo San Bartolomeo at the base of the Rialto Bridge. She mingled with the milling crowd. 'How do I lose him?' she thought - 'My mask. Of course, my mask - it's still round my neck.' She quickly put it on, and instantly became indistinguishable from all the other revellers. 'I'm just another Casanova look-alike,' she thought. 'He'll never find me now.' She peered out through the almond shaped slits, as through keyholes from within a darkened room. All masks. All joy. All colours. No black.

On top of the Rialto and in good light from the rows of tacky little gift shops, Jessica felt a lot safer – for one thing there was still no-one dressed in black anywhere in sight. She got out her mobile and rang Bianca - there was no answer. She went over to the other side of the bridge where she found the signal to be stronger and tried again. Still nothing. 'Shit!', she said out loud, and now assumed that Bianca's mobile had been damaged during the attack. But then her heart began to pound with a new dread, as she became consumed with a fear for the worst. She pushed and shoved her way to get off the bridge and back to the campo. At the bottom, she hadn't a clue which way to turn, and grabbed at the nearest costumed sleeve, shouting. 'Strada Nuova'. The stranger pointed. She went as directed, and fortunately for her it was the right way. She ran off against the thinning tide of revellers back towards the palazzo, desperately seeking Bianca as she ran. Tears now streamed down her cheeks as, gasping for breath, she prayed that she would be spared the sight a white-masked man attired all in black.

What she was unaware of, was that her pursuer had more important things on his mind than chasing after an hysterical student. With a long journey to make, he had long since squeezed his way out of the crush and into one of the minor streets, dissolving into its narrow darkness and away.

As Jessica neared the bridge over the Rio di Magretti, it dawned on her that she had neither seen 'B' looking for her, nor had a call from her. She had never been more frightened in her life. She stopped and looked all around her, and checked that she still wasn't being followed. The magical city of yesterday was now unfriendly, sinister and macabre. 'God I hate masks,' she thought, 'this whole trip is turning into a bloody nightmare.'

She turned the corner and walked down the fondamenta keeping close to the wall, squinting into the gloom of the near invisible quay. The plopping of the cold Adriatic water against the canal side, and the hard, rough, resistance of the stone wall, completed her alienation from all the things she loved.

'Bianca where are you?' She shouted "B', are you there?' But the stygian blackness offered up no reply. "B", she screamed, and made for the door.

She pushed the bell and banged on the door till it hurt. 'Angelo, Angelo,' she shouted. The faint sound of running feet was followed quickly by a stark flash of light as Angelo opened the courtyard door.

'Miss Jessica,' said a startled Angelo, 'what you doing here?'

'Is 'B' in here Angelo?'

'No Miss Jessica, she with you.'

'She's been attacked Angelo, right here, outside the door, and now she's gone, and I don't know where she is.'

'Calm down, Miss Jessica,' pleaded Angelo. 'She is probably looking for you right now, up there,' he said, gesturing towards the bright lights. 'How you so sure she was attacked? I see you go to the Casanova Ball, what, half an hour ago.'

'We forgot to take any cash with us. Can you believe it? We came back for some, and we saw this man, right here.' She gulped for words. 'And then…he hit her…and…and then he chased after me!'

Angelo, silhouetted against the glare of the courtyard security light, was just about to put a consoling arm round her, when she dashed off towards the main road. 'I've got to find her,' she cried.

Back up on the Strada Nuova now less busy, there was still no sign of her. She stood on the bridge to make herself seen, but still nothing. Jessica really feared for the worst now, and imagined that, perhaps bound and gagged, Bianca was already being carried off to some remote island in the lagoon, or being taken out of the country by a gang of evil kidnappers. Who would dare to imagine what terrible fate might be awaiting her?

She walked briskly back down the fondamenta to the door and the waiting Angelo, fully expecting to see a smiling Bianca standing beside him, ready to come out and end her ordeal with a big hug. She didn't. After a few moments, a more composed Jessica looked about her. It was then, on the ground in the shadows, that she saw something that truly terrified her. It was Bianca's carnival mask, and, half a metre away, her mobile phone.

7

The laughter and music of carnival now belonged to another world. Just forty metres separated a distraught and confused Jessica from the festivities she had left behind with Bianca only half an hour earlier. Now, here, she was on her hands and knees, fumbling around in the dark, on the cold hard flagstones of a foreign quay, searching for any reassurance that her best friend was alive and well.

She could make out the handrail, but the steps leading down to the black and uninviting water were all but invisible. Angelo joined her in the search, but clearly there was nothing else to be found. Jessica, still on her knees, called up to him. 'Angelo, phone the police. *Please* Angelo - right now. I'm really scared.'

'Miss Jessica, I'm sure Miss Bianca is OK. I think she look for you. She will be worried that the man who chase you will do *you* harm. Get up, please Signorina. I'm sure she will be back any minute, you see.'

She stood up, and joined him in the shaft of unforgivingly exposing light from the security lamp. 'Angelo, 'B' never goes anywhere without her mobile, never. Now I know something is seriously wrong, and we're wasting time. Look, what if that man stopped chasing after me and came back for 'B' because he couldn't find me? He might have her and is hurting her right now. Angelo, you've got to ring the police - *now!*'

'OK, OK,' he replied. 'I do as you ask, but I know these policemen here in Venice. They may not be as simpatico as you would like. Look, I phone right now.'

It was a busy night for the Venice Police, and they appeared to be in no hurry to get to the palazzo. It was nearly half an hour after their first call before the police launch finally turned off the Grand Canal and entered the Rio di Magretti. It's spotlight pierced the night like a rapier. The bravado manner of their arrival was obviously a declaration by the officers that they were going to do their talking from the boat. They said that they were fed up with dealing with drunken teenagers, and especially British drunken teenagers. Dismissive of Jessica's pleas for them to at least spend a few minutes searching for Bianca, they just told her to ring again in the morning if she still hadn't turned up.

'But she was attacked, officer. Here's her mask and mobile phone,' she urged. 'See, telefonino, mask,' she said, waving them abortively at the launch and its grimacing and unhelpful crew. 'How many men have you seen tonight dressed all in black? This is carnival for God's sake, someone must have seen him.'

'Signorina please, there must be dieci mille, no, twenty thousand persons on the streets of Venice tonight. Where do I start to look? Eh? Where? You tell me!'

'Officer, I *beg* you,' implored Angelo, 'the signorina we seek is too sensible; she is not the sort of signorina to go and leave her friend like this. I know her....' But he was interrupted by the police phone.

'Si, si English eh, where?....Oh, si, si, OK ciao Antonio. More of your English lager-louts Signorina. Your compatriots make plenty of work for us all over Venice tonight. Arrivederci - ring us in the morning.' The driver slammed the engine into gear, and the boat lurched backwards, reversing at high speed back down the side of the palazzo into the Grand Canal, and away towards the railway station.

An hour or more must have passed since they had last seen Bianca. Angelo went off to do his rounds, and Jessica changed out of her costume. In her eternity of worry she had lost all sense of the time, but Angelo's sudden disappearance made her conscious of it. Checking her mobile, she found it was ten-thirty.

'That means it's nine-thirty at home,' she thought, as first she phoned Randy, and then Tony.

The response of both men was the same - to get to Venice as quickly as possible. They both knew that Jessica was not the sort of girl to over-react, and the anxiety in her voice would have been enough to convince them that they were needed immediately. With his own plane, Randy was soon on his way to Northolt Airport, but for Tony, flying abroad was a rather more mundane affair. The first scheduled flight wouldn't get him to Venice until 9.10 the following morning.

8

Tony Chapman had just arrived back at his home in Maldon from a trade fair in Manchester, when his phone rang. He tossed down his overnight bag, took out his BlackBerry and checked the screen. It was the call he had been expecting from Jessica. He turned the speakerphone volume right down before pressing connect, fully expecting to hear her struggling to make herself heard over the raucous din of the 'Casanova Games'. A deathly silence, followed by an unexpectedly ominous tone to her voice, soon dispelled any notion he may have had that she was enjoying a night out. She spoke with a directness full of fear and dark urgency.

"B' has gone missing, Tony,' she said. 'We were attacked, and this man came after me - he wouldn't give up - he kept on and on, and what with my costume and everything, I never thought I'd get away from him...'

'Are *you* all right?'

'Tony, I'm scared.'

'Exactly where are you?'

'I'm back at the palazzo. Randy's security-man, Angelo, is here, and he's looking after me; she's just vanished, Tony - we can't find her anywhere.' She paused. 'Darling, speak to me.'

'How long ago did this all happen?'

'About an hour.'

'I'll get out to you as soon as I can - have you contacted Randy and Helena?'

'Before I rang you; I only spoke to Randy; he said Helena's abroad on a buying trip.'

'I guess he'll be on his way already.'

'What if 'B''s been kidnapped, Tony? We even joked about her being worth millions. She might have been targeted - that man could have been part of a gang - she might already be on her way out of the country!'

'Don't let's go there, Jess,' he said. 'Look, if she saw *you* being chased, then *she* might be worried about *you,* and is out there somewhere trying to find you.'

'We've searched everywhere. We called the police and they couldn't give a shit, they're useless. I've let her down, Tony, I feel so awful…Randy was petrified that one day this was going to happen…we've always been so careful.'

'Darling, whatever's happened it's not going to be your fault, and try not to let your imagination mess with your common sense. Stay with Angelo, and don't leave the palazzo on your own. If 'B' appears, text or call me straight away, OK?…I love you, Jess.'

'Love you too.' She said, and hung up.

From the despair in her voice, he knew that at a time like this, he was the only person who could possibly give her the comfort and support she needed. She was suddenly vulnerable, and her call concealed an urgent plea for help. The girls had often holidayed together, but Jessica had never been to Venice before, and Bianca, for all her extravert nature and worldly confidence, wasn't the sort of girl to go off on her own - ever. Carnival or not, Venice on a winter's night can be a barren, raw and uninviting place. He had to reach her as soon as possible, but the first scheduled flight from Stanstead to Venice Marco Polo wasn't until morning. It left him with an anxious wait.

His eyes dwelled for a few moments on the image of Jessica's face, smiling to him from the glowing screen. He went into the sitting room to fix himself a much-needed drink. He had been captivated by her from the moment she stepped into his office, a little over eighteen months earlier. She had answered his advertisement for a model in the Halstead Gazette, as she wanted to earn herself a few euros before going back up to university. At five feet ten, and with strikingly good looks, she thought modelling for his 2015 art materials catalogue might be fun, and they soon struck up a close relationship. Tony had found himself fascinated by the contrasts of innocence and worldliness in this forthright young woman, for whom getting away to university was an essential part of her struggle for independence - and freedom from the overbearing influence of her father.

Her long-time best friend, Bianca, also an only child, had been a huge and positive influence on her; but 'B', being the daughter of a world-famous celebrity father, placed Jessica in the proximity of the international world of entertainment, and its hangers-on. This caused a most unwelcome tension with both her parents. Maybe it was because she craved her independence so much that she would sometimes cling to Tony too assiduously, creating a minefield of tact and diplomacy for him, which no-one around her had either the inclination, or the patience, to clear.

Randy doted on his 'darling girl', and Tony knew that he would be beside himself the moment he received Jessica's call, and heard that something might have happened to her. 'What must the poor guy be going through right now?' he thought. 'I bet he'd give away his whole fortune just to know she was safe - I wonder if he's told Helena yet?'

He went into the kitchen to get some ice. On the wall by the door hung one of Alex's framed letters in that amazing calligraphy of his. Normally, he would have passed it by without so much as a second glance, but tonight, weary from a day stretched to its limits, and capped with Jessica's distress-call, he found himself dwelling on it. What had been a rich and exciting time in his life, full of untold promise, had ended so abruptly. He cast his mind back to his friend's funeral five-and-a-half years earlier. How that whole episode now appeared so distant, and so brief, as, gradually, it intruded less and less into the new life he had established. The trouble was, the more content he became with his 'new' life, the less he could ever entirely avoid the nagging reminders of an uncomfortable chapter in his past. Even though he had come to consider himself fortunate to have a convenient shut-off mechanism for his emotions, allowing him to rebuild his life away from past troubles and past mistakes, he still never got round to removing Alex's letter from his kitchen wall. The innocent A4 sheet of paper, with its fluid tracery of ascenders and descenders, may for years have been whispering guilty memories, but, now, unexpectedly, it was shouting a very present urgency. But it was Jessica who needed him, not Alex.

The discovery of the books and manuscripts in Randy's palazzo reminded him that he'd never bothered to follow up on Alex's Shakespeare authorship research. He had always meant to get to grips with the enigma one day, for his own reasons, but never allowed it to become a priority. Alex had discovered so much during those summer months, back in 2010, and Tony knew in his heart, that he owed it to Alex to carry on from where he had 'left off'. It was something his ex-wife, Imogen, Alex's sister, never let him forget, and her gnawing persistence had made him increasingly obdurate during their brief marriage. 'I'll get round to it one day,' he would say.

He straightened himself, rubbed his eyes, took a welcome sip of his drink, and mused for one last moment over the sheet of inscribed parchment-paper in its delicate black-japanned frame. 'Poor old Alex,' he thought, 'if only I'd taken your last letters to the police, if only I hadn't deleted your last phone messages, if only I hadn't gone away.'

'Hindsight,' he thought, 'you interfering bastard. What are you masquerading as now - a counsellor? Insinuating yourself into my recollections like a sympathetic friend?'

Guilt may have shadowed him from a safe distance for the last five-and-a-half years, but these seemingly unrelated events now unfolding in Italy, looked as though they were about to unearth a whole crypt-full of memories which he thought were well and truly buried. He was feeling wrecked after the four-and-a-half-hour drive down from Merseyside, and mulling over his past wasn't exactly the most sensible preparation for the uncertainties of the day ahead. His thoughts quickly focused on Jessica and

Bianca, and his concern for their safety and well-being. He went back to the drinks cabinet, fixed himself another vodka-and-tonic, added a splash of Limoncello, and went into his study to check on the earliest flight times to Venice.

9

SAT. 27th. VENICE:

Randy touched down a little after 3.00 am., and taxied into the private parking area at the northern end of Marco Polo Airport. Within a few minutes, he had been checked through customs and was in a water taxi speeding across the lagoon towards the city. The familiar twenty minute journey to the palazzo seemed to take for ever, and it was a very tearful Jessica who greeted him on the steps when he arrived. She had been Bianca's best friend for over ten years, and Randy knew her, and embraced her, like a second daughter.

As the taxi reversed out of the narrow Rio, it was immediately replaced by a police launch. Randy had contacted the Polizia Veneziano from the airport, and had told them, in no uncertain terms, that he wasn't going to have an investigation into the whereabouts of his missing daughter handled by a couple of night cops. As the blinding intensity of its spotlight picked out every detail of the surrounding buildings with uncompromising clarity, they pulled up to the steps. Commissario Montano jumped onto the quay, as his sergeant took one last sweep around the canal and its buildings with the spotlight. The driver cut the engine, but its dying roar was instantly replaced by the siren scream of a transfixed Jessica.

She stood and stared, pointing at a pattern of colours, that glittered in the oil-black water under the scaffolding, and danced rhythmically across the palazzo wall. Everyone turned and looked. It was their worst possible nightmare. Bianca must have been floating there all night, just out of reach. Ophelia-like, her titian hair flowed and mingled with the rainbow silks of her costume. The whole horrifying spectacle might have been staged for the cinema or the theatre.

They all stared.

'Kill the light!' Ordered the Commissario. 'Phone for an ambulance - now!' He shouted. 'Mr. Middleton, please, go inside, you shouldn't see such a thing. Everyone, go inside, please, we will deal with this.'

'I'm staying Commissario,' said Randy, 'I'm not leaving my darling girl.'

The detective got a long hooked pole from the rear of the police launch, and with it, ran to the base of the scaffolding. He reached for the dead Bianca, and eased her to the quayside.

'Light' said Montano, and with indecent suddenness they were exposed in its glare. The uncontrollably sobbing Jessica was helped into the courtyard by a shocked Angelo. She took a moment to glance back in order to remind herself that this still wasn't just more of some awful dream.

Angelo, with his arm round her shoulder, blurted out apologies in an incoherent mixture of English and Italian, blaming himself for the whole disaster, 'Bianca morta, Bianca morta,' he wailed, 'is all my fault, mi tanto dispiace, e e calpe mia, Miss Jessica mi dispiace, Signorina Bianca morta...'. Further police launches were soon on the scene, but had to shuffle themselves about straight away to make room for the ambulance. In his distress, Randy, dumbfounded by the chaos, crouched down to kiss the stone-cold hand of his daughter, as she lay on the flagstones at the top of the steps.

The Fondamenta Magretti and the Rio were quickly cordoned off, and a forensics team sprang into action. The medicos swarmed over Bianca, checking for any sign of life, and noted the time as they pronounced her dead. Randy looked on, like an uninvolved bystander, as the ritual of his daughter's removal unfolded. The routine efficiency of the medical team complete, he watched helplessly as the ambulance disappeared slowly down to the Grand Canal, fading into the darkness, taking away his only child, taking away his darling girl.

In a tragedy of this magnitude, involving the daughter of a high profile media personality, there was bound to be the type of publicity and public scrutiny that Commissario Montano could well do without. The eyes of the world were going to be on him, and he knew it. For Bianca's family and friends though, it could mean a speedy and thorough investigation. However compassionate he might like to have been, the Commissario had to pursue what few leads were on offer as urgently as possible, and he only had a confused and tearful student, and a half-hysterical security guard to assist him. Up in the first floor kitchen some preliminary statements were soon being taken. An English-speaking policewoman was most sympathetic in helping Jessica to stay calm, and to relate her version of events. Montano joined them.

'Please, Signorina, I know this is a difficult time for you,' he said, 'but could you tell me what you remember about this man who attack Signorina Middleton. Was he tall or was he short, was he, as you say in England, 'well built'? Any detail, will help.'

Her sobbing lessened a little, and she took a sip from her mug, cupped in both hands. She sat with her heels on the stretcher of a neglected seventeenth century chair, her knees tucked up defensively as though to protect herself, not only from the icy cold Adriatic wind, blowing in through the courtyard door, but from what had suddenly become a hostile and unrecognisable world.

'He was all in black except for his mask. Everything - even his gloves. He had a small bag, and that was black too.'

'And the mask, Signorina, what was it like?'

'Just one of those ordinary ones, white, plain, and a bit sad looking. I could see a bit of his hair at the side, but it was all so dark, I couldn't tell you what colour it was.'

'Was he tall, thin, 'well built' perhaps?'

'Tallish, average, and pretty fit because he ran after me. Not unlike the man who came from the consulate yesterday.'

'What man from the consulate, Signorina, this is the first time I hear of him?'

'Mr., Mr.,...oh God, I can't think straight. He had a public school accent, and waltzed around with that superior air, the way they do.' She paused for another sip of coffee. 'Drummond. That was his name - George Drummond. 'B' and I took to him instantly - It's not going to be him, is it?'

'Let's not jump to conclusions, Signorina; these are early days. You mentioned the consulate. The British Consulate, I presume?'

'Yes, that's right. He had some identification papers with him. None of us looked that closely. Well, I suppose 'B' did; but, from what I could see, it all looked official - his photo, coats of arms and stuff.'

'Is there anything else you can recall about his appearance?'

Jessica went over all the details she remembered about the friendly and engaging visitor she had been chatting to only eighteen hours previously. There were indeed similarities with Bianca's attacker.

The Commissario went into his phone menu, and brought up the British Consulate. Within seconds the emergency twenty-four-hour help-line number was ringing. He waited while it went through all the options he had no interest in, and then it told him to wait for further assistance. It then deferred to the Consul's private residence. He waited again.

'Sheridan here,' came the voice on the other end.

'I am sorry to trouble you at this hour, Signor Consul, but one of your nationals has met with an untimely death, and I require some information from you most urgently.'

'Who is this, please?'

'Commissario Montano of the Polizia Veneziano. You may ring the Questura and ring me back if you wish.'

'There's no need for that. Fire away, Commissario - how may I be of service?'

'Do you have an employee called Drummond, signore, a Mr. George Drummond?'

'No, why?'

'Then I would like you to come to the Palazzo Magretti-Bellini as soon as you are able please. Tell the officers at the cordon you are here to see me personally.' And with that he rang off. Before he could continue interviewing Jessica, a voice came echoing out of the decorated voids above.

'Commissario'

'Si'

'Il portego in il secundo piano, per favore.'

Commissario Montano excused himself, and went in search of his fellow officer. He found his sergeant standing by the balcony doors. 'She mentioned a bag, Stefano. Does it look like a break-in?'

Sergeant Stefano had found all the palazzo windows locked, and the doors to the top floor also secure. That left the loggia doors on the first floor, which were bolted as well as locked, the main entrance, and the second floor balcony, as the only means of entry. He had noticed that the key to the balcony doors wasn't fully turned in the lock. The doors appeared locked, but they weren't. They opened the door. A close inspection revealed no damage, or evidence of a forced entry. What was clearly discernable however, was a line of footprints, made of what appeared to be builders dust from the boards outside. They called up two forensics and fingerprints officers, and after leaving them to do their work, returned to the primo piano nobile.

'Have either of you been up to the secundo piano since the disappearance of Signorina Middleton?' demanded the Commissario.

'I haven't,' answered Jessica.

'Si,' answered Angelo. 'I check all doors and windows are locked. Is my job.'

'And everything is safe and secure signor?'

'Si,' Angelo replied, his face quickly showing the first flush of dishonesty. His mind was filled with confusion, as he wondered how he would find the right moment to admit that he knew there had been a robbery.

'No, signore, everything is not safe and secure, and you have chosen to lie to Commissario Montano. For the balcony door it is not locked. It wasn't locked when my sergeant checked it ten minutes ago, and therefore it is was not locked when the Signorina was attacked. So, Signor Angelo, how do you explain that, eh?'

'But, but I checked it was locked. On my round - every hour - I check.'

'Not well enough it would appear, Signor. How many times have you checked since the Signorina she disappeared?'

'Er, let me think, er, twice, no, three times.'

'Not every hour then, Signor. For it is now more than six hours since the Signorina she was reported missing!'

'I am excellent security guard. I work for Signor Middleton many years. Please, you ask him how reliable is Angelo.'

'Just how do you make your security sweep, Angelo?' asked Randy.

'I go to the top Mr. Randy, and as I come down, I go round each floor room by room, as you say, clockwise. Top floor always locked and bolted - no need to search. Second floor, first floor, ground floor, all done.' It was at this moment that Angelo chose to admit that whilst doing his rounds, he had discovered the theft of some of the artefacts from the front drawing room.

'What artefacts?' asked a surprised Montano.

'You didn't say anything to me about a robbery, Angelo,' said Jessica sharply.

'I don't want to upset you miss.'

'Anyway that door wasn't always kept locked,' she added.

'Oh!' cut in Commissario Montano. 'And how do you know this, Signorina?'

'Because, when Bianca and I went on the balcony to look at the city yesterday, it wasn't locked, that's why.'

'Miss Bianca, she often not lock doors and windows…'

'Don't you *dare* go blaming 'B'. It was *your* bloody job to make sure *we* were safe.' She shouted.

'Jess, Jess, that's not going to do any good is it?' pleaded Randy.

'The robbery, Angelo; exactly what time was it when you

realised someone had been in?'

'At ten-thirty. Miss Jessica, she saw me go. I am so sorry, Mr. Middleton.'

With Jessica and Randy so upset, and Angelo squirming and more or less begging for his job, Montano was now decisive, and rounded on the hapless security guard.

'One or other of two things happened here, it occurs to me,' he began. 'Either a cat burglar came by and chanced his luck, or our 'Mr. Drummond' came back last night. Whoever he was, he was very clever to get in and out - possibly with a little inside help. With all respect, Mr. Middleton, security guards are not the best paid profession. An insecure door on carnival night - a night when you know that the palazzo will be empty, Signor Angelo, may not prove to be a coincidence.'

Angelo was shocked and speechless that the finger of guilt should be pointed at him. Before he was able to utter a sound in his defence, the Commissario continued. 'Mr. Drummond may be a friend of yours, and you invited him here to look over the objects he stole. You knew they must be valuable, Signor, and, as you well know, there is a ready market for anything that is old isn't there? I would like to ask you a few more questions, but not here I think - Sergeant?'

'Are you sure about this, Commissario?' interrupted Randy. 'I've known Angelo for seven or eight years, and he's as honest as they come.'

'Let me be the best judge of that, Mr. Middleton. Take him to my launch. Just to help with our enquiries you understand.'

The protesting and gesticulating Angelo was summarily removed from the palazzo. Handcuffed and cautioned, he was showily manhandled down the long stairs to the courtyard and Commissario Montano's waiting launch. He was immediately whisked away into what was left of the Venetian night.

With Angelo despatched to the Questura, the police headquarters in Castello, the Commissario turned to Randy. It proved to be a real test of his tact and diplomacy. He was keen to get his investigation on the move, but confronted by the distressed state of both Middleton and Jessica, he was forced to back off. He rang the mortuary to find out if there was any news on the cause of Bianca's death. An initial diagnosis showed that from the amount of water in her lungs, she actually died of drowning. The cuts and bruises on her head, arms and hands, were clear evidence of a violent struggle. However briefly, she had fought for her life.

When Randy chose to go into the kitchen to fix himself a drink, Commissario Montano approached him and asked if he would be so kind as to check what was missing from the palazzo, as it might speed up the catching of the intruder. Randy thought for a moment. Should he phone his wife now or later?. He checked his watch.

'Let's get it over with,' he answered, and took the sergeant with him to search all the rooms.

An even more confused and upset Jessica received some comfort from the understanding policewoman who brought her another mug of coffee. She thanked her, and still shaking and trembling, burst into tears. She wanted her boyfriend, she wanted her Bianca, and she wanted her yesterday.

Randy returned after a couple of minutes with the sergeant, and was holding an antique book in his hand. 'Two of the old books that we found have gone, Commissario. They were very much like this one. And so have all the handwritten sheets of paper. But that seems to be everything; just small portable things, I suppose.'

'Were there many sheets, Mr. Middleton?'

'I'm not sure, as I never counted them; around three dozen, forty, something like that.'

'It may be that the visitor your daughter entertained yesterday was a fraud, Signor, as no-one by that name works at your consulate here in Venice. We will check all British Consulates in Italy of course - then we will know for certain.'

'Damn, damn, damn,' said Randy in response to the news. 'Now what?'

'We will check all British passport holders, especially men following the description given by Signorina Jessica, as they leave the city by the airport and the ferries. I am now sending my officers to the railway station and the car park at Piazzale Roma. If he is leaving Venice by taxi or train, we will have him in a couple of hours.'

'And the hotels?'

'Don't worry, Mr. Middleton, we check them all; and the CCTVs from around the city. We will find him.'

Randy looked from the courtyard balcony at the group of officers in conference by the doorway to the fondamenta. A sad, yellow, presaging dawn edged the clouds outlining the surrounding buildings. Commissario Montano kept his telefonino clamped to his ear throughout the proceedings. 'I wonder if they would be that motivated if I weren't so bloody famous,' he thought. He took out his mobile and phoned Helena. Emotions surged up from unplumbed depths of his being. He choked as he tried desperately to control his breathing. His vision blurred as tears filled his eyes once more. He took another deep breath, and pressed the key. Then an inexplicable terror came at him…For God's sake don't answer…Don't ever answer. But answer she did.

'Hello darling, it's lovely to hear from you - heavens is that the time?'

10

By the time the British Consul arrived the early morning traffic was already churning up the choppy green water of the Grand Canal. The Pescheria on the opposite bank had been busy for a couple of hours, noisy with the clatter of fish boxes, boats coming and going, and the seemingly irreverent shouting of the fishermen and the buyers. His water-taxi eased into the Rio Magretti under the police line and moored at the steps. He was greeted by Commissario Montano who filled him in on the essentials of the situation so far.

'I have spoken to several of my staff, Commissario,' said the Consul, 'and this man Drummond is completely unknown to any of them.'

'He showed official looking documents to gain entry, Signor Sheridan, and he phoned ahead to announce his impending arrival. He was most confident and well prepared, si?'

'Is there anybody here who saw these identity papers, Commissario, I want an idea of what they looked like?'

'Si, the young lady you will find in the casa. She was a close friend of the unfortunate Signorina who was killed last night. Mr. Middleton, who owns the casa, is also here. It was his daughter who died.'

The Consul stepped quickly across the courtyard and up the stairs. He knocked, and entered the lobby announcing his presence. He greeted Randy with a firm handshake, and offered his condolences. Richard Sheridan, ex-Guards, and a tall and imposing man in his late fifties, asked if he might see Jessica. She came into the portego from the kitchen and introduced herself.

'I am sorry to have to be so down to earth, Miss Marston, but, if we can help the police in any way, then I think we must.'

'That's OK, Mr. Sheridan. I know you've got a job to do; it's just that I can't really believe this is all happening to me.'

'Montano's a jolly good chap, you know. I've dealt with him several times over the years, and, if anyone can help get to the bottom of this awful business, it's him, believe me.' He was painting as optimistic a picture as he dared under the circumstances, but the gently sobbing Jessica was unmoved. 'Can you remember any details about this identity card? What did it look like exactly?'

She gave what description she could, having seen it for literally only a few moments. 'He showed it to 'B' and she looked at it quite closely,' she said, 'and then he put it back in his inside pocket.'

'From what you describe, it sounds like the real thing. Do you remember if he mentioned any person at the consulate by name?'

'No, no one. I wasn't really involved; he addressed himself to 'B' all the time he was here. It was almost as if he was a family friend. He seemed really nice.'

'Drummond, if that's really his name,' said Randy, 'couldn't have known I wasn't going to be here, so he must have been prepared to meet me. Surely his ID would have to be nigh on perfect, or I would have been straight on the phone to you.'

'That had gone through my mind, Mr. Middleton. Few people get to know what our official documents look like for obvious reasons. As I see it, either one of my consular staff is capable of giving away security information, or this Drummond fellow was working entirely on his own and taking one hell of a bloody risk. Trouble is, I trust all my people, and I haven't a clue where to start!'

9.30 am.

The sombre mood of the morning was interrupted by the sound of a commotion outside. The voices got louder until a group of figures appeared silhouetted in the doorway to the courtyard balcony. Commissario Montano left Sergeant Stefano holding a man by the arm, and came in.

'Signorina Marston, this man says he knows you, is that true?'

Jessica avoided answering the detective's question, leapt out of her chair, and threw herself into the arms of the man she'd been waiting for so anxiously.

'Tony, am I glad to see you? You can't believe how awful this has all been. We were attacked right there - by the door,' she said, pointing outside. And with her words breaking up, went on, 'and now…'B's dead…Tony… she's gone.' He held her trembling body tightly, and she clung to him for protection, as though she might be the next to suffer at the hands of a dangerous man. She was relieved that he had got to the palazzo so quickly. Randy had done what he could to look after her, but half the time she was caring for him. They went and sat down. Tony caught Randy's eye. They knew each other well, and the nod of the head they gave each other said nearly everything.

'I daren't even think about it, Tony, I can't contemplate our lives without her.' As he spoke, two of the forensic team came down the portego, and walked between them. 'I'm - empty. I feel like I'm…nothing.'

Jessica gave a description of 'George Drummond' to the Consul. Tony stood up and addressed him.

'Tony Chapman,' he said, offering his hand.

'Richard Sheridan, British Consul here in Venice, how do you do.' The detached formality of the civil servant distanced him from the emotional tsunami that had swept over everyone else in the room, but Tony needed an update in order to get his head round the events of the last few hours. He decided that this wasn't the man to help him. He bent down and gave Jessica a kiss on the forehead, then went out onto the balcony to talk to the Commissario.

'Have you any idea who we're looking for?' he enquired.

'Well, Mr. Chapman, we have an intruder, a thief, a cat-burglar, who entered the casa and helped himself to some renaissance artefacts. It appears that, as he was leaving, he was surprised by the two young ladies. He attacked Miss Middleton, and, whether he intended it or not - we do not know - his actions resulted in her death. He then chased after Miss Marston, but as you can see - she is safe and well.'

Back in the portego, the Consul was preparing to leave.

'I'm off to see if I can get any leads from my staff Mr. Middleton. All I can glean, I'll pass on to Montano here. Here's my card. Ring me any time you need assistance, making any arrangements, that sort of thing.'

'Thank you Mr. Sheridan, I'll ring if I need you, and thanks for coming over so promptly.'

'All part of the service. Good bye for now. Good bye, Miss Marston, Mr. Chapman, and, if you don't mind my saying so, watch out for the paparazzi. They scan the air waves over here and they'll be gathering along the quay as we speak.'

Jessica hadn't thought of media, and it dawned on her that the twenty-four-hour news channels were bound to be picking up on the story. She thought it wise to ring her parents and prepare them. Also, if it was 'Breaking News', then it might be judicious to get out of Venice as quickly as they could. She got up and walked down the portego.

'Mummy, I've got the most awful news,' she began. By the time she reached the loggia overlooking the Grand Canal, she had finished telling her mother the basic facts. '…and we're coming home just as soon as we can get a flight. Yes, that's right Mummy, with Tony. Byee.'

She looked back up the barren portego, to see Tony, Randy and the Commissario deep in conversation.

'We have found no evidence of fingerprints, and no DNA yet. Our man was very thorough, signores. We may be finished by lunchtime, Mr. Middleton, and then, but not before please, you may use the Casa as you wish. We found evidence that your daughter was in contact with the courtyard doorframe, and the metal post at the top of the steps leading to the water. Some silk fibres on the steps indicate that she fell on them before entering the water. Analysis of them will confirm if they came from her fancy dress costume. That is all I can tell you at present.'

'And the assailant, Commissario,' asked Tony, 'any news of him?'

'It is too early to say, Mr. Chapman. We are checking all the hotels and pensiones. As soon as I have any news of him I will inform you straight away, but please, you must be patient, and leave the investigation to the Polizia Veneziano, si?'

'Of course,' added Randy, and the two of them sat down with Jessica, who was finishing off her coffee.

A few moments later, Commissario Montano came up to them, his telefonino seemingly glued to his ear.

'Seventeen single male passengers have flown back to England on British passports last night and this morning from Marco Polo,' he said. 'Twelve of them arrived in the last three or four days. Unfortunately none of them was called Drummond. We keep searching. Remember, please, we do not know when he came to Italy, what is his real name, or if he is still in Venice, or indeed, still in Italy.'

'What about the Shakespeare connection, Commissario, isn't that your best line of inquiry?' suggested Tony. 'It was the subject of everything that was stolen.'

'They were also the only things of value small enough to be easily carried, and for which our robber may have, as you say in England, 'a ready market.' Please Signor Chapman, leave the detective work to us. I have seen many robberies like this before. The scaffolding is like an invitation card to a thief - especially on a building such as this. Maybe our cat-burglar is a lone opportunist who uses the distractions of Carnivale to do his dirty work. 'Mr. Drummond', or whoever he is, may have nothing to do with the burglary, or the unfortunate Miss Middleton. You see, I keep the open mind.'

'Do you have an open mind where Angelo is concerned too, Commissario?' asked Randy.

'I frighten him a little, Mr. Middleton. If he has anything to tell us we shall soon hear it.' Leaving them to ponder the helplessness of their situation, the Commissario left for his launch and the Questura.

Following up on his rejected suggestion, Tony asked Randy if he could remember the names of the two stolen books, and whether they definitely had a Shakespeare connection.

'I haven't a clue Tony, and quite frankly, at the moment I don't care.'

'I'm sorry Randy, I didn't mean to…'

Their conversation was cut short by the sudden appearance of a woman, silhouetted in the lobby doorway. The elegant figure, all in black, entered the portego unannounced. 'Where is she, Randy?' she said, and after a few seconds delay - 'I *must* see her.' It was Helena, who had been on a buying trip to Florence when Randy phoned her to break the news.

'She's at the Ospidale darling,' he said, and went straight over and put his arms round her. 'Come on, I'll get a taxi.'

11

'Can we go home Tony, soon?'

'Let me check the flight times.' He took out his phone. 'You sure Montano doesn't want to speak to you any more?'

'I signed a statement just before you arrived, and he hasn't said I can't leave.'

'I'll see if I can find him and tell him we're on our way home.'

'By the way, have a look in the front room, up there on the left,' she said. 'You'll find something very interesting.'

Jessica ambled over to the bedroom she had shared with Bianca for their tragically short stay. She stood in the doorway and looked at Bianca's clothes scattered all over her bed. Tears ran down her cheeks, and dripped onto her T-shirt. 'You lazy cow,' she thought, with an ironic smile. 'You're the only person I know who could still be that untidy even when you're dead!'

Tony went to the scene of the robbery. He knew what Jessica had meant him to see from her phone-call two days earlier. One of the two remaining forensic officers was rolling up the last of the crime scene plastic tape, as the other packed their equipment with meticulous care into his kit box. They indicated to Tony that they were done. Then he spotted, in the unfurnished and faded opulence of the room, the renaissance writing box. Through the fingerprint dust on its lid, he could discern the Coat of Arms of the Seventeenth Earl of Oxford. He ran his fingers over the shield, its star trying vainly to shine through the forgotten centuries of neglect. He felt as though he was invading the private space of the eccentric lord he had been studying for so long.

His passionate interest in the Elizabethan aristocrat had come quickly into focus when Jessica had told him about the find on the Thursday afternoon. Bianca's death now shed a very different light on things. 'I don't believe in coincidences,' he thought. 'First Alex, and now Bianca. Two people dying so close to the mystery of the Shakespeare Authorship problem - there has to be a link. If there is a coincidence, it's the fact that I knew them both.' He had never told Jessica about Alex, and kept the whole episode in his life to himself. Wise decision or not, it looked as though circumstances were inevitably going to lead to the opening this particular Pandora's Box.

He closed up the front, and fastened the clasp on the Tudor writing box, and took it along to Randy's office.

'You ready yet?' he called.

After she had packed, Jessica folded all Bianca's things, and put them in a neat pile on her bed. As she left, it occurred to her that there was no-one to lock up.

'Hang on, Tony,' she said, and ran upstairs to lock the balcony doors, and remove the troublesome key. She came down, checked the loggia doors, and took the keys to Randy's desk in his office. She knew Randy wouldn't have given security a thought, so she rang him to tell him they were leaving.

'I'll pop them in the top drawer OK?'

'Thanks Jess,' said Randy, 'don't worry about the front door, Montano's leaving a couple of his men, either until Angelo gets back, or till I can arrange for his replacement. Well, safe journey.'

'Thanks Randy, I guess we'll see you back home.' She was on the verge of saying, 'at B's funeral,' but stopped in time. 'Love to Helena, Byee.'

'That writing box is a museum piece if ever I saw one,' he said.

'I thought of you the moment I saw it. I knew you'd love it.'

Jessica went over to Randy's desk and opened the top drawer to put the keys safely away. There, to her astonishment, lying in full view, were the three manuscript pages that Bianca had removed from the front drawing room the day they'd arrived.

She found herself in something of a dilemma. Should she leave them where they were, tell Randy, tell the police, or take them? Commissario Montano had shown no interest in following up their suggestion about a Shakespeare link to the robbery, and she couldn't ask Randy and Helena, as they were at the hospital, and preoccupied with their grief. If she just left them where they were, a vital lead in solving the crime might be overlooked.

'Tony, come here a minute.' She took out the handwritten pages and showed them to him.

'Oh, my God!' He exclaimed. 'Where were they?'

'In the drawer. I'd forgotten all about them. 'B' removed them on Thursday for a closer look. She obviously put them in here for safekeeping.'

'Were they all like these?'

'More or less, yes.'

'And was Randy absolutely certain that none of the things he found could have ever left the palazzo, that they must have been here and nowhere else since the sixteenth century?'

'Positive, because the fresco was painted in the late 1570's. 'B' and I checked for ourselves. It was all in the Venice newspapers too. The artist died in 1578, shortly after he finished it.'

'And Oxford left Venice for England in March 1576,' said Tony.

They both had very mixed emotions about their discovery. At one moment they were desolate over the loss of a dear friend, and the next, able to enjoy the exhilaration of a find that might lead to her killer. Jessica felt the pull of conscience and unseemliness more than Tony, who found it impossible to escape what he knew was being offered by this unique opportunity.

'I wonder if the British police would be more interested than the Italian?' He said. 'I know these are Randy's and not ours, but, if he would let us borrow them, at least we could see if the CID back home would take us more seriously. Well, we've got nothing to lose have we?'

'Whatever, sweetheart. I'm too tired to think straight, and I want to get home, all right?'

Tony grabbed a sheet of writing paper, and wrote a note to Randy:

Jess has just found three of the pages we thought were stolen. She said Bianca had separated them from the rest for closer study and put them in your desk. If it's OK with you, we'd like to take them back to England with us, to see if we can get a more positive response from the CID. The three pages are: One headed 'The Jew' and has drafts for Portia's famous soliloquy on it: one with verses that might be from Venus and Adonis, though I can't be sure, and some lines that look a lot like Loves Labours Lost, and the final one almost certainly jottings and drafts for Taming of the Shrew. I promise you we won't show them to anyone but the police, and, even then, we won't leave them in their possession.

See you soon,

Regards,

Tony & Jess

Looking at his note, written in almost perfect copperplate, he recalled his friend Alex, with whom he used to communicate regularly in longhand years before. He had been an 'Oxfordian' too, spending the last couple of months of his brief life researching the Shakespeare Authorship question. What he wouldn't have given to be able to show these pages to him. He also felt a pang of dishonesty, for, however honourable his motives, he was well aware that, without the owner's permission, he was the second person to remove some of these unique pages from the palazzo in the past twenty four hours. He slipped them into an A4 envelope, picked up his bag, and joined Jessica, who was waiting for him on the courtyard balcony.

The couple made their way to the fondamenta to await their taxi, but a commotion and a flashing of lights to their right alerted them to the presence of the paparazzi and TV crews. They dashed back into the courtyard. Jessica was quite unprepared for the suddenness of this intrusion into her life. The taxi soon arrived, and with the assistance of the police guard, they got into the boat almost unseen. The pair were now safely out of the sight of prying eyes, and on their way to the airport.

As they skirted the island of Murano, it was Jessica who broke the silence. 'I'm going to get that man if it's the last thing I do.' She said. 'Oh God, I sound like a B-movie actor. This is all so unreal; it's as though somebody else is talking for me.'

'*We*, are going to get him,' added Tony.

'Do you really think we can though, Tony. I mean seriously, two ordinary people like us?'

'We'll just have to become extraordinary people then won't we? Despite all Commissario Montano's experience, Jess, that robbery looked to me like stealing to order. 'B's death could well have been quite unintentional, but that thief was determined, and scared, if you ask me. I mean, why else did he go chasing after you? I know we haven't got much to go on, but, like you, I think the answer lies in England.'

He looked out of the window, but the spray on the glass almost completely obscured the view. 'We're going to have to put our thinking caps on once we get home,' he said, inviting a reaction from Jessica, but she was already dropping off to sleep.

The engine suddenly slowed. 'Jess. Jess. Wake up! We're almost at the airport.'

12

Tony and Jessica entered the baggage reclaim hall, and wandered over to the carousel. Refusing to join the race to grab a trolley, Jessica kept well away from the mêlée, and hid behind one of the huge grey roof supports to phone her parents and tell them they had arrived safely. She also wanted to asked them if either television or radio news had picked up on Bianca's death.

Her mother was in the kitchen clearing up after a late lunch.

'Your father should be in arrivals Jessie love - wait a moment and I'll see what's on.' At the touch of a button on the remote, an LCD screen, already tuned to BBC News 24-7, dropped into view from under one of the wall cupboards. To her dismay, the "Breaking News" panel was already running the story. It ran: "Media Celebrity Randy Middleton's daughter dies in Palazzo tragedy - Body found in canal." 'Oh, dear girl!' she gasped. 'Darling, it's on right now.'

Tony followed Jessica and her father, Peter Marston, for the short journey out to Halstead and Great Colne. It was late February, but, as they swept along the gently curving rise and fall of the dual carriageway, there wasn't a hint of winter. At weekends, every road in Essex seemed to be busy, and this Half-term Saturday was no exception, but they were soon able to leave the hurry-scurry of the commuting shoppers behind as they turned off the main road, through the tall stone gateposts, and into the courtyard in front of the Old Rectory.

Peter and Julia had bought the property about fifteen years earlier from a local farmer, Angus Basset. He had become famous all over north Essex and south Suffolk for Basset's Pies, and all their friends called their red-brick home 'The Pie Factory', on account of its being so huge. The Marstons had been sorely tempted to downsize now that Jessica was getting independent, but couldn't face taking the first step.

The day had been exhausting for both Tony and Jessica, and they were completely drained. In the last twenty-four hours, the couple felt they had run the whole gamut of human emotions - fear, anger, love, loss, elation, loneliness, disappointment. Tony knew that this was not the time to leave her; even though she had her parents to care for her, he knew they were unable to give her the kind of support she needed.

'Have you asked your parents if it's all right for me to stay over?' he asked.

'They're not happy, as you might have guessed. It's OK though.'

Tony came down with the envelope containing the pages, and went into the garden room. He sat on one of the two long sofas, between which was a generous glass-topped coffee table. He removed the pages and placed them in a neat row on the spotless surface. As he waited for Jessica to come down, Julia came in with a couple of cups of coffee.

'They look old, Tony,' she said.

'They are, Julia. Randy found them in the 'Magretti.' This is the work of one of the best playwrights at the court of Elizabeth I. I think they're going to prove to be extremely valuable, and I've got a horrible feeling 'B' was killed because of them.'

'Oh! Tony - you're frightening me. How can a few pieces of paper be *that* important? - And what about Jessie - she isn't in any danger is she?'

'I'm sorry, Julia, I didn't mean to scare you. I'm sure Jess is quite safe here with you and Peter. But as for these sheets of paper, well, it's a long story, and I think the question of the Shakespeare authorship is very probably in the mix, even though the Venice police don't seem to think so.'

There was an uncomfortable silence. The tension was broken

by Julia.

'Who found her Tony? Please tell me it wasn't Jessie?'

He looked at her and nodded his head. 'Sorry, Julia,' he said.

She stifled a sob, and put her hand to her mouth as if to prevent her next words being uttered. 'Oh, my poor baby,' she said in a half whisper, and went off to be alone with her worries.

Tony read through the pages. What irked him was to have them in front of him, while all his references were twenty miles away at his home in Maldon. His thoughts turned to his Uncle Brian, or 'BJ' as most people knew him. What would he have made of these pages? Seven or eight years earlier his favourite uncle had introduced him to the hypothesis that Edward de Vere, the Seventeenth Earl of Oxford, was possibly the true author of Shakespeare's works. His membership of an 'authorship society' added weight to this conviction, and Tony felt certain that if 'BJ' knew that he had original Shakespeare-Oxford material, he would be euphoric. The trouble was, it would be in front of his society members, and the news posted on the internet, before you could say 'Globe!'

But the precious Renaissance sheets weren't his to do with what he wanted. Randy would be furious, and rightly so, if he were so indiscreet as to go public with them, especially as Bianca hadn't even had a funeral yet. He looked at them again and again, lying in a row on the table in front of him. He hungered for the stolen ones. What treasures did they hold, he wondered? And who had them now, and was their possessor intimately connected with the tragedy a thousand kilometres away?

5.40 pm.

It was dark, and the rain on the lofty windows hinted at sleet. As Jessica hadn't appeared, Tony went to see if he could find her. He found Julia in the TV lounge.

'Is Jess all right, Julia?' he asked.

'She's having a well-earned rest.'

'Do you mind if I go up and see her?'

'Look after her, Tony,' she said, 'she's leant on 'B' so much since going up to university, sharing the flat with her and everything. It was so kind of Randy; but now, well, you never know how things are going to work out do you? Who knows, it could even be the making of her?'

Tony left her and went upstairs. He found Jessica asleep on her bed, still fully-dressed. 'Damn me if you don't look just perfect,' he thought to himself 'maybe too perfect.' He had had two or three relationships since his divorce two years earlier, but he hadn't fallen for anyone as deeply as this. He didn't doubt for a moment how badly she wanted him; the trouble was, he knew she wanted to get away from her parents and the 'pie factory' just as much. When she left to go on her 'Carni - varli weekend' with Bianca, he hadn't expected to see her for a week, hoping that a little more of that girlish grammar school insecurity might have worn off by the time she got back. But here she was, twenty-four hours after putting on her carnival costume, back in her parent's house, asleep, and still with all that growing-up to do. Now that Bianca was gone, it was as though all the bright colours had gone from her palette. He sensed from Peter's silences that *he* knew something in her had changed too. Events were accelerating Jessica into leaving home, and Tony's heart went out to the father who was helpless in the face of the inevitable. He eased the duvet over her shoulder, and went back downstairs.

Peter was in the kitchen making a pot of tea for Julia and himself, one of his many daily rituals. Jessica's parents had no time for 'heretics' as they called Tony, or anyone else who challenged the orthodox view of the Bard. They were donating to the Globe soon after the death of the tireless campaigner Sam Wanamaker, and were regular visitors to the RST in Stratford-upon-Avon and the Globe on Bankside. They preferred to keep their 'Jessie' away from such subversive ideas, and, in fact, she was far from convinced that Tony was right anyway. 'It's all circumstantial,' she would say. 'So is the case for the glover's son from Warwickshire,' he would reply.

It was difficult for Peter and Julia to disguise their prejudice where Tony was concerned. The trouble he had gone to, to help their only child, did little to ameliorate their bigotry towards the northern comprehensive boy, who was making such an impression on her. He was almost six years older than her too - and with a failed marriage behind him; what sort of prospect was that? Conversations round the dinner table went uncomfortably quiet whenever the subject of Jessica's love-life was raised. His successful business, importing quality art materials from China, didn't help either; on the contrary, it just further undermined the feelings they had for the England they loved. To them, Tony's attacks on Shakespeare typified a modern fashion for subverting their history, their heritage, their souls.

<hr>

SUN: 2.00 am.

It was pitch black, and Jessica woke to the sound of the wind in the trees, roaring like the tide on an unseen shore. Raising her head from the cold wet pillow, her eyes open or closed, the image of Bianca's drowned body appeared so vividly to her that its shimmering colours could have been projected onto her bedroom wall. Before it could fade, white masks rushed at her from all directions, gaping and grimacing - menacing and hungry. She was engulfed by such intense feelings of fear and loneliness she felt she would scream.

She sat up, hugging the duvet. A distant clock chimed two. In just twenty-four hours, without any warning, her happiness and her optimism had been ripped away. Her best friend, who held one of the keys to the outside world, was gone. Her family wouldn't understand - couldn't understand - her sense of desolation. How she needed Tony now.

She removed her shoes, and tiptoed out of her room and across the landing to Tony's room. She stood by his bed, got completely undressed, and slipped in next to him. He shifted a little as their bodies assumed a single form - her back in contact with his front, she could feel him all the way from her neck to her toes.

As his elbow nestled in her waist, the natural fall of his arm left his hand cupping her breast, her nipple hard in the palm of his hand. The radiant heat from her skin began to consume him like an inextinguishable fire. He fought his passion, his breathing quickened. This wasn't the time and he knew it. He relaxed. 'You all right?' he whispered.

'I am now,' she answered.

He gave her a gentle reassuring squeeze. She wriggled in acknowledgment His presence was enough for her, and they drifted off to sleep.

10.40 am.

Jessica poured herself an ice-cold apple juice, grabbed a cereal bar, and joined Tony by the window in the garden room.

'We haven't got a single lead except those, have we?' she said, nodding at the row of pages on the coffee-table. She flopped into the cream leather sofa opposite him.

'After the funeral, I want to go to Stratford,' responded Tony, 'I want to get into the mind-set.'

'I need to do something like that myself,' she said, and after a short pause, added, 'And you know how I feel about having those as well, don't you?' pointing at the handwritten pages. 'It feels wrong,' she went on. 'First I'm robbed of my best friend, and now I've helped to rob her father.'

'Here,' said Tony, gathering the sheets together, 'best not to see them.'

'Oh, and that'll make everything just fine, I suppose.' She snapped. 'Out of sight - out of mind.' She looked him straight in the eye. Her unexpended teenage petulance could prove pretty testing. He had nowhere to go.

'That was tactless of me, sweetheart, I'm sorry.'

'No, it's OK, it's me. Oh I don't know, Tony, I'm all over the

101

place, and I don't know what to think anymore.' She finished her apple juice and placed the glass noisily on the table. 'They are a constant reminder though, aren't they?'

This wasn't the Jessica he knew, the carefree, final-year student with her boundless optimism and exciting future stretching off into infinity. Her emotions still raw from her ordeal, it was as though she'd been forced against her wishes to grow up over night .

'Yes they are,' he said, 'but don't forget, they might, just might, help to catch whoever was responsible.'

MAR. 9th WED: 12.00 pm.
SAFFRON WALDEN, ESSEX:

The funeral was a miserable affair. An attempt by the vicar to turn it into a celebration of Bianca's life did not endear him to Randy or Helena, or anyone else for that matter. Her death had left a huge hole in the lives of all her family and friends, and a priest who didn't know her wasn't going to ease their sorrows with a string of platitudes, however well intentioned.

Tony, Jessica, Peter and Julia went back to the Middletons' afterwards. It was the first time Tony had seen Randy and Helena since the events in Venice, and he was in two minds whether to mention the three pages from the palazzo. At a quiet moment, when Randy offered Tony a drink, and he felt it appropriate to bring up the subject, Randy pre-empted him by saying. 'Thanks for not phoning me when you left the note, by the way. I told Montano about them, and he said to be sure to keep them in a safe place in case any of the stolen ones turn up over there in an antiques shop or an auction. Want's them available for comparison, he says.'

'I still think he's barking up the wrong tree, Randy, and I'd tell him so to his face too. He's wasting valuable time, if you want my opinion. Did he say whether he had any more leads?'

'I spoke to him again only yesterday, and he's convinced that all the evidence points to 'B' happening to be in the wrong place at the wrong time. "Killed after the burglary by a person or persons unknown." He said, and that only a fool would case a scene for a robbery in front of three witnesses, and then come back a few hours later and do it. He thought you and Jess were "English Romantics.'"

'I'll give him 'English bloody Romantics.' What a cheek, and him with no fresh leads to go on! Bloody hell! And what about Angelo? What does Montano think he is - a Mafia godfather?'

'Oh, they've let him out on police bail, so he can't leave Venice. He has to report to the Questura every day - he's just going to love that. He was a damned fool over that second floor balcony key though. Not like him at all; if anything, he's too punctilious where locking up is concerned rather than too lax. I wondered if he had taken his eye off the ball with the girls there. You know, allowed himself to get distracted; but he swears he didn't.'

'As I suggested in the note, maybe we can get the police over here interested?' said Tony. 'I could show them the 'pages'. They may be quick to see a link.'

'If the police over here can find a lead by using them then fine Tony, but I don't want to see pictures of them all over the television and the papers, or anywhere else. Can you be absolutely sure that no-one except you and the police see them?'

'I'll do my best.'

'As long as it's as good as my best, young man, and don't go showing them to that uncle of yours either. What was his name again?'

'Brian - 'B J,' remember?'

'Yes, that's him. I'm aware you've got lots of respect for him; but, like all small society buffs, he wouldn't be able to resist spreading it all around.'

'I'm sure you're right. Tell you what, Randy, I'll phone you before I intend to use them, and, until then, I'll keep them under lock and key. How about that?'

'Sure.'

'Actually, we're off to Stratford this weekend, to get a flavour of the place.'

'Oh, yes,' said Randy, rather surprised. 'You've never been back since all that Alex business have you?'

'No, you're right, I haven't,' he answered. 'I'm not looking forward to it, particularly, but I've got to go, for Jess's sake as well as my own.'

'What was her reaction to the Alex affair?'

'I've never told her.'

Randy took a sharp intake of breath. 'Do you think that's wise?'

'Probably not, but what's done's done, or what's not done's not done. That was almost six years ago now, Randy, although it doesn't seem like it. I knew I'd have to tell her sooner or later; I'm keeping my fingers crossed she'll understand, and won't think any the worse of me.'

Randy glanced towards the open patio doors, and the figure of Jessica silhouetted against the garden, it's lake and bare trees. 'I'm going to miss the second daughter I never had you know. She's bright, she's sharp, and she's your problem now.'

Tony looked across at her, and she returned his gaze with a half-smile. 'Too true, too true. Look, thanks for giving me so much of your time, and I promise the 'pages' will be safe.'

'Thanks Tony. Now, if you'll forgive me, I've got some of my family to see.'

13

Katie was going through the ritual of checking the e-mails when Dryden arrived. Reaching the top of the stairs, he walked across the airy reception area, through the glazed doors, and into the records office of the Shakespeare Centre.

'Anything interesting?' he asked.

'Morning Mr. Dryden, chilly one isn't it? One from Christies with an attachment; I'll have a closer look in a minute, otherwise it's the usual well-intentioned spam.'

'Mmm,' he mused, tossing down a bag of freshly-ground coffee onto the counter of their indispensable kitchen, 'I wonder what little gem they've found for us today?' He checked the time and went into his small but meticulously organised office next door. He soon heard the familiar clink and chink of Katie making the first pot of coffee of the day.

'There's an anonymous portrait coming up at the end of March,' she called, 'a bit naive and in fair condition by the look of it, but the provenance is definitely rather shaky.'

He was in no hurry to check what the painting was like, or whether it was going to be important enough to put it to the Trust, and eventually put in a bid. Katie had an intuitive gift for implying the value of things with the tone of her voice, or her body language, or both. As office manager, and his PA, Katie Lancaster, had run the Records Department for more than nine years, and treated everyone as though they were members of an extended family. She had two archivists to look after, but as the Trust had no need to employ them full-time, they each worked a three-day week.

He left his topcoat on as he sorted through the post which she had put in a neat pile on his desk. 'Thanks Katie,' he said, taking a sip of coffee, 'perfect.'

Mark Dryden was the assistant archivist. Professional, charming and discreet, he had worked for the Trust for eight years. He kept himself physically and mentally fit and possessed what passed for Mediterranean good looks. It wasn't uncommon for people to ask why he did such an apparently mundane job. 'It suits me, and I suit it,' he would answer. He was also much in demand for his amusing and authoritative lectures, and had written several successful and popular books on Tudor and Jacobean culture.

He made his way back downstairs, and stepped out into the traffic-free street. There was no commonsense reason why he went all the way up to his office and then back down again to get his paper it was just part of his well-ordered daily routine.

There were no sightseers about yet to see him stride purposefully the hundred metres or so to the newsagents, but, any who had seen him would have guessed that you wouldn't find many jeans or T-shirts in his wardrobe.

'One Euro forty, Mr. Patel,' he said, inviting a response.

'One pound and five pence, Mr. Dryden,' replied the smiling and engaging Asian, harking back to the days of sterling. Mr. Patel and his family had come to England over fifty years ago. He was a confirmed anglophile, and what could be more British than to live in Warwickshire, and in Stratford-upon-Avon, the home of England's most famous son, William Shakespeare?

A group of hardy Chinese tourists were already digitally recording each other in front of 'The Birthplace' by the time Dryden left the shop. He slipped the business, sport and climate news sections into a waste bin, and almost subconsciously refolded his Daily Telegraph to expose the crosswords on the back page. He knew exactly how he liked things, it stabilised his world for him, keeping any notions of chaos at a safe distance. This is not to say that you would describe him as a control freak - far from it; at times he would even surprise himself with confident acts of impulse.

Council vehicles were already parked at the north end of Henley Street, and groups of workers busied themselves with preparations for the celebrations in April to mark the quatercentenary of the great dramatist's death. A man who prided himself much for his self control, Dryden was more than a little taken aback to sense a quickening of the heart at this overt display of evidence that the most important event for more than half a century was about to devour the town.

He left the workmen to transform the street, and with the sun not yet fully risen, shrugged off the cold February air and went back up to his first floor office. The ever dependable Katie had already put a fresh cup of coffee on his desk. The familiar smell of the fifty/fifty Kenya/Costa Rica was guaranteed to settle him down for the day.

Or so he thought.

'Isn't that the most awful thing, Mr. Dryden? Such a beautiful girl too, and with everything to live for.' His paper had unfolded itself on his desk, and Katie was looking at the photograph of Bianca on its front page.

Not even the *Telegraph* could turn down the heaven-sent opportunity to hi-jack Bianca in order to up their sales for a day. Being born with looks like hers left her very much at the mercy of the world and forces she could never have hoped to control. It came as no real surprise that the media grabbed her once again.

He felt sick.

He went into the kitchen, which overlooked the north end of Henley Street. 'A really terrible business by the look of it, Katie. It was on this morning's news - I don't know whether you saw it? My heart goes out to the girl's family.' He paused for a moment. 'Isn't her father that famous TV celebrity?' He thought it propitious to play the ignorance card, in order to distance himself from his involvement in the affair. As he, too, looked at the picture, he was finding it increasingly difficult to come to terms with the enormity of what he'd been involved in. He had no idea of precisely what had befallen Bianca after he had fled the scene three days previously. He was as shocked as anybody to see and read the news reports. He turned the page to read the continuing story on the inside pages. He was pleased to see that coverage of the robbery was minimal, and that the reporter hadn't picked up on the Shakespeare connection. Happy in the knowledge that he had the stolen pages and books securely locked away at his home, he knew an event of this magnitude was always bound to carry an unpredictable element, and who was to say some smart young journalist wasn't going to point his ambitious little finger straight at Stratford?

Dryden consoled himself that, for all their problems, he had covered the bases pretty well, leaving nothing to chance. He prided himself on his thoroughness and adaptability, one of his best qualities being an instinct for seeing the best solution to the unexpected, but he could get quite paranoid if things went wrong, even on a trivial matter. He was the first to admit that this was one of his least endearing qualities. Seeing Bianca's familiar face staring out at him so soon after he had been talking to her, not only gave him a most uncomfortable feeling, but forced him to go over, yet again, every detail of his two-day journey. The spectre of error, uninvited, entered his mind. He was filled with an urgency to rid himself of this most unwelcome of visitors; had he in fact overlooked some vital detail after all?

As soon as Katie left the office, he phoned John Fletcher.

'Back all in one piece then?' Came the reply.

'Yes John, no problem.' It was going to be one of those conversations where the unsaid and the implied were the crucial components.

'And the merchandise?'

'In my safe. I had a good look at it yesterday, and it's a damned good job I went out and retrieved it. You wait till you see it.'

'I told you not to worry Mark. I had every confidence that you'd be able to handle everything.'

There was a pregnant pause.

'Bill Harvey was very helpful John, friendly and efficient - and tactful enough not to ask too many questions.'

'A good man, Bill,' said John. 'I've used him a couple of times before. He's dependable and resourceful. Keeps himself to himself - if you know what I mean? We must make a date when I can come up and see you. That material is going to need thorough analysis.'

'Speak to you soon,' said Mark, and he rang off.

With the news of Bianca's death now spread all over the television news channels and the papers, he knew exactly what John had meant by his "keeps himself to himself" comment. They were all used to keeping matters secret, and sometimes this meant from each other too. It called for a particular type of inner strength, one that lifted you to a superior place - one where faith and trust might be tested to the limit.

The Sundays all went with the story, but the details had been muddled. It wasn't until the Monday editions that the order of things began to make any real sense. Commissario Montano was uncharacteristically tactful about British tourists and teenagers, being sensitive as to how the British press would vilify him if he generalised on the subject of lager-louts. He was also aware that Randy Middleton wasn't to be underestimated. Here too, the usually frank and forthright Commissario exercised uncommon restraint. Any ambiguous response by the celebrity on one of his shows might be seen as a sideswipe at him, and far too public to be brushed aside.

Dryden tried to put to one side the 'unfortunate' incident involving Bianca. He was disturbed to find that there had already been several occasions since his return when he found himself going over his actions step by step. He put on the pretence of being relaxed, but, in reality, he was struggling to keep an inner turmoil under control.

He had taken time to study the stolen pages on the Sunday after his return. As he feared, the evidence, written so carefully and so clearly on the handmade sheets, if seen in its entirety, and in the context of its discovery, would blow apart the carefully maintained case for the Stratford man's claim to the authorship. The matter wasn't made any easier by yet another article in The

Times seriously questioning the orthodox view on Shakespeare. Because of the world-wide interest in the quatercentenary celebrations, generated so effectively by the Trust and the media, authorship-challenging articles were now attracting a growing audience. He had taken a back seat in responding, leaving other members, directors, and Trust officials, to take the flack. They were finding it increasingly difficult to shake off their inquisitors; it was like trying to rid yourself of a persistent Jack Russell snapping at your ankles - the more you tried to kick it away, the more fun it had, and snapping with a renewed vigour.

'Thank God there are no satellite speed-governors on this road yet,' he thought to himself, as the twenty-minute journey south into the hills neared its end. Swinging round the last few bends, he left the hedged confines of the Cotswold lanes for the uncomfortable half-mile of the concrete and tarmac patched track that led to his farmhouse. He pulled into the gravelled courtyard, and parked at the side of the seventeenth-century grade two listed building. More grey than honey-coloured, it was huddled round with an eclectic group of pretty outbuildings, added one at a time over the past three centuries. He opened the side door, and, as he entered the immaculately kept kitchen, was greeted by a purring pair of well fed tabbies. He knew Troilus and Cressida wouldn't go hungry whenever he went away, as they regularly rebalanced the local eco-system with a diet of mice, shrews, rabbits, pigeons and a host of other birds and assorted carnage, no matter how much he fed them.

He was soon relaxing in the comfort of his living room. He sat back in the deep soft settee, and took a long draught of his vodka and orange from a satisfyingly heavy crystal tumbler. 'No-one makes a screwdriver like the Americans,' he mused, remembering, as though borrowing someone else's memory, the one that 'Chuck' had mixed for him by the Moonie Falls, at the bottom of Havasu Canyon, two decades earlier.

He had already removed the 'Magretti' file from his safe and had the 'pages' spread across the coffee table in front of him for a second time. He surveyed the works of the Earl of Oxford before him. The potential contained in these few sheets of paper was huge. Their value at auction might be tens of thousands of euros for each one, but their monetary value was not his concern, nor indeedtheir value to historians and scholars - it was silence. Then, out of the blue, a brilliant, though potentially dangerous idea seized him. As he thought long and hard about the sheer audacity of it, the more it took root, and the more he loved the genius of it.

He knew that these precious pages had hardly been seen by anyone; just the Middletons and maybe a couple of others. They hadn't been studied by experts or catalogued, just laid out to dry a few days ago. He probably already knew more about their contents than anyone but the author himself. What if one of these pages was 'discovered' in the run-up to the Great Gala opening on April 23rd? - but with some added detail to tie it indisputably to William of Stratford. OK, he thought, so it might be seen as one hell of a coincidence, but these things happen. It was too good a chance to miss, and an opportunity like this was only going to happen once in a lifetime.

Any guilt he had had over the events of the past few days evaporated as elation usurped his finer feelings. But how to effect it, that was the question - and when and where? Time was pressing, and the Great Gala was no longer beyond the horizon. He knew an operation of this kind couldn't be hurried. He needed time that didn't exist.

Dryden stood up and walked over to the window. In its leaded blackness all he could see was his own dark reflection, silhouetted against part of the softly lit room. He stared into the void containing the unseen low rolling Cotswold Hills. He ran over the possibilities of success and failure in his mind in uncompromisingly equal measures. The buzz of excitement started to consume him. 'Can I pull it off,' he wondered? 'If any one of the small group of readers of these pages recognises the one I choose, then the game's up, and what if one of them thought to photograph them? And then there's the experts, and media scrutiny; surely if the one doesn't get me then the other will. I'm going to have to be perfectly precise in every department to stand even the slightest chance of success.' With the Gala opening now only eight weeks away, timing would be critical. The more he thought about releasing one of the pages, the more he loved the idea. It would silence the critics, galvanise interest in the celebrations, and distance John and himself from the events in Venice, all in one go.

It all seemed too good to believe. He turned and looked down at the table with its unexpected treasure. 'I'm usually pretty good at dealing with situations like these,' he thought, 'but is the world going to crash about me as everyone smells a big fat rat?' One thing soon became certain; the magnitude of what he was contemplating required more than an evening at home and a couple of screwdrivers.

By the time he'd tidied around and put the pages securely away in his safe, and then locked up, his thoughts were already mellowing. Maybe it was just the emotional high, a reaction from the trip abroad. Perhaps it was his imagination filling in the spaces left by tiredness. When there's no partner to share things with, no-one there to help rationalise the motions of an excited intellect, then the ego can speak with an awfully seductive voice. Before reaching the top of the stairs, the disappointing voice of reason had already begun to convince him that it was just too high risk to contemplate seriously. The beauty faded, and he said to himself quietly, 'Don't let your heart rule your head.' He wanted to hear the words as well as think them.

14

The cutting winds, having already blown their way across fifty or sixty miles of East Anglia, were determined to give spring a hard time for a few miles yet. The leafless limes and walnut trees offered little protection to the diminutive figures of Tony and Jessica as they tossed their overnight bags into the back of Tony's Audi.

Peter and Julia came out all wrapped up.

'Have a nice time dear,' said Julia.

'We're not going for a nice time, Mummy.'

'Please don't be sharp with me, Jessie dear you know what I mean. Now, are you sure you've got everything?'

'Sorry, Mummy, but nice doesn't readily spring to mind, and yes, I've got everything, so don't worry. I'll give you a ring, OK ?'

'Look after yourself, love,' said Peter, giving his daughter a kiss on both cheeks.

'You too, Daddy.'

'Thanks for looking after me,' called Tony, as he got into the car. 'She'll be fine. I'll take care of her.'

The dark green car sped the few dozen metres to the gates, throwing up a bit too much gravel for good manners. With little more than a perfunctory slowing down, they swung out onto the village main street and away towards the A604 and the Midlands.

They were both hoping that a few days in the heart of Shakespeare country would help to focus their minds. They were sensible and rational enough to admit that this could all be for nought. What hard evidence did they have that Commissario

Montano didn't? None. Did they have any proof that the thief stole those items specifically - to order, perhaps - and was so determined that he was prepared to kill to obtain them? No. Tony found that going over the circumstantial evidence again and again was beginning to play tricks on his mind. Over the last week, wish fulfilment had developed a persistent habit of linking up a lot of his previously unconnected brain-cells, convincing him that he was dealing with facts. It was becoming increasingly difficult to remain completely unbiased, and now long held memories were beginning to surface, making things even worse. He hoped secretly that Jessica's grounded scepticism would prove one of his most reliable allies. She was pretty astute where reasoning was concerned, and you don't get four A's at 'A' level just handed to you; but it was her intuition that he really valued. It gave her an enviable clarity of vision, virtually free of confusion, regret or self-pity.

For her part, Jessica had noticed a single-mindedness in Tony since Venice, and particularly since they'd decided to take a look at Stratford. Was it because of her, or had the events in Venice had a more profound effect on him than he was prepared to admit? Did he know something about Stratford that she didn't? If so he certainly wasn't saying. He also knew how much she wanted to get away from home, but he had never asked her if she wanted to come over to Maldon to live with him, even though they loved each other. One day she was going to need commitment from him - but when?

The journey along the lanes, main roads and motorways might have passed unremembered had it not been for Jessica's commenting on a huge blue and white road sign on the M6.

'My God, Tony, look at that!' She exclaimed. The sign in question read - 'Welcome to Warwickshire, Shakespeare's County'. 'That is *so* bigger than a 'Welcome to England' sign! Don't these Midlanders just love their Bard! They really *do* mean business, don't they? How much further is it to Stratford from here?'

'It must be at least - thirty miles,' he answered. 'Do you think we're going to see a succession of roadside shrines as we get nearer - gradually getting bigger and more elaborate as we approach the sacred precinct of dramatic invention?'

She smiled in response to his flowery 'dramatic invention,' commenting: 'Ah, how refreshing it is to hear the unbiased voice of reason.'

They drove on through the near monochrome landscape of the early March morning, and were soon directed off the A46 to 'Shakespeare's Stratford.'

'Tough on all the good taxpayers of the borough who thought they had a stake in their own town then,' said Tony. 'I guess it'll be 'Nelson's Norwich' and 'Lennon's Liverpool' next!'

'You're becoming a grumpy old man, Mr. Chapman,' joked Jessica, but inside she was earnestly hoping that this wasn't a sign of bitterness to come. She was even more certain now that something was lying heavily on his heart, and that sooner or later he was going to come out with it.

They swept round the one-way system at the entrance to the town, crowded with a bewildering profusion of road signs, crossed Clopton Bridge, and were soon parked at The Alveston Manor Hotel.

'You've done this before haven't you?' she said. 'You drove the last ten or fifteen minutes like a seasoned commuter.'

Tony took a deep breath and sighed. 'Yes, Sweetie, you're right. I came here several times a few years ago, so I'm quite familiar with the roads around Stratford, or 'Bardsville' as a friend of mine used to call it.' With no further comment, he got out, took their bags from the boot, escorted Jessica to reception, and checked in.

Twenty minutes later, the couple were tiptoeing their way with extreme caution, through a careless mosaic of duck and goose droppings, as they made their way along the riverside walk to the RST. Jessica had been to performances at the main theatre and the Swan, both situated in the same building, shortly after the major restructurion of the mid to late 'noughties', but had never seen the 'Shakespeare sights.' Tony took her on a whistle-stop tour of the town's main attractions. She found she was in for quite a few surprises.

He led her up Sheep Street and right into High Street. They crossed the top of Bridge Street at the traffic island and turned left into Henley Street. To the accompanying sounds of bongo drummers, a rap-rendering of *Romeo and Juliet*, and a Romanian - or possibly Ukrainian - version of a Beatles hit, the couple eventually reached 'Shakespeare's Birthplace'.

'Notice anything?' asked Tony.

'How do you mean?' she said, looking over the Tudor half-timbered house. 'I see a very famous building.'

'Well, you've seen 16th and 17th century buildings before; we passed several getting here.'

'Oh! I see what you mean now. This doesn't look like any of them. In fact, now you mention it, it doesn't even look old. It's like someone's idea of what a Tudor house should look like. A sort of 'Elizabethan Ideal Home'.'

'That's because the building you are looking at isn't old,' he said. 'It should be the one built around 1500 and acquired later by John Shakespeare, William's father. This is a mid-Victorian rebuild based on an engraving, copied from an eighteenth century watercolour by a man called Richard Green - which was painted in around 1762 I think.'

'That can't be true. Everyone knows Shakespeare was born here. You *are* having me on aren't you?'

'There were two properties here until the middle of the nineteenth century Jess. One was an inn, 'The Swan and Maidenhead', the other a butcher's shop. In their wisdom, the good burghers of the town demolished all the surrounding properties, gutted these, saving all the best timbers, and did a complete makeover. And of course no-one actually knows for sure where, or even when, 'William' was born.'

'Oh Tony, come on! Everyone knows he was born here, even if it's had a facelift.'

'Sweetheart it's true. I wouldn't lie to you. It's just as likely that he was born in his father's other house in Greenhill Street, away from the dirt and smell of the glovemaking business. The guidebooks still tell you, quite categorically, that the poet and playwright was born here. Yet there isn't a smidgeon of proof.'

'You'll be telling me he wasn't born on St. George's Day next.'

'I hate to tell you this!'

'Oh, really,' laughed Jessica. 'This is getting ridiculous. It's celebrated every year. They have parades - the whole works.'

'The happy coincidence of the divine 'William' being born and dying on the same day, was a harmless conceit by Nicholas Rowe at the beginning of the eighteenth century. When he began to compile the first biography of the bard, he found no birth date, so, taking the traditional gap of three days after a birth before baptising a child, he just went back three days from the baptismal date. He could have gone back a week if it suited his purposes. The truth is - we'll never know the true date.'

'I had absolutely no idea that his origins had been messed about with like that. How long has all this been known?'

'About two hundred years,' he replied. 'They don't want it made too public in case the tourists get disillusioned. Come on, let's get away from all these crowds and take a look at New Place.'

A few hundred metres back towards the theatres, on the corner of Chapel Street and Chapel Lane, was an open grassy space where, four hundred years earlier, stood the impressive five-gabled house called New Place. It had been the second largest house in Stratford-upon-Avon and the home of William Shakspere for the last twelve years or so of his life. They peered over the wall at the few remaining stones amid the carefully tended lawns.

'So this is where the great man lived out his retirement.'

'So they say,' answered Tony. 'But a couple of things do bug me whenever I think about this place, especially when you consider who lived here.'

'Try me,' she offered.

'OK, now remember, this man, greatest of all wordsmiths in the English language, leaves behind illiterate children and grandchildren. It is a known fact that his parents and his wife were all functionally illiterate. He lives over the road from the

King's Free School, and would have watched the boys, and heard them, six days a week, every week, for many years. And yet, out of his considerable fortune, he gives the school, which equipped him for the most brilliant and illustrious of careers - nothing. When I watch a Shakespeare play, I find it hard to believe that the universally acclaimed author, so in tune with the human condition, could possibly have been that mean-spirited. He left his home nothing; well, except £10 for the poor.'

'Why are you telling me all this, Tony? I can't see it helping to solve the riddle of 'B's death. Are you sure you haven't got an ulterior motive?'

'I want to take you to the parish church,' he said, turning to her, 'I've got something I need to tell you.'

As they walked along Church Street to the final destination on their tour, Jessica slipped her arm through Tony's. He was deep in thought, and didn't say a word all the way to the north entrance of the medieval edifice.

Jessica broke the silence as they neared the porch.

'This is where we find the famous monument and gravestone isn't it?'

'Yes it is. Do you want to take a look?'

'Of course.'

Through the North Porch, and just inside the back of the main body of the church, was a small shop. Two Chinese women were deliberating at length over which souvenir guide book to take home. Tony couldn't resist going to their assistance. He gave Jessica a little wink.

He assured the grateful tourists as to which of the colourful and informative guides was sure to provide them with the most rewarding memories of their time in this sublime place, so sacred to the peoples of the English speaking world. They bowed, they paid, and they left, but not before photographing Tony and Jessica, and then each other.

'I needed something like that,' he said, and walked her up the nave. In the chancel was a party of about thirty Hispanic schoolchildren. Most of them looked as if they had no idea which town they were in, let alone which country just that it was obviously too near the north pole. Their body language said it all; they were clearly itching to get back to a land with a sensible climate - like Spain. Tony and Jessica waited for the Iberian invaders to vacate the hallowed and vaulted sanctum, paid their euro, and went in.

'No name,' was Jessica's opening comment, as she looked down at the famous gravestone. 'And surely we aren't meant to believe that he wrote that absurd piece of doggerel. It's the language of the alehouse, the defensive prattle of the Jacobean labourer.'

'I couldn't have put it better myself, Jess, but look at the monument, up there on the wall. Now be objective, what is your first reaction?'

'It's nothing like the Droeshout engraving we see everywhere, or the Chandos Portrait in the National Portrait Gallery. It's as though they're pictures of three very different men.'

'Everything here has been messed about with. The original figure was of a leaner man, his moustache was down turned, and he had his hands together on a woolsack. As it was erected in the lifetime of his widow, Anne, and his children, we can be pretty sure that that was a fair likeness There was no pen or paper either, they were added later. What intrigues me most though, Jess, is the inscription stone under it. That epitaph has been the subject of more research than you can imagine.'

'It seems to have been knocked about too,' Jessica noted. 'See those marks along the edges, and when you read it, it doesn't make any real sense for a poet and playwright. There's no mention of Ovid for a start, and why Olympus - the home of the gods; surely Parnassus would have been more apt as home of the Muses of the Arts?'

'Either you had a damned good teacher, or you stayed up late last night to do your homework! Those observations are spot on, and have you noticed, there is no Christian name? In my experience that's almost without precedent. Also, no mention of his wife or children, or of his other achievements in London or here in Stratford. It's all very odd you must agree, and someone I knew reckoned he'd cracked it - you know, solved its mystery.'

'Then why haven't I heard about it? Why isn't it in all the books?'

'Let's go outside shall we, and I'll tell you?'

They walked along the slabbed path bordering the north wall of the church until they reached the low wall at the east end that overlooked the river. They sat on a bench and watched the pleasure boats as they plied back and forth on the slow current, and the families relaxing and playing games in the park beyond.

'This isn't going to be easy Jess,' he began. 'Nearly six years ago, a friend of mine was killed, possibly murdered, right here, and his body dumped in the grass-cuttings over there, before rolling down the bank into the river. It was four days before he was found down there by the weir. The police never arrested anyone, and as far as I'm aware it's still on their books as an unsolved crime. We'd known each other right through school. We were so close, it was almost like having a twin; we each seemed to know exactly what the other was thinking. Even though we went to different universities, we were still in constant touch right up to his death. It must sound really odd for you to hear me talking like this?'

'No, go on, I'm fascinated - anyway, I knew there was something you wanted to get off your chest. You've been as tense as hell for days.'

'I'm absolutely convinced that if we can solve what happened here, it will lead us to Bianca's killer.' Alex, my friend, had become engrossed in the mystery of the Shakespeare authorship, and had discovered something here in Stratford, that was so important, he paid for it with his life. Tony stopped as though his world had suddenly come to a halt. He looked away and thought for a moment. 'I've also got a few things in my past to face up to, sweetheart,' he said. 'But first, you have to know what happened to Alex.'

Part Two

A REVELATION
(ALEX'S STORY: 2010, JUNE - SEPT.)

Prospero,

"……………..; and by my prescience
I find my zenith doth depend upon
A most auspicious star, whose influence
If now I court not, but omit, my fortunes
Will ever droop……"

The Tempest, 1,2.

William Shakespeare.

15

When he arrived home from university that evening, Alex Paris found a letter addressed to him propped up on the small oak table in the hall. He recognised immediately the colour and format of the envelope, and the way his name and address was written on it in a handwriting so stylish and regular, it might almost have been printed.

He glanced briefly at its Bristol postmark, and picking it up, noted that it was light and thin. 'Only a single sheet,' he thought. 'Well, whatever the bugger's been up to this time, it doesn't look as though he's got a lot to say for himself.' Letters between Alex and his best friend, Tony, had become less frequent over the past twelve months, as inevitably, IM and emails had replaced their handwritten communications. Upstairs in the front bedroom, a room he had occupied for almost the whole of his twenty-one years, he tossed his bag onto the bed and sat down at his computer. With a little apprehension, he opened the envelope, removed the single sheet, and began to read:

'Dear Alex,
I'll cut straight to the chase – there is definitely a God…'
'Here we go again,' he thought, 'another Miss World contestant!' he read on '…*the proof, and ample (note the considered choice of adjective) evidence of His munificent works is to be found behind the bar at the* Landogger, *as I write. Received wisdom has it that she is the template God uses…'*
'And this is cutting, "straight to the chase?"' Alex scanned the next few lines until he found the real reason for Tony's letter –

what he was apologising for.

'...and so there must be a madman on the loose in Bristol! She loves the outdoors, Alex, and I'm off to the 'Lakes' with her sometime soon. Sorry and all that, but we can arrange things for later in the Summer can't we? I promise I'll keep you posted,

Yours,

Tony.

P.S. Be a pal and don't say a word to Immy – she'd have a fit!

The PS with which Tony had closed the letter was a reference to Alex's sister Imogen. She and Tony had been childhood sweethearts, but they were now behaving more like an engaged couple rather than the 'brother and sister' of their teenage years. They had decided to keep their relationship 'open' until they had finished their degrees. This was proving a lot easier for Tony than for the feisty and independent Imogen, and even though his twin sister was well able to deal with Tony, Alex still felt rather ambivalent about his friend's request.

Most of the correspondence between the two friends had been in handwritten letters for several years. A school art project on calligraphy five or six years earlier had led them both to create 'historical' writing styles. It started out purely as a bit of fun, but it soon developed into much more.

Something that had intrigued them both was how unique and expressive everyday handwriting used to be; but here they were, in the first decade of the twenty-first century, witnessing the "terminal decline", as Alex put it, of a skill developed and refined over many centuries. Whilst at school, the two friends developed a theory that the human personality was irretrievably dissolving into cyberspace. In an effort to retain as much of their own 'pure' inheritance as was practicable for two zeitgiesty youths studying for their exams, they created their individual handwriting styles in order to express at least some of their inner spirit before they, too, became dependent on 'Windowsworld'.

For Alex, the art of calligraphy had its flowering in the sixteenth and seventeenth centuries, before 'everything turned into copperplate'. In his opinion this was the only time that written English thrilled the eye like Arabic or Chinese. The unique style he designed for himself was a cross between Tudor English and an early Italian hand. He liked its compact look, with gratuitous flourishes to its extended ascenders and descenders. To his dismay, Tony turned out to be a lover of copperplate! - as evidenced by his disciplined control of the pen, in the neat rows of italic handwriting on the sheet of paper in his hand.

The last week of the summer term had arrived with a fearful suddenness. Focusing on his final essay and handing it in on time had been stressing him out, but Tony's impromptu removal of the prospect of getting away to the Med for a couple of weeks, left him with little alternative but to crack on with it. At least he could now devote himself totally to his studies - top the year off with one last 'A.'

Alex's decision to go to Birmingham University had involved something of a compromise. He would have loved to have got away from both home and home town, but as Birmingham offered one of the best courses in Drama and Theatre Arts, he opted for the compact life that came with living only a ten minute cycle-ride from the campus.

During his first eighteen months of research into Elizabethan and Jacobean Drama, he had trawled through literally thousands of books, periodicals, printed plays, programmes and theses. He became amazed by the sheer depth and range of Shakespearean study, finding that every conceivable aspect of English life of the period had been explored and analysed through the countless biographies of the Warwickshire playwright.

Writers, historians, actors, lawyers, politicians, scholars, they all had a different take on the great man, not to mention the many sceptics who didn't believe that William of Stratford was the true author in the first place. It seemed quite absurd to him that anyone with a modicum of intelligence could doubt such an established fact as the identity of the English speaking world's greatest playwright, and yet a great many people had. Alex had dismissed all challenges to the orthodox view of the authorship as nonsense, regarding them as 'barking up the wrong tree'. He felt the claims for none of the contenders deserved to be taken seriously for a multitude of reasons, not the least of which was that the allusions to William Shakespeare's life and times in Stratford and London as expressed in his works, were so well established. The more he delved into those works the more he was in awe of him.

Scanning the catalogue in the Birmingham Reference Library one particularly unproductive afternoon, he was about to call it a day, when his eye happened to light on an obscure double volume. It was an American publication by an American author, but its subject was the analysis of a book written by an English schoolteacher around the time of the First World War. 'Now why', he thought, 'did she go to all that trouble I wonder?' Curiosity got the better of him, and he soon had the books in front of him. 'Right, Mrs. ...' he opened it to the title page, '... Lloyd-Miller, let's see if all this is just some personal passion of yours.' He was on the verge of taking them straight back, when he realised that they were about yet another theory that Shakespeare's works must have been written by an aristocrat. However, there was something in the modest and self-effacing manner of this Durham schoolmaster, the author of the book in question, and the way in which he set out his stall, that made Alex persist. He was very glad he did. As it drew towards closing time, he found all his assumptions about the conventional accounts of the Shakespeare authorship severely challenged. He had shrugged off all the other claimants like a minor winter's cold, but this claim for the Earl of Oxford persisted like a heavy bout of flu.

The following morning, back at the university, he was straight up to the English Department to tackle his tutor on the thorny subject of doubt about Will, the peerless renaissance playwright. 'I'm halfway through an essay on collaboration in Shakespeare's last plays,' he said to the bemused professor of English Literature, 'and the bastard has just disappeared! - I've still got hold of the best playwright in the English language, but the *man* has vanished!'

'We have the oeuvre, Alex,' his tutor replied, 'the plays and poems, the words, that's what is important. You are by no means the first student to feel desperate at the paucity of biographical evidence to support the bard; its something we all learn to live with. Try not to get distracted from your core studies by taking seriously the amateur scribblings of a load of snobs who insist that an aristocrat must have written it instead.'

'But there isn't a single instance in the history of western culture, where there is a question mark over the identity of a major figure - with this one exception - I've looked,' said Alex, 'and the same goes for so-called 'spontaneous genius' - not one example in the history of literature. Shakespeare had to have been highly educated, and must have moved in the highest circles - and he definitely spent time in Italy and Venice.'

'Keep off the subject, Alex, I insist. You will only be wasting your time.'

'But I want flesh and blood - I now see it as essential, and I don't find it in Stratford-upon-Avon.'

'It's better to have the Stratford man than no-one at all. Can't you see where all this'll take you?' Alex shrugged his shoulders. 'Well I'll tell you - into a labyrinth full of wasted lives. Get yourself back on track, and immediately otherwise I'm going to be very disappointed with you.'

Alex conceded to his tutor's demands in front of him, but, in truth, the wall of intractability so hastily erected by the professor, with its unexpected rendering of emotion, made him more determined than ever to get to the bottom of the mystery. He was left with the frustration of having only four days to satisfy his course requirements to complete his final essay, whilst at the same time having severe doubts as to the identity of the person he was writing about.

That same evening, back at his home in Bournville, he couldn't wait to get a letter off to Tony. Out came paper, pen and ink, and, without a single correction, he wrote enthusiastically to his friend of his discovery. As he began to write, he recollected Tony talking about the Seventeenth Earl of Oxford, being the man behind the works of Shakespeare. Tony had come across the theory through an uncle of his who was a confirmed 'Oxfordian'. Alex always thought that his friend used the theory just to wind him up. Now he wasn't so sure.

As the letter unfolded, revealing his thoughts, he became acutely aware of an eagerness to save himself from the sense of isolation brought about by stepping aside from conventional wisdom.

'What convinced you, Tony,' he wrote, 'that it was Oxford and not one of the other claimants?'

'The *'First Folio'* and family, Alex,' replied Tony, 'Shakspere's family were all illiterate, and there isn't a shred of evidence to link them to the written or printed works in any way. The records tell us Will was very much a man of his time; a theatre entrepreneur, and a rich property-dealer and landowner of the rising middle class. Compare that with the *First Folio:* decades of work, written in a style regarded as archaic at the time, and virtually all of it extolling the virtues and vices of court life of past ages. I doubt whether any publisher would have looked on the project as much of a money-spinner, do you?'

'You think Oxford's daughters were behind it don't you?' asked Alex, whose hunger for answers had him switching from pen and paper to IM.

'The *'Folio'* was dedicated to Mary Sydney's two sons, William and Phillip Herbert. Phil was married to Oxford's youngest daughter, Susan - how's that for a coincidence? It seems obvious to me that they oversaw the logistics of production and publication. You remember that in Tudor times it was considered highly dishonourable for a nobleman to write plays for the general public, don't you? Well, 'Eddie's girls' would have felt it was their solemn duty to protect their family honour. I reckon the 'family firm' would have used its considerable influence to get their late father's works to the presses - but under an assumed name, of course.'

As their communications continued over the next few days,

Alex became more and more convinced he was on the trail of the right man. The Earl, he discovered, had lived a life closely linked to both literature and the theatre. He was awarded degrees from both Cambridge and Oxford Universities, and studied law at Gray's Inn. Not only did he patronise and support many writers and playwrights, but he is on record as being the best court playwright of the day. He was also a friend of the Third Earl of Southampton to whom two of Shakespeare's major poetic works are dedicated. Two of his daughters married into the families of writers and patrons of the theatre and the arts. Not everything resolved itself easily, however.

'That stuff about the use of a pseudonym sounds all very well, Tony, but it's not Joe Bloggs's name on the cover, it's Shakespeare's - explain that away!'

'The Earl probably employed Will as his play-broker for years, Alex, and adopted his name as a convenient pseudonym. Oxford's family would have trusted him to keep his mouth shut - just as long as the money kept rolling in. The documentary record has it that in both London and Stratford, 'Will' had little conscience where making money and expanding his property empire were concerned. There is no record as to how he acquired his fortune - and, don't forget, he died, safely out of the way in the middle of rural England in 1616, seven years before the 'First Folio' was published.'

'Susanna, his eldest daughter, was the main beneficiary of Will's estate; surely she would have had a hand in getting her old man's jottings to the printers?'

'Neither she nor any other member of the Shakespeare family had any connection to the printing of the collected works.' replied Tony. 'His family would have been blissfully ignorant of the goings-on in the faraway capital.'

The correspondence that flowed between the two friends all served to increase Alex's feeling that there really was a strong case to be made for this relatively obscure and unpredictable aristocrat. If the theory was true, one of the hardest things to explain was how the Earl had so successfully managed to conceal his identity for two decades, while he was writing the most popular plays of the day. Maybe his authorship was an open secret, but never put to paper: like knowledge of President Kennedy's philandering in Washington D.C. and elsewhere - everybody knows, but nobody says. Once Oxford was dead perhaps it was his children and grandchildren who continued to protect the family name, who knows?

It had, for centuries, been known, that William Shakspere came from an illiterate family, and left one behind when he died; but it came as quite a surprise to Alex when he discovered that absolutely no paper trail of any kind leads from the world of theatre and literature in London to the property dealer, wool trader and usurer from Stratford-upon-Avon. No-one in Warwickshire in the seventeenth century, it seems, ever mentions that one of England's greatest son's was in their midst.

Now a fully signed-up sceptic, Alex found he wasn't the only person to realise that, if one were to write down the CVs of the Earl of Oxford and William Shakspere of Stratford-upon-Avon, it would be patently obvious which one had to be the accomplished author and which one wasn't.

He was behaving more like an investigative journalist than an undergraduate, and, for the first time in his life, experienced the excitement of being on a genuine quest. He began to feel like a prospector, obsessed by the vision of a seam of the purest gold, or a knight searching infinite and unconquerable lands for the Holy Grail. He had virtually forgotten about the cancelled holiday with Tony when he decided to ring him for some communal updating.

'Not that I'm obsessed, of course,' he chuckled down the phone, 'but I'm off to Stratford next week to do a bit of sightseeing - and hopefully unearth a bit more about 'Mr. Bard'.'

'And to put a few pointed questions to those Stratfordians too, I hope,' added Tony. 'Don't let them palm you off with a whole load of maybes, probablys and most likelys will you?'

'No chance, pal, and don't worry, I'll keep you up to speed

OK? By the way, are you still going 'rambling' with your 'Miss World contestant', or has 'la bicyclette de Bristol' disappeared into the ether?'

'Still on board, mate, and don't laugh, she wants to explore wildernesses even more remote than the Lake District. I've managed to convince her that I've got some remote areas that are fun to explore as well, and she won't need a GPS and a tent either! You can bet your sorry ass it'll be more than a couple of rocky mountains I'm going to be climbing!'

'Lucky bastard! - See you when you've got your breath back!'

'Bye, Alex, have a better one.'

16

The 'Ophelia Guest House', B and B, AA recommended, English this and Tourist Board that, with its slabbed front garden and four monstrous and tasteless hanging baskets, was just a five-minute walk from Stratford-upon-Avon's Market Square. Alex kept pace with the crawling commuters as he struck out for the main sights of the busy and prosperous town. On his way, he was wryly amused to see a sign pointing to 'Ann Hathaway's Cottage'. 'That must be where the glover's daughter-in-law came from,' he mused, and wondered what shame her family might have suffered as three autumn months dragged by, back in 1582, before the marriage of their pregnant daughter to William Shakspere took place. She was well past her prime, and Alex felt certain she tricked William into getting her pregnant on the orders of her father, Richard, eager to unload his aging and increasingly ineligible daughter.

A few minutes later Alex was confronted by a map of the town. It was a cheerful sort of aerial view, and displayed clearly all the popular tourist sights including the 'Birthplace', and Holy Trinity Church, or the 'death place', as he had renamed it!

He pressed on to take a look at Henley Street and soon found himself engulfed by an unruly mob of philistine French schoolchildren. Even at this early hour they seemed to be practising for an international shouting contest. How many of this ice-cream licking horde could give a damn about English History, let alone it's drama, he wondered; and did the actual truth really matter to tour parties like these, just as long as they were served up a diet that didn't upset their expectations?

Seated at an empty café table opposite the 'birthplace', he got out a notepad and started to write down a list of the principle areas of questioning that had come to concern him His research had convinced him that the publication of the *'First Folio'*, was, almost certainly, a Masonic venture, probably financed and produced by the Herbert brothers. They were, to quote the First Folio, the "incomparable paire of Brethren" to whom the volume was dedicated. "Brethren" hinted strongly at a secret Brotherhood; if indeed it did, he thought that that would most likely be the Rosicrucians, forerunners of the Freemasons. Not only that, William was the Lord Chamberlain, whose role was to oversee all stage production, and drama publication. He was also rumoured to be the most senior Rosicrucian or Freemason in England. Phillip, who succeeded him as Lord Chamberlain, being married to Susan, Edward de Vere's youngest daughter, brought them into the Oxford family fold. Their friend, the poet and playwright Ben Jonson, who, it is now widely believed, edited the *First Folio*, used to stay at their home, Wilton House, near Salisbury.

The last mystery that he wanted to solve was the questionable provenance of the Shakespeare Monument on the chancel wall in the parish church. In his will, the thorough-going Tudor/Jacobean businessman, William Shakspere, left not a single item connected to the worlds of literature or the theatre - not even a quill - and yet a few years after his death a monument is erected to him - as a writer! Or so we are meant to believe. This was considerably altered soon after its installation, and Alex was convinced that the Freemasons, or some other secret brotherhood, were behind any changes. Stratford-upon-Avon was, he felt, awash with unanswered questions and he was more convinced than ever that, somewhere in the Shakespeare Centre, just across the road from where he was sitting, was a key that would finally unlock the mystery of the authorship.

After a busy ten days in Stratford, Alex had just about drawn a blank. He had tried to get information out of the Shakespeare

Centre so many times that his presence there almost constituted harassment; he had been asked to leave more than once, and found it impossible to gain access to any original texts. He was told repeatedly the same thing - "Put your request in writing and we'll get back to you." Systems and protocols were all very well for scholars with years at their disposal in which to do their research; Alex was a man in a hurry, but his pleas to the officials to cut corners fell on deaf ears. The aggressively defensive attitude of the assistant archivist, Mark Dryden, made him feel quite uncomfortable on several occasions, but he persisted. However, one day, when discussing the Parish Church where Shakespeare is buried, the impatient Alex said, in sheer desperation, that he would "dig up the chancel and the whole bloody churchyard" if he had to. At this, Mark Dryden ordered him out and put a watch on him, just in case the "aggravating little student" decided to take the law into his own hands.

In his search for information during that long hot summer, his forays into the British Library, the Freemasons Archives, and both the Wilton and Hatfield papers all yielded little of value. Hundreds of researchers had been there ahead of him and he was getting very familiar with the results of many of their studies. But when he saw the size of National Records Office at Kew, he knew he had to take another look at his methodology.

He stopped off at Hackney, in east London, to see what remained of the church where the Earl and Countess of Oxford had been buried. Only the 13th century tower of the old St. John's survived. He found welcome refuge in its cool, blue-grey shadow, pointing away from a neighbouring London Transport bus depot and a warehouse-like Tesco supermarket. Out of place and out of time, it looked, and was, abandoned. The old churchyard was now little more than a thoroughfare; he surveyed its motley assortment of forgotten gravestones, monuments to lives no longer mourned. Then it dawned on him - there must have been a well established trade, importing marble and other high-quality stone for sculpture and monuments. One avenue he had never explored, he realised, was the very stone from which the Shakespeare gravestone and monument were carved. Perhaps there was a record of it being quarried, transported, carved or even delivered and installed. Stratford-upon-Avon was, and still is, in the diocese of Coventry, but it was dependent on Worcester cathedral. He was soon on his way to Worcester.

High up in the roof space above the South Transept, the Cathedral Library housed an extraordinary archive. The extensive catalogue contained a section headed: Records of Special Collections and Correspondence: 1131 - 1665. Alex thought its enigmatic title looked promising, so he requested access to it. It was here, as he sifted through volume after volume, and box after box, of 16th and 17th century record keeping, that he chanced upon a collection of invoices, orders, letters and lists, that recorded repairs and additions to Diocesan buildings.

Amongst them, Alex spotted a document which shed light quite unexpectedly. It was an order for a load of building stone to be delivered to the rectory at Alcester, a small market town on the road from Worcester to Stratford. It had a note added at the bottom in a second hand which said, 'Slabbe of darke marbul of ye finest qualitie for Mr. L. Chambers Gent., To S super A, mason.' Luckily the order was dated and signed: 'FCV, 1626.' Why, he wondered, was the order added to an existing delivery by Mr. FCV? And who was important enough in Stratford to have only the best marble ordered in this manner?

It didn't take him long to find that there were no families called Chambers in Stratford at the time - what if 'L.Chambers' was a not very subtle way of saying that it was for the Lord Chamberlain? There was no mention of its dimensions, so he could only speculate as to what it was for. His thoughts turned to that peculiar gravestone, to the bard that lay in the chancel floor. Was this the original? A replacement perhaps? With Stratford once again proving his best lead, he copied out everything on the order sheet with the greatest care, packed his things, and set out once again for 'Stratfraud', as he now referred to the internationally renowned tourist destination.

Alex made straight for the Shakespeare Centre on Henley Street, and in the records office up on the first floor, asked if he might see any records they had for stone and marble for monuments rather than buildings. He was rebuffed in the usual way - "put your request in writing," etc., etc.. It was no use protesting, or even arguing that, "If you would help me out, just this once, I'll be out of your hair and gone", as he hit on a day when the intransigent Mark Dryden was in.

'And what do *you* know about Mr. FCV, Mr. Dryden?' said Alex, and pointing to the archive-packed shelves behind him, added, 'and how much have you got on him in there?' He turned on his heels and stormed out. It was another setback, but he now had the bit between his teeth and was impatient for answers to the riddle of the 'slabbe' - and those initials.

It was too late to contact the Warwickshire Records Office or Stratford Town Council, and the soporific heat of the late afternoon made it feel more like north Africa than England. He bought a bottle of iced water and ambled his way over to Holy Trinity to have another look at the 'Monuments'. He had studied them so often - too often perhaps - and began to wonder what his family, or indeed Tony, would make of how he had spent the last ten or twelve hours. They'd probably all tell him to "get a life." It was all getting a bit too much, and, since he didn't want tiredness or his emotions clouding his judgments, decided on a much needed break. Leaving the church's cool, vaulted interior behind for the churchyard, he soon found himself standing on the low wall overlooking the river. The water looked so inviting that he thought that, just for the hell of it, he would dive straight in; but common sense, combined with a persistent thirst, told him that a couple of pints at the 'Dirty Duck' was more his style. Anyway, he could see that the water was barely a foot deep!

The late summer sun seemed more reluctant than ever to set, as though light and heat were conspiring supernaturally to suspend time, enticing everyone to extend their day into the seductive comfort of the darker hours. England was acquiring a Mediterranean lifestyle, whether it wanted one or not; but for Alex, on any hot, dry day, globally enhanced or not, nothing soothed the throat quite like the caress of an English Real Ale.

17

Mark Dryden was getting quite desperate to find a solution to the problem to the troublesome student with his dogged attitude and persistent enquiries. He contacted a colleague of his, John Fletcher, to see if he had any suggestions. Dryden's mention of the letters FCV was enough to spur his friend into action.

'How did he come across it Mark? Have you any idea what he was researching?'

'He was enquiring about stone for buildings and monuments, if that's any help. Otherwise I've no idea; but there was no doubting what he said just before he stormed off.'

John Fletcher left his office at the Foreign Ministry (FCO) in Whitehall immediately after Mark Dryden had hung up. In less than two hours he had made the ninety miles from central London and its rush-hour to Stratford-upon-Avon.

From the moment Alex left the Records Department, Dryden had kept a watchful eye on him, and knew precisely where he was spending his evening. He asked John to meet him in the Falstaff Bar at the RST, just fifty metres from the 'Dirty Duck'.

John arrived at 7.30, and, after a cordial and fraternal greeting, they left immediately for the fifteenth century inn. They approached the raised terrace in front of the pub cautiously, but, there was no sign of Alex. They went up to the door, and Mark caught sight of him, standing at the crowded bar. As he didn't want to be seen, if at all possible, Mark left John to go inside and get their drinks. They sat at a large, heavily constructed picnic-style table to the side of the crowded terrace. It overlooked the gently flowing River Avon, just twenty yards away, and gave them a clear view of the only entrance. With some urgency, they discussed their options.

'One strategically placed post on the internet, and the carefully crafted work of centuries will be undone. I don't want him getting any closer to revealing our secret, Mark. Do you?'

'No, I don't. And it was because I suspected that he might be on the verge of causing untold damage that I rang you.'

'Do you think he knows of the existence of the 'Brotherhood'?'

'I don't think he does, but I can't be sure,' replied Mark. 'He spoke in terms of 'FCV' being someone's initials, but he's so bloody persistent you can be certain he'll be digging deeper.'

It was imperative they find out exactly how much Alex knew; explore the limits of how well informed he had become, and what he was doing with his knowledge. Was it all here in Stratford, or was he emailing it. It looked as though they were going to have to negotiate with him, but at the same time giving away nothing about themselves or their activities.

'It would be foolhardy,' said John, 'for the two of us to hand it to him on a plate - the opportunity to be so ruinous.'

'Perhaps we could drip-feed him all he needs to know in order to keep him happy. Steer him away from the 'Brotherhood' and any importance he might be attaching to 'FCV'. It worked with the Bacon and Marlowe societies for years. The Oxfordians are no different, because that's where this chap is coming from.'

They finished off their gin and tonics, and John returned to the bar to order two more. All evening they kept a sharp eye on the door to the bar. It was a long and nervous wait, but after nearly three hours, and when the two friends were on the verge of giving up ever seeing Alex again that evening, there was suddenly some activity at the entrance. Two attractive young women came out laughing and joking, closely followed by a quite exuberant Alex. He obviously fancied his chances with one or other, or possibly both, of the girls he had spent his evening chatting up, and pursued them through several groups of boisterous drinkers towards the exit at the edge of the terrace.

'That's him, John,' indicated Mark, shielding his face with his empty glass as though draining it. 'So that's what he's been up to. Why can't he spend more of his time making use of his God-given testosterone and behave like any normal person of his age?' John didn't answer - he just watched.

The last of the theatre crowds had long since dispersed. The threesome left down the short flight of steps to the pavement and walked away from the RST along Southern Lane, towards the Parish Church. Mark Dryden and John Fletcher got up and followed them at a discreet distance. When the youthful trio reached 'Old Town' at the end of the lane, Alex put his arms round his potential conquests and they skipped away across the deserted road - but, before they disappeared into the warren of terraced streets on the other side, a sixth sense made Alex look over his shoulder. He saw two tall dark figures on the street corner, watching him.

The two friends, realising that they had missed a golden opportunity to talk to Alex, left him to his own devices and made their way back towards the town centre. 'You can score with almost anything in there,' said Mark nodding to the Avonbank Gardens on their right, 'and I don't mean women either, but at least the authorities know where it's going on.'

'Is it really that bad out here in the sticks?' asked John.

'Didn't used to be, but, with Turks, Romanians, Ukrainians and whoever, we've all got little choice but to adapt. The Middle East is on everyone's doorstep now, as you well know. There are so many junctions and sliproads on the Heroin Road between here and Afghanistan, it may as well be designated the 'H1'! None of us are immune from political imperatives are we?'

'Too true,' replied John, 'but they're the least of our problems tonight. From what you've told me, that young man has become a real thorn in the side, and he is already too close to us for my liking. We need to find him tomorrow and talk to him.'

'I know where he's staying from the forms he's filled in, and his home address. He moves in small circles - I'll find him. Don't worry. You can rely on me to do whatever it takes to protect our work; but look, I'm already late and I must get going. Let's see what tomorrow brings, shall we?' After a fraternal handshake, the friends said good bye, and went their separate ways.

18

Having been unsuccessful in pulling either of his 'Miss World' contestants, Alex returned to Old Town and the Parish Church. He vanished quickly through the main gates and into the tunnel of trees and its dense canopy of leaves that led to the church's north porch. He wanted some time alone to mull over the day and its pros and cons.

The church and the trees lent a blackness to the churchyard that was so dense you had to force your way through it. He felt his way towards the east end of the medieval building along its north side. He stopped. Straining his eyes and ears, he peered into the churchyard's eerie alien void. Nothing - but he had an uncanny feeling that somebody was watching him. He crept forward, looking around continually until he felt reassured there was no-one there, and that his fear was no more than the workings of an overactive imagination. He climbed onto a tomb and sat for a while in order to collect his thoughts. The silence was broken only by the distant hubbub of the town centre traffic, the intermittent squawks of geese and ducks and the sound of rushing water over the nearby weir.

He took out his mobile and shone its LED torch it across the ground below him. There, lying in the well-tended grass, were several flat and unadorned slabs of various sizes. One, in particular, caught his eye. It was perfectly rectangular, smaller than most, and made of dark marble, quite unlike any of its neighbours. What struck him almost immediately was how familiar it appeared - and this wasn't four pints of 'Hookie' talking either! The modest stone was identical in size and colour to the inscription stone below the Shakespeare monument on the wall in the chancel, no more than twenty metres from where he was sitting. Common sense told him that a replacement, or even an original slab, if there ever was one of course, couldn't possibly lie undiscovered for four hundred years - not out here where hundreds of visitors walked past it every day! But, just to be certain, he would turn it over anyway and take look at its underside.

He jumped down and attempted to prise it free, but, no matter how hard he tugged at it's edges, the soil refused to loosen its secure and long-held grip. He needed a tool of some kind, and, went back to his lodgings to see if he could find a suitable implement. With no access to the garage, his evening's activities came to an abrupt end. On reflection, he realised that buying a tool was probably the most sensible course of action; after all, it would be a tricky request to explain to the guest house owner. 'Er, excuse me, Mr. Smith, but tomorrow night, under the cloak of darkness, I fancy digging up a gravestone in the parish churchyard. Have you got something suitable I could use?'

Early the next morning, he was off to the ironmongers in the centre of town. It was a rare Aladdin's cave of a store which was unusual to come across in a town centre, even in those days. It didn't take him long to find the ideal tool - a bolster chisel, normally used for splitting bricks or stones.

Alex now had the rest of the day to kill, and started with a great favourite of his, Waterstones Bookshop. Its uninspiring interior housed a feast of Shakespeariana and books of local interest. By pure chance, he happened on two books which only someone with his particular focus would have related together. The first was in the section devoted to topics of local interest entitled - 'Unsolved Warwickshire Murders'. One chapter in the macabre paperback concerned a Stratford drunk and ne'er-do-well who became celebrated in the eighteen-seventies and eighties. Claiming to be a direct descendant of one of William Shakespeare's best friends, John Coombe, George Coombe would wander from pub to pub, reciting at length from many of the famous plays to earn himself a beer, but usually ending up making a general nuisance of himself. He claimed to have unequivocal proof that "Shakespeare never writ Shakespeare".

The town was still buzzing from the recent opening of the Memorial Theatre, when one day, he produced his proof in the form of several letters handed down to him. He either lent, or gave them, allegedly, to a member of the Birthplace Trust. He went on to say, in a most public manner, that the 'Trust' denied ever having had them, and when George demanded his property back, he was told in no uncertain terms to keep away. Fights broke out in the streets, and the whole business got rather messy. To cut a long story short, he ended up being beaten to death, his body being found on the towpath of the Birmingham and Stratford Canal, a mile or so out of town.

The second book, a more academic work, concerned the last days of the workhouses in Great Britain. In its thoroughly researched pages, Alex came across the case of the 'Mad Woman of Lincoln', also known rather mockingly as 'Lady Macbeth.' One of the workhouse's last few sorry residents, she lost her mind and spent her final days ranting and raving disjointed quotes from Shakespeare in the neglected and crumbling institution on the outskirts of Lincoln. Her story might have gone unnoticed but for three things which caught Alex's eye: firstly, that the principle benefactors of the workhouse where she lived out her miserable existence were the Freemasons: secondly, that her real name was recorded as Mary Coombe - 'origin unknown' (George Coombe's wife, he recalled, was also Mary); lastly, the author had included a photocopy of her admission document - signed by an 'FCV.' The fate of the Coombe children was never established, but, according to the Warwickshire Murders book, George's widow...'went mad and died in the Warwickshire County Lunatic Asylum at Hatton, just outside Warwick'. Two Mary Coombes with a Shakespeare/Stratford connection required further investigation, not to mention the strange coincidence of the reappearance of the initials - FCV.

Alex flew out of the bookstore to check the details of the two stories in the Library and Information Centre back in Henley

Street. He found that the same officials' names cropped up in both cases, and they were senior figures in the police, the town council, and the Birthplace Trust. Although he had no proof, he bet that they were all Freemasons too. The 1901 Census revealed no Mary Coombe at the Hatton Mental Hospital, either as a patient, or in the burial records. Was he being paranoid to speculate that these were amongst the reasons why Mark Dryden was getting so tough with him, or, if he was honest with himself, wouldn't he treat a stroppy student in the same way if he was a Trust official? Whatever the facts might be, he had found two convincing and exciting new leads.

The remains of the day were interminable. He was more certain than ever that there was some kind of cover-up going on, but, before he was prepared to go public with his findings, he had to take a look at the 'slabbe' - just to put his mind at rest. Later that evening, as dusk finally yielded to the coppery glow of the street lights, he wondered, somewhat optimistically perhaps, if he might be fortunate enough to meet the same grammar school girls again. Unfortunately, Shottery Manor, home to the famous school, didn't offer up any of its finest for him, and his evening was spent drinking alone.

The night was as black and hollow as the street lights would allow as he made his way to the patch of ground outside the chancel, near to where the old ossuary once stood. He approached his task with the sense vulnerability characteristic of performing secretive acts; the feeling that an audience was watching him, a primal fear denying him his peace, his heart pounding hard enough to break free from his chest. After one last look round, he knelt down on the grass, and drove the chisel into the ground at the edge of the slab. Levering on it firmly, he soon freed it from its centuries of rest - up it came, dirt, worms and all.

Initially it appeared to reveal very little, but his disappointment was short-lived, as he picked and scraped away eagerly at the clumps of soil stuck to its surface. He could see evidence of letters carved into it. In the blue-white light of his torch, slowly but surely, he exposed neat rows of roman capitals jealously hanging on to their last few fragments of gold, a sure sign that the stone had spent some of its early life indoors. In the bottom left corner were the letters 'FCV'. 'I knew it,' he said, in a loud whisper, 'there *is* a covert group behind this whole business after all. Those initials prove it. They must have used their membership of the Freemasons as a cover for centuries'.

He cleaned off as much dirt as he could, and propped it against the nearby tomb. Not wishing to attract unnecessary attention to himself, he switched off the flash on his camera, and photographed it with both camera and phone. After copying the text into his notebook, he replaced the 'slabbe' as best as he was able, and then e-mailed the images to his home computer. Finally, he phoned Tony, leaving a message to tell him what he had discovered, and to tell him to get back to him.

Back at his lodgings, frustrated by the fact that he couldn't contact the one person he could trust to keep quiet about the find, he decided to stay over one more day. He wanted to write up his conclusions regarding his summer of discoveries, and to check whether he had overlooked any other references to the mysterious 'FCV.'

He compared the text on the famous inscription stone on the chancel wall with the one he had just discovered. The reason for its replacement was immediately apparent. He could see straight away from lines two and three, that it told the 'passenger' that, now that William Shakspere was dead, the name of Edward de Vere, as the author Shake-speare, was being buried with him. The 'WE' who were expressing their gratitude, were obviously the 'FCV' whose legend was inscribed in the bottom left-hand corner. The installation of the 'Slabbe', with its cryptic message so simple to decipher, was an error of judgement the FCV had to rectify quickly, and that's precisely what they did.

He wrote and posted a last letter to Tony, urging him to get into contact, and spent the remainder of the day extending the results of his research into accepted areas of Shakespearean scholarship.

His findings still contained a lot of circumstantial evidence, but he couldn't afford to spend too long on the authorship issue, as the autumn term was only a few weeks away and coursework studies beckoned.

On his last day in Stratford, Alex rose earlier than usual. The previous night, he had written his letter to Tony in a combination of excitement and apprehension. Excitement about the momentousness of the discovery and all the media attention and hype it would inevitably bring, but apprehension that because of the disturbed ground around it, the inscription stone might be discovered by somebody else. Somebody who might go public before he was ready to himself. He packed his things and had a light breakfast before setting off for the churchyard. Concerned that he hadn't replaced the slab neatly, and might have left obvious traces of his activities, a last check of the site was essential. Only then could he afford to relax before catching the early commuter train back to Birmingham.

He had indeed left marks in the grass the previous night, and some scratches on other slabs and the tomb. He put his bag down and did a little tidying up.

Without him noticing, a tall, dark figure appeared beside him.

'You really meant it when you said you were going to dig up the churchyard then, didn't you?' he said.

'If only you knew what I've found,' said Alex, looking up momentarily at the man's face, silhouetted against the pale pinks of the early morning sky, adding rather naively, 'and you are going to have a lot of explaining to do when this goes on the net and hits the front pages in the next day or two.'

Alex was blissfully unaware that the person he was addressing would stop at nothing, to prevent him from going public with his discoveries

'Are you a member of FCV?' asked Alex; but there was no answer, and there was to be no idle banter either, no discussion, no negotiation. A swift blow to the neck propelled him against the nearby tomb. It was sufficient to silence him. Once he had been relieved of his valuables, his bag was emptied of all his recent research, and thrown into the nearby bushes. His body was then concealed in the pile of grass cuttings at the top of the steep riverbank.

His assailant had to think quickly. Realising that the body could well be discovered quite soon, attention may well be drawn to the 'slabbe,' and the disturbed grass and soil around it; there would be fingerprints, DNA. He had no choice but to get rid of it - and immediately - but where? Surely, he thought, no-one will think of the river? He picked up the 'slabbe,' - and then paused. He had known of the existence of the 'slabbe' for many years, but he never dreamt that he would ever find himself holding it. He had very mixed emotions as he read its cryptic text, and in the bottom corner, what to him were very familiar letters - 'FCV.'

After checking that there was not a soul in sight, he threw it into the murky shallows below. Confident that the local police were unlikely to connect the mugging of a student with the theft of a small gravestone from the churchyard, and with there being nothing to link him to either event, he felt safely in the clear, and left.

* * * * *

The text of the 'original' inscription stone, found by Alex in chapter 18:

IVDICIO PYLIVM GENIO SOCRATEM, ARTE
MARONEM, TERRA TEGIT, POPVLVS MAERET,
OLYMPVS HABET.
STAY PASSENGER, WHY GOEST THOV BY SO FAST?
READ IF THOV CANST, WHOSE NAME DOTH
DECK THIS TOMBE, EVER MORE. WITH, IN THIS
MONVMENT, IS SHAKE-SPEARE PLAST: WHOM
ENVIOVS DEATH DID TAKE: THANKS GIVE WE,
FOR WHOM, NOW IS SILENCE: SIEH WOVLD THAT
HE HATH WRITT,
LEAVES LIVING ART , BVT NAME, TO SERVE
HIS WITT.
FCV   *OBIT ANO DO 1616*
                                         AETATIS: 53, DIE 23 AP

Text of the inscription stone to be found beneath the bust of William Shakespeare, in Holy Trinity Church, Stratford-upon-Avon, England:

IVDICIO PYLIVM GENIO SOCRATEM, ARTE
MARONEM, TERRA TEGIT, POPVLVS MAERET,
OLYMPVS HABET.
STAY PASSENGER, WHY GOEST THOV BY SO FAST,
READ IF THOV CANST, WHOM ENVIOVS DEATH
HATH PLAST, WITH IN THIS MONVMENT
SHAKESPEARE: WITH WHOME, QVICK NATVRE
DIDE WHOSE NAME DOTH DECK Y TOMBE,
FAR MORE, THEN COST: SIEH ALL, Y HE HATH
WRITT, LEAVES LIVING ART, BVT PAGE, TO SERVE
HIS WITT.
                                    OBIT ANO DO 1616
                                    AETATIS. 53 DIE 23 AP.

Stratford Herald : Mon. Sept. 13th : 2010.

ANOTHER 'DRUGS DEATH' BODY FOUND FLOATING IN AVON POLICE IN STRATFORD are

bracing themselves for a new wave of gangland killings after the body of an unknown man was found floating in the River Avon on Saturday morning. He had been dead for about 3 days, said the Police.

Shocked American visitor Walter Whitmore, 35, boating with his wife and children, discovered the bloated corpse half-concealed in the reeds above the weir.

The river has now been cordoned-off from Holy Trinity Church to the weir as a 'Crime Scene'.

'The six-feet tall, twelve-stone man could have been a student,' said Senior Investigating Officer, D.I. York, at a news conference this morning. 'He might even have been British,' he said. 'His hands were too clean and well-manicured to be those of an itinerant farm-worker. However,' he added, 'this does stop him from being mixed up with the East European drug scene.'

BLOODSTAINS

Over the weekend, attention focused on the churchyard close to the east-end of Holy Trinity Church, where forensic officers discovered bloodstains on a tomb near the riverbank.

A freshly exposed patch of bare earth near the bloody 18th Cent. tomb was explained by Inspector York. 'It's not the first time we've had gravestones stolen in Stratford,' he said, 'and I'm sure it won't be the last,'.

'Ridiculous!' was the sole response of the Church authorities, to the rumour that someone had been seen digging for 'Shakespeare's bones,' near the chancel, close to the site of the medieval charnel house.

'What do you expect when they keep on letting all these bloody Transylvanians into the country,' remarked one local resident, who asked not to be named. 'Nothing, not even our beloved "William", is sacred to these people if they think there's a few euros in it for them.'

Anyone with further information should contact Warwickshire Police (Stratford CID), on 01789 414111.

Stratford Herald : Fri. Oct. 8th 2010.

'DRUGS DEATH' MAN CREMATED

Aʟᴇxᴀɴᴅᴇʀ Pᴀʀɪs, 21, identified as the 'Mystery Man', whose body was found floating near the weir three weeks ago, was cremated yesterday at Northfield Cemetery, Birmingham.

A Police spokeswoman said last night that they are no closer to making an arrest. 'We are following up what few leads we do have that Mr. Paris was probably killed accidentally while being mugged,' she said.

'It's most likely that somebody wanted cash for a fix,' added D.I. Watson, brought in from West Midlands Serious Crime Squad to head the investigation. 'Paris just happened to be in the wrong place at the wrong time,' he said. 'We've had trouble with dealers using the itinerant farm-workers as cover for years, and their activities continue to make huge demands on our already overworked officers.'

Antony Chapman, 21, a close friend of the dead man, said 'It's nonsense to suggest that he was associated with the Stratford drug scene.'

The Bristol University student remained convinced that there was a 'Shakespeare' connection to the death of his best friend 'Alex,' when we spoke to him yesterday.

'He was in Stratford doing research into the life of William Shakespeare,' he said. 'He rang me to say he was on the verge of a great discovery only the day before he died.'

The investigation continues.

Part Three

Launcelot,

"…truth will come to light, murder cannot be hid long,…
…in the end truth will out."

The Merchant of Venice, 2,2.

William Shakespeare.

19

'Alex seemed convinced that some sort of 'brotherhood' connected to the Freemasons were at the bottom of things, didn't he, and yet he said nothing about them being involved back in 2010?' said Jessica.

They had decided to complete a 'Circular' walk, and were in the park opposite the church, heading back towards their hotel.

'The Freemasons have had a finger in the bard's pie for ages. Stratford was still so poor, two hundred and fifty years ago, they had to drag in David Garrick, the greatest thespian of the day, to save them. A hundred years later, there was enough cash around to pay for the original Memorial Theatre. The foundation stone was laid by Lord Leigh, Provincial Grand Master no less. Where did all the money come from, you may well ask?'

'The Freemasons?'

'And again, when its rebuilt successor, nicknamed the 'Jam Factory', was opened in 1929, it, too, was a Masonic event. If our culprit is to be found in the Midlands, we will have to investigate their involvement.'

'And what of his great discovery; did you find out what it was?'

'He alluded to it, but held back at the last moment; so, no, I never knew exactly what it was. My guess was that he had come across an original manuscript which would prove conclusively that William of Stratford was no author. Sounds familiar or sounds familiar?'

'Like the ones Randy found in Venice, you mean?'

'Maybe, Jess. I can't be certain, but it sure challenges your belief in coincidences doesn't it? I find myself close to two untimely deaths, and manuscripts on paper seem to connect them.'

5.15 pm.

It was a gentle and uncommonly quiet two and a half hours. Tony was deep in thought, driving on autopilot, and there must have been several ten mile stretches of the journey back to Essex for which he had no recollection at all. Jessica saw that he was much more at ease with himself, and hoped that getting such a major issue in his life out into the open was not going to alter him. As a twenty-two year-old woman it wasn't easy to take in what the deep platonic friendship between these two men had really meant. As he told the story, it was as though Alex was still actually alive, and that he was eager to tell Alex something, apologise perhaps. It almost seemed that part of him belonged to Alex, and part of Alex still belonged to him. He gave the whole episode such an immediate and powerful presence that she soon found it resonating through her own more recent memories of her time with Bianca in the Palazzo in Venice. Even though the episode had been several years earlier, it still ran very deep, and she knew there would be more to come. When it did, she just prayed that whatever changes they made in him, they wouldn't take him away from her. Her emotions had had a sort of adrenalin fix, and at one moment she loved her man more than ever before, and, at the next, she felt that she hardly knew him at all. It wasn't only Tony who had found the trip to Stratford cathartic.

After he had dropped Jessica off at the Old Rectory, Tony drove straight home, his mind throwing up assorted frustrations that shattered his peace. He didn't want to show it to Jessica, but he was becoming consumed by an urge to prove the Italian police wrong, to find out who was really responsible for Alex's death, and to solve the Shakespeare authorship question all in one go. He was getting increasingly concerned that he might lose her to this new passion. She had embraced the facts she had learnt in Stratford, and Alex's story, but, would it be enough to keep her on board when it was the demise of her best friend that had taken her there in the first place? He was aware of the selfish motives behind his actions. Was it too much to expect someone as inexperienced as her to understand what he was doing?

He drove up to his house and was greeted by the uncompromising glare of the security lights. He got out of his car and strode wearily up to the front door. Bathed in the silent brilliance, he opened the door and went in.

'God, that girl's really something,' he thought, as he tossed his keys onto the table in the hall. He went into the living room to fix himself a drink and flopped into the deep soft sofa. His tired eyes dwelled for a while on the Jim Dine on the wall in front of him. It was a painting-cum-drawing, a mixed-media piece of a skinny girl in what, at a glance, looked like a hasty, almost careless mishmash of watercolour and pastel. On closer inspection, it revealed an enviable control of the artist's chosen media and a deep feel for the form of this near anorexic young girl, whose skin clung to her skeleton with apparent desperation. Rather like a depiction of life and death, fused in a single image, and a great favourite of his, he had a sense that he wouldn't look at this A1 sheet of handmade paper in quite the same light again. The painting next to it held his gaze for a very different reason, not because of the image or its slightly battered Italian cassetta frame, but because, behind it, was a small safe. Small yes, but large enough to house, perfectly flat, Randy's three precious renaissance pages.

Whether or not the British police would take their theory of a motive for the killings more seriously than Commissario Montano and his Polizia Veneziano he just couldn't say. It was quite likely that, in England, it would be even harder to get the authorities to take them seriously because of the inherent prejudice, here in Britain, to publicly questioning Shakespeare's authorship - 'Oh no, not that old chestnut!' he could hear them all saying. The best way forward could be to have someone to help on the inside, but he didn't have any contacts in the police. There was only one person he knew who might be in a position to help. He checked the time - it was almost eight - 'Not too late surely,' he thought. He fumbled his way through a pile of unsorted mail on his desk until he found his old address book. Although he felt close to his Uncle Brian, they never e-mailed or had made much more contact over the past few years than exchanging Christmas cards.

'Hi! Uncle Brian?'

'Now there's a voice form the past,' came the reply. 'What can I do for young Tony?'

'Is it convenient to talk for a couple of minutes, Uncle, I'm sorry it's a bit late?'

'Of course Tony, I've always got a few minutes for my favourite nephew. You haven't found something new and exciting on our friend Edward de Vere have you?'

'Not exactly, Uncle, no.'

He first got to know his uncle - 'BJ' to nearly everyone since his schooldays - at a family get-together shortly before going up to university. He was tall, fit, and had a friendly, if formal, air. Tony took to him immediately when some other relations, also on his mothers side, rounded on him for what were known to be his well voiced views about the 'Bard'. They would get disquietingly emotional with him - 'His name's on the First bloody Folio for Christ's sake,' they would say, 'Wasn't there enough twaddle on the subject spoken about Bacon?' But 'BJ' would respond with quiet rational arguments for which they had no answer, making them even more furious. Tony found the interchanges so amusing that he would move in closer, to see how his uncle was able to control the situation so adroitly.

'I've got to handle this with tact,' he opened, 'even with you, Uncle, because a friend of mine is involved and has asked for my assurance that I will not divulge certain matters that concern him.'

'It all sounds rather intriguing; but why have you chosen to involve me with your problem?'

'Well, I'm hoping you may be able to help me by finding someone in the police who is prepared to listen to what I have to say, in an unbiased way. Someone you can be certain I can trust. You see, Uncle, a relation of my friend has died, and, although it may have been an accident, my friend thinks it might have been deliberate. Manslaughter, or even murder.'

'Why me, though, why not take your suspicions straight to the police?'

'It happened abroad.'

'And the authorities there - your friend has tried, I suppose?'

'Yes he has, and has got nowhere, which is why I want someone on the inside as it were, to find out what is going on.'

'Did this 'accident' occur in Europe?'

'As a matter of fact, yes, but that isn't the only thing I'd like to ask him about. Do you remember my friend Alex who died in Stratford about six years ago?'

'Yes I do, go on.'

'Well there were always a few unanswered questions over his death, and it might be he could help there too.'

'You haven't gone and got yourself mixed up in something… irregular, shall we say?'

'Oh good heavens, no, Uncle, no, no, nothing like that.' Tony hadn't realised how his story would sound to an outsider. When he reflected for a moment he understood how bizarre his request sounded.

'Calm down, young man, calm down. You have to admit, it all comes across as rather suspicious, and there's not a great deal for me to take to a fellow professional to convince him to give up some of his very valuable time.'

'I'm sorry, Uncle, you're right. I must admit, it does all sound a bit weird. Please trust me when I say I wouldn't trouble you if it wasn't a serious matter, and I daren't run the risk of some eager young constable walking into his station canteen and blurting out, 'Hey guys, you'll never guess what I've just heard?' Now can I?"

'You can't be any more explicit?'

'If you can help me out, Uncle, I'm sure your contact will tell you if he thinks it'll interest you.'

'Leave it with me, Tony. I've got a couple of good men I might approach. I've a feeling you'll tell me all about it when you're good and ready anyway.'

'Thanks for giving up your time, Uncle. I can't tell you much more without leaving you even more up in the air than you must be at the moment. Coincidences rankle with me, as I'm sure they do with you, and I don't want to burden you with unnecessary information. If the officer you know can get into past files, and expose any irregular goings on, and in the process see if there is any sort of connection between the two incidents, then I'll be so grateful. I'll pay for his time of course.'

'Don't worry about that, Tony, I'm getting a clearer idea of the sort of investigation you are seeking, and a chap I know who has recently left the 'Met' should see you all right. It may be a week or two before you hear anything you realise.'

'That's so kind of you. Anything that he can discover that puts my friend's mind at rest - and mine - will be greatly appreciated. We must have a get-together; it's been years since we've had a good talk.'

'Yes, we must, and you can tell me more about your mystery. Speak to you soon.'

It hadn't been the easiest of conversations, but at least there had been a positive outcome of sorts. Tony didn't want to bring up the matter of the stolen pages, or even Venice, as he knew that his uncle would immediately put two and two together and come up with Randy Middleton. The investigation into Bianca's death had inevitably slipped from the front few pages of the quality national dailies, but her face still regularly adorned the inside pages of the tabloids, and insensitive journalists were already asking when Randy was going to be "back on our screens". All Tony could do now was wait for contact from the ex-detective, putting his faith in the hands of his uncle's judgement and a man about whom he knew absolutely nothing.

20

The phone ringing so early on a Friday evening was quite unusual, so Tony checked the screen carefully before answering - 'Number withheld'. He let it ring another couple of times and then clicked on speakerphone.

'Chapman', he said in a business-like tone, expecting to hear an oriental voice make him yet another climate-saving offer only a fool would refuse.

'Steve Watson, ex D.C.I. Steve Watson to be more accurate. That's Antony Chapman, I presume?'

'That's correct.'

'An uncle of yours rang me earlier this week, Mr. Chapman, and gave me the impression that you were in need of some assistance.'

'Yes, that's right. My, that's very prompt of you, Mr. Watson.'

'Well, old 'BJ' sounded a trifle anxious, even for him, and, as it seems you two are quite close, as you might say, an' I owe him a couple, here I am.'

'Thanks, yes, well, it may all turn out to be for nothing, Mr. Watson...'

'Steve - no need to be formal.'

'OK - Steve - if we can meet up somewhere, I can run the whole situation past you, and you'll know whether you are in a position to help.'

'I see you're on the edge of Maldon - how about the 'Brewers' in Danbury, d'you know it?'

'The Brewer's Arms on the main road? Yes, I know it.'

'How about seven tomorrow then, eh - strike while the iron's hot, as you might say?'

'Let's make it seven-thirty, if that's all right. How will I know you?'

'Yeah, that's OK. I'll be in the bay window, round to the left in the bar - and, don't worry, Mr. Chapman, I'll know you.'

MAR. 19th SAT: 7.30 pm. DANBURY, ESSEX :

When Tony and Jessica arrived at the white, concrete-rendered Victorian inn, they pulled into a small, and virtually empty, car park to the side, stopping next to a silver Volvo sports coupe. It displayed all the latest in hydrogen powered technology, had two aerials, and a dashboard full of communications wizardry. The passenger seat and floor-well could barely be seen for paperwork, maps, cigarette packets and empty fast-food containers.

'You don't think our man is leaving a few too many clues, do you?' asked Jessica, with a smile.

'We'll soon see. I just hope he's at least half as efficient as his car,' answered Tony.

They went straight into the bar. There was only one person sitting at the table in the bay window, and, as the couple made their way through the orderly scattering of cast iron tables and chairs, the man stood and stretched out his hand.

'Evenin', Mr. Chapman, Miss,' came the slightly hoarse and self-consciously cheerful greeting. Steve Watson proved to be a stocky five foot eight or nine, and spoke in the detached manner of someone who is always busy, or, at least, likes to get by on creating that impression. He was still wearing his topcoat, an indication that he wanted to be brief, perhaps. Grey and balding before his time, his face hadn't worn well. He had the dissipated appearance of a man whose only purpose in life was have what he wanted on his own terms, and who only checked the mirror to reassure himself that he was looking at the same person who was there yesterday.

'Nice to meet you both.'

'Good evening, Mr. Watson. This is my partner, Jessica, and please, call me Tony.'

'An' I'm Steve, remember? Now, what can I get you?'

'No, Steve, this one's mine. Jess, your usual?'

She nodded and shook the ex-inspector's hand.

'Same again, Steve?'

'John Smith's, Tony, ta - best make it a half, though.'

Tony went over to the bar, leaving Jessica to the tender mercies of the brusque 'private eye'.

'This is all a bit of a mystery then, Miss,' he began. 'Old 'BJ' was quite insistent that I should get in touch - made it sound important like.' He took a large draught, draining his glass. He placed it back on the table the way an impatient workman would a hammer on his workbench.

Jessica didn't rise to the bait, but said quietly, 'I'm sure Tony will tell you all you need to know.'

He summoned up the remains of his bonhomie with a leering grin but said nothing. She disliked and mistrusted middle aged men who fancied their chances with her. Usually she thrived on attention, and could even find it unsettling if a man didn't give her a second look, as though he was deliberately trying to drain her of her ego. This man had sadly misjudged her, though, and should have had the sense to realise that the meeting was to be treated purely as business - and that it belonged to Tony.

'Here we are,' said Tony, putting the glasses on the table. He sat down, took a sip from his double tonic, and began. 'Two friends of mine have died in what I can only describe as mysterious circumstances, Steve. One recently and one nearly six years ago.'

'And you want to see if yours truly can find a link, yeah?'

'Well, partly, yes, but, as there are question marks over both deaths individually, I would like you to look at them separately. See if you think there is anything suspicious about the way they've been investigated, and then if there is a connection - as I - we - think there is - then we can take it from there.'

'Did they know each other, these friends of yours?'

'No they didn't, but their deaths are oddly similar. For instance, both of them died after being hit against stone. One was killed outright and the other drowned, but both of them were found floating in water.'

'No weapons then?'

'No.'

'So both could look like accidents, or unintentional killings?'

'Exactly.'

'Are the investigations ongoing?'

'The death in Venice is recent, and, yes, the case is 'ongoing', as you say, but the death of my other friend, in Stratford-upon-Avon, occurred six years ago. No-one was ever brought to trial, so I assume the case is still open. The police up there believed that immigrant workers mixed up in the local drug trade were responsible.'

'And you think there might've been a cover up, I suppose?'

'That's one of the things I'd like you to establish, to see if my suspicions are justified. I knew my friend very well, Steve, and he wouldn't go near drugs; but that's not the point, it's the fact that the case was wrapped up with such indecent haste that I found disturbing.'

'Now hang on a minute, young fella; you're trying to tell me that the Warwickshire force did a cover-up, or that they couldn't be bothered, and you've waited six years to tell anyone?' The ex-D.C.I. was getting protective of his profession, and for the first time showed some emotion.

'I've come to you on a recommendation from someone whose opinion I respect greatly, Steve. If you feel you're not up to lifting the edge of the carpet to see if there's any dirt underneath, then now's the time to tell me.'

'Don't get me wrong, young fella, I've seen corruption all over the place, big and small, but you've given yours truly almost zilch to go on. I need some stuff - you know - times, dates, places.'

Tony admitted that he had been skirting around the issue, but was prepared to take the ex-police officer into his confidence. He started with the attack on Alex, and, although the detective said he would take a look into the procedures of six years ago, he promised nothing.

'Someone was looking for a fix. Your Alex was an easy target if you ask me: alone, carrying the usual set of portable valuables. But as for a connection to Shakespeare, well, I'll have a look, but it all sounds a bit bloody far-fetched to me - if you'll excuse my French, Miss,' he added, in an aside to Jessica. 'I'll dig around and see if anything was deliberately overlooked, or sidelined. There's loads of ways to move an enquiry this way 'n' that, and Steve Dubya is the man to find out if and how it were done. Now, what about this second one, Venice, you said?'

'This death is the reason why I'm so sure there's a Shakespeare connection,' said Tony. He went through the facts as he knew them. It was difficult not to go into the sort of detail the detective would need to check out how the investigation was progressing under Commissario Montano. He decided to explain things in generalities without mentioning who was involved by name, keeping quiet about Randy, Helena, and the fact that not all the books and pages had been stolen. If and when the private detective proved himself, then, and only then, would he bring his famous friends out into the open. He felt honour-bound to protect their names as long as possible. He also wanted to protect Jessica, as any enquiry into Bianca's life was bound to reveal her.

'Can't be more specific?'

'Not at the moment Steve. Concentrate on Stratford if you will, and I'll talk to my friend about extending the enquiry into his daughter's death before I give you any more to go on. Is that OK ?'

'Right, leave it in the capable hands of yours truly. I'll give you a bell as soon as I've got summat, but y' gotta be patient because these sort of things can't be hurried.' He was on his feet in a moment, drained his half of John Smith's, and after quick handshakes, bade them farewell, and left.

'Not quite what I expected,' said Jessica, 'from what you told me about your uncle Brian I thought we were in for, well, if not Poirot then Morse, at the very least!'

'Life's full of surprises, isn't it, sweetheart?' Tony took time to finish his drink. 'Let's wait and see, shall we? I've no reason to doubt 'BJ's judgment, yet. This guy, Watson, has only just retired as a D.C.I. from the Met., so he must know his stuff.'

'I still don't like him. I find him creepy. I mean, fancy earning your living nosing around in other peoples private lives, ugh!'

'Jess, we're not in this to *like* anyone. If he's 'BJ's best choice for discretion and getting the job done, I'm going to trust him because at the moment he's all we've got.'

Back in his car, the private detective lit up, took out his mobile, and dropping his professional manner, rang a Red-top journalist friend. 'Baz, you old tart, Steve - and before you ask - on top of the world. Now, what school did that Middleton girl go to?.... Yeah, yeah, the one in the canal.... Colchester Girls, eh? I'm not surprised....Oh, one other thing, d'you know if the 'crabs' over there in the Bride of the Adriatic have got any more on who did her in?....Still an accident then?....Thought as much.... Well, seeing as you ask, you know that prat on TV - Randy Middleton?....her old man, yeah, that's the one.... He's trying to find out what he can by the back door - surprise, surprise - and he's put up a young pair of hoorays to front for him.... Sure, anything I find out, you'll be the first to know, tarrah.'

21

'Can we do something about all these damned boxes and files, Katie, they must have been here for more than a month? It's beginning to look like a charity shop storeroom in here!'

It was quite normal for the Trust to receive bequests and donations of literary material, but, since his return from Venice, Dryden had been more sensitive than usual to the inconvenience caused by this latest delivery.

'It's all got to be sorted and catalogued before it can be moved, Mr. Dryden, and I've only got one pair of hands.'

'Then get another pair! Look, I've still got a job to do, and this last bequest is all pretty mediocre stuff. Can't you just shove it off into a storeroom somewhere, and forget about it until the Gala is over?'

'I mustn't allow them to get mixed up. Someone devoted half a lifetime to building this collection and…'

'For God's sake, woman! Don't keep going on about them as though they are a collection of national treasures or something. You've only got to look at the state of these in the top box.' He lifted some of the tatty books and folders with both hands, as though half-heartedly tossing a salad. 'Surely, even *you* can tell at a glance what you're in for. Can't you just get them out of sight, because there's no way I can do any meaningful work while I've got to clamber over them every day? - And, what's more, they smell!'

Katie was shocked by Dryden's hostile attitude. She was certain it was due to stress, caused by the pressure he was under in the build up to the quatercentenary celebrations, now only five weeks away. Her experience in running the records and archives departments was respected by all the staff, but to be treated in such an off-hand manner by him was a bit hard to take. She bit her lip, and got on with the job of checking the contents and then carrying the heavy boxes through to the small storeroom at the back of the lecture theatre .

Their situation wasn't made any easier by the increasing media interest into the 'authorship' question. They were having to deal with the thorny problem more and more often; clearly it was not going to go away. The latest example was a very well received TV programme the night before, whipping up speculative argument once again.

The phone rang. 'Shakespeare Centre …. For heaven's sake, no, I don't have an official statement to offer on last night's programme,' he fumed, and, listening with increasing impatience, added, 'contact the Director, and, no, I will not offer you my opinion for you to be going on with …. No, ring the Directors office, good-bye.' Why the call came through to their office he had no idea, but that wasn't what really made him so angry. It was that the authorship question was now gaining a momentum of its own and was successfully invading both his work space and his private world.

The phone rang again.

'Deal with that, Katie, will you?, I'm up to here with interruptions.'

The call was another request for a visit from abroad. She answered in her exemplary, diplomatic manner, affirming to the caller, in her best BBC emotion-free tone, that - 'all the best and most important books and documents are with the conservation department. I'm afraid you won't be able to see them until they go on display next month …. Yes, that's right, when the general public gets to see them, too.'

'Can't you refuse them?' interrupted Dryden. 'This is getting beyond a joke.'

'No, Mr. Dryden, I think that would be most unreasonable. Provided we can show them something genuine, they'll be happy, and we will have created the right feeling of openness and generosity.'

'All right, do whatever you think is right, but, please, don't ask for any extra help. Give them something out of that latest bequest - that should keep them happy - anything old will do. Where are they from?'

'Verona. I'm sure they would be quite satisfied if they could be shown anything with a connection to northern Italy.'

Dryden went into the kitchen to make another pot of coffee. The barely adequate window shed a surprising amount of light for such a cloudy and blustery March afternoon. He took a deep breath and sighed equally deeply, and, for a few welcome minutes, gazed absentmindedly across Stratford's untidy hotch-potch of roofs.

In those timeless moments, a montage of images crowded his mind as he recalled the events of a fortnight before. He had found himself haunted repeatedly by the Daily Telegraph's front page photograph of Bianca. Night after night, he had lain awake for hours in a conscious prison of guilt, unable to escape the image of her radiant and beautiful face. Would nothing relieve him from this nightly, and now daily, turmoil? Surely this must be somebody-else's nightmare? He was watching the clouds as they scurried off to shade the east of the county when, to his surprise and relief, the idea, so brilliant in its simplicity, that came to him on his return from Venice, flashed back into his mind. He wondered why he hadn't done something about it sooner. What jolted his memory must have been contained in those few words of Katie's: "…show them something genuine….something with a connection to northern Italy." He collected his thoughts. The kettle was about to come to the boil. He was quick to turn it off before it did. He made the coffee, depressing the filter of the cafetiere with measured slowness. He was regaining control rapidly, but he didn't want his change in attitude to alert the perceptive Katie. She would have to put up with his short temper for a little longer, but maybe he could soften it with a suggestion of an apology.

'Who will rid me of this troublesome dramatist?' he mumbled.

'What's that, Mr. Dryden?'

'Nothing, Katie, nothing.' He paused. 'Would you like a coffee?'

'Well, seeing as you ask, Mr. Dryden, yes, actually I would. I think I've earned one, don't you?'

'Mmm,' he responded. 'These are going to be busy weeks.' That was as near to an apology as he was prepared to give her. She was putting him in his place, and quite rightly so. He knew it would have been both disingenuous and a waste of time to argue it.

'When are the Italians coming - is it RAI ?'

'I've got them down for the 7th of April provisionally, and, yes, it's RAI, one of their regional crews.'

'Remind me to be out. What day of the week will it be?'

'Let me see… Thursday.'

'Good! I wouldn't have been in anyway.'

She left, letting him see her knowing smile. That was as near to forgiveness as she felt Dryden deserved, and she returned to her office. Dryden returned to his, and closed the door. If there really was any mileage in the idea of releasing one of the 'pages', then it was vital to get the order of things down on paper quickly while the inspiration was fresh. He took a sheet of A4 out of the printer, and printed the words PAPER TRAIL in the centre, and like a child doing a school exercise, brainstormed the concept of a 'providential discovery' all round them.

Amongst the words and phrases was 'will they smell a rat???' 'Aye, there's the rub,' he thought, 'the press are bound to be onto it like a shot.' He was going to have to be so careful, and so calculating, to make sure that no evidence of a deception or a forgery could be traced back to him. The media would be all over the Trust like a bad rash. It would be worse than the flu pandemic of three years ago. Likewise, there would be no stopping the academics and researchers who had spent their lifetimes scrutinising every fragment of Tudor and Jacobean writing paper in their search for evidence of the Bard's hand. But what an opportunity. He had dismissed the idea as perilously risky before, but, now, a fresh light radiated from the idea, instantly ridding his mind of those earlier doubts. To the very core of his being he knew it would work. All he had to do was to choose the right page, and the right book. The doctored page would be secreted away, to be 'discovered' by an ecstatic Italian TV crew.

He looked down at the remaining piles of grocery and wine boxes stuffed with grimy and dusty old books, and the bundles of files tied up with an assortment of strings and cords. The musty smell of decades of damp and neglect permeated his office.

'Did you lock the door to the lecture theatre store room, Katie?

'No, I'm afraid I didn't, Mr. Dryden, I'll do it right away.'

'Don't worry, I'll do it. I just want to see the back of these boxes before I go tonight. Have you got the key?'

'In my top right hand drawer, underneath everything, Mr. Dryden, it's the shiny one.'

'Thanks, Katie, good-bye.'

'Good-bye, Mr. Dryden. See you in the morning.'

He finished outlining the details of his plan and took time to inspect the top box more closely before taking it to the store room. As he thought, it was all pretty mediocre stuff, and he recognised nearly all the titles. In the main, they were late Victorian and early twentieth century volumes and easily available. He carried all the boxes through to where the bulk of the bequest had been stacked so neatly by Katie. He went through every box. He despaired at the paucity of the material and the apparent lack of discrimination by the collector, who obviously valued quantity over quality. Thankfully, a couple of the boxes did contain some genuinely early publications, albeit in an appalling state. Before removing anything from the boxes, he went back to the kitchen to find a pair or rubber gloves. Even at this early stage, he didn't want to run the chance of leaving evidence of his fingerprints or DNA on what might possibly be his chosen material.

The contents were, in the main, in a terrible state. Damp had got at them, and on much of it there was mould, not to mention the combined effects of cats, mice, insects and the rest. The first volume he removed came apart with no effort, and the same was true for several others, as he searched desperately for anything worth saving, let alone meriting his special attention. He pushed the storeroom door wide open to help ventilate the confined space and rid it of the combined acid sweet reek from mouse droppings, gum arabic, leather and cat urine. He was beginning to wish that he had never opened the boxes when his eye fell on what would prove to be the perfect choice. He lifted it clear of the rest and placed it carefully on a table in the lecture theatre. The covers, spine and endpapers were all long gone, as the deplorable condition of the remaining outer pages testified, but the title page still said everything. It was a copy of volume 2 of Sir William Dugdale's *Antiquities of Warwickshire*. As he opened it, it came apart into seven or eight sections of assorted sizes. It was going to need immediate conservation if it wasn't to collapse into seven or eight more. With a touch as delicate as a surgeon, he opened the folio pages one, by one, until he reached page 680, the chapter containing Stratford super Avon. He slid out the whole section and put it to one side. He then carefully inserted the remainder of the book back among its fellows in the box, exactly as he had found it, and restacked the boxes. After he had put it between some clean sheets of paper, he slipped the fragile book-section into his *Telegraph* for the journey home.

22

Mark Dryden spread the 'Magretti' pages across his table once more. Handling archive material on a fairly regular basis as part of his job meant that he automatically donned either fine cotton or surgeon's gloves. This had the added advantage that no contaminants were transferred to the paper from him personally.

He had already divided the pages into categories: poems, letters, play drafts, notes on itineraries and so on. All the sheets which he'd classed as play drafts were divided into comedies and non-comedies. The majority were recognisable as studies for *The Merchant of Venice*, but there were rough drafts for passages from *Much Ado About Nothing*, *The Taming of the Shrew* and, most remarkably, *Othello*, which wouldn't appear on the stage for another thirty years after these lines must have been written. The family home of Oteli del Moro, whose ancestors included governors of Cyprus, the setting for the play, he recalled, was only a five minute walk from where the Earl of Oxford had stayed. As he surveyed the table for the most suitable page, he turned each one over, and put to one side those with nothing on the reverse. It was from these that his choice would be made.

As he searched for his chosen sheet, he couldn't help but be impressed by the legibility of de Vere's handwriting. Usually it takes quite a while to read through a Tudor manuscript, as many of the characters require deciphering, and the largely phonetic spelling needs translating. De Vere's however, was so clear and contemporary in appearance that most of it could have been read by a child. He decided to go along with the conventional chronology of dating the plays, and selected a page with an extract from *The Merchant of Venice, Act 1*, a passage where Portia and Nerissa are at Belmont discussing suitors. Any scientific tests carried out on the paper would place it around the time he knew it must have been made, and, as Edward de Vere left for the continent at the beginning of 1575, that would probably mean 1574. This was still dangerously early - William of Stratford would have been only ten years old, but it was the best he could do, especially when he had no idea where it was made. The spacing of the wire lines of the laid paper were typical of English-made paper of the period, so he felt it safe to assume that the Earl had taken all his paper with him in his writing box.

The ink was quite another matter. The oak-gall and carbon were easy to carbon-date, but, as water contained radio isotopes, scientific analysis would make dating a reconstituted ink simple and straightforward. Tap water, even if it were distilled, was therefore out of the question, and so was rainwater, as additives could still be traced. Spring water was the answer, and fortunately he kept a small bottle containing some which he had had scientifically tested and proved to be several thousand years old. He kept it with a forging kit in his safe.

He placed his old writing box in a space he had cleared for the purpose on a table in his study. Opened up, it displayed a wide range of writing and drawing materials, collected over many years from auctions, second hand shops and car boot sales. For his present task, the most valuable item was the bottle of ink dating back to the sixteenth century, which he brought back from Venice. The syrupy contents, wet from the last time Edward de Vere dipped his quill into it, would soon be reconstituted with the ancient and precious spring water. He removed one of the goose quills from a drawer, recut it, and split it on his thumbnail to check for resilience and flexibility. He prepared a second, and put them to one side. He now mixed the ink and checked its consistency by writing word after word, adding drops of water until it flowed perfectly. He was now almost ready to tackle the page itself.

For a page to appear to have spent maybe two hundred years pressed between the pages of a book, it was most important to show evidence of a faint depression. To effect this, he first photocopied the chosen sheet and measured it diagonally both ways to be certain that his copy was absolutely identical to the original. He then took a sheet of acetate , and after checking it for thickness, spray mounted the photocopy onto it. With a scalpel he then, cut the acetate through the photocopy to leave himself with a clear cellulose facsimile of the Tudor original. He peeled off the photocopy and discarded it, and removed any adhesive with white spirit from the acetate. He was careful to remove any traces of the spirit with soap and warm water. He then checked the accuracy of his cutting against the original. Satisfied with the result, he removed the sharp freshly cut edges by sanding them with flour paper. This elaborate procedure was vital if the deception was to succeed. He now gently folded the acetate, a little off centre, and between several sheets of smooth paper used a bone folder to increase the sharpness of the crease until the fold was dead flat.

He now turned his attention to the damaged book section. He selected page 688, the illustrated page at the bottom of which was Hollar's famous engraving of the monument to William Shakespeare. It was the perfect page to be identified with an improvised bookmark, like an old sheet of writing paper roughly folded in half. He gently atomised the open pages with a little of the spring water. This would open the fibres of the paper, and allow the folded acetate to make its impression in the seventeenth century pages more readily. He quickly placed the acetate in the book section, closed it up, and put it in his book press under plenty of pressure. Here it would remain until he needed it.

He was well aware that a lot of practice was needed to free up his handwriting. It would take many hours of patient application to bring to his hands the relaxed ease of a sixteenth century penman. He took a clean sheet paper, and wrote a line of m's, a line of l's and then a line of o's. He repeated this procedure many times, before cleaning the nib, and placing the pen to the side of the sheet. He went into the kitchen and made a cup of Darjeeling, with just the lightest squeeze of lime. The long day held no tiredness for him. The hours slid silently by - the Monteverdi Singers having sung their last chorale more than an hour ago. Troilus and Cressida were intertwined in their feline heaven on his best armchair. Time ceased to exist.

He straightened his back, flexed his shoulders and scanned the sheets of fresh text. It was coming on, and by tomorrow it would look as though someone else had written it - a sure sign that success should be just round the corner. A success that ultimately depended on the right choice for the fake text. The decision as to what would hopefully fool even the experts was critical. Success would mean he had created one of the most talked about pieces of paper in the western world. Failure to pull the wool over their eyes would mean that his world, Shakespeare's world, Stratford's world, would be in tatters.

He turned to a little volume of the records of William Shakespeare's life and business dealings in Stratford. Flicking through it's pages, it reminded him of not only how little he knew about this rural entrepreneur, but how he kept his two worlds so separate: the Stratford man is never mentioned in London, and the London theatrical man is never mentioned in Stratford. In many ways, this made his task easier, for he could create the only document to tie these two worlds together He knew the existing documents relating to Shakspere's property dealings well, and chose to add a note about the purchase of New Place. The substantial house had a large garden, added to, over the years, by buying up charitable lands and a couple of barns. Something about Shakspere quibbling over the inclusion of a barn with the land would be in character, he thought, and set about inventing the text.

After another hour of practice, he was content with the way his handwriting looked, and straight away turned his attention to the sheet from Venice. In a couple of minutes he was finished. He now removed the book section from the press and extracted the folded piece of acetate, and after folding the doctored page identically to the acetate, placed it in the faint depression checking it matched perfectly. Again he atomised it gently so that the ink would leave the faintest of traces on both pages, plus some discolouration caused by more than a century of contact with Dugdale's book, so much of its life spent in poor and damp conditions.

He stood up, closed the book, and removed his surgeon's gloves. The scene was now set for a member of the visiting Italian TV crew, with Katie's unwitting help, to make the discovery of his or her lifetime.

23

Things had gone worryingly quiet for Tony and Jessica in the fortnight since they had enlisted Steve Watson's help. He had asked them to be patient - 'as these things can't be hurried', as he had put it, giving them their one and only update a couple of days later - but complete silence for two weeks was surely a test for anyone's patience. They had been reluctant to contact Randy or Helena as they must still be grieving, though, at the same time, they worried, that their lack of contact might look as if they didn't care particularly deeply, and had just got on with their lives. This restless ambivalence ended with a pleasant surprise - an e-mail from Helena inviting them over for lunch.

'Randy is having a business meeting the weekend after next, and I'd love you both to come over and cheer me up. I'm doing pretty well, under the circumstances, but if neither of you have got anything arranged for Saturday week, drop me a line and we can all meet for a chat before I go back to Florence,
Love H.'

'I do hope she isn't going into denial and burying her grief in her work,' said Jessica.

'Let's find out next Saturday - we're not doing anything special, are we?'

'Not that I can think of,' she replied, and immediately typed their acceptance. 'Don't you think we should take the initiative with Steve Watson as well? Surely he's been able to find out something for us to go on? It would also mean we would have more information for Randy and Helena.'

'He wasn't particularly forthcoming the only time he rang, was he? Maybe I'll get back to old 'BJ' and see if he can come up with someone else who can to devote a bit more time and effort to us. Even if it still means no breakthroughs, at least we might get more regular updates on both investigations - hopefully.'

'By the way,' said Jessica, 'as you two wrote so many fancy letters to each other, what happened to all the ones Alex sent to you?'

'I don't know what I'd do without you sometimes!' He exclaimed. 'Why the hell didn't I think of them before.' Straightaway, he was down on his hands and knees ferreting about under tables and desks, pulling out files, cardboard boxes and all manner of storage containers. 'It's all here, somewhere, you know me, I never throw anything away - just in case.' The study floor rapidly disappeared beneath the flotsam and jetsam of his years of hoarding. 'You never know when you might need something,' he said. This was one of those rare instances when he was going be proved right.

'Here they are,' he said triumphantly, holding aloft a battered Tyrwhitts shirt box. Opening it, he secretly prayed that his chaotic filing system wouldn't let them down.

Tony and Alex had corresponded every four to six weeks, on average, over a period of around four years, so although there were about forty letters, it was only the last few they were particularly interested in.

'Thank God, they all seem to be here. His final letters should be these on top,' he said. 'Can you check the dates as I give them to you, and then put them in chronological order?'

'Did he send you any of your dreaded e-mails?'

'I think he did, yes, but, after all this time I don't think they can possibly still be there. I tidy my unwanted files and e-mails so regularly, there's no chance.'

'And do you think Alex would have done the same as you and kept everything you wrote?'

'He might have done. There's a remote chance that the Paris's haven't thrown his personal stuff away, I suppose.'

'The who?'

'The Paris's - his parents, up in Birmingham. I haven't seen them for years, myself - ever since, before you know what.'

'If you mean before your divorce, why don't you just say so? Is *she* still on the scene up there?'

'Couldn't tell you. I used to send her Christmas cards, but she never reciprocated, so, last year, I didn't bother. She never entered my mind till you mentioned her.'

'It was *you* who said "you know what" - meaning - you know who.'

'Jess - she's history. She might be up there, if we go, or she might be happily married and living in Australia, for all I know.'

'What do you mean - "if *we* go up?" Don't you think this is something you should sort out for yourself?'

'Hold it there, Jess, please. There's nothing there for me any more, and I think you know it. My marriage to Immy is all over and done with, so let's not confuse things by dragging out a load of old memories - deal?'

'Deal,' she conceded, suspecting that this was the beginning of something rather than an end. Her 'deal' was a quick-fix peacekeeping response, and she sensed he knew it too. 'I'll come with you if you really want me to, especially if we get nowhere with all these,' she said, gesturing dramatically at Alex's letters, 'but don't expect me to be 'Miss Nice'.'

'Deal,' he said, wondering if she was right, and it really was something he should do himself.

'You're going to have to be 'Mr. Tactful' too, aren't you, asking them for help after all this time?'

'Now, just leave it out, Jess. All right. I'm not sure what you're idea is, but, if it's to get a reaction out of me, you're going the right way about it.'

'Sorry. Sorry. I didn't mean anything by it. I know Alex meant a lot to you, and I don't want to cause any upset. Peace?'

'Sure. Let's just get on with sorting these - huh?' He cast a long look over the letters. 'If we're going to get to the bottom of this whole business, every avenue has got to be explored. I've got to ask the Paris's because I'm pretty sure there's nothing amongst these - I've read and reread them so many times.' He looked up at her. 'Now, are you with me or not, Jess?'

'Yes. I'm with you,' she replied.

They continued their study of the exquisitely written letters, concentrating on those dated at the end of August and the beginning of September, 2010.

'This last one refers to another letter which he never sent - or possibly never even wrote,' said Jessica.

'I certainly didn't receive any more than these. I remember that one well. He mentions the amazing find he's so sure he's about to make, and mentions the next letter. As you can see, I never received it.'

After a few moments deep in thought, Jessica asked, 'Tony, why are some of the characters bolder than others?'

'It's when he reinks the nib. When you're writing with a calligraphy pen the nib only holds enough ink for so many words. Periodically, you get darker, freshly inked characters, usually at the start of a word. Sometimes you can see the ink gradually running out just before he re-inks again.'

'You mean to tell me he went to all the trouble of carting around pens, nibs and bottles of ink, just on the off chance that he might write you a letter?' She gave him a quizzical look. 'I don't think so. Anyway, the bolder characters appear at all manner of spacings; sometimes they're right next to each other - there's no regularity to them at all - and how can you be sure that these letters weren't written with one of those calligraphy fountain pens, or even a felt pen?'

Tony took a much closer look and had to admit that she was right, as there were none of the tell-tale marks of a dipping pen anywhere. On each of his last three letters, Alex had gone over some of the characters to make them bolder. It was unmistakable. Once he was aware of the subtle changes he couldn't miss them. Alex had encoded information - but what on earth for?

'What a bloody fool! - How did I miss seeing what is now

so obvious? Christ almighty, Alex - what a time to start playing games!'

'Are you sure it's a code?'

'Do two and two make four?'

'How do you decode it?'

'Oh that's simple enough. The codeword will be encrypted near the beginning of the first letter.'

'Darling, I know what you're suggesting, but I just can't see the point of what he's done. It's a letter that probably only *you* are ever going to read. By the sound of it, he's getting stressed-out because he thinks he's being followed - but he can't be sure. He is about to make his 'great discovery,' and he takes time off to encode a 'secret' message... Why? I mean, call the police if you're being stalked. Ring your parents - or your sister, but, come on, isn't this all just too 'Boys Own'?'

'All I can think of is that he only wanted me to know for the time being - you know, so that he wouldn't look a fool if it was all for nothing. He wasn't stupid, Jess. He was damned bright and very much on the ball. What I'm saying is that, although this looks like a game, he would have been deadly serious. He knew that what he was saying would have alerted me, and he never cried wolf, never. I can't believe I never saw the clues. Anyway, he had no idea he was going to die did he?'

'Well if it really is what you say it is, did you two always use the same code?'

'The method was more or less the same - finding the codeword sometimes took a while.' Jessica was getting confrontational in a way he hadn't experienced before, and he needed a way to relax the situation. He decided to use her competitive spirit, and got her to do the decoding. He picked up the earliest of the three last letters. It was the first one to show the irregular use of bold characters. 'Be a love and get some paper out of the printer.... thanks. Now, let's write down all the bold characters.'

They printed the letters in order, but they didn't spell a word. Reversed they spelt nothing, nor did they yield up an anagram. They even tried foreign languages, but still nothing was forthcoming.

Tony went back to the letter for a closer inspection.

'Now why on earth did he write that?'

'Write what?'

He pointed to the phrase following - "I am now in execution of a …bold (and) noble enterprise" - it read - "if you follow me".

'The first bit is a quote from '*Julius Caesar*', so he's telling me he is using a Caesar code, but what do you think he means by - 'if you follow me'?'

'It's certainly ambiguous,' she answered. 'It could mean - if you get my drift, or - if you follow in my footsteps, as in continue his research. It could mean to literally go exactly where he went - if we knew where that was.'

Suddenly, Tony thumped the table in delight, and sat up. 'You cunning bastard, Alex! You've been telling us exactly where to look all along - we're supposed to be using the characters that follow his bold ones - here, you do it Jess.'

She went straight to the second paragraph. She underscored all the characters following the bold ones to make them more instantly identifiable. - 'My searching has come along famously since my trip to Worcester. I found a document which had … etc., etc..' She beamed all over her face as the codeword appeared.

'MONUMENT. I don't believe it!'

'Scary isn't it?' He said, 'finding the key to someone's private world. Decoding the final two letters will be a boring slog, enlightening, but boring.'

'Let me be the best judge of that if you don't mind - Mr. Control Freak. Come on then, show me how it's done.'

'OK, first print out 'monument' with no duplicate characters.'

Jessica printed MONUET at the top of the sheet

'Now print the rest of the alphabet - in order - following those six, so that's VWXYZAB and so on, and finally print the whole alphabet carefully above the cipher alphabet……..good, now we can begin the serious business of discovering what was bugging him.'

'I hope we're right - this is a hell of a lot of trouble to go to.'

'We are, make no mistake. Now that I'm looking at them in

a fresh light, Jess, I can see how stressed-out he must have been in those last few days. He's encoded something all right. Now, where were we? - Let's have a look at the rest of the letter.'

Jessica printed out the characters methodically, just as she had earlier - the salient section read - 'I went straight back to check up on the titles at Waterstones ....'

'That gives us TGKCUI which spells - F...O...U...N... D...S...my God - that's amazing!' she said excitedly, 'let me do some more - 'before some dizzy anorak snaps them up. You know how anxious I can get...' they give us - M...O...K...I...N...- what on earth is a MOKIN?'

'It means he believes he's found the 'smoking gun' - what do you want to bet the next two characters are Gs?'

'Well I'm damned! So they are, but - smoking gun? Help, Jessica, please.'

'It seems he believed he had discovered irrefutable proof that Shakespeare wasn't the author after all. Dangerous knowledge to have in your possession, alone in Stratford, at night, especially when it appears someone else has a vested interest in the knowledge staying a secret. Alex opened a Pandora's Box, Jess, and somebody slammed it shut just after he had a look inside.'

* * * * *

ALEX'S CODED LETTERS:
Letter 1 :

Dear Tony,
*I've tried phoning you but without much luck, and I'm keen to update you on my progress researching Mr. Bard and Mr. Oxford. 'I am now in execution of a ...**bold** (and) noble enterprise' - If you follow me.*
My searching has come along famously since my trip to Worcester. I found a document which had been quite overlooked.

I'm not exactly Mr. Popular with the SBT at the moment – the Italian looking guy is starting to take things personally.

Give me a call to say you received this

I'll write again soon explaining more.

Yours,

Alex

Letter : 2

Dear Tony ,

I've left you messages but you seem to be off the radar. Please contact me either here in Stratford, or at home in Bournville – If you follow me. I went straight back to check up on the titles at Waterstones before some dizzy anorak snapped them up. You know how anxious I can get. I've saved all kinds of useful info in a file called jumble box – all authorship stuff in one place, very joined up as you might have said. As you're well aware I can't develop a confident strategy unless I'm well organised.

Get back to me Tony, I think I need your help.

Yours,

Alex.

PS   Have you ever come across any references to a group calling themselves FCV? If you have then let me know.

Letter :3

Tony,

I don't want to sound too anxious but – where are you when I need you? Ring or write – you're the only person I can confide in. In my next letter or e-mail you'll find plenty of things to keep your fellow pro-Oxfordians ecstatic. If you could just find time to make a journey up here however brief you'd really find it worth every minute.

Just when I thought there were no more lines of enquiry left,

I realised that the solution had been drawing me to it for weeks. It's so easy to get excited and over-eager. Once I had my leap of the imagination, I kept myself to myself and did nothing, wondering if I could really and honestly be the person to stumble on the answer that obsessive searchers had missed for two hundred years.

I'll know for certain tomorrow morning – It should make everyone sit up!

Ring me Tony, ring me for God's sake – where are you when I really need you?

Alex.

PS   Have you ever come across any references to a group calling themselves FCV? If you have then let me know.

* * * * *

It took no time at all to complete the decoding – 'Found smoking gun details to follow', and they went quickly to the third letter and its more sinister tone. It revealed an ominous message – 'Official cover up . will not author . they have proof . being followed.'

'He sounds really frightened to me,' said Jessica. 'And what's this 'FCV' all about? And who are 'they'?'

'No idea. It was something he must have stumbled across in his research. I've had a look through all my stuff, but never found any reference to it. Perhaps the 'FCV' are 'they'.'

'How does the writing of the letters fit in with the time of his death?'

'The pathologist put his death at some time on the Wednesday morning. These are dated Monday the seventh and Tuesday the eighth. That means he must have written the lost letter on the Tuesday night or before breakfast on the morning he died.'

'Surely any normal person would have just rung you – where was your mobile?'

'Switched off.'

'For three or four days! Tony! – Twenty-first century! – No-one has their mobile switched off for *one* day, let alone *four!*

'Well mine was. OK?'

'Why?'

'That's my business.'

'You've made it mine now - so come on, Tony, you owe me.'

Tony went quiet, finished his now cold, hot-chocolate, and fell back into the settee. He looked up at her, sitting erect on the front edge, less than an arm's length away, her head turned towards him.

'Well?' she added.

'I went for a long weekend's walking holiday in the Lake District with girlfriend of the day, and she insisted on 'back to nature', and 'no phones'.'

'For a long weekend!' she squeaked in sheer disbelief, 'Four days! You're kidding me! - Even when they're on holiday, no-one in their right mind has their mobile turned off - but for four days!'

'Well we did. Now don't make things worse than they already are by rubbing it in. How do you think I've felt for the past six years wondering if my best friend died because of me. If only this, if only that. Alex was a loner essentially, and I was probably his main communications link to the outside world. He could handle himself pretty well you know, but girlfriend pressure can be a tough one to call.' The moment he'd opened his mouth, he knew he'd invited trouble. She widened her eyes and looked straight at him, - 'Oh-oh,' he thought, 'here it comes!' .

'Oh, yeah! - You switchee off phone - me switchee on sex!'

'I know how it must appear, but it wasn't only that. I mean, come on, Jess -we were young and free and twenty-one.'

'And now you're a Chelsea Pensioner, and all covered in dust!'

'Well thanks for that,' he snapped back. 'I've had my share of nightmares thinking about that day, you know - Alex fighting for his life while I'm humping my way up Langdale Pikes!' Tony stopped and sighed. 'I feel guilty and yet not guilty, but, at the end of the day, whether I'll be judged right or wrong, I still owe it to his family to try and sort it all out. Someone's hands are still dirty in this business, and I don't believe they're an itinerant farm worker's.'

The tragic irony of Tony's situation almost made her smile, and but for the tragedy of Bianca's recent death, she might have. 'Have you ever spoken about this to anyone else, I mean, was it the reason your marriage finished?'

'Imogen was devoted to him and couldn't forgive me when it all came to a head. She was right, too. I know I've got a selfish streak, and I was arrogant in a way I didn't recognise then, like shutting away important things with the trivia, expecting them to stay hidden for ever - but life's not quite like that, is it?'

'No, it isn't. 'Perspective's got a life and energy all its own,' as our Art teacher used to say - and he wasn't just talking pictures either.'

'The police have got to see all this, Jess,' he said, waving a hand across the paper-strewn coffee table. 'With or without Steve Watson's help, we've got to build a case so strong they can't shut their eyes to it.'

24

'Hi, guys, so pleased you could make it.'

'Always look forward to one of your lunches, Helena.'

It was now six weeks since the tragedy in Venice, and Tony and Jessica were unsure what to expect. For such an ambitious couple, Randy and Helena had been truly successful at staying together as a family. They had worshipped Bianca, but now that she was gone, both Tony and Jessica wondered how long it might be before the energy of their independent lives pulled them in different directions. First impressions were that all seemed fine as they cautiously restarted their social life.

'Come and meet Eddie,' she said, 'he's been faffing about for years, saying he's going to get his 'Big One' off the ground and into the can, and he's here to convince us that, this time, he means it.'

Tony and Jessica both recognised a tension and self-consciousness in Helena's step. It was so unlike the woman they thought they knew, and they sensed it sprang from sleepless nights of loss. She took them through the spacious modernist, almost art deco, interior to arrive at the terrace where Randy was deep in conversation with Eddie Gascoigne and Jimmy Tyrrel. Their wives, Rosaline and Alice, made up the party. Once all the introductions were out of the way, business was put to one side and gave way to a more relaxed and social who's-whoing.

'I saw some of your work for the Olympics, Eddie, and, I must say, I was impressed,' said Tony.

'That's very kind of you. 2012 wasn't quite the disaster we all thought it was going to be, and we did quite well out of it, considering. But, as for poor old London, God knows when they will have paid for it all. And I hear that you have an interest in the Tudor scene and all matters Shakespearean. We were just discussing Venice as you arrived, weren't we, Randy?'

'I think I told you, didn't I, Tony, Eddie came with me to the 'Magretti' on the day of the mini-tempest?'

'Yes, you did. So that makes you one of the only people to see the Earl of Oxford's bits and bobs, Eddie. What did you make it all - especially his writing box?'

'Bit of a stormer. It's with the conservators isn't it, Randy?'

'Yes, the British Museum are giving it a health check. The pages are safe?' He asked, turning back to Tony.

'Locked away, safe and sound.'

'What pages are those, if you don't mind my being nosey?' asked Jimmy.

'You can tell him Tony. We're all friends here,' said Randy.

'There are certain things the press don't know concerning the robbery, Jimmy. A few days before it, Randy and Eddie found some artefacts, including quite a few sheets of writing. They had belonged to an English aristocrat called Edward de Vere, the Seventeenth Earl of Oxford. 'B' had taken three of those pages for closer study when she had a few minutes, so the burglar missed them. Now, I've got them. In the circumstances, Randy played down any potential importance of the find as he didn't want gangs of ego-seeking experts banging on his door and ringing at all hours.'

'You're sure all that writing was Oxford's, aren't you?' asked Eddie, who was well acquainted with the authorship debate.

'Not a shadow of doubt.'

'Going to give the anti-Stratfordians a pretty strong argument when it all comes out isn't it?'

'Like carbon fibre.'

'Don't tell me you've got proof that Shakespeare wasn't 'Shakespeare',' said Jimmy, with a look of astonishment.

At that moment Helena and Jessica came out with some plates of antipasti and a couple of chilled bottles of Prosecco.

'It's looking that way,' added Jessica.

'What about the Italian Police. Don't they have any say in the matter?' asked Jimmy.

'Montano, he's the Commissario in charge,' said Tony, 'doesn't see a Shakespeare motive behind the crime, or believe the theft was to order, but I think differently. It remains to be seen who's right. We've got a private detective looking into another crime which may be related - but that's another story.'

Without saying a word, Helena got up and left the table.

'Too soon, Tony, too soon,' said Randy. He excused himself and followed her into the house. An unfriendly and isolating silence descended on the company.

Alice Tyrrel, who was a close friend and business partner of Helena's, and had been running their retail business ever since the tragedy, was the first to speak out.

'I'm trying to feed her back in gently. Getting her to Italy for the first time since you-know-what isn't going to be easy, gentlemen,' she said. 'Randy is going on 'Peter and Katie's' daytime TV show on Thursday, and she's worried about what might come from that as well. Normality is kicking in hard and fast, and she just isn't ready for it.'

It was Tony who, after an uncomfortable pause in the proceedings, took the initiative. 'Tell me, Eddie, what's your big story, or is that a trade secret?'

'By the time we've finished, Tony, the whole world will be familiar with the Battle of Lepanto,' he began. 'We're doing a kind of 'East-Meets-West-Side-Story', but without the Bernstein - you know, an R&J style love story using some of the most exotic locations in Italy and the Middle East. For Montagues and Capulets, read Muslims and Christians.'

'The radicals are going to love you to bits!'

'Chance you've got to take, old boy - nothing ventured and all that.'

'The Magretti-Bellini?' asked Tony.

Eddie glanced to where Randy had been sitting. 'Bit early to say. Not banking on it - if you get my drift. The topical angle is the

Islamic threat to Venice - microcosm - macrocosm. Interesting coincidence four hundred-odd years on, wouldn't you say?'

With their hosts absent, the six chatted idly about everything but the tragedy that had befallen the Middletons. Eddie recounted the tale of the fresco, and the discovery of the Earl of Oxford's artefacts. This led to discussing Stratford, and the surprise that Eddie was working there at the moment.

'We were there, what, three weeks ago wasn't it Tony?' put in Jessica.

'Well I'm going to be there, on and off, right up to the four-hundredth 'big do' with 'E2' et al, and probably a few days beyond. Channel Seven have given me a free hand to do a 'Stratford Undressed' version of the whole unseemly show.'

'You don't sound like a particularly big fan of England's 'Man of the Millennium' Eddie?' said Tony.

'Got no time for all that Bardology. My pals at Channel Seven know my views. They knew where to come for something cynical and spicy.'

'We might see you up there, Eddie,' said Jessica.

'I'll buy the first round,' he replied.

25

Holly Grove came as quite a surprise for Jessica. It nestled in a small housing estate squeezed between one of Birmingham's largest hospitals and an even larger chocolate factory. They parked in the adjoining Laburnum Road, and, on getting out, she was quick to notice the distinctive Arts and Crafts style of the houses. Their steeply pitched, lichen-speckled roofs crowning a wealth of early twentieth century architectural detail. To the nearby sound of passing trains and factory generators, they walked the few yards past carefully manicured gardens to the Paris's home at the end of the cul-de-sac.

Tony's call the previous day had been warmly received, and, yes, most of Alex's belongings were still in his old room. Christopher and Elizabeth, his parents, didn't want his room to become a shrine to their only son, but their initial reluctance to throw any of his things away had inevitably turned into a problem they daren't face.

'Hello, Tony dear, it's so nice to see you after all this time. You don't look a day older.'

He kissed her on both cheeks. 'You're looking wonderful Elizabeth, how do you do it?'

'Flattery always got you everywhere - and who's this?'

'Jessica, my girlfriend - Jess, Elizabeth.'

'Hello, Mrs Paris,' she said, rather guardedly. 'It's nice to meet you, and thank you for giving up your time to see us.'

'Oh, it's no trouble, dear, any little thing to help...Chris is down the garden, Tony.'

He knew exactly why Chris was keeping out of the way.

Losing Alex had virtually destroyed him, and even a daughter like Imogen couldn't compensate for his loss; but Tony appearing almost without warning was bound to reopen old wounds - his greenhouse provided him with emotional insulation. He had hardly spoken to Tony since Alex's indecently hurried inquest, blaming him for getting his son such a bad name in the press.

'You must have some tea - have you driven all the way from Sussex?'

'We'd love some, Elizabeth, and it's Essex, remember?'

'Essex, yes, of course,' she replied, and went into the kitchen to add a pot of tea to the already prepared tray. 'You remember his room, don't you? I've put all his writings and research on his bed. He never threw anything away, you know; he kept all your 'copperplate' letters. We haven't looked through his stuff, of course, not for ages - just help yourself, Tony - I'll put away what you don't want.' She opened a small china tea caddy, and removed a couple of tea bags. 'I suppose I really ought to do something about it all.'

'I'll take a look now, shall I, while you're making the tea?'

He disappeared upstairs with Jessica, and they went into the front bedroom. Six colourful storage boxes were lined up in two neat rows, each one carefully labelled - School - University studies - Shakespeare - Books, and so on. Two boxes in particular took their eye - Shakespeare and Books, for on top of the latter was a box containing his calligraphy equipment and some manila folders. They went through the folders one by one, including the one that contained all Tony's letters, but nowhere was the 'last' letter to be found. A thorough search of the other boxes also yielded nothing. As time was getting short, they quickly looked around for any other evidence of his personal belongings. Tony opened the wardrobe. Inside, it looked like a collection for a white elephant stall. Neatly piled up was all his sports stuff, computer, toys, CDs, more books and magazines, his clothes and various bags.

'His bag,' said Tony, pointing at a medium-sized backpack, peeking out from between some tennis rackets and a skateboard.

'That's the bag he had with him in Stratford. If my memory serves me correctly, a member of the public handed it in to some lost property place or other - before his body was even found. Let's see if there's anything still in it.' He slipped the dusty, dark blue canvas bag out from its forgotten resting place and opened it. Protruding from the worn lining was a triangle of white paper. He took it out. 'Well, well, well - what have we here?' he said, holding up an envelope which had his own name and address on it.

'Surely the police must have had a look at what was in his bag?'

'They did, because they had Chris and Elizabeth in to identify his clothes and other personal things. And they never spotted this either, did they?' Tony felt through the lining to see if anything else had been overlooked, but his search yielded nothing. 'It was a week or ten days before this bag came to light. Why the police never took its existence more seriously I couldn't tell you.'

They sat on the bed and, just as he turned the letter over to open it, Elizabeth called up from the bottom of the stairs.

'Tea!'

'Coming,' they answered in unison. He put the letter on top of the 'Books' box with the folders, and took it, together with the 'Shakespeare' box, down to the foot of the stairs. Tony felt that the Paris's only needed to know that he was interested in Alex's authorship research material. As the police hadn't taken on board the importance of Alex's work, he would tell them, perhaps something in the boxes or folders might persuade them to take another look at the case. It was a long shot but worth a try. As they sat down to tea, and a slice of Madeira cake, the subject never arose.

'Would you like me to take it all away?' Tony asked.

'Oh no, dear, that's very kind, but, now it's out, Chris and I'll do it.'

'Elizabeth, you would have done it by now if you could face it, wouldn't you? Am I right or am I right?' Her eyes were edged with pink. 'Even if I only take the boxes, how about that?'

'You were always very kind, Tony.'

She sat staring vacantly at the tea tray, its embroidered cloth and the partly eaten Madeira cake. Within a few minutes, the remaining boxes were downstairs, and after a couple of trips, all were in the boot of Tony's car.

After saying their farewells, they were soon threading their way through Kings Norton and the sprawling outskirts of the city, and making their way to the M42. Jessica had the foresight to keep the all-important letter with her. She opened it and read the contents aloud.

Tony - forget codes, if you haven't received any of my messages or e-mails, then I hope to God you get this one. Keep it safe - and here's why.

The night before last I found the original inscription stone from under the Shakespeare Monument. On it is clear proof that Oxford was the author. I'm sure it was Mary Sidney, her two boys, Will and Phil, and Susan Vere who put it all together. It's signed FCV- what do you make of that?. I've photographed it - camera and phone, copied it out, and even done a rubbing in my notebook - covering all the bases, eh?

I'm certain someone in the Shakespeare Centre knows all this - except for the location of the 'slabbe'. I'm also positive that someone really is following me.

I'm going back home tomorrow, and I'll be in touch again soon. I'll tell you something, I could do with that Uncle BJ of yours to help make complete sense of all this.

Don't forget - keep this letter safe. Fantastic isn't it?

Yours,

Alex.

'And I thought he'd found a long-lost manuscript. But the original inscription stone - bloody hell! He doesn't say where he found it does he?'

'Not a clue I'm afraid. That's all there is,' said Jessica. 'You can tell he was tense, but not scared for his life or anything.

This isn't in his perfect calligraphy either,' she added. 'Would the police investigation have followed a different course with this do you think?'

'Thanks Jess, I could do without the reminder,' he said. 'He's still going on about the 'FCV' as well, isn't he? If he's right, and they are some kind of secret brotherhood, then just who the hell are they? Anyway, let's wait till we get back home, and see what things look like when we put it with all our other evidence.'

MALDON: 7.30 pm.

They spread every relevant document across Tony's dining room table. The notebook containing the rubbings Alex had mentioned was missing, and, without his camera or mobile they had no images. Looked at in the cool light of day, it didn't look much at all. Even when they added their experiences in Venice and the awful events around Bianca's death, it still didn't seem to be enough to put before the CID. The question now was had they missed anything, some small detail, perhaps, that might convince the police they should look at the case again?

'If that inscription stone - the 'slabbe' - as he called it, was to be found, I bet that'd convince them to take another look,' said Jessica.

Tony cast his mind back to Stratford and the last days, indeed the last hours, of his friend's life. It occurred to him, in the light of what he now knew, that the inscription stone must have been quite close to his B & B. The time frame meant that, at walking pace, it could only be five or ten minutes from 'The Ophelia Guest House'.

'Am I thick or am I thick!' He said, turning to her. 'The bare patch of soil in the churchyard that was mentioned in the papers. It must have been the inscription stone. It explains everything, don't you see? Why else would the police have wanted to keep the investigation out of Stratford? The killer obviously removed it. I reckon the police bloody-well knew all along, and they were in on a cover up because they knew who the killer was. Either that or someone in high places got them to do it because *they* knew who did it.'

'Why hasn't Steve Watson come up with any of this?' She asked. 'He's supposed to be the detective not us!'

'I'm going to give him a ring and see if he's found anything new.' It was well into the evening, but not too late to give their 'Private Eye' a call.

'The only new stuff I've got is that Mr. Montano and his Carabiniwhatsits in Venice are interested in one of our chaps at the Consulate,' chirped Steve.

'I didn't say anything about whose death it was in Venice, Steve - so where's all this come from?'

'Come on, Tony. Your friend's friend dies abroad - dies by drowning after 'falling' against stone - famous father wants his name kept out of things - I mean, er, does the Pope shit in the woods?'

'OK, fair cop - no pun intended - but as you've sussed which case it is, is there anything else we should know?'

'Only that that Angelo fella isn't completely out of the frame yet. It seems he had some form over here, and his family got up to a few tricks over there as well.'

'Oh, yes.'

'Only small beer, no violence or 'owt. I wouldn't waste any sleep on his account, though, because I don't rate him - but, then again, temptation's a funny thing, my son, and the most unlikely people can be tempted.'

'Nothing on the Stratford case?'

'Pretty cut 'n' dried, if you ask me.'

'What about the stolen gravestone, there was never a satisfactory explanation for its removal was there?'

'God, I'd forgotten all about that. What do you want to drag that up for? Your mate wasn't into stolen flagstones was he - part of a gang of international floor thieves?'

'Just thought I'd ask, Steve. It was one of the few unanswered questions in the case, that's all.'

'You'll only find yourself going up a dead end, Tony, my son. Well, I think that's about it for now - soon as I've got something concrete, I'll get back to you, OK? Tarrah.' And with that he hung up.

'Well, what did he have to say?' Jessica asked.

'Not a lot. He must have twigged I was talking about Bianca before we left the pub that night. The only news of sorts was that Montano is quizzing someone at the Consulate, and that Angelo was no angel!'

'Why's that? I thought he was rather nice.'

'It doesn't matter how nice he was; apparently, he's got some form.'

'That makes him even more interesting.'

'Does it? That was quick, you only knew him for a few hours!'

'He looked after us. He was quite caring - in an Italian sort of way!'

'Oh! And exactly how do Italian men 'care' for young English women?'

'You're jealous, Tony - fuck me, you're actually jealous!'

'Jess,' he said, turning to her, 'I've got more important things to worry about. This isn't a game.'

He scanned the table again for promising leads. 'I can't get used to 'Dubya's brusque manner either. I think it's going to be up to us, you know.'

'Maybe he's up to his eyes and ears with paying clients.'

'Maybe. Anyway I'm not going to trouble 'BJ' with finding us an alternative. We'll make do with Steve, for all his sins. You know, if the 'slabbe' had ever come to light, I'd have heard about it. Either the killer took it with him, or, amazingly, it might still be out there, waiting to be found.'

'Small enough to be carried away do you think?'

'Yes, but how would you explain carrying a slab of marble through the churchyard first thing in the morning? I want to go back and take a long hard look at that burial ground - who knows what a thorough search might turn up?'

'He was robbed of everything valuable wasn't he - money,

camera phone?'

'His phone. His phone Jess - what if he…..'

'…..Sent a photo to his own computer?'

'It was in his wardrobe, for God's sake, and we were just looking at it!' He wagged his head in disbelief. 'If I'd offered to clear out all his stuff.'

'As you damned well should have, Tony. That wasn't one of your best moments.'

He sighed. There was a pause, and then he continued. 'I've got to ring them, Jess - Not tonight, tomorrow. I'll never rest until I know whether he left a picture or message for himself.'

APR. 11th MON: 10.00 am

It was just after ten when the phone rang.

'Hello,' said a curt female voice.

'Immy - is that you?' asked Tony in complete surprise, as he certainly never expected to hear his ex-wife's voice.

'It's Imogen, Tony. What the hell do you think you're doing phoning - wasn't yesterday enough for you?'

'I had no idea you were there, Immy, sorry - Imogen. I was expecting to speak to Elizabeth.'

'Well it's me, and she's far too upset to talk to you. You're a fine one, turning up with virtually no warning. That was so typically bloody thoughtless. Now, what's your game, Tony?'

He refused to rise to the bait, kept calm, and came straight to the point. 'I've found new information that might shed light on what befell Alex. I thought that with all his paperwork I'd have enough to go to the police - you know, reopen the enquiry, but, when I got back I remembered his computer and….'

'Ah, now we come to it. You're not here to apologise or anything. You want me to leave Mum and Dad, who need my support to get them through what you've so rudely started, and give up the rest of my day to sit in front of some damned computer so that you can unload your latest guilt trip.'

'Now that's below the belt.'

'Is it, Tony, is it? You're the one who screwed up the original enquiry with your country hike with miss control freak and her phonophobia. Then you come waltzing back into our lives with your teenage sex-toy, all sweetness and light and your - 'don't worry, Elizabeth, I'll get rid of his things for you' - you hypocritical bastard. More like - 'I'll just get rid of history and guilt by clicking on delete, and, ooh, look, all the bad memories have gone, I do feel better.' Dad was right about you all along.'

The line went quiet. He could hear Elizabeth and Chris arguing in the background - what had he started? There was a lot of truth in what she said, of course; it was just that he didn't want to hear it. She was referring to the fact that, when he came back from his 'phone-free' Lake District holiday, in a hasty moment, he had deleted all three of Alex's messages from his mobile phone mail box. They had referred to the contents of the three coded letters which he and Jessica had just decoded, as well as the missing 'last' letter they had just unearthed. Alex hadn't been specific about what his discovery was, only that it was irrefutable proof that the Earl of Oxford was, and William Shakspere of Stratford wasn't, the author of the works of Shakespeare. The police might have acted very differently in the light of them.

'I'm only asking for a little help and understanding, Imogen, that's all. I didn't want another row.'

'Another row is it? How you have this convenient way of turning things round to make everything *my* fault - Mum was dead right as well, Tony - you haven't changed a bit.'

'For God's sake, Imogen, climb down for two seconds, will you - help me out, just this once, and maybe we can all get closure, OK? I promise never to trouble you again.'

'Go on.'

'It shouldn't take more than a couple of minutes - are you happy with computers?'

'Get on with it, Tony, or I'll hang up.'

'OK, now, all I would like you to do is to plug in his computer and monitor. Then, check his last e-mails. What I'm hoping is that he sent some pictures from his mobile. If they're there, Imogen, would you please e-mail them to me? You have no idea how important they may be.'

'Just don't hold your breath,' she snapped, and hung up.

26

'Was she on fire, or was she on fire?'

'Aren't you glad you didn't meet her?'

'Why? From where I was sitting, you couldn't build a firewall fast enough, Tony. If she can still get smoke and flames out of your phone after more than two years, then you are by no means, Mr. Squeaky. I think she's still got something to say, and it could be interesting.'

'I freely admit that, when we were married, I wasn't at my best. But you don't want to hear all this.'

'Don't tell me what I do, or do not, want to hear. You can be so damned self-righteous at times. From what I can make out, keeping things from 'Immy-ex' was the main reason why you two split up - you have so not learned anything, Tony, if you can't hear that huge and roaring silence.' She stood up, and went into the kitchen to make a pot of coffee. Without turning round, she added. 'You need to go into advanced search, and see what humility and redemption throw up - if you've got the courage.'

He could do without the amateur psychoanalysis, but he forgave her as he sensed what she must have felt, having his ex-wife reappearing like that, with no warning. To some extent she was right, too; there was some unfinished business with Imogen.

Without moving a muscle, he watched her make the coffee. It was like seeing the ideal way in which a human being was supposed to perform the task. He felt no-one in this world could surpass her for the beauty and economy of her actions. The effortless ease with which she performed this most mundane of tasks had him transfixed. He had just had a reminder of the kind of emotional analysis he had had to endure during two years with Imogen, followed swiftly by a hint of this woman's potential. Comparison was inevitable, but Jessica had more breadth, more patience and more humour - and a figure to die for.

'God you're sexy when you're getting milk out of the fridge!' he said.

She depressed the filter, and, without the slightest sideways glance, said. 'And stop watching me. It makes me feel uncomfortable.'

'Liar.'

She looked across at him and gave him a broad smile, and then quite suddenly, disquietingly, looked grave. ''B' was lovely, Tony, wasn't she, I mean - really lovely?'

'Like a film star, Jess. Bright as a million stars.'

'We owe it to her, just as much as to your friend, Alex, to find out who could have done such a thing, don't we?'

She placed the drinks on the table, and plonked herself on a chair next to him. The room was getting a real mess, so they made a concerted effort to make sense and order out of it all. Tony tried to imagine himself as a stranger, coming across it for the first time.

'It's difficult to know whether it could convince anybody,' he said. 'Be a love and switch on my email, just in case Immy does send us anything.'

She strolled over to the study, went to the computer, and clicked on the icon. 'It's already here, Tony!' She immediately clicked on attachments, 'And there are pictures.'

'Bloody hell! How on earth did she manage that so fast? Is she in IT or something?' He rushed over to study the hazy images. 'They're not very clear are they? Of course, he didn't want to alert anyone by using the flash - Let me have a go at sharpening them up on Photoshop.'

The two photographs, taken from slightly differing angles, were indeed of the inscription stone Alex had written about in his last letter. The enhancement tools didn't make all the words legible, but enough to get the gist of the original epitaph. There was a short note accompanying them -

'If these are of any real value, I'm sure we'll read about it in the papers.

Don't bother to contact us again.'

'She didn't even put her name,' observed Jessica.

'She wanted me out of her hair as quick as she could - can't blame her I suppose. Let's print off a few copies of them, add them to the rest, and then see what it all looks like.'

With some accompanying explanatory notes Tony had written, what they now had in front of them started to look a lot more grown up. They made up four packages - one for Tony's solicitor, one for the Warwickshire Police, and two for themselves - one of which was locked away in Tony's safe. The next thing on their agenda was a trip to the Warwickshire Police Headquarters to see if the results of all their efforts would be taken seriously.

APR 16th SAT: 12.30 pm. WARWICK :

They parked in the confined visitor car park to the right of the typical 1960's municipal building and climbed the short flight of steps to the entrance. Their appointment was with D. I. Southwell. She was an attractive thirty-something, and you quickly got the sense that she was empowered by her looks and curves. She greeted them cordially and put them at their ease with her well practised interpersonal skills. With a sweep of her arm, she directed them to a door to their left. The business of the day was to be conducted in a small, sparsely furnished interview room.

'What's all this about new evidence you've found on one of our unsolved cases, Mr. Chapman?'

Tony knew it was best to keep the proceedings formal. He wanted a result, not a friendly chat. He placed the envelope containing all their 'new evidence' on the table between them.

Without offering it to her, or opening it, he related the story of Alex's death.

'I remember it very well, Mr. Chapman. We ended up chasing itinerant farm-workers right across the South Midlands and back - some to-do I can tell you, but, no convictions to show for all our efforts, I'm afraid.'

'I was surprised how abruptly the investigation concentrated so entirely on the itinerant workers. Any other leads were dropped completely. Why was that, Inspector?'

'I can't go into details of policy or procedure here you realise, Mr. Chapman, as authority for that sort of thing can only come from my superiors. I would be in a stronger position to answer your questions if you could give me an idea what you have uncovered that brings you a hundred and fifty miles. I see you haven't come empty handed.'

'Before I show you the contents of this envelope, Inspector Southwell, there are one or two things I need to know.'

'Go on,' she said, glancing from Tony to Jessica and back again. She found her open and engaging smile returned with serious expressions.

'Can I be certain of your confidence and complete trust, Inspector, because, without them, I can't proceed?'

D.I. Southwell was quite taken-aback by the unreserved directness of Tony's approach. She responded positively, mainly due to the manner in which the request was made. Put differently, it could have been taken as arrogant, even confrontational.

'That sounds like a loaded question. I think you owe me an explanation,' she replied.

'Very well. I have good reason to suspect that the death of my friend was deliberate, and in no way at all connected with the drugs scene, East European or otherwise. Furthermore I believe that the investigation was calculatedly mismanaged to deflect suspicion from whoever was really responsible for the crime.'

The Inspector sat up in her seat. 'That is a very serious allegation. I hope you can back it up.'

'Forgive my directness, Inspector, but, as this is such a serious matter, I thought it best to come straight to the point. Oh! There is one last thing - then I promise I'll be open and transparent with you.'

'You don't want much do you? What is it?'

'Do you know if any of the original investigation team are still working in the force either here or in Stratford? You see, after everything the two of us have been through, I should hate to think that, unbeknown to us, or you, for that matter, someone here might still be in a position to stop a fair reinvestigation.'

'There are very few murders in South Warwickshire - and most of those are East European families settling old scores. We take a lack of success very much to heart, Mr. Chapman. Failure sits uneasily with us. Nothing would give me greater pleasure than to get a result, and to close the Alexander Paris case. I was on the case in its early days as a D.S., as it happens. It was my first 'suspicious death', and one of my few unsolved cases. But I was taken off the case after three or four weeks - well, actually, I requested the move, as did two or three other officers. Slimming down an investigation is perfectly normal, even after only a couple of weeks.'

'Why did you request a transfer?' asked Jessica.

'I wasn't happy with the SIO..'

'That would have been Inspector Lodge wouldn't it - is he still here?'

'Oh, Tony Lodge. No, Tony retired a couple of years ago. He was great to work with. He was replaced as SIO, only a couple of weeks into the investigation, for no apparent reason, by a D.I. Watson from West Midlands Serious Crimes. He was promoted to the Met..'

'Who did you say?' asked Jessica.

'D.I. Steve Watson, madam - do you know him?'

'Oh, there's a D.C.I. Watson in Chelmsford,' cut in Tony. 'Or rather ex-D.C.I.. He works in the private sector now I think.'

'It certainly sounds like him,' said the Inspector.

'And you didn't get on?' added Jessica.

'Couldn't keep his hands to himself madam. None of us could

wait to see the back of him.'

'And did the investigation change direction when he came on the scene?' continued Tony.

'Again, I can't answer that, but, perhaps, this would be as good a time as any to have a look at the contents of that envelope and see if it sheds any new light on things. I'll get my sergeant. He's a Stratford man I'm sure he'll be interested'

Tony and Jessica spread the contents of the envelope across the table. At the same time, they related a concise version of the events in Venice, hoping it would add weight to their convictions of a Shakespeare/Stratford motive for both crimes. The officers were sceptical about the 'authorship' link in the motive argument, but the tone of Alex's letters came as something of a revelation. Having been on the case in its early days, the inspector expressed her dismay that a second line of enquiry was never kept open. Her reaction to this new information, however, gave Tony renewed hope that something might now be done.

'Can I keep these?' asked D.I. Southwell.

'Of course. I have a complete copy, as does my solicitor.

'A wise move, Mr. Chapman. Now, I'll put these in front of my 'Super' on Monday morning. I think he'll find them just as interesting as me. I can't make any promises, and in the end it's the Chief Constable who decides if a case is to be re-opened.'

They thanked the Inspector for giving up her time, and came away feeling quite optimistic. They had made their case, and they had made what they felt sure was a sound contact. But, as for the bombshell! As soon as they were in the car, Tony got out his phone.

'What the bloody hell does Watson think he playing at? Why didn't he tell us he was involved?' said Tony, his finger hovering over the connect button.

'Exactly. Why didn't he?' said Jessica. 'No wonder he didn't find anything in Stratford when we asked him. And what about your Uncle 'BJ'? He put us on to him in the first place - don't tell me he's mixed up in it too?'

'Don't be ridiculous Jess, he's my uncle.'

'Sorry, Tony, but you have to admit, it's one hell of a coincidence that the person he recommends to us, is in an ideal position to block our lines of enquiry.'

27

They zig-zagged their way past the Lord Leicester Hospital and West Gate on their way out of Warwick. It was uncommonly hot for so early in the year, but, like everyone else, they had had to come to terms with the effects of climate change, a subject that wasn't going to go away. But their minds were on neither the weather nor the flat and featureless urban mile of the Stratford Road.

'You didn't press her on the matter of whether there are still detectives here who were on Alex's case six years ago,' said Jessica.

'Slipped my mind in the end. I'm still trying to come to terms with what it all might mean. I'm glad I didn't ring Steve 'Dubya' - God knows what I might have said in the heat of the moment. Did you see her sergeant's face when he saw the photographs of the inscription stone? It was almost worth driving up here just for that!'

Tony negotiated the huge Longbridge Island over the M40, and they were soon in a stream of assorted traffic climbing the A46 on their way to the final destination of their weekend, and what they hoped was going to be one of the most unusual and exciting events of their lives.

'What are we getting mixed up in, Tony?… Don't you feel the least bit frightened?'

'No, sweetheart. A bit apprehensive perhaps, but not frightened.'

'How well do you know your Uncle 'BJ'?'

'Oh, so-so , you know - how well does anyone know a relation they haven't seen for years? I always looked on him more as a friend than an uncle. It was as though there wasn't any generation gap. It was 'BJ' who got me all excited about the authorship question in the first place. He's in the Lord Oxford Society and keeps pace with all the current research - or at least he used to. He's always been one of my favourite human beings. I think you'd like him.'

They rounded the one-way system at the entrance to the town and were amazed by the presence of hordes of pedestrians. Ahead of them, Bancroft Gardens had been transformed into a huge Shakespeare Exhibition and Theme Park.

The market town had been devoured.

They checked in at the Alveston Manor Hotel, and, up in their room, Tony wasted no time in getting out the two photographs of the 'slabbe'. He checked his watch to work out how much daylight was left. He knew the churchyard was a fair size, but he hoped the two of them could mount a pretty thorough search in a single afternoon. The corner of the tomb the 'slabbe' was resting against should be easy to recognise from one of the photographs. If the 'slabbe' was still in existence, he reckoned it might not be far from it.

They left the hotel, crossed the road, and, using the Shipston Tramway Bridge over the River Avon, entered Bancroft Gardens. Its beds were crudely daubed with 'cheerful' municipal planting, but, above ground, still garnished with the last of the abundant Spring blossom. A brief riverside walk, skirting the RST, brought them to the Parish Church.

There were many more tombs than they expected, and a lot more slabs. Gravestones were not only standing, and lying, in the carefully tended grass, but were also the main constituent of the many paths. They also edged a lot of the paths, supporting the raised lawns.

In the pretence of searching for long lost ancestors, Tony and Jessica spent over three hours in an almost fruitless quest. They found the tombstone in Alex's photograph, but the slabs nearby could be quickly discounted on account of their being too large or not made of marble. It seemed that their first theory, that the killer had removed it six years earlier, was right after all. They sat on the same bench where they had sat a few weeks earlier. The mound of grass cuttings, now piled a little higher, was still there, not ten metres away.

'Fact,' said Tony. 'Alex was right here. Fact - his killer was right here. Fact - the original inscription stone was right here. Now, imagine you've just killed someone and disposed of the body. The slab is at your feet. What do you do with it? You can't leave it here for some passing tourist to find.' He turned to Jessica. 'What would *you* do?'

'Chuck it in the river,' she said, 'As long as there's no-one around, of course. The only other thing you could do would be to take a chance and carry it through the churchyard to your car - a bit hard to explain if you're stopped by the vicar, though - 'Excuse me, sir, but isn't that one of ours?''

'Couldn't have put it better,' he said, and walked over to the low wall that topped the river bank. It was a drop of about ten feet to the water. Clearly visible in the murky shallows, were an assortment of what looked like building stones, probably left over from church repairs, and dumped there by centuries of builders. 'Fancy a trip on the river?'

'I like a man who knows how to give a girl a good time - I thought you'd never ask.'

'Come on then, we'll have to hurry, those boat-hire guys start packing up around now.'

They were in luck, and managed to hire the last rowing boat before 'Stratford Willy's Pleasure Boat Hire' closed for the day. Tony rowed them under the bridges, past the theatres and on towards the weir and the Parish Church which dominates the lower reaches of the widened and straightened river.

The last of the rowing boats and motor boats pottered about randomly or idled their way back up-river. Before long, Tony and Jessica were virtually alone. They manoeuvred themselves towards the shallows beneath the retaining wall. Jessica steadied the tiny craft with one of the oars, whilst Tony dug around, and levered at the submerged blocks with the other.

'There are quite a few - and of widely differing sizes as well.'

'Tony,' said Jessica, 'Essex man pokes holes in river-bed in search fiasco!'

'Ha, ha! I'm afraid it's going to take longer than I was hoping, and that's for sure,' he replied. He looked up to check their precise location in relation to the wall and the bushes. 'It's all big stones in the centre of this stretch, but more mixed at each end. We need an early start, tomorrow.'

They eased the boat out of the water margin and slowly made their way back upstream.

'I need some swimming trunks,' said Tony. 'Unless you would like to take over the search at this rather interesting juncture, of course?' Adding with a Cheshire cat of a grin, 'Have you brought your bikini?'

'In your dreams!' she replied.

28

Tony and Jessica had a restless night and rose early. They showered and dressed but didn't go straight down to breakfast. The couple had some serious thinking to do. Jessica could understand what was driving Tony, but felt that an obsessive streak in his nature was being unearthed. She was finding it hard to believe that this was the most productive use of their time.

'Tony, whichever way I look at it, searching for a slab of marble - which may or may not exist - in a cold and murky river, in the middle of Stratford, on a Spring Sunday, is a pretty iffy enterprise. Come on - be honest!'

'Bear with me, Jess. Let me put my roving imagination to rest, yes?'

'What were you going to do if we did find it - had you given that any serious thought? Give it back to the Church? Claim it as treasure trove? Take it to the Police? Or maybe take it home, and hide it and say nothing; no, that's hardly a realistic option is it? Come on, 'Indiana Jones,' what were you actually planning to do?'

'My original idea was to photograph it, and then take it to the Police, if you must know,' he said. 'And I haven't come across anything to make me change my mind. I'm fairly sure we can trust Southwell. Unless, of course, you can come up with something better.'

'Don't look at me - it's your hair-brained scheme. I'll go along with you, up to a point, but I've only got so much patience.'

Tony defused the moment before the tension made one of them say something they might regret.

'I'm getting hungry. Let's go down and get some breakfast.'

Jessica saw this as a defensive move from Tony. He must have been aware that she was alluding to the fact that finding clues to Bianca's untimely death had been put on the back burner. He hadn't mentioned her for days.

As they entered the restaurant, she was on the verge of broaching the subject, when they were met with quite a buzz of excitement from the unusually talkative and animated groups of guests.

They had neither seen nor heard any of the day's news reports, so were blissfully unaware of the subject deserving all the attention. One look at the copy of the Sunday Times on the sideboard explained the mystery. They stared wide-eyed and open-mouthed at the compact newspaper. There, in colour, on the front page, was a photograph of a small page covered in writing, and, next to it, what was obviously the reverse with rather less writing on it. 'Providential Discovery - So Shakespeare was Shakespeare All Along!' said the heading. They ignored any pangs of hunger, and sat down to read the accompanying text in an air of astonishment and bewilderment.

It was Jessica who spoke first. 'It's one of ours - Randy's, that is.'

'Are you certain?'

'Positive. Absolutely positive,' she affirmed. 'There were three or four pages from '*The Jew*'. 'B' and I sat on the floor back at the Palazzo and read through them. I remember them distinctly because we did '*The Merchant*' for 'A' Level, and were just incredulous at what we were reading. Hang on, isn't one of our three ….' But before she could finish, Tony was up and gone. He was back in moments with the photocopies of their three pages.

'Identical - it's a perfect match,' she exclaimed. 'Now where on earth has it come from, and who the hell found it?'

On the inside pages was the full story of the discovery, and a lengthy explanation as to how a member of a visiting Italian TV crew had found it a week earlier - just as Dryden had planned. All the details were there; the distressed and decaying copy of

'Dugdale's Antiquities of Warwickshire'; the depression in the pages; experts brought in from London and Cambridge to verify the find. Not a stone left unturned.

'I don't believe a word of this, Tony. It's bullshit - all of it. Either that's one of Randy's or it's a damned good fake.' Jessica was unusually emotional, and suddenly leapt to her feet. 'Someone is having us on, Tony. Of all the places in the world where that page could have turned up. I mean - here in Stratford - no coincidence there, then!' Her tone had the effect of quietening the room, and many of the guests looked their way.

'Cool it, Jess, cool it. We don't want to attract a lot of unwanted attention.' She took a few deep breaths to calm herself, and sat back down. They had some breakfast, and resolved to go up to the 'Birthplace Centre' as soon as they'd eaten - this looked like being a long day, and not to be tackled on an empty stomach.

'It's all too neat and tidy, Tony. Everything's just too con-bloody-venient. Who in their right minds could believe all this crap? Anyone intelligent can detect that so fish-like smell surely?' She tucked into a second croissant. 'These are gorgeous!' she said, 'They must be straight from the oven.'

'Well, it's put paid to my paddling lesson, that's for sure.' said Tony.

9.30 am.

A crowd of a thousand or more thronged the north end of Henley Street in front of the Shakespeare Centre. Tony and Jessica squeezed their way gradually to the front, and joined the media scrum at the entrance. The Staff appeared to be fighting a losing battle with the eager and impatient mass, but eventually instigated a 'keep left and keep moving' system. It still took nearly an hour to reach the first floor lecture theatre, the scene of all the excitement generated by 'The Providential Discovery.'

The 'Page', in a transparent plastic wallet, was held aloft by Katie. She stood behind, and near the centre of a long trestle table at which sat a row of Trust officials. Amongst them were the Chairman, the Director, the Chief Archivist and the Assistant Archivist, Mark Dryden. They were answering a barrage of questions: 'Tell us more about the owner of the book', asked one journalist. 'How did he get hold of it?' 'Exactly how long had it been sitting here?' asked another. 'Could it have been planted?' asked a third. The Director was handing out copies of a prepared statement, the one all the papers had already printed. The dismembered copy of Dugdale's *'Antiquities of Warwickshire'*, on a table of its own, was illuminated by the strobe-like flashing of dozens of cameras.

As the couple shuffled their way towards the front, carried along by the slow human tide, Dryden caught sight of Jessica. The jostling crowd of reporters, academics and the simply curious, couldn't have dreamt why he went white, and appeared so shocked. He stuttered another answer to an enquirer, and quickly pulled himself together. He glanced up at her. Was this really the same beautiful student whom he last saw in Venice three months ago? That hair, those eyes - it was her, all right. His mind flashed back to that February day, when, without a care in the world, the two girls had shown him round the Palazzo with unconditional friendliness. But why was she here? How was she here? For the page? For him? He couldn't take his eyes off her for a moment. Would she see through his disguise, his accent? And who was this with her - a boyfriend, a work colleague, an investigator perhaps? The couple got ever closer. The tumult in the room was matched only by the tumult inside his brain and his chest. His heart pounded as though his very soul was trying to break free. Where was the cool, controlled professional now, just when he needed him? Jessica was soon standing right in front of him.

'Tell me, where in Italy did the TV crew come from?' she asked. 'It wasn't Venice was it?'

'I'm not sure madam,' he replied, 'it might have been, or possibly Verona. Excuse me - Katie,' he called, 'was the Italian TV company from Venice or Verona?'

'Verona, Mr. Dryden.'

'Thank you, Katie. Yes, Verona madam, they were looking for connections between Shakespeare's works and locations in northern Italy for a culture channel over there.' He was pushing his luck by continuing the dialogue, but as she hadn't recognised him - why not?

'Thank you,' she said, and shuffled on towards the table with the book.

'Do you know if the TV crew is still working in Stratford or the Midlands?' asked Tony.

'I really couldn't say, sir. We were their first port of call, if my memory serves me correctly, and they had a busy schedule. But whether or not they're still in Stratford, or even England?' Dryden answered, with a shrug.

Tony turned to Jessica 'They appear to be distressed by all the hassle, but if you look at them they're lapping it up. That piece of paper could add a million a year to their coffers,' he said. 'Come on, lets see if we can track down those Veroneses.'

10.45 am.

As they left the muggy and airless lecture room, they were unaware that Dryden had already left too. He was now in the nearby Records Office on the phone to John Fletcher.

'John, you're not going to believe this, but I've just been talking to that Jessica girl ....Yes, that's right, the one from the 'Magretti-Bellini' ....No, she didn't recognise me. She's also got a man with her.'

'Untune that string, and hark what dismal discord follows,' came John's voice from the other end.

'What's that? What did you say?'

'Nothing. We've got to meet,' he said. 'We can't undo what you've done, but we have to discuss what we do next. I'm going to come down tomorrow. Make sure you're free.'

'I can be.'

'You will be, Mark, you will be.' He snapped. 'You're near

Stretton-on-Fosse, aren't you?'

'Yes. If you ….'

'I'll find you on Satnav. It'll be late in the morning, I can't be any more exact.' John hung up.

Dryden felt wrecked. He went into the kitchen and put the kettle on. He couldn't face the crowds in the lecture theatre. He was desperate for a few minutes to himself. His day had started like a dream, but it was going to end like a nightmare. The deception had been better received than he could have imagined. He was able to sit back and enjoy the show. But Jessica appearing like that was such a shock - so unreal. She represented his worst fears. How come she was here, and so soon after the announcement? Surely *she* hadn't found him when there hadn't been even the slightest sniff from the police in three months? Maybe the man with her was a private eye after all.

His contemplations were interrupted by the boiling kettle. He waited for the simmering to stop before filling the cafetiere. He took a few minutes to look out of the window as the coffee infused. The trees were all in full leaf and shrugging off the last of the blossom - summer was pushing on with indecent haste.

'Mr. Dryden,' said Katie. 'Mr. Dryden, you're needed in the lecture theatre.'

'What? Who?' He turned to her, his eyes piercing straight through her. 'I'll be there in a minute, all right.' He stabbed her with the words for stealing his precious peace. She stared back into his eyes, frightened, as though he were an unknown - an intruder. She had done nothing to deserve this, and fought back in silence.

As his gaze relaxed, he blinked and took a deep breath. 'Sorry, Katie, I didn't mean to be rude, I don't know what came over me - it's not like me to be so stressed is it? I'll be along in a couple of minutes - I'm just so damned thirsty, and that room has turned into heaven and hell at the same time.'

29

Getting out of the Birthplace Centre proved almost as difficult as getting in. Once they were out through the crowded lobby and back into Henley Street, they could breathe freely again.

'How people can find enjoyment being in crowds, I'll never know,' said Tony.

'For the buzz, old man, for the buzz,' said Jessica.

He indicated to their right. 'Come on, this way's best,' and they made their way from all the hype and hysteria to the quiet of the Market Square and a welcome table at a small, French-style café. The citrons pressees were perfect. Tony took the photocopies of the three pages out of the envelope and studied them.

'That forgery of theirs sure puts these in a new light, doesn't it?' he said, 'but before we take another step, I think we ought to have Randy's take on the day's news. What do you think?'

'Ring him straight away, Tony. Someone is playing fast and loose with history and stolen goods, and if it is tied to 'B's' death as well, then we have to get onto it right away. With Randy's blessing too, if he'll give it.'

'Hi, Randy.'

'Hi, Tony! I guess you've seen the papers, then?'

'Yes we have. Jess and I are in Stratford now. We've just been up to the Shakespeare Centre to have a look at it.'

'It's one of ours, isn't it?'

'Jess knew it straight away - there's no doubt in her mind whatsoever.'

'I guess you'll want to go public with them, and you want me to give you the nod, yeah?'

'It's all going to be in the timing, Randy. I won't do anything hasty, you know that, but it might be necessary to use the 'pages', because we've now got the police interested. We showed Warwickshire CID all the new stuff we put together on Alex's case, together with 'B's', and stressed the link to Shakespeare and the robbery in Venice. I'm pretty sure we can trust the D.I. who listened to us - I'll do everything I can to keep you and Helena out of shot, whatever happens.'

'Are people going to believe you though, Tony? Remember, not a single expert has cast his, or her, beady little eyes over them, unlike the one in today's papers. The sort of delays made by authentication procedures could take months and lead to the trail going cold. Which reminds me - have you got anyone in mind yet?'

'No, I haven't. As I said, we've only just come away from the Shakespeare Centre; but looking at that table-full of dignitaries a few minutes ago, I can hardly believe we're going to find a killer amongst them. We've had a surprise to do with our private-eye, Steve Watson, though, I told you about him didn't I?'

'The 'Cockney Columbo,' yes, I remember. What's he been up to?'

'Apparently he headed-up Alex's case for a while and wasn't particularly popular up here. Our D.I. Southwell has some history with him, and she'd like to see him put in his place for her own reasons. Although she wouldn't say so directly, you don't have to be a Rebus to work out that our Steve Dub'ya had a wall built round the Alex investigation so impregnable that a couple of dozen Skyhawks couldn't even punch a hole through it!'

'Is he still going to prove useful?'

'We think he might be serving us up with what *he* thinks *we* want. How useful? - Only time will tell.'

'Be careful Tony. If you are getting close, you're not far from a dangerous man.'

Tony had tried to keep any worry about being in danger as far from Jessica as humanly possible. It was difficult not to look across at her and give the game away. He switched the conversation back to the 'pages'.

'Sure, Randy, of course, so it's OK to use them?' he said, nodding in Jessica's direction.

'Just make sure you keep your wits about you. Give my love to Jess.'

'Cheers, Randy. Ours to Helena.' He rang off.

'He knew all about it then?'

'Yes, and now we are free to use these and everything in there,' he said, casting a glance down to the envelope lying on the newspaper between them on the table.

She looked up at him. 'What are you thinking?'

'One day in the non-too-distant future, Randy and Eddie will have to go public with these pages. They're going to love that! But, as for the here and now - we need a strategy.'

'Let's have a look at that report in the paper and see what the experts actually said,' said Jessica. 'How could they have been fooled?'

Tony read through the relevant paragraphs. 'The sheet of laid paper is undoubtedly English in manufacture, and late sixteenth century…' It says here. '…Subject to a more thorough and detailed forensic examination, there is no reason to doubt its authenticity…' It goes on a bit, and then says, '…It is true that the hand is very similar to other Tudor hands, but this is only to be expected.' Christ, I could have written all this - who is our expert? Ah, here we are, Marjory Jourdain - 'Britain's foremost authority on Elizabethan and Jacobean manuscripts.' Well, she should know, according to this, she had it for a week. And the handwriting verified by a forensic graphologist - from Cambridge no less. Nothing but the best for our Will, eh?'

'They could be knights of the realm for all I care. It's still a con.'

'You don't suppose it came from the same sequence, but appeared from another source - you know, one that got away?

'Tony! For God's sake! You'll be telling me you don't believe me next. What's the matter with you? - I told you - I read it in Venice - with 'B'. That whole charade up there is an elaborate and calculated fraud!'

'Stratfraud.' said Tony.

'What?'

'Stratfraud. It was an in-joke of Alex's. It was what he used to call Stratford - either that or Bardsville.'

They left the Market Square and headed for Bancroft Gardens, down by the river, and centre for the Town's festivities. 'Let's see if we can track down the 'Boys from Verona', they could well be our best starting point.' he added.

'What about the Freemasons and the mysterious 'FCV'. Alex seemed certain they had something to do with it, didn't he?' asked Jessica.

'Yes. How we approach a secretive group like them though, I've no idea. The Masonic Hall is in Great William Street, by the way, no more than a hundred yards from the back door of 'The Birthplace' - that's a nice coincidence, isn't it?'

They wove their way through coach parties of oriental tourists and continental school-children to reach the top of Bridge Street, a couple of hundred yards from their destination. It was impossible to avoid the excesses of festival. Everywhere they turned, it was like a cross between Blackpool sea-front and The South Bank. They were assailed by flags, banners and bunting, triumphal archways celebrating each of the plays, and street performers and musicians. The whole town had been converted into a quasi-cultural Disneyland.

'Why don't we just show the world our genuine pages and be damned,' said a frustrated Jessica. 'We know they're the real thing, and, now that Randy has given us the go-ahead, we should be able to force their hand. I want whoever was behind that fake to be exposed, and the sooner they're unmasked the better.'

'It's too soon, Jess. As things are, we don't stand a chance against all this,' he said, gesturing up at the mass of street decorations now enveloping them, 'not to mention the tidal-waves of media adoration.' The pair sought sanctuary on the refuge which ran some distance down the centre of the road.

'I remain to be fully convinced.' she said, somewhat

dismissively.

As Tony stopped to talk to Jessica on the narrow, slabbed reservation in the middle of the wide, bustling thoroughfare, two bright-red tourist buses came up, one on each side of them. They were covered in brilliantly-coloured computer-drawn images of half-timbered cottages and of 'the Bard', and, amidst the cacophony of amplified information being blurted at the passengers on their open-topped observation decks, he had to almost shout to make himself heard.

'Just think for a moment,' he said, 'if you and I put Randy's three pages, Alex's letters and photos, and all our other bits and bobs on one pan of a pair of scales, and you put four centuries of English historical and theatrical tradition, university English and history departments from around the world, thousands of scholars, academics and researchers, publishing houses, international tourism and the economy of central England on the other....does that help to convince you?'

'I'm beginning to see what you mean.'

'This is as deep as it gets, Jess - this is England's divine cultural centre. Even the ghosts of Leonardo, Michelangelo, Beethoven and Tolstoy can't enjoy the luxury of all this. Back up there in Henley Street, you've got 'Bethlehem,' with its inn, stable and manger. By the river you've got your very own Calvary, complete with tombstone. Not only that, you've got a Bard who wrote his own Bible! - What more could you want? Now, if D.I. Southwell can unearth some dirty goings-on from six years ago, it'll help to tip those scales. But if we could add the weight of that manuscript forger and the original inscription stone to our pan - then bingo!'

'I was forgetting about our river adventure. When are we going to attempt a search? Now?'

'Tomorrow, I guess. I hadn't given it much thought after today's revelations.' He stopped suddenly. 'Tomorrow, Jess. It's tomorrow when Southwell will hopefully be getting Alex's case reopened.'

'Well?'

'All this 'Providential Discovery' rubbish could ruin our

argument. It could make us look even more like Commissario Montano's romantic English fools! I've got to get on to her and tell her what we know.'

They crossed Waterside and skirted the huge tented exhibition area to find a quiet area from which to phone. The Inspector wasn't amused when Tony admitted to holding onto information. He managed to persuade her to put the facts before her seniors, and promised to show her the photocopies of the three pages as soon as he could. He prayed that he had done enough to tip the scales in his favour.

12.30 pm.

The couple entered an outdoor theatre area in front of the Royal Shakespeare Theatre. A sizable crowd was watching the erection of a giant spinnaker-like awning. Several tiers of seating and the main stage had been in place for some time, but so that Her Majesty, the royal party and the other dignitaries should remain dry, or shaded as the case may be, there was something of a rush to complete the covering.

'Do you see who I see?' said Jessica.

'Where?'

'With the film crew. Isn't that Eddie whatshisname - you know, Randy's friend?'

'Eddie Gascoigne, you're right, it is. He said he was making a documentary for Channel 7 up here. He could prove a valuable ally. I'll bet he knows the whereabouts of every film and TV crew for miles around, including 'the boys from Verona.' Let's go and say hello.'

Keeping well out of shot, they manoeuvred themselves as close to the action as they dared. Eddie appeared to be directing the whole operation, the erection company obediently falling in line with his demands. Rather like so many weddings, it was film and photo first - bride and groom second! After ten minutes, the fuss was all over, the awning was up, and Eddie's film was in the can.

Both crews took a break.

'Eddie!' called Tony.

'Tony. Jessica. What a pleasant surprise. What are you two doing up here - some Shakespearean sleuthing, no doubt?'

They greeted each other like old friends, even though they had only met once, a week earlier at Randy and Helena's.

'And what about the news splashed across all the Sundays - you two must be a bit gutted?'

'Surprised, astonished perhaps,' said Jessica, 'but certainly not gutted. All that discovery nonsense will soon be exposed for the shameless fraud it undoubtedly is.'

'Blimey, girl, that's a bit strong. Mind you, there are already stories doing the rounds.'

'Come on then, Eddie - all the dirt!' said Tony.

'Well, a little bird, or should I say 'ucello' told me that the miraculous discovery had an ancient fish-like smell about it.'

'Everything you know please, Eddie,' said Jessica impatiently. 'You were in on the find in Venice, so don't tell me you weren't suspicious when you read it?'

'OK, Yes, I was. And I have to admit to doing a double-take on it, too, because it really took me by surprise. Look, I'm parched. Let's go over there and have something to drink,' he said, and led the way to a temporary Italian-style coffee bar in the shade of the trees. They sat down on some shiny metal chairs, at a shiny metal table. Eddie turned to the bar and held up three fingers. 'Tre Americanos per favore, presto!' he called, and gossiped on. 'The poor sod's Polish - he won't understand a word of that! Anyway, back to business. Last Thursday, Salarino and his crew from Verona were up in the Records Office - you know where - being offered some original old stuff to film. One of his 'amicos' thought it was a piss-poor offering. He even said so there and then, by all accounts. All the good stuff is going on show in here from tomorrow, you know,' he said, indicating over his shoulder.'

'Yes, we'd heard - and?'

'Well, basically, they were shown tat. I mean, those guys had just hauled all their kit a thousand kliks across Europe - and to be shown that! You could've found better in any second-hand bookshop - I could've done better! A few printed plays and uncatalogued pamphlets, and a couple of very tatty books - shameful! No wonder they were so pissed off - wouldn't you have been? But the gloom was soon illuminated by shrieks of delight, and the rest is now part of history, m'dears.'

'You mean - anyone being presented with that choice was bound to find the page?' said Jessica.

'Your deduction - not mine,' he answered, 'but that's the flavour of the giorno.'

'What about the experts, though, Eddie, you can't nobble them? Their reputations would be on the line,' said Tony. 'We're talking British Library and Cambridge University here, not some outfit of half-wits from the sticks, ready to be overawed by the grandeur of things and eager to sign up to their fifteen minutes of fame.'

'You know what the world's like, Tony; you see what you want to see; find what you want to find. I'm not suggesting for a moment that they were Shakespeare Trust patsies. They're kosher for sure, but, pressure to please, wish fulfilment! We live in a funny old world.'

'No, we don't.' said Jessica. 'My best friend has just been killed, and that's not the least bit funny.'

'Apologies, Jessica. Really, no offence meant in any way, but what if that manuscript is genuine?'

'Bullshit!' she snapped back. 'You are one of only half-a-dozen people in this world who can sleep tonight safe in the knowledge that it's a fake, so don't give me that crap.'

Her invective silenced both men. Tony cautiously restarted the discussion.

'How do you think it got into that book, Eddie, you must have thought about it? You saw that manuscript before Jess did, back in Venice, and you know the Earl of Oxford wrote what was on it - well, what was on one side of it, at least.'

'From the press reports, it could have been done any time in the last three or four months. Have you any idea how many people visit the Shakespeare Centre every day, let alone every month? But did someone up there fake it and plant it? - The jury hasn't even been sworn in yet! Only God and Shakespeare's ghost know the how of it my friends, because I certainly don't.'

Eddie was in a spot. If he agreed to go along with them, he would be a fully signed-up 'heretic' - not an easy stance to take in his profession. It was all very well to be openly sceptical about William of Stratford. Signing up to one of the contenders for his crown was a very different matter. The trouble was, he knew these amateur sleuths were right, and it was only a question of time before the truth about the authorship would be front-page news - and they were not of the 'giving-in' variety.

'There's something damned fishy going on and that's a cert. Randy and Helena still hurt like the holocaust over that girl of theirs, and I'd love to do something for them, but where do you start? You can't just go around accusing people. If you go up to the Shakespeare Centre and start nosing around, all the doors will be shut in you face - and rightly so. You haven't a shred of proof they're in any way involved. The Venice police think you're barking up the wrong one, and they are the professionals after all. With all due respect, Tony, what have *you* got that will convince me?'

'Two things I hope, but you'll have to wait till tomorrow for confirmation. I can tell you one other thing, though. Yesterday, Jess and I virtually convinced a senior officer in the Warwickshire Police that there are grounds to reopen a murder case from six years ago that was strikingly similar to the way Bianca died. If we were successful, we should have them on board in the next couple of days, and they will be out to establish a link between the two crimes, three if you count the burglary. Now, can we count on your help?'

Eddie looked them both in the eye.

'My heart's ruling my head here. If I say yes, what help could I be to you? I'm a busy man, guys. I've got a crew here who depend on me, and I've got contracts to fulfil.'

'I've got an idea,' said Tony. 'What are you doing in the

morning?'

'I've got a production meeting at eleven, and then…'

'Let me have your mobile number, and do your best to keep the morning completely free - at least until eleven, OK? Oh, and can you have one of your cameras at the ready?'

'Can you tell me what this is all in aid of?'

'Just in case it's all for nothing, Eddie - wait for a call in the morning.'

'If you say so - Aye, aye, here comes the league of mentalmen! Can't stop - Tony, Jessica, it's been a pleasure. Ring me any time before eleven. Ciao.' And with a flamboyant and pretentious farewell, he disappeared off his own media whirl.

30

The events of the weekend had made Tony and Jessica more determined than ever to connect the deaths of their friends to a cover-up of some kind involving archival material. Alex's notes and conclusions from his researches might never have been found, but they felt absolutely certain that what he'd discovered six years earlier would prove vital in making headway. Alex was sure of a Shakespeare Centre link to the Freemasons, and possibly the police too, possibly the elusive FCV. But he had no proof. Perhaps tracking down his 'stalker' might establish that final link in their search for the truth. The task ahead looked monumental, but at least their meetings with Eddie and D.I. Southwell had furnished them with renewed optimism.

With Eddie on board and his connections in the media they might be able to cut some corners - get rapid access to the SBT archives, for instance - or quiz the Italians. Being partly motivated by his long friendship with the Middletons, Eddie's presence could only be a positive. He had no truck with 'Bardology' either, and, with his mischievous streak, might see a contribution to solving the authorship debate as fun for its own sake.

They wondered what D.I. Southwell had made of the news reports so soon after they had been talking to her in Warwick. She must have had a shock! But would it assist their argument to get Alex's case reopened, or quite the reverse? To an outsider, the discovery of the page might appear to completely undermine their case - make them look like a couple of cranks. Her superiors might say 'stuff and nonsense' and tell her to forget the whole business. At least she was still on board after Tony's call to her the previous day.

Steve Watson hadn't furnished them with any news of progress from Venice on either the robbery or the identification of the 'man in black'. If he really was obstructing their enquiries into Alex's case, then why would he not block Bianca's as well? This man from the North, the Midlands and the South was proving quite an enigma. They had only met him once, and that was over a hurried drink in a pub they'd never been to before or since. His purposeful manner initially gave rise to optimism; his no-nonsense attitude that of a man who got things done. But he was turning out to be a dead loss, and they were wondering if there was any point in keeping him on board. His lack of contact was, by degrees, becoming less of a cause for concern.

The one thing that bugged Tony more than anything, was Alex finding the original inscription stone. Having a photograph of it made things worse rather than better. In his heart of hearts he knew there was only a snowballs of ever finding it, but he couldn't relax until he'd given it his best shot. Jessica must have thought he was a bit crazy to be so determined about rediscovering it, to go to all the trouble of mounting a search, but he was thankful, that for all her rationality and reason, she was prepared to go along with him - just this once!

The weather had taken a turn for the worse. It was only the following morning, but difficult to believe it was the same season, let alone the same week. They thought it wisest not to tell D.I. Southwell of their plans to search the river. For one thing, it was probably illegal, and, for another, she was almost bound to stop them on grounds of health and safety. The summery spring Sunday had been obliterated by a surfeit of March winds and April showers. It all made navigating Stratford Willy's motorboat the half-mile downstream to the Parish Church the challenge of a transatlantic ordeal. Fortunately, no-one else was fool enough to join them, and their only company - other than assorted waterfowl - was a lone walker on the opposite bank.

They manoeuvred the little white craft into the reedy shallows beneath the soaring mediaeval spire. Dry winters were now the norm in England, and low river levels made the water-margins increasingly accessible. This was the case here on the Warwickshire Avon, where some of the discarded building stone of centuries now stood proud of the slow-flowing water.

They made a most improbable sight - a young woman struggling with her long wet hair with one hand and the handle of an outboard engine in the other, vainly trying to steady a boat whilst a young man, leaning over the side of it with his backside in the air, his sleeves rolled up, was groping about among the rocks and stones in the Khaki-coloured current!

Tony was attempting to establish which, if any, of the slabs or stones matched the description of the one mounted on the wall in the Chancel above them. After nearly two hours, and with time rapidly running out, as they gradually edged the craft along towards the limit of what was practicable in their search, several pleasure-seekers in a variety of boats came up to them offering their assistance. Tony politely refused their advances, explaining that although his friend's camera was probably ruined, thanks to his clumsiness, he felt honour-bound to retrieve it anyway.

The rain gradually eased off. It was now gone half-past ten, but it was brightening, and the wind had abated to a fresh breeze. Jessica was tiring rapidly, and had almost had enough as Tony plunged his red-raw arms and hands once more into the river. He was about to admit to her, very reluctantly, that she had been right all along, when he found himself shifting a piece of trapezoid shaped marble. It was a little under a square foot in area, and about two inches thick. He was just discarding it when his fingers detected letters carved on its underside. He lifted it clear of the water and turned it over. To his amazement, he read some words he knew only too well - JUDICIO PYLIVM - and underneath - TERRA TEGIT - The beginning of the first two lines of the missing stone.

'Of course!' He exclaimed. 'It was broken in the fall.'

'Have you found it?'

Tony washed it as best as he could, and lifted it into the boat.

'It's in pieces Jess. I've been searching for the whole slab when I should have been looking for fragments.' He put it on the seat, dried his hands as best he could, and got out his mobile phone. 'Eddie, I'm sending you a photo - now - can you get yourself and your camera up to the east end of the Parish Church - five minutes ago - or sooner?'

'What's so important?'

'You are in for a big surprise, believe me!'

'I'm on my way.'

Tony photographed Jessica, holding the broken fragment, with the Church in the background. He did this with both his phone and his camera. He then resumed his search, and after fifteen minutes had retrieved two further fragments to complete the rectangular slab. Eddie arrived just as Tony lifted the third and largest piece clear of the surface.

'Put it back in, and make it look a bit trickier getting it out,' he called down from the low stone wall. 'Soon as you like!' Both of their cameras were fitted with satellite dating and timing, which made the discovery legally verifiable. Eddie continued to film - Tony and Jessica made their acting debuts as convincing as they could.

An unwelcome group of onlookers were gathering at the wall to see what all the fuss was about, but Eddie saw them off in his inimitable style.

'Oi! What the bloody hell do you lot think you're doing? We're trying to shoot this in one take.' They retreated obediently, and it allowed Tony time to carry the three pieces up the steep bank to the waiting Eddie. Once Jessica was also at the top, they explained what all the fuss was about.

'You're telling me this was originally on the wall in the Chancel, and was exchanged for the one that's there now because the Earl of Oxford's daughter thought it gave the game away?'

'Precisely.'

'I know my Shakespeare history pretty well, guys, and I can tell you for nothing that, if you're going to try to convince the world of that, you've got a mountain to climb, not just a slippery river bank. What I also find hard to believe is that you two have come up with this after couple of days when far more dedicated and obsessive searchers have come up with zilch after scouring this place for the last couple of centuries.'

'It's a long story, Eddie,' said Tony, 'but the crux of the matter is that, nearly six years ago, my best friend was killed, just over there, for the pleasure of unearthing this slab.'

'Thanks, Tony.' said Jessica.

'Oh, Christ! I didn't mean to frighten you, sweetheart.'

'I don't like this place, Tony, and I'd like to get away - the sooner the better.'

'Soon, Jess, soon. Film this quickly, can you, Eddie?'

He assembled the broken pieces to make the complete slab, and pointed to the small delicately carved characters in the bottom left hand corner. 'It's not just the cryptic message carried in the main text of the epitaph that's of special interest, it's these initials, 'FCV' that give the show away. They conclusively link the role of William Shakspere here in Stratford to the Earl of Oxford and the Herbert Brothers, and eventually, the Freemasons.'

11.15 am.

When they were happy with the way they had documented the find, Tony rang D.I. Southwell to inform her of the morning's goings-on. Realising that what they had found could well be evidence in a murder case, Tony knew the police would have to keep the broken slab under lock and key. He had his fingers crossed that the next few minutes would prove that they had a genuine ally in the detective.

'I'll be over as soon as I'm free, Mr. Chapman,' said Southwell, 'and perhaps then you could explain to me how you obtained permission to search the river! Be that as it may, I have two pieces of news for you. Firstly, I have tell you it's not going to be that easy convincing my superiors to re-open the Paris case. With the Shakespeare Gala bearing down on us, it's all hands to the wheel. Secondly, someone has been hacking into our computer - quite recently it seems. Some files have been deleted and others tampered with - all around the time of the Alexander Paris case in the Autumn of 2010 - hardly a coincidence, I think you'll agree.'

'Where will that take you?' asked Tony.

'We'll need to talk to Steve Watson, of course, and we'd also like to make some discreet enquiries up at the Shakespeare Centre. As money not only talks but shouts, I will be looking closely at some of the bigger investors behind the 'Trust' and the whole RSC - if we are given the green light, of course. Now, exactly where are you?'

'Holy Trinity, Inspector. We'll wait at the east end till you arrive - and thanks for being so open.'

'Before I say 'don't mention it', have you got any more tricks up your sleeve?' asked the Inspector, 'because, if so, you'd better tell me now.'

Having blotted his copybook twice already that morning, Tony knew it was best to play things straight or he really could run the risk of losing her.

'I'll explain more when I see you, Inspector. But if anything is going to convince your superiors to re-open case and forge a link with the recent happenings in Venice as well, then what we've just fished out of the river is it.

31

The lone figure on the far side of the river watched Tony as he manoeuvred the boat away from the bank and made his way upstream after leaving the 'slabbe' with the police. He had been watching the couple since earlier in the morning as they struggled against the wind and rain to keep the craft under control at the site of the discovery. In fact, he had been observing their comings and goings throughout most of the weekend. He knew precisely what they had gone in search of, and thought how stupid and inept they were embarking on what was sure to be a fruitless quest. How wrong he now proved to be. He had wrongly assumed that the 'slabbe' had been removed five-and-a-half years earlier and safely disposed of. Whatever the reason for its not being recoverable, the cat was well and truly out of the bag now.

The troublesome duo and their comrade-in-arms, the blasé photographer, were becoming more and more of a problem and needed dealing with. 'These are little people', he thought to himself, 'and have no idea what they have started'. He walked back to his car, but took a moment to look across the park to the figure of Tony, almost lost amongst the other pleasure-craft now filling the river, as he powered himself back to 'Stratford Willy's Boat Hire'. 'You're full of elation now, little man, but you need a dose of real fear to bring you back down to earth - and I'm just the man to provide it.'

32

'Would you mind telling me what the fuck's going on, John? I thought that Paris business was all done and dusted. I've just had a call from one of my D.I.'s who's determined to have the case reopened. With all the new shit she's putting together, it's going to be impossible to refuse her.'

'Did you get those files sorted out, Harry?'

'I'm not a bloody idiot! Now where the hell is all this coming from?'

'I know exactly where it's all coming from, and I've got everything under control. Now can you be certain there are absolutely no hard-copies around?'

'John - this is me you're talking to! I know the death of the Middleton girl is in the mix too. Now I want to know if it's got anything to do with all this "Providential Discovery" crap as well - I mean, this could run and run - just how far does it go?'

'I can't tell you right now, but it's vital that you to meet up with Mark and get your stories straight. Do it as soon as you can because that D.I. of yours is going to start sniffing around pretty soon - probably later today, I shouldn't be surprised. I'm on my way to see Mark now.'

'Where are you?'

'On the M40 coming down the Stokenchurch Cutting, so I'll be with him in about fifty minutes. Ring him and tell him we've spoken. Tell him about your D.I., and, for God's, sake tell him to stay cool.'

Harry Gower, now the Warwickshire D.C.C., was a D.C.S. back in 2010, and responsible for the transfer of Steve Watson from West Midlands Serious Crime Squad to Warwickshire Police. John Fletcher had seen to it that the fewer people who knew the exact details of Alex's death the better - even Harry wasn't certain who was actually responsible. As a fellow Freemason, he knew he could always rely on Mark Dryden to keep quiet, but the unpredictable element of the 'fly' Steve Watson meant he was always having to look over his shoulder. He'd come and gone in six months - nobody ever got to know him. He never discussed his life or his past and left you with the feeling that, not only you wouldn't like his friends, you'd rather not know about them at all. Being revisited by memories of such a forgettable colleague was like the rude arrival of a bad dream.

Although Harry's role had initially been a minor one, he could see his whole career going down the tube thanks to the recent developments in both Italy and Stratford. Like Mark Dryden, he was a member of Garrick Lodge, and he decided that, if he couldn't meet him any earlier in the week, then it would have to wait until their regular Lodge meeting at the Masonic Hall on Thursday. It was to be a most important meeting for all the Brethren, as arrangements for their crucial role in the Gala opening ceremony, in front of the Queen, were to be finalised. It was their solemn duty to be present.

33

It was lunchtime, and the last of the rain was being dismissed by the blustery winds as John Fletcher pulled up outside Dryden's farmhouse. He knocked on the kitchen door and invited himself in. He stumbled over the cats as they purred about their empty bowls, but, before Dryden could even get to the kitchen, the impatient Fletcher was in the hall.

'Give me all the files, Mark, please - and I'd better have the books and manuscripts from Venice, too.'

What was known to only a very select few was that the facts surrounding the authorship had been known for centuries. A secret file of information to that effect was being protected by these two men. They were its present custodians, members of a long line of dedicated and trusted keepers, dating back to the early seventeenth century, and sworn to absolute secrecy.

Their first commercial venture had been *'Mr. William Shakespeare's Comedies, Histories, & Tragedies'*, known today as *'The Complete Works of Shakespeare'*, also referred to as the *'First Folio'*. Publication of the volume in 1623, was overseen by the Herbert brothers, and their mother, Mary Sydney, Countess of Pembroke. Over the centuries, a succession of high-ranking men, using their membership of the Freemasons as a cover, had maintained the secret, controlling any further 'damaging' evidence whenever it appeared. As Shakespeare's works became more famous and influential, people demanded to know more about the man behind them; but of course, nothing could ever be found.

By the time the Monarch became Patron of the 'Royal

Shakespeare Company' it was too late to think of turning back. They were now the custodians of a monumental and international, cultural fraud. What had started out as a harmless conceit to protect an aristocratic family name, had mutated into a burdensome, anachronistic monster.

'It's not that urgent, surely, John?'

'We can't take any chances, Mark. This whole business has got far too messy as it is. This isn't some sort of damage limitation exercise, you know - this has to be watertight. Everything you've got has to be as far from Stratford and the prying eyes of the police as possible - and immediately. Warwickshire CID could be coming down your drive right now. There is no way I can be here, should they arrive - it would be disastrous.'

Dryden went to his study and removed the files and books from the safe.

'Is this all because of that Jessica girl and that man of her's?' he asked.

'Earlier this morning they found the Inscription Stone. The stone which *you* should have removed, you damned fool, but let's not go there - has Harry been on to you yet?'

'We're going to meet at Thursday's Lodge meeting.'

'No urgency there, then!'

'Come on, John!'

'No, Mark, *you* come on! You two get your stories straight today, and be bloody careful who rings who, and how, because your phone records are likely to be checked. I just hope no-one looks too closely because my number is in there, Lord knows how many times.'

Reluctantly, Dryden handed all the Shakespeare/Oxford files and documents to John Fletcher. He had an unexpected premonition that he wouldn't be seeing them again.

'Let me have everything you've got on the 'Fraternity' as well, Mark It's far too risky to leave anything about us lying around so close to Stratford.'

Dryden removed some files entitled 'FCV' from the top shelf

in his study and handed them to his friend.

John Fletcher immediately turned on his heels and in a few seconds was outside, loading everything Dryden had given him into the boot of his car. 'I'll be in touch,' he said, 'and, remember, don't ring me using your land-line or your regular mobile.'

He left the hapless Dryden to face his fate.

As he watched Fletcher's car disappear back up towards the main road, his phone rang.

He ignored it.

34

Half-an-hour had passed since Eddie rushed off to his production meeting. D.I. Southwell had come and gone too, leaving Tony and Jessica alone, gazing down at the deserted river margin. Neither a succession of spring floods nor winter and summer droughts had moved the fragmented slab during its five and a half year rest in the shallows. Now it was gone, and undoubtedly destined, when freed by the police, to a life of fame.

The exhilaration of discovery had ebbed away with remarkable speed. It left them feeling oddly deflated, as though their success couldn't match the magnitude of their expectations. Other than Eddie's filming, all they actually had for their troubles were a few photographs in Tony's camera, a couple of e-mails to his home computer and his solicitor's, plus the satisfaction of knowing that Alex had been right all along - the initials on the 'slabbe' had been a testimony to that.

After all the fuss of the previous weekend, he felt it was only fair to e-mail the Paris's, and ask them to thank Imogen - after all, without her co-operation the discovery wouldn't have been possible.

Jessica walked the Riverside path back to the RST half a mile away while Tony returned the motorboat. Their strenuous efforts had left them exhausted and with a good appetite. They agreed to rendezvous at the Wanamaker Restaurant for a well earned lunch and to make plans for their next course of action.

They walked down the bright modernist interior and chose a table at the window overlooking the waterfowl-infested river, now busy with pleasure-craft. The paved esplanade below was jammed with an eclectic mix of Oriental tourists, European families, leather-clad motor-cyclists and white-haired seniors.

'How can it be so crowded, even on a Monday?' asked Jessica.

'It's still the Easter Holidays, don't forget,' said Tony. 'This is Britain's most popular inland resort. It positively groans under their weight every weekend, as well as during the school holidays.'

She continued to gaze out of the window. 'Alex mentioned an Italian-looking guy at the Birthplace Centre in the first of his coded letters. We haven't seen anyone like that since we've been here, have we?'

'Only the chap we spoke to yesterday, I suppose,' answered Tony. 'Actually he did have something of a Mediterranean air about him, now that I think about it. He seemed nice enough, but otherwise, no. He didn't actually say his stalker was the same person as the one giving him a hard time from the Trust,' added Tony. 'He was convinced someone was shadowing him, but never described him in any detail.' He slipped off his coat and put it on the back of his chair. 'There's a conspiracy of some kind here, Jess - the trouble is, we haven't a clue how many people are involved. And *you* haven't spotted anyone else like your 'George Drummond' or whoever he is, have you?'

'No. But then again - I haven't been searching for him.'

The waitress arrived to take their order and they both decided on a starter as well as a main course, choosing potentially the largest dishes on the menu, and asked her to bring some much needed drinks.

It was now as hot as any summer's day outside. The wind had died down after banishing most of the clouds, and only a few puddles were left to reflect flickering spotlights onto the ceiling. Tony turned to Jessica.

'How many employees do you think there are up in the Trust offices with access to the archive material?'

'Haven't a clue. Half-a-dozen, ten, maybe. Not a lot.'

'And how many, I wonder, are qualified to go front of house

and face down an inquisitive public? Two, three? I've got a hunch the whole public face of the Trust was on show yesterday.'

'But 'smooth George' at the Palazzo was younger than anyone up in that lecture theatre; and he had a goatee and specs. Anyway his accent was completely different from, what was his name - Dryden? - far more public school. He swanned round Randy's palazzo as though he was the Doge of Venice himself!' She took a sip of water.

'Montano said no-one called George Drummond had entered or left Italy around the time of 'B's death, and nobody at the Consulate had ever heard of him either. Like that manuscript page, he was a complete fake, Jess. He was putting on an act. He was putting on an act for you and 'B'. What if he'd changed his appearance - just enough to fool the authorities - and Bianca and you?'

'Tony - this *is* the real world, you know.'

'I know what you're thinking, but take away the glasses and beard, Jess. Remove a bit of hair-dye that makes him look younger. It doesn't take much to deceive the eye - or two impressionable young women - or CCTV cameras.'

'You're so trying to convince yourself, Tony.'

'Pull up a picture in your mind, Jess. Close your eyes, and go back to Randy's Palazzo. What do you see? A man of similar height and build? English and well educated….'

'Stop right there. Just stop what you're doing. You're getting obsessed and putting ideas into my mind. I have to admit, there is a similarity; but I would have to see him again, close-up - talk to him, if possible; then I could tell you, one way or the other, but I don't want a head full of thumbnails!'

'Let's have some lunch and then we can pop up to the Shakespeare Centre before we go back home. See if he's there. Put our minds at rest. What do you think?'

'OK, if it'll make you happy,' she said.

Jessica looked across the river to the weeping willows cascading into the murky, choppy water, impatient to get into full leaf.

'Had you thought of ringing Steve to tell him about finding

- 'the slabbe'?'

'His reaction would be rather interesting, wouldn't it?'

'Try him.'

'I think I will.' He got out his mobile. 'Hi, Steve - any news?'

'What-ho, Tony my son, how y' doin'?' He was sitting on a bench on the opposite side of the Avon from the RST. As he tucked into a bag of chips and ketchup, quite unnoticed, he looked up at them at their table by the first-floor window. 'News?' he said, 'Not a lot, as it happens - what about yesterday's papers then, eh, and all this media crap? - Bet you never expected that?'

'No, we didn't. It came as quite a surprise, I can tell you. We're still not sure what to make of it all. I've got some interesting news for you though. You know I was convinced that it was only going to be the discovery of manuscripts that would eventually lead us to the person behind Alex's killing? Well, it wasn't. Alex had found the original inscription stone - the one that was replaced with the one that's still on the Chancel wall. We found it again this morning - what do you make of that?'

'That's very enterprising of you. How did you manage to pull that off?'

'It's a long story, Steve, but it means there's a definite reason to look at a second motive for his death, doesn't it, and see if anyone actually did interfere with the original investigation?'

'I'll take another look at the good old 'Warks' Constabulary, if you like, and see if anyone's credentials look fishy, but I wouldn't hold me hat on if I were you. They're all pretty kosher. Remember, I've had one nose around already.'

Tony sensed that Steve was being very cagey in his response to the suggestion that he should dig deeper. He wondered if Steve's "one nose around already" comment was an oblique reference to D.I. Southwell's revelation about computer hacking. As far as they knew, Steve was still unaware that they knew of his earlier heading-up of the case. Anything to do with the ex-D.I. was becoming a game of tact, suspicion and economy with the truth.

'I'm certain there was something going on, Steve. Give it another try - yeah?'

'If you say so my son, but I've only got twenty-four in mine, same as you, you know - tarrah.' And with that he rang off.

1.35 pm.

As they finished their lunch, Tony became increasingly impatient. Several e-mails to his phone during the morning, signalled that he was needed back at his office in Essex. China had been losing its competitive edge for some time, as it came under increasing pressure from the Global Carbon Trading Organisation. It was urgent that he prepare the ground to find new sources for production and supply of art materials. The sooner they set off for the Shakespeare Centre the better.

Henley Street was still bustling with tourists, and the Birthplace Centre was only marginally less busy than the day before. Jessica had very mixed feelings about the situation. As she approached the doors to the lecture theatre, she felt herself being overwhelmed by a sense of panic. She entered the room and vividly recalled escaping, in fear of her life, through the crowded streets of Venice, two months earlier. Was she about to confront her would-be attacker? The lecture theatre was pretty-well packed. She looked immediately to the top table and then around the room. Mark Dryden was nowhere to be seen.

'Damn!' said Tony. 'I was really hoping to pass on our suspicions to Southwell. Another day perhaps?'

'Can't have everything,' she said, but was secretly relieved that she wasn't going to be face-to-face with the man who might have killed her best friend, and, given half-a-chance, killed her too. She didn't want to alarm Tony with what she felt, but couldn't conceal her eagerness to leave as quickly as she could, preceding him through the double swing-doors and along the lobby to the stairs.

At the top of the stairs she got the shock of her life. Rushing up two steps at a time was Mark Dryden, who virtually collided with her.

'I do beg your pardon,' he said, and then, as he looked, and looked again, couldn't conceal *his* shock at whom he was addressing. He covered his surprised reaction with some quick thinking. 'You're....you're the young lady who was here yesterday, aren't you?'

'That's right.'

'Did you and your young man find the Italian TV crew?'

'No - no, we didn't.' She tried not to look too interested as she concentrated her thoughts and memories. As she looked into his eyes, an uncomfortable sickness started to well up in her stomach. 'We were told they returned to Italy last week - so no luck.' She averted her gaze and turned her head to where she was sure she would find Tony.

He came up close behind her and offered Dryden his hand.

'Tony Chapman,' he said.

'Mark Dryden, Assistant Archivist,' came the response, as he continued to regain his composure. 'I hear you missed your TV crew, Mr. Chapman. I suppose, after ten days, it would be a long shot to find them still here, would it not?'

'You're right, Mr. Dryden, it really was rather a lot to expect. We weren't surprised to hear that an Italian company was involved, as so many of Shakespeare's works are set over there. You must be very excited at such an important discovery - and right on your doorstep too.'

'You never can predict what is going to turn up, or when, or where, or how.'

'Well, we must be on our way, mustn't we, Jess? Nice to have met you, Mr. Dryden - Good-bye.'

'Good-bye,' said Dryden, 'and good hunting!'

Outside, under the brilliant and remorseless glare of the early afternoon sun, Jessica urged Tony to find somewhere to sit down - preferably in the shade. They found a small café in a busy side-street full of gift-shops and boutiques.

'I thought my legs were going to give way,' she said, sitting at the only free table at the back. 'It was *him*, Tony. It was *him*.'

'How can you be so sure?'

'How many people do you know who say 'would it not?'. It's so mannered and unusual, and I couldn't help noticing when he used the phrase in the Palazzo. It struck me as too proper - do you know what I mean?'

'He'll have recognised you too, you know that, don't you?' He said, in a manner that did little to reassure her. 'Let's have a long cold drink, collect our thoughts and figure out what we ought to do next.'

'You can be a thoughtless bastard at times,' she said, and threw the menu at him.

They checked out of their hotel and made ready for the journey back to Essex. Tony decided not to inform D.I. Southwell of their convictions with regards to Mark Dryden unless he heard that the case was to be reopened. Jessica's identification of Mark added nothing to Alex's case, but it might well add to Bianca's considerably. As it concerned a crime committed in Italy, a call to Commissario Montano might be more in order.

Tony contacted Randy to keep him up to speed, and suggested that perhaps *he* might like to ring Montano, as a call from him would carry more weight than one from the 'English Romantics!'

'That might be taken as twisting an already deeply plunged knife, Tony,' Randy said. 'Angelo called me earlier to say that an off-the-cuff remark I made on Peter and Katie's lunchtime show last week has been spread all over their Tabloids. The Venice Police are furious with me by all accounts, but you give him a call, by all means - anything to speed things up.'

'As soon as I get back, Randy, I will. We're just leaving Stratford. Be sure to give our love to Helena. See you soon.'

As she got into the car, Jessica asked 'Did Mark give you a 'Masonic' handshake?'

'Yes, he did, as a matter of fact,' said Tony, 'I didn't take any notice at the time, but it all ties in, doesn't it?' As he drove out of the hotel car park, he suddenly called out. 'What the hell's wrong with this car? Don't tell me - of all the times to get a puncture!'

He rang the hotel reception to ask if they knew of a tyre repair garage that was open, and to enquire if they could stay one more night, if the worst came to the worst.

'Kwik-Fit Tyres should still be open, Mr. Chapman. They're the nearest - just the other side of the Bus Station, but I'm afraid we're fully booked for tonight,' came the reply.

He changed the wheel as quickly as he could, and made it to the garage just before it closed.

'You need a new tyre, sir.' Said the mechanic. 'This one's got a hole in the wall, and it can't be repaired. Looks like a knife-hole to me.'

'A what?' Said Tony.

'Well you see, sir, if you look at the puncture, there are no marks to suggest that you caught a kerb or anything else. Just a neat slit. Wait there a moment, please, sir.' The mechanic walked round the car. 'I'd better have this other front off an' all - someone has took a dislike either to you or to Audis, by the look of it!'

He was right. It too had a cut in the wall; it was just deflating more slowly than the other. Tony went to see Jessica in the functional and overtly masculine reception area. He had no intention of alarming her with talk of sabotage, telling her that the car would be fixed in a few minutes. He gave her a reassuring kiss and got himself a drink of water from the dispenser.

He strolled back to the tyre-bay entrance and looked around. He felt more vulnerable than ever before in his life. Not only did someone know they were in Stratford, but knew which hotel they were staying at, and knew his car. He was being warned off in a very unpleasant way. He knew exactly how Jessica must have felt on that day back at the end of February, when she couldn't wait to leave Venice quickly enough. Stratford too had become an alien and hostile place.

They left for the three-hour journey home, Tony driving more carefully than usual in the nose-to-tail traffic along the winding road out to the A46. The day had taken its toll on Jessica. She pushed her seat back, reclined it and relaxed. It wasn't long before she was falling asleep. Their investigations were making some headway, but living and working a hundred and fifty miles away added an unwelcome stress. He pressed on along the succession of by-passes through Warwickshire. He thought more and more about the mystery man who had been stalking Alex back in their student days, and wondered if he'd just been talking to him. Or maybe it wasn't him at all, but a Masonic friend of the quietly-spoken man from the Birthplace Centre. Maybe a visit to the Masonic Hall was needed.

The holiday traffic had thinned by the time he swept round the Coventry South-Eastern by-pass and he started to make up for lost time.

An hour into their journey, he prepared to leave the M6 for the A14. Joining the inside lane for the run down the slip-road, an articulated truck up ahead braked severely. Tony did the same. Immediately he was alerted by a buzzer and flashing alarm to say that his brake fluid pressure was virtually non-existent. With his foot now hard on the brake, nothing was happening, and the car seemed to be going faster rather than slower - the truck was getting frighteningly close. He changed down and changed down again. He grabbed for the handbrake and glanced hurriedly at the sleeping Jessica. He yanked at the handbrake with all his might.

'Jess - your seatbelt!' He screamed, and changed down again. There was no hard shoulder, and the outside lane was full. With his tyres screeching and leaving a cloud of blue-white smoke, a wall of truck now filled his vision. His options had run out. He swung the steering wheel to the left, but, as he did so, his off-side front caught the near-side corner of the truck. The metallic green Audi spun, rolled and cart-wheeled down the embankment, finally coming to rest at the bottom, the right way up, in a stream, at the edge of a field.

Tony opened his eyes to the sight of an empty passenger seat and an open passenger door. He had been saved by his air-bag, and hers had deployed, but where was she?

'Jess!' he screamed. 'Jess!' he pushed open his door and climbed out. Squelching through the muddy stream he shouted again, 'Jess! Jess!' But still no answer. He now feared for the worst. A small crowd of onlookers, who had left their vehicles, came running down the bank to offer assistance. The air was rapidly filling with petrol fumes. 'Get away!' yelled Tony. 'It's going to explode!'

35

As Peter and Julia walked into the recovery room adjacent to A & E in the University Hospital in Coventry, Tony was just coming out.

'That's the last time you're seeing my daughter, you careless.... bastard.' Peter virtually never swore, and struggled for a means to express his feelings adequately. 'You don't care what you do, do you? Just so long as you get your own way, and now you've almost killed her....so get out of our way.' He brushed the speechless Tony to one side.

'How is she, Tony?' asked Julia as she passed him, swept along in Peter's wake.

'Pretty shaken, but no bones broken,' he said, adding, 'they want to keep her in overnight - just to be on the safe side.'

'I'll give you "safe side"', snapped an irate Peter, turning back to him as he approached Jessica's bed.

'Daddy, I'm all right - really,' she said, 'I was a bit concussed and I've got a few grazes and bruises, but that's all.'

Her parents overwhelmed her in wave after wave of doting kindnesses. They had already booked one of the Hospital's hotel rooms, to be close to her, and, as she succumbed to their effusiveness, Peter started on a strategy that he hoped would remove Tony from her life.

Tony could only watch from the door and despair. 'You poor, lovely girl,' he thought, 'can't you just ask them to leave you alone so you can get some sleep?' The ward-sister came in, alerted by Peter's angry outburst, and asked him to please be quiet for the sake of the other patients as well as for Jessica. Tony had a lot of sympathy for Peter. He would be retiring in a few years and he knew it was breaking Peter's heart to look on as his daughter gradually inherited the world he had prepared her for. Tony wondered who all the doting was really supposed to benefit. 'Who are you doing it all for, Peter?' he mused.

He walked off down the spotless, echoing corridor and rang D.I. Southwell to see if she had heard from the Fire Service about the cause of the crash. She confirmed his suspicions. A distinct trail of brake-fluid, starting about a hundred and fifty metres back up the slip-road, finishing amid the rubber skid-marks, pointed to an obvious causal link. A Fire Officer had had a close look at the Audi's brake-lines once it was on the recovery vehicle, and a nick, probably made by a pair of pincers, was clearly visible. She added that she would add this information to the evidence she was putting before the Chief Constable in the morning.

Peter and Julia saw to it that Jessica was moved to a private room as soon as was practicable, and ignored Tony completely. He left them and walked away through the colourful and airy reception area to the cafeteria, but was alerted, before he got there, on hearing his name called over the Hospital Radio system. He went back to reception to be met by a representative of a car-hire company sent by his insurance company. He had arrived with a replacement for Tony's written-off Audi Hybrid. Tony went back to find Jessica's private room.

'I'm fine, love, honestly.' she said, 'I feel a bit stiff here and there, but I'm sure they'll let me go home tomorrow. Are you certain you're fit to drive? You still look ever so washed-out.'

'Sure,' he answered, 'the consultant doesn't want me to - delayed concussion and all that - but I'll be fine. Now are you sure *you* feel OK?'

'Sure - and don't go blaming yourself - there was nothing more you could have done.'

'Tyres *and* brakes Jess. Somebody was *very* determined to stop us from investigating these cases any further. I want to know what kind of person could do this to us, but I don't want you to find yourself in any more danger because of me. So...'

'I'll decide that, Tony - OK ?'

'Jess, please.'

'No argument, Tony. Daddy and Mummy are not going to stop me from discovering who killed 'B'. *I* decide all right? You haven't forced me into this, and I'm a big girl! I'm in this because 'B' was my best friend, and I'm certain that, together, if we're careful, we can find who was responsible and find out exactly why they did it.'

'I'm falling in love!' he said, with a huge grin.

'Let me get some rest and I'll see you back home.'

'Hope it's tomorrow - bye,' he said, and, with a kiss, left her in the care of the nurses, and to the devices of her parents.

He still felt a bit shaky, as, to the distant roar of the M6, he searched the huge car-park for his replacement car. If his own car had exploded, as he thought it might, or caught fire even, the outcome could well have been very different. Without her seatbelt on, Jessica had slipped under the airbag, and had been folded up in the foot-well; not thrown out onto the grassy bank as he had assumed. She was fortunate not to have broken legs and a broken back - or worse.

Even though he had no obvious injuries, the paramedics at the scene of the accident, as well as at the Hospital, had advised Tony not to drive for at least twenty-four hours; but, with her parents there, he was only going to be in the way, so getting on the road and back to Essex was probably best.

36

Shortly after he arrived at his office, Tony took a call from Jessica in Coventry to say she hoped to be discharged later that morning and could leave as soon as the duty doctor gave her the all-clear; she should be home by lunchtime.

A little after 2.00pm, his secretary called him in from the warehouse to read an e-mail which she didn't understand. When he saw it, he was horrified. It said quite simply, "Mr. Chapman, you have a very pretty girlfriend." It came with an attachment - a photograph of Jessica. He knew precisely when and where it had been taken; she was sitting at the café table in the Market Square in Stratford. It had been taken two days earlier. He had a feeling of empty nausea. Sweat formed all over him in an instant. He went cold, blood rushing from his head. He sat down, still staring at the screen. He was being targeted through Jessica. To be reassured that she was in no immediate danger, he rang her mobile.

'Hi, Tony. We've just got back.' she said.

'Oh, good; you're OK, then?'

'Yes, of course. I told you the doctors would give me the thumbs up; I'm made of tough stuff! - Darling, are you all right?'

'I'm fine.'

'No you're not. Something's wrong - I can tell from your voice.'

'No, honestly, everything's fine.'

'Stop it Tony. Something *is* wrong. Don't *you* start overprotecting me as well. Tell me what it is.'

'I don't want to upset you. I'll talk to you when I see you this evening.'

'You're frightening me Tony....'

Hearing his daughter in distress, Peter grabbed her mobile-phone.

'Get off the line now, Chapman. Can't you see what you're doing? Jessie is in no state to talk to you; her mother is a nervous wreck, and I'm keeping hold of her phone.' No sooner had he hung up, than the office phone rang. It was Jessica, using the Marston's land-line.

'Tony, tell me what this is all about...' The line went dead. He rang back, but it was engaged. He tried her mobile - it was switched off. He fled from his office and headed for her home in Great Colne, apprehensive as to what he was likely to find.

He turned into their drive and sped noisily across the gravel up to the front porch. Before he was out of his car, Peter was out through the front door.

'Get away from here Tony. You're not seeing her.'

'Don't be stupid, man. She needs me just as much as she needs you.'

'You think you're the be-all and end-all don't you? Just get in your car and go. I mean it.'

'Think about Jess and Julia, Peter. How do you think this'll look to them? Can you imagine how they must feel, hearing us arguing like this?'

'They're more upset than you could possibly imagine,' Peter went on, 'they're genuinely frightened, and its all your doing. What's this new scare, eh? What have you cooked up this time?'

'Let me see her please, Peter; this isn't getting us anywhere.'

Tony headed straight for the front door, but Peter blocked his path, pushing him back with a blow to both shoulders at the same time.

'No!' He insisted.

'For Christ's sake, man, I'm seeing her and that's that!' In a moment, Tony had pushed past him, and was in the hall.

'Jess - it's me,' he called.

Jessica came into the hall from the sitting room. 'What's happening, Tony? I want to know what the hell could have suddenly got you so upset.'

'Really - it's nothing to worry about.'

'Don't bullshit me, Tony,' she shouted, 'I'm an intelligent bloody woman - so don't treat me like an idiot. You were terrified on that phone. Why?'

'Stop that!' ordered Peter, 'I'll not have all that shouting in this house.'

'Shut up, Daddy! Just shut up!' squealed Jessica.

Peter recoiled at the outburst from his bruised and bandaged daughter.

'All right, all right; I'll tell you,' said Tony, 'but I promise you - you're not going to like it.

'Pretend I'm sitting down,' she said, 'go on, tell me.'

'I've received an anonymous e-mail,' he said, and proceeded to tell her about its contents, including the photograph. She stifled a scream, and cupped her hand over her mouth.

'God, Tony, what have we got mixed up in?' she said, and burst into tears.

———

LATER:

'You're a guest in my house, and Jessie's still my daughter, whatever you might think. While she's here, she does what I say, Tony, and you are not welcome if you can't accept it. Make up your mind.'

Tony stood up and finished his coffee. As he considered Peter's ultimatum, he looked out from the garden room across their beautifully designed and maintained garden, to the wooded, gently undulating hills beyond.

'This is all so perfect - and so sad,' he said.

'What *are* you waffling on about?' asked Peter. 'She's safe here.'

'I couldn't hope to make you understand,' he said. 'I'm going to say good-bye to Jess and Julia. So, if you will excuse me?' He went into the kitchen and placed his mug carefully in the dish-washer. Julia had a neatly refolded copy of the day's *Telegraph* on the central island, and was studying the Sudoku on its back page.

'Must be one of the forms heaven takes?' he said.

'I'm sorry, Tony - what's that?'

'Never mind, Julia; I'm off. I'll just go and say cheerio to Jess, OK? Good-bye.'

In the silent, spacious and tastefully furnished sitting room, he found Jessica curled up in a chair-and-a-half. Her left arm was in a sling, and there were support-bandages on her right wrist and elbow and both her knees; she was leafing through an illustrated volume on Venetian Palazzi.

'How are you doing?' he enquired.

'Better all the time,' she answered. 'You?'

'Better all the time,' he said, and they both smiled. 'Butter him up and get your phone back. Ring me once you've got it. I want to be back in Stratford for that Masonic meeting on Thursday evening. Will you be up for it, do you think?'

'I should hope so; anyway, I hope to be rid of some of these bandages and plasters by then. If I can't call you, I could drive over.'

'For God's sake don't drive yet, sweetheart; leave all the driving to me - for now at least.'

'If you say so, boss,' she said.

They kissed; but as Tony prepared to leave, Jessica held onto his arm.

'He's starting to drive me round the bend, darling,' she said. 'He's getting paranoically protective - you must have noticed?'

'I've been waiting for the watchtowers to go up for months!' he said, giving her arm a gentle squeeze. He ran his hand through her hair. 'Time to move away?' he mooted.

'It's been getting progressively worse since going away to Uni, and I'm not sure Mummy has even noticed. It's something we never discuss.'

'What don't we ever discuss?' said Julia, who had entered the sitting room unnoticed, and was standing just inside the door.

Jessica looked at Tony. She took a deep breath, and praying that she wasn't jumping the gun, turned to her mother.

'I want to go with Tony, Mummy,' she quickly looked back at him. He looked down at her, smiled, and nodded his head. 'Please, Mummy, Daddy's suffocating me. You must know it's because I love you both so much that I've got to go.'

Julia crossed the room to where Jessica was sitting and sat on the arm of the oversized armchair. She took hold of Jessica's bandaged hand. 'I've never seen you happier than when you two are together,' Julia said. 'We might not have discussed it, Jessie love, but I've seen this day coming for the last two years or more. It's going to be a nightmare trying to convince your father you're independent of him. Leave it to me though; I'll find the right moment in the next day or two.'

'Mummy, you're a star!' she said.

37

Tony was just getting into his car after saying good-bye to Jessica, when his phone rang.

'Hi, Tony, can you help me out?'

'Eddie, what a surprise! I don't know, it depends what you're after?'

'If I'm going to make something decent out of your 'slabbe' discovery my friend, I need a few more pics, and you're my main man.'

'Sounds interesting, Eddie. When you say 'make something', what have you got in mind? A news item?'

'I'm looking for enough to put a minidoc together, and get it on the news channels. You know - *Sky, Virgin, 24-7* - and hopefully *Newsnight* before the weekend; something to make the 'Bardologists' straighten their backs, Tony! It's a heaven-sent opportunity; too good to miss, and not just because of the four-hundredth and all that crap, either; that page discovery has dumped things right in our laps - it's a chance in a mill'.'

'Who's doing *Newsnight* do you know?'

'The old Doyenne herself, Dame Kirsty - I know her; she thrives on a portion of cultural controversy - she'll lap it up!'

'Precisely what are you looking for from me? I presume you want it all yesterday?'

'Randy's three pages for a start, pal. He's in the States right now; I've just spoken to him, and he's up for it. Personally, I think he wants to give kick-ass to the Commissario!'

'Helena?'

'She's over here to clinch a prime spot for a new retail outlet in Birmingham's Skypoint Tower, and she's fine about it too - ducked out of the Milan trip to sign the papers, I hear.'

'Anything else?'

'Pictures and info' on that Alex pal of yours. You never know, it might help to flush out the bugger who really bumped him off. Oh! And any interesting bits you've got on the Earl of Oxford that I can't pull off the net. I only need ten or fifteen minutes-worth altogether, but it's got to be as visually rich and memorable as we can make it, coz we've only got this one chance - know what I mean?'

As Tony drove away towards Maldon, Eddie continued to enthuse about ideas for his short film. He had a distinct feeling there was a bit more to the request and that Eddie probably had his eyes on a scoop; aiming to get the story onto the front pages in the States, and Europe too, if he could; and why not? If it helped to expose Mark Dryden, and connect him with the two deaths, surely it could only be a good thing? It was so tempting to tell him about Jessica identifying Mark as the man she'd seen and talked to in the Palazzo, but he held back. He didn't want some lawyer rubbing his hands with glee because an all-too-zealous Eddie had inadvertently overstepped the mark.

The aches and pains from being tossed about in his car twenty-four hours earlier were abating and he wasted no time in the run down to Witham on the A12, before taking the tedious twisting lanes to his home on the outskirts of the historic East-coast port.

He pulled into the drive in front of his house, got out , and walked up to the front door. He turned and looked at the car. As he took out his front-door key, he was suddenly overcome with a light-headed, fainting sort of feeling. An irrational fear gripped him and he couldn't move - tears welled up in his eyes. He felt confused and began to sway. 'What the hell's happening?' he thought, and seized the column that supported the porch. Without warning, his knees gave way and he found himself sitting against the front door. He took a few deep breaths and rubbed his face vigorously. 'Bloody hell!' he said, and, after standing up slowly, inserted the key in the lock. 'Of course you're safe here, you damned fool!' he said to himself, turning the key, and going in.

He fixed himself a drink and set to collecting all the imagery which he thought Eddie would find most useful. It only took a few minutes to scan some old holiday photographs of Alex and download some suitable bits of film, but what took rather longer was cobbling together a CV for him. Once he'd e-mailed it, he rang Jessica to check she was all right, assuring her that, once she'd packed all her essentials, he would be over to pick her up in the morning.

38

Commissario Montano was furious that someone in his office could have leaked information to the press. He had stopped at his favourite bar on the corner of San Provolo for his usual latte and brioche, breaking the short walk from his apartment to the Questura. The 'Sundays' had all run a report on the same TV chat-show, screened in England the previous Friday. They had gleefully reported how Randy 'Pop-Idol' Middleton had accused the Venice Police of dragging their heels over the investigation into his daughter's death. It was even said that he (Randy) had information that the investigation was being scaled down. Lies of course, but Commissario Montano's superiors weren't amused at the slur, and wanted him to get things on the move before the whole of the Italian Police Force became an international laughing-stock.

'Flagged up on some Red-Top editor's laptop, I suppose,' he fumed. 'British bloody journalists!' He made the five minute journey to his office in four. Sergeant Stefano was already waiting for him.

'Get me the British Consulate - presto!' He said.

The morning's issue of the *Gazzettino* was on his desk. 'Man in Black Keeps Venice Police in the Dark.' went the headline.

'Very witty,' he mumbled, as Stefano handed him the phone.

'Signor Sheridan, I am coming to see you this morning.....yes, in a few minutes. I leave my office as we speak....Prego.'

The Police launch, carrying the Commissario and his sergeant, sped down the Rio di San Lorenzo into Rio di Laterano and off towards the Grand Canal. It was sweltering for mid-April, the relentless sun beating down on Montano's unprotected and balding pate. He stood for the short journey along Venice's main thoroughfare to Piazzale Roma and his waiting car. As they rushed past it, he didn't give the Palazzo Magretti-Bellini a second glance, now back on the market, and still shrouded by Sr. Zenobi's blue plastic. The Commissario had his mind fixed firmly on the two Consular officials and what sort of story they were probably dreaming up in the twenty minutes grace he'd presented them with.

He was soon striding impatiently between the trees in the modest piazza towards the Consulate with his Sergeant in tow.

'Watch out for these 'Brits', Stefano,' he said, 'they think life's all a game - like their game of creeket.'

Richard Sheridan was waiting for him in the entrance lobby. Dispensing with the formalities, Montano fired the first salvo.

'Firstly I wish to speak to your receptionist, Signore. I presume she is here?'

'Yes, Commissario - Emilia!' It was pretty clear that Montano was out to give them a tough time. His bark was usually far more intimidating than his bite, so the Consul, deferring to the Commissario's urgent manner, went along with him to get the ball rolling.

'Would you like a private interview room, Commissario?' he offered.

'It should not be necessary, grazie.'

Emilia had already been interviewed twice, and her recollection of the events at the end of February remained unchanged.

'He wore a dark suit and white shirt, Commissario. He was tall and quite athletic, very smart with a goatee beard and what looked like designer glasses.' She was describing the man she only knew as George Drummond, who breezed in and out one morning during carnival week, two months earlier.

'Thank you, Signorina. I say to you again, any detail you recall, no matter how insignificant it may appear to you, ring Commissario Montano. Si?'

'Si, Commissario, yes, I will,' said the receptionist, and went back to her desk.

'Signor Harvey, he is here today - yes?' Montano continued.

'Yes - Emilia, call Bill and ask him to come through, would you?'

A couple of minutes passed before he appeared - the Commissario was not amused at being made to wait.

'I will speak to him alone, Signor Consul. You have a room, you say?'

He ushered a slightly bemused Bill Harvey into the vacant room. Montano's pride, and possibly his last promotion, were at stake over the high-profile case. Murders were so rare in Venice that Bianca's death had attracted a huge amount of media interest - and, of course, she had been very pretty. Not only did the whole of the Polizia Veneziano want a result urgently, but so did the Carabinieri and the Vigili Urbani. All eyes were on the Commissario, and he was beginning to show the pressure. Bill knew from his attitude he meant business. Montano asked him to sit down - which he did.

Montano took a handkerchief from his top pocket, refolded carefully, and mopped his brow. He looked across at the nervous Bill, and began to pace slowly round the room. 'You are most fortunate Signor Harvey, to have a job where you can take your time. It is a luxury I do not have.' He returned the handkerchief to his jacket pocket and turned quickly to the seated diplomat. 'In our last conversation you denied seeing this... 'George Drummond'. Do you still deny seeing him?'

'Yes, I do,' he said.

'So you are quite happy to call one of your fellow employees a liar, signor, and yet still greet her every day with a smile?'

'That's a bit strong, Montano old chap, now come on....'

'It's Commissario to you - *Mister* Harvey - and I do not "come on" for you or anyone else!' He snapped. 'You may use your Public School manner on each other as much as you like - "old chap" - but it does not wash with me. Now, our 'Mr. Drummond' had an identity card. It must have been so good that it would have fooled

267

Mr. Middleton - an intelligent and successful businessman. If that card had been brought from England, he would have no reason to visit this Consulate - which is where I believe he obtained it. You see Mr. Harvey, I believe the young receptionist - not you.'

'Now steady on Commiss….'

'No! *You* steady on, Signor. You are in charge of security, si? And is your responsibility to issue the security pass, is it not?'

'It is.'

'And just where do you keep the blank passes, Signor?'

'In a drawer in my office.'

'Not locked in a safe? Ha! Show me - now.'

'If you'll follow me Commissario.'

Bill stood up, scraping his chair backwards across the cheaply-tiled floor as he did so, and showed the Commissario and his Sergeant to the door. In the corridor and next to Reception, Montano pointed up at the CCTV camera.

'How many cameras are there between the entrance and your office?'

'Two, Commissario. This one and one in the lobby downstairs.'

'And on the day of 'Mr. Drummond's' visit; they were both working?'

'Only the one downstairs if my memory serves me correctly.'

'Oh! How very convenient. The camera which would have filmed him against the light as he arrived works; but the one which would capture his face clearly does not. When he left, did the camera in the entrance lobby reveal his image, or did it miraculously "not work" also?'

'I'll have to check.'

'Whose responsibility are they Signor?'

'Mine.' answered an embarrassed Bill.

'Even more convenient!' laughed the detective. 'Your office, please.'

After showing the Commissario and Sergeant Stefano in, Bill followed and went straight for his desk. Montano told him to stop.

'No, Commissario, you will not order me about in here. This is a Consulate, and I have diplomatic immunity.'

'You are not immune from the laws of the Italian State while you are here, Signor. I have here a warrant to search this, and any other office I need to in order to pursue my investigations. I am sure you will not obstruct the Polizia Veneziano in their work?' Bill was speechless. Montano indicated to his sergeant to go through the drawers of Bill's desk.

Starting at the bottom, the sergeant began his search.

'Not even locked!' said Montano, 'No wonder you British lost your whole Empire!'

Within moments, Sergeant Stefano held not only blank security passes in his hand, but a collection of security tapes and DVDs. Before he could express his dismay, however, the Commissario was interrupted by the sudden arrival of the Consul.

'What is it Bill? - and what's all this about, Montano?'

'At a guess, I'd say - incriminating evidence, Signor Sheridan.'

'Put it back immediately,' he said, 'you have no right whatsoever to remove anything from that desk, this office or from this building. This is British Government property, and I want you to leave - both of you, Commissario.'

'No, Signor. I will not. Not unless you wish to have a diplomatic incident on your hands. You see, I believe you two gentlemen are in, what I think you English call cahoots.' He took out his telefonino and started to dial. 'First I call my friend the British Ambassador in Rome, and then my colleague in Scotland Yard who deals with matters Italian, as I am sure they will...'

'Hold it right there Commissario. I'm sure we can....'

'Come to some arrangement - pooh!' He carried on pressing the keys.

'For God's sake, Montano!'

The Commissario stopped. A smile lit up his face as he looked at the two terrified officials.

'If what I think is on one, or perhaps two, of those tapes or discs, signores,' he said, 'then you fine gentlemen are going to have a lot of explaining to do and I may find myself arresting you as accessories to murder.'

'Now that's going too far,' said Sheridan, 'You can hardly blame me for having any part in the palazzo robbery, or the death of Bianca Middleton. I've done everything in my power to assist you.'

'Not everything, Signor Honorary Consul: perhaps the silent Mr. Harvey would like to add something?'

'I'm sorry Dickey,' he began, 'it all started with a call from the FCO in London. I can't say who, you realise, confidence and all that. I was assured that it would save a lot of embarrassment to HMG if I could assist someone to gain entry to the Magretti-Bellini. No name, just that he was coming out the following day, and er - say no more. That's all.'

'Not quite all signor Harvey. You have lied to me to save your skin, kept your secret with your "someone" in London, and possibly aided the escape from my country of a murderer.' He took the tapes and discs from Stefano, and waved them at the officials. 'Let us see what is on these.'

It wasn't long before they were watching the relevant films on Bill's computer. There, in his minimal, though very effective, disguise, was Dryden, running up the stairs, two steps at a time.

'Well, well, Mr. Drummond, or whoever you are, now I see you. As your receptionist said gentlemen - "fit and athletic-looking." He is fit, you must agree?'

'What the hell did you think you were doing, Bill?'

'How was I to know, Dickey - it was nothing - doing a chap a favour. You know the sort of thing?'

'You're a bloody fool, man - and with a media A-lister like Middleton, too! What the devil must have been going through your mind - nothing, I shouldn't wonder?'

'I wasn't to know all that was going to happen, was I? Anyway, we still don't know if he had anything to do with the girl's death, do we?'

'Pigs might fly, Bill. Pigs might fly. Well, there's no point in crying over spilt whisky, as my dad used to say. We've just got to find ourselves a way to avoid being hung out to dry once this lot hits the net.'

'Perhaps we can do each other a favour Signores.' Said Montano. 'I want some good news for my superiors - presto. For the morale of my men, I want to quieten the media. That security disc is essential for me to do this. Let us just say that it arrived 'mysteriously' on my desk - si? In an unmarked envelope, perhaps. Mr. Harvey, you will have to explain how it managed to 'escape' from your system. That is your problem, but it might just save both of your jobs - and your necks! - Well?'

The consular officials looked at each other.

'Give us two minutes, Commissario,' said Sheridan, and the two men went into a huddle over by the window.

'He's forcing us to do things the 'Italian' way, Dickey,' said Bill, 'and it doesn't look as if there's much option but to go along with him.'

'Maybe, but there might just be some wiggle room. We have to make sure no-one can source that disc directly to either of us.'

'Why don't I make a copy?' suggested Bill. 'We can keep the original, and let Montano have the copy. I can claim to have been doing a regular service on the system, and misfiled some tapes and discs. I can still claim never to have seen 'Drummond' He could have come in when I was out of the office - snooped around - found himself an ID blank, and slipped back out unnoticed. It'll keep my London source happy, too. How about it?'

'I need an answer gentlemen.' called Montano.

'I can't let this disc out of the building,' said Sheridan, 'but what I'm prepared to do is this - with your kind co-operation, of course.' He explained their plan, and awaited the Commissario's response.

'Make the copy now. Stefano - you are deaf, blind - and dumb!'

'Si, Commissario.'

Twenty-five minutes later, Commissario Montano and his sergeant were at his desk, on the third floor of the Questura, going through the airport security films. It wasn't long before they had a match to 'Tom Underhill', caught on camera at the departures desk, but not traced in England after his arrival at Bristol International. Simple enhancement techniques proved it could be none of their other few remaining suspects. He e-mailed his findings to Avon and Somerset Constabulary, and asked if they would waste no time in identifying his suspect after his arrival in the UK.

39

Sergeant Bedford slowly raised his head, and looked up the stairwell. Two to go, he thought, and continued his slog up to the Incident Room on the second floor. The box of security discs and tapes he was carrying wasn't particularly heavy, but he was. The journey down to the evidence store in the lower basement, and then all the way back up again, was getting too much for the sixty year-old.

As soon as he was at the top, he kicked open the Incident Room door with a resigned showiness and stormed in. Trying in vain to conceal the obvious signs of exhaustion written all over his red and puffy face, he dumped the box noisily onto the nearest desk.

'Where are you, Marchie, you little geek?' he yelled.

'Here, Sarge,' answered the rookie detective constable from the opposite corner of the room.

'And it's Sergeant to you, you geeky little toe-rag. Now get you arse over here and grab hold of this box of goodies - come on, shift yerself.'

'Yes, Sergeant,' he replied.

D.C. Aaron March, fresh out of the Police Training College, was still not wholly certain that the macho world of the police was for him. He was keen to put his considerable computer knowledge to practical use, and since signing up with Avon and Somerset Constabulary, had found several opportunities to make good use of what he believed were two of his best assets - dogged persistence and infinite patience.

His immediate superiors, most of whom were unlikely to rise any further in the force, enjoyed making his life a misery, so he was never happier than when left alone with his computer. As a result, he was quite philosophical about being ordered around by the boorish sergeant. He picked up the grey plastic storage box and walked smartly back across the large open office space to his work-station, followed at a distance by the sweaty, puffing bulk of Sergeant Bedford.

'In their infinite wisdom,' said Bedford, 'the powers about two rungs down from God have asked us - I lie, told us - to get a result from this box of crap. Look upon this as your lucky day, Marchie, my boffy little friend, for we may all be able to bathe in *your* glory. As the chosen one, you get to search through all the security discs and tapes herein!'

He banged his podgy fist affirmatively on the lid of the box, splitting it open in the process. He then pushed the young constable to one side, and commandeered his chair.

'And somewhere in here,' he said, condescendingly, 'we should find some happy holiday snaps from our friends in Italy - wherever the fuck they are.'

'Have you got a name, or a date, I can enter, Sergeant?'

Bedford's hands hovered above the keyboard, his fingers moving slowly as if playing a silent tune on an invisible piano. He stared at the screen with an expression of loss, bordering on fear. He struggled out of the chair, and squeezed his way out of the work-station. 'Stick 'Commissario Montano,' 'Venice' and 'Underhill' on your blasted screen, and see what you get,' he gushed, and shuffled off, bumping into everyone's desk and work-station as he went. Without turning round, he called back. 'You've got twenty-four hours to come up with a match.'

From the tone of Commissario Montano's e-mail, Aaron March realised that D.S. Bedford had been playing down the importance of the task. He was well aware that he was now dealing with one of the most high-profile crimes of the year, and wondered if professional pride was at the root of his sergeant's dismissive attitude. Checking through all the file dates, he noticed that it was D.S. Bedford who had been given the job of searching the City-Centre CCTV films for evidence of the elusive 'Tom Underhill' back in February.

A routine check of Bristol International's database confirmed a false address for the passenger arriving from Venice. Bedford had drawn a complete blank, and clearly had no intention of going through the hours and hours of fuzzy night-time films all over again.

Aaron started with the airport films, and watched as 'Tom Underhill' walked briskly through the baggage reclaim hall; picked him up again going through departures, and saw him finally, as he hailed his taxi for the twenty minute run into the city centre. He read through Sgt. Bedford's interview with the taxi driver, who had remarked how odd it was for a passenger to be dropped off at Temple Meads Station so late at night. "There were no more trains arriving or departing at that late an hour on a Friday," he had said. "Maybe he had arranged for someone to pick him up."

The constable spent the next couple of hours patiently sifting through the variously formatted films, keeping a keen eye on the time shown in the bottom corner of each one. In Bristol City Centre, even after midnight, there were still hundreds of people wandering the streets, going from bar to bar, club to club. He could see why Bedford had got nowhere. However, not very many of those out on a Friday night carried bags, and he concentrated his efforts on them.

After a long and frustrating search, he noticed a man with a bag, similar in build to 'Tom Underhill' getting into a car at the far end of the Watershed Car Park. At first he discounted him as suspect, as he had no beard or glasses, unlike the passenger at both Venice and Bristol Airports. He also thought the man arrived there too soon after the taxi-driver had dropped off his customer at the top of the station concourse. But when he followed the short route, through Queen Square and across Pero's Bridge to the Waterside, he found his man almost running towards the car park on three separate cameras. With the bit now firmly between his teeth, Aaron concentrated on the moment the car pulled out of its bay in the underground car park. Just as it did so, the film came to an end. He rewound the last few seconds, and replayed them frame by frame. On the final two frames could be seen the blurred registration plate. 'Gotcha!' He said. He downloaded the images, and using an American Military Image Enhancement programme, which his employers knew nothing about, soon had a clear copy of the registration plate in front of him. A few clicks later, and the DVLA computer had delivered the owner's name and address.

'Shit!' He whispered to himself. As the registered owner's name was neither Underhill nor Drummond, but Dryden, he thought that he'd followed the wrong man. He looked up at the clock. 7.30. He'd been on his computer for more than five hours without even realising it. The Incident Room was deserted but for a solitary cleaner, sweeping away lethargically at the far end, lit by the last moments of a brilliant orange, setting sun. He walked over to the drinks machine, got himself a cup of coffee, and went back to his computer. He studied all the films from Temple Meads to the Watershed and its car park again and again, but nothing seemed to shed any fresh light on the mysterious traveller. With no credit card transaction for payment, and no clear image of his face as his car exited, Aaron was left with his first conviction that the Venice police's suspect was none other than Mark Dryden. He checked the address, and seeing a GL postcode, thought he might be a fairly local man; but a closer inspection revealed Stretton-on-Fosse to be not a Gloucestershire address but a Warwickshire one.

He typed up his report to the Commissario in Venice, adding that he should contact Warwickshire Police, as the address of his suspect did not come under Avon and Somerset's jurisdiction.

'A couple of clicks and this'll be at the Questura,' he thought. He stood, arched his back and exercised his stiffened neck. He bent over his desk, about to send the file, when he stopped for a moment to consider who his immediate superior was. Without hesitation, he saved the file and logged off, hoping he wouldn't live to regret it.

APRIL 19th: TUES: 8.10 am.

'Shouldn't you be searching for the "Midnight Cowboy", Marchie?' called Sergeant Bedford, mockingly, from the far side of the Incident Room.

'It's on your computer - with my report, Sergeant,' came the reply.

'Christ almighty! Don't they sleep in your bloody family?' He pulled up the results of the constable's investigation on his monitor, and printed it off, complete with the advice to Commissario Montano. 'Remind me to stick a gold star and a smiley-face in the front of your exercise-book,' he said. Having been so consummately upstaged by the youngster, Bedford was now out to save face by any means at his disposal. 'I fuckin' hope you haven't sent this,' he said.

'I thought that was your responsibility Sergeant.'

'You thought! You thought! You cheeky little sod. You're here to do what *I* tell you to do, and leave the thinking to me - is that understood?

'Yes Sergeant,' he replied.

Bedford had no intention of letting his superiors know how inept he had been back in February, so he chose to sit on the information for a couple of days in order to give himself time to contrive a story about how arduous the search for the suspect had been, and how Aaron March wasn't as clever as he thought he was. He also had no intention of being told what to do by an Italian policeman. 'I'm not having some spaghetti-eater tell me to "waste no time in identifying his suspect", he thought, and waited until the following day before he cleared the results with his D.I, and then e-mailed the file later the same evening; late enough he hoped, to miss the Commissario.

40

Harry Gower gave D.I.Southwell a week to see if she could tie up all the loose ends in the Alex Paris case and make an arrest. Her first priority was to talk to Steve Watson, something she certainly didn't want to do back in 2010.

The only phone numbers she had for him were either unavailable or discontinued. She knew he must have a car registered to him, and used the DVLA to find his address. She remembered Tony mentioning Chelmsford, and guessed, quite rightly, that there weren't many S. Watsons to choose from. She was soon dialling his ex-directory number.

'Hello.'

'Steve Watson, ex-D.C.I. Steve Watson?'

'The same.'

'D.I. Southwell, Warwickshire CID.'

'Lizzie! Hello, gorgeous! And how are the best tits in the Midlands? I hope you're still looking after them!'

'I'd prefer to do things the easy way, Steve, if we can.'

'OK, OK, keep your knees together, girl, Steve Dubya isn't gonna eat you - mind you…'

'Fuck off, Steve. This is business.'

She came straight to the point.

'The Alex Paris case: who got you transferred from Brum?'

'No idea, my love. Ask me another.'

'Come on, Steve, was there a handshake in it - a backhander of some kind? The case is re-opened man, so don't lie to me or I'll pull you in.'

'You can pull *me* in any time you like my lovely, but I still can't

278

help you. An anonymous letter on my desk one morning. Say no more.'

'That investigation ground to a halt in two or three weeks after you arrived and took it over. Were you given a only short period to wrap it up, or is there something else I don't know?'

'Look, luvvy, Tony Lodge was getting past it, and tripping over his Zimmer. They wanted someone who could drive it along and get a result. Now stop being so bloody suspicious. Some fuckin' druggies got that student - pure and simple. You want answers? - Look east, Lizzie my love. Look east.'

'You haven't heard the last of this one.'

'Hey! Sports club changing room - always a thrill!'

'Bastard!' she replied, and hung up.

Steve was livid that someone who had once been his subordinate could challenge him like that - especially a woman! He knew the two deaths were linked; the question was, how could he be absolutely certain nothing would stick to him - that he wasn't implicated? If he could find out who the killer was before 'Lovely Lizzie' he should be in the clear. When a call to 'BJ' didn't provide any leads, he used his trusty press contact.

'Baz you old tart, and before you ask - even better still... Yeah, yeah, the Essex tossers are still on board - it's like watching puppy-idol! Now, business - that bent D.S. in Avon and Somerset who owes us one, you know, the clapped-out old van?...Bedford, that's him. This is his big chance to go global for fifteen minutes. Get on to him and see if he knows if they're likely to collar the 'Middleton Murderer' this side of my Summer holidays...What do you mean they already have?....When?...Yesterday! Jesus Christ...Who is it? - Don't fuck me around - just tell me?.... Thanks, mate - I owe you one.'

41

Dryden was in his office when his mobile rang.

Steve had never met Mark Dryden, but knew of him from the investigations he'd made into Alex's death. The ex-D.I. needed to get things straight with him before the news from Bristol found its way to Lizzie Southwell and she got to interview him. He still had Dryden's mobile number and gave it a try.

'Dryden,' said Mark.

'Steve Watson. We never met back in 2-10, but I remember you all right.'

'2-10?'

'Cut the crap Dryden, it was me what saved you from all that Alex Paris shit. Lodge would have had your balls if I hadn't been there in time with the Cavalry.'

'Oh, *that* Steve Watson - well, what do you want with me now?'

'Yes *that* Steve Watson - and don't come the innocent routine either. It's you what's opened up the black hole so big it's already sucked half the known universe up your arse, so, before the other half goes the same way, when Detective Inspector Lizzie Southwell comes banging on your front-one, you make sure you keep everything bottled, or I'll be banging on it - and a fucking hell-of-a-lot harder and louder than her.'

'Who the hell do you think you are to threaten me?'

'I'll tell you exactly who I am. This could well be your last peaceful night on planet Earth. If one word from you collars me, you're going to need a seventh frigging continent to hide from me, coz I'm the best Dryden, and I'll find you - make no mistake.

Nowhere'll be safe from Steve Dubya.'

'What's suddenly brought this on - Paris was buried nearly six years ago?'

'It's not six years ago that should have you bricking it, Dryden; it's Carnival time 2016 your little grey-ones should be linking up for. You see, a mate of mine tells me that the boys in Venice have got the names - Underhill, Drummond and Dryden all lined up like three pretty maids, and are just about to e-mail everything they've got to 'Lovely-Lizzie' in your Warwickshire CID. - Now tell me you're still as relaxed as when you were tucking into your Corn Flakes this morning?'

'All right. All right. I've got the message,' he replied. 'Whatever they start asking me, I'll keep your name out of it. You'll be safe - now, please, just get off my back.' He then added that he now needed time to himself to plan his next move; a job he could do best if he knew he wasn't going to be hassled any further.

He hurriedly finished off the last of the day's essentials, tidied his desk, and went into the main office.

'Sorry for the short notice, Katie, but something's come up that's going to keep me busy for the rest of the day. I'm going to be off-limits - OK? See you tomorrow.'

42

D.I. Southwell decided to pay the Shakespeare Centre a visit. With the Inscription Stone fragments safely wrapped up and in a secure evidence locker in Warwick, she and her sergeant made their way to Stratford-upon-Avon and the red-brick building at the northern end of Henley Street.

It was late morning and there was still plenty of interest in the newly discovered manuscript. They went up to the first-floor offices. A good crowd filled the lobby and a continuous stream of visitors was entering and leaving the lecture theatre.

They entered the main office and addressed the receptionist.

'I'm Detective Inspector Southwell, and this is Sergeant Heywood. Could we have a word with the most senior person present, please?'

'Certainly, Inspector, I'll get the Director. He's in the Lecture Theatre - just give me a moment.'

Southwell apologised to the Director for arriving unannounced and explained how she wished to remove any suspicion that there might be a link between the Trust and much-publicised events in Venice earlier in the year. Also, that she wanted to tie up a few loose ends in the matter of Alexander Paris from five-and-a-half years ago.

The Director gave her free access to the relevant departments to check employee records. At least six males fitted roughly the description of the intruder at the Palazzo given to her by Jessica - Dryden amongst them. When it appeared that he was absent on the 25th and 26th of February, and wasn't in his office today either, she asked to see Katie.

While they were waiting, the Inspector rang her Headquarters, and asked them to check International flight departures and arrivals. It transpired that no-one called Mark Dryden had flown in or out of the UK around the last weekend in February, or used rail or ferry links. As far as they could ascertain, his car hadn't left the country, and neither had he.

Katie came into the office. She and the CID Officer were about the same age and build, and viewed each other somewhat competitively. D.I. Southwell displayed a powerful, no-nonsense presence, and Katie couldn't help but view her as an intruder rather than as a guest, albeit an uninvited one. She pulled a secretarial chair towards her desk, making sure it was left facing the window. She walked round to the window-side of the modest and functional desk and, leaving her laptop open, sat down and invited the Inspector to do the same - which she did.

'Miss Lancaster, Mr. Dryden is usually here on Thursdays, but, according to your records, not on the last Thursday in February.'

Katie cast her mind back to the cold winter's day and thought for a moment. She didn't answer immediately but keyed a few words into her laptop. Still looking at the screen, she replied. 'That's right, Inspector; he came in first thing, but clearly wasn't himself. I told him to go home, have a whisky and hot lemon, and to keep himself warm. There was a nasty bug doing the rounds at the time. Why do you ask?'

'His office is empty, I see. Isn't he usually here on Wednesdays?'

'You've only just missed him. He's out on business, and I can't be sure he'll be back today. Is there any particular reason for seeing him personally, or may I help?'

'Just eliminating him from our enquiries, Miss. Nothing to trouble yourself with.'

It wasn't long before they had eliminated the other employees on whom suspicion might have fallen. Southwell switched her questioning to the 'Providential Discovery'.

'I have heard some doubts raised about the genuineness of the manuscript and its discovery which filled the papers last weekend. I have to admit, Miss Lancaster, that if I were a cynic, I would say that the find was too good to be true. What is your response to such a suggestion?'

'I was there when it was found, Inspector. I was amazed - as were we all. I don't doubt the genuineness of the find for a moment.'

'Exactly what happened - take me through it?'

'The RAI television crew came up, and I showed them into the Lecture Theatre. We had arranged for them to see some original documents.'

'Who selected them?'

'The Senior Archivist and myself. All our best books, letters, manuscripts and whatever were to go on show. They were with the conservators, getting them prepared for the 'Gala' exhibition. To be quite honest, we had little of any real value left to make their trip worthwhile - but - as it happens!'

'The old book in question had been here for some time, I'm told.'

'That's right. It was in an archive collected over fifty or sixty years, and bequeathed to us by a late Trust member. His widow apologised for the state of it, as it had been left in a leaky garden shed. It was in an assortment of boxes and in an appalling state. Little would have been of much use to us, even if it had been in perfect condition. With all the preparations for the 'Four-hundredth', it was put to one side soon after it arrived in mid-February.'

'Whose responsibility?'

'Mine. I'm in charge of the Records Office and the security of all the books and documents held here.'

'"Put to one side," you say. So objects of possibly great value can be left lying around for weeks - or even months - where any member of the general public can interfere with them - steal them even - and it's all your responsibility?'

'Well put that way, Inspector....'

'That's the only way *to* put it, Miss Lancaster. I think your security procedures need reviewing - don't you?'

Katie found herself on the defensive. What had started off as a friendly chat about staff attendance had turned into an attack on her credibility. Her hackles were up and she mounted a defence.

'I had a cursory look through the bequest shortly after it was delivered. It was in locked rooms virtually all the time it was here; and, in my experience, strangers do not wander about the Centre. You are free to check any of our CCTV tapes at any time - perhaps you'd like to make a start this afternoon? I can arrange things for you right now - it's no trouble.'

'You are telling me, then,' responded Southwell, 'that no-one, at any time since the Trust acquired them, could have interfered with any of the boxes or files of documents in question?'

'Extremely unlikely - but not definitely.' she answered.

'That's all I wanted to know. Thank you, Miss Lancaster.' The Inspector had regained the upper hand and decided to drive home her advantage. 'Experts verified the find too? They didn't question its veracity?'

'I really think you should address these sort of questions to the Director or other senior staff. They are better qualified to answer them than I am. It was a member of the visiting Italian TV crew who spotted the sheet. Someone had used the folded sheet as a bookmarker, perhaps a hundred, perhaps even two hundred, years ago.' Katie was really on the defensive now, but against her better judgements, pressed on. 'Unlike you, Inspector, I don't see anything as suspicious. As I said before, I was present throughout the time they were here. You think it was planted, or brought from Italy by one of the TV crew don't you? As part of some elaborate hoax - well, it couldn't have been. Anyway, the most highly qualified expert in the country was here to see it. She confirmed that the manuscript must have been between those book pages for at least a hundred years.'

The Inspector had Katie on the run. She said nothing for fifteen, maybe twenty seconds - they could have been hours. She shifted the centre of questioning again.

'How long have you worked here?'

'Eight years - a little more, maybe.'

'Do you remember being pestered by a research student about five or six years ago. Alex something?'

'Yes I do. A very likeable young man, rather good-looking too; but he made such a nuisance of himself, and outstayed his welcome. It was all most unfortunate. He was killed in a fight over drugs or something like that - I think his body was found down by the weir. I don't remember all the details.'

'Did he upset anyone here?'

'Not especially, as far as I remember.'

'You said that you've worked here for eight years or so. Have very many of the staff done the same?'

'Quite a few, yes. Let me think - Mr. Bedingfield, Ms. Whetstone, Mr. Elviden, Mr. Dryden; quite a few. People like to stay, Inspector. They love their work here. We're like a family - Shakespeare's family!'

'I would like you to do one last thing, if you would? Send me a list of the long-serving members of your 'family' - here's my card. You can e-mail them direct to my office.'

She thanked Katie for being so co-operative, and left through the airless and claustrophobic lobby.

Downstairs and outside, amidst the visitor and tourist hubbub, the two detectives wove and negotiated their way through representatives of the five Continents to a quiet spot near their waiting car.

'Well, Tom, what did you make of that?'

'Would you like some ointment for those scratches in your eyes Ma'am?' he offered.

She looked up at him out of the corner of her eye, and smiled.

'Not very different from what I expected, Boss. Polite, professional, open. Fought her corner when you put the pressure on - nice to see! Good middle-class stuff, I'd say - solid and reliable.'

'Any suspects?'

'Couldn't say, Boss. Three, maybe four, guys in the frame, but,

I mean, they're hardly killers, are they?'

'How do you know, Tom, how do you know - have you met many killers lately?' she asked.

A minute later they were in the car, heading off to the southern border of Warwickshire. She felt it looked less likely that Dryden was involved in the recent crimes in Italy, but that was for the Venice Police to sort out. She was interested to hear what he recalled about the events of six years earlier.

Tom drove them out along the Shipston Road, and through a succession of unremarkable villages, until they reached a roundabout at the Fosse Way. He turned right.

'Archivists and the like always make the most of even the smallest discovery, Boss; so it seems incredible to me that, if someone at the Shakespeare Centre *was* in on it, that news of the original Inscription Stone turning up six years ago should have been kept quiet until now.'

'Only if someone had a damned good reason for keeping quiet about it, Tom; and I'd like to know if Mark Dryden, Esquire, has got anything interesting to say for himself.'

The Satnav brought them to the entrance to the lane leading down to Dryden's farmhouse. They bumped their way for nearly half-a-mile until the buildings came into view.

'Do you think he's the "Italian-looking guy" Chapman told us about, Boss? The one who gave Alex Paris such a hard ride.'

'We might be just about to find out, Tom. I think that's him.'

Living in such a remote place in the arable landscape, Dryden received few visitors, so was more than a little surprised to see a police car approaching his house. John had rightly warned him that the police were possibly onto him but he was taken-aback at the suddenness of their unannounced arrival.

Tom pulled up next to his car so as not to block the way out. He didn't want to make it look as though they were already treating him as a suspect and a prisoner in his own home. They noticed that he was putting an overnight bag into the boot of his car.

'Off on holiday, Mr. Dryden?' asked D.I. Southwell, stepping from the police car.

'Just a short business trip, Officer. May I ask the reason for your visit?'

'We would like to clear up a few points concerning a Mr. Alexander Paris,' she said, offering her Warrant Card. 'He died in Stratford in the summer of 2010. Perhaps you remember him?'

'Ah. The research student who fell foul of the Stratford drug-scene. I do remember him. Have you caught whoever did it?'

'No, Sir. No such luck. However, some new evidence has come to light, and the case is being re-opened. Which is why we are here.'

Dryden started to move towards the house, and, as he removed his sunglasses, wondered what could possibly have been unearthed to bring the CID all the way out here.

'I can't be too long,' he said, 'but shall we talk inside, out of this heat?'

He opened the kitchen door and showed the officers in. A freshly killed and partially devoured rabbit was in pride of place in the middle of the floor. 'Oh, dear!' he said, 'they're so quick and so efficient. It's a wonder there's any wildlife left around here.' He removed the carcass, and threw it into some long grass, well away from the house, and came back in. He was furious with himself for not foreseeing what now seemed so obvious. To be unprepared for the police turning up was quite unforgivable. How he wished he'd got his story sorted with Harry Gower straight away, instead of waiting till the Thursday-night Lodge meeting. He got on with washing his hands but didn't betray his feelings, remaining calm, and relaxed.

'Tell me what you remember about Alex Paris, Mr. Dryden.'

'He was very persistent…Detective….'

'Detective Inspector Southwell, and this is Sergeant Heywood.'

'Well, Inspector, I remember, at the time, wishing that we had more researchers with his dedication and enthusiasm. His impatience had the better of him, though, and he refused to go through the formal channels in 'pursuing his lines of enquiry,' as you yourselves might put it.'

'This is off the record, Sir, but D.I. Lodge had a word with you a couple of times, didn't he?'

'Yes. That's right. He said that somebody had come to him with the theory of a 'Shakespeare' motive for the young man's death. It all seemed pretty far-fetched, but I could see he was serious. If you're investigating a crime committed in Stratford, Inspector, and you think there's a link to the Bard, I suppose the obvious place to start asking questions is the Shakespeare Centre.'

'And did you ever meet Mr. Paris outside the Shakespeare Centre?'

'No, never.'

'So he never talked to you about his research?'

'No.'

'Do you know of, or have you ever heard of, a confidential file of information which questions the authorship of Shakespeare's Works?'

'Good heavens, no! Is that what Inspector Lodge was on about? If it was, Inspector, then that student certainly had a lively imagination. At the "Centre" we deal with the gathering of facts and making them available to the public. We do not speculate or hypothesise, and we leave the "Heretics" to their own fun and games!'

'Changing the subject; I believe you were part of the selection process for choosing the items filmed by the RAI TV crew.'

'No. That was my colleague, the Senior Archivist. He rustled together a few scraps with Katie. You should really address your questions to her you know; she knows almost everything there is to know about the 'Centre."

Having failed to trip him up with her question, she watched for his reaction closely as she responded. 'We've just come from speaking to her, and she proved most helpful.'

He didn't bat an eyelid.

'Well, Sir. We mustn't keep you from your trip. I'm sure we'll speak again.'

The Officers got up from their bar-stools and made for the door. Thanking him for his time, they said they hoped his cats wouldn't fill his house with dead rabbits while he was away, and that his trip would be successful. As she was about to get into the car, Southwell turned to him and asked.

'Oh! One other thing, Sir. You haven't been abroad in the past few months have you?'

'No I haven't. Why do you ask?'

'No reason, Sir. Safe trip.'

As the detectives drove away, he busied himself at the back of his car knowing that they would be watching him in their mirrors.

'Well like a good servant, I guess you had to do the bidding of your masters,' he thought. 'What a dutiful pussy you are you are, what a dutiful pussy you are! But please, don't be so condescending that you think you can play your mind-games with me and win.'

Once they were out of sight, he removed his overnight bag, and, after a quick check to make sure there were no helicopters or drones around, took it to one of the farm-buildings which he used as a garage. After loading his classic nineteen-seventies Alfa Romeo, he drove it out of the garage and replaced it with his Saab. He then left for the mile-long drive across the farm tracks to join the main road. This, he hoped, should avoid the police if they had staked out the regular route to the farmhouse - the only route shown on Satnav or maps.

Dryden's intention was to lie low and keep well out of sight until he'd fulfilled his duty at the Gala opening. The only time he thought he might be at risk before then was in attending the Masonic meeting on Thursday evening. He had no choice but to attend, in order to corroborate his version of events with Harry Gower. It was going to be risky, but a chance he had to take.

43

Tom Heywood ran from the Incident Room, and along the corridor to D.I. Southwell's office. 'Check your e-mails, Boss,' he said, 'are you in for a big surprise?'

She had only just arrived at the station and her Sergeant's enthusiasm was bubbling over like a milk-saucepan left on the heat.

'The one from Italy, Ma'am,' he added, 'look whose name is on it.'

'Well, well, well, Mr. Dryden, you have been a busy boy, and telling porkies to auntie Lizzie too. That'll never do. Maybe 'Essex Boy' and 'Essex Girl' were right after all, Tom. This Montano guy has really had his cage rattled hasn't he? - He even talks about opening extradition proceedings.'

'What do you want to bet this is all because of Randy Middleton opening his big gob on that TV show last week? The Sundays were full of it.'

She sent a reply immediately, explaining that, although they didn't know of Mark's present whereabouts, they hoped to interview him during the day. She would keep him informed of developments.

They used IM and the Commissario's response came back moments later. As soon as he had cleared things with his superiors, he said, he would be flying to the UK, and could they recommend some reasonably priced lodgings for him and his sergeant?

'Our man from the Trust has been a *very* naughty boy by the look of things, ma'am, and is due for a thorough talking to!'

'Too right, Tom. This afternoon, or better still, this evening,

I think we'll go for a drive in the "Cute Cotswolds", as my American relations insist on calling them, and see if the elusive Assistant Archivist is back from his business trip. Let's go and rattle *his* cage a bit, eh? And see what he has to say for himself now.'

44

Mark Dryden was used to taking the short walk to the Masonic Hall along the terraced corridor of Great William Street. The arrow-straight road, bordered with ribbons of parked cars punctuated with white vans, led, in less than a hundred metres, directly from the garden of 'The Birthplace' to the Hall. The regular meeting of Garrick Lodge took place on the third Thursday of the month, but tonight's was no normal Lodge meeting. The Extraordinary Meeting had been called to finalise arrangements for Saturday's Shakespeare Gala opening by the Queen. It was to be chaired by the Provincial Grand Master accompanied by the Lord Lieutenant of Warwickshire.

When Dryden mounted the concrete steps and walked into the entrance hall, he let himself in for something of a surprise. All the Brethren from the three Lodges who used Stratford's Masonic Hall had been instructed to attend, but there were barely two dozen present. He was aware that numbers in his own Lodge were dwindling but hadn't taken in just how few practicing Freemasons were left. He recalled how mounting social criticism of 'secret societies' towards the end of the twentieth century had caused Freemasonry to fall foul of political correctness, and many senior figures in the society had opened their doors to the public. With their exclusivity gone, and some of their rituals openly mocked, the overall result was an uphill struggle to find new blood.

Looking around, he realised how increasingly unlikely it was that he was ever going to find a recruit in there to take over his role as guardian of the secret Shakespeare file. For the first

293

time since joining the Lodge, he was not in possession of the file, since John had it in London, and it left him feeling bereft - as though he had no justification for being there. He was surrounded by friends and colleagues but felt isolated and alone. It was as though God himself had been stolen. He had a moment of unexpected realisation; he now knew that keeping secret the truth about the authorship was far more important to him than being a Freemason.

All the familiar faces were there, including the senior Trust officials, but it was the less familiar figure of Harry Gower, beckoning to him from the bar, that caught his attention. Dryden went up and greeted him, and ordered a couple of gin-and-tonics.

'I'm not going to be able to do much to protect you out in that public arena,' Harry said 'Lizzie Southwell is a feisty little madam once she's got her arse in gear. She's cute, and she'll smell a rat if I mention you, so, for an hour or two, I'm afraid you're going to be rather exposed.'

'I can handle it, Harry, don't worry; it's that pest, Steve Watson, showing up again that I don't like. He's a law unto himself, and you never know what pie he's got his meddling little fingers in.'

'What's he been up to that's got you so riled?'

'I had a threatening phone-call from him yesterday, telling me to mind my own business, and to be sure to keep his name out of it - or else. He is so coarse. He sounded just like a playground bully.'

'No change there then?' said the Deputy Chief Constable, who kept quiet about the fact that he too had been contacted by the unpopular ex-DCI.

'When you had him transferred down here….'

'All done on paper, Mark, and all destroyed. I guarantee Steve Dubya will have done the same.'

'It's not so much the unpredictability of the man, Harry - unlike you, I've never met him; it's the undercurrent of violence in everything to do with him that I find unsettling.'

'Ten years in Mosside and almost the same again in the West

Midlands, and there can't be much at the bottom of the barrel *he* hasn't had to scrape off' said Harry. He bought a second round of drinks and turned to Mark. 'Lizzie won't find anything on you in our files, by the way, but things do look destined to get messier,' he said. He looked Mark straight in the eye. 'There's something else you ought to know. The Venice police are sending one of their best men over. He's in charge of the Middleton case. I don't need to spell out what that could mean do I?'

'Damn!' said Dryden, 'that's all I need; first it's the 'dynamic duo' from Essex; then it's Watson, followed closely on the rails by Southwell, and now, coming up on the outside with a late run, it's the Doge of bloody Venice!'

'I wish I could treat this as lightly as you, Mark, because this could be seriously serious. This…Commissario Montano knows that you travelled to Venice under a false identity, and that you used another identity to obtain an official security pass to get you into the Middletons' Palazzo. Now, I hope you've got a good cover-story, because you're on your own on this one.' He paused, and looked at the grim and silent friend. 'A girl's dead Mark. Dead. Are you sure there's nothing you want to tell me?'

'I've never killed anyone, Harry, believe me. Montano might be able to have me for illegal entry and exit, but I'm damned if he's going to pin the Middleton girl's murder on me. What evidence could he have anyway? The only things to tie me to the Palazzo would be a positive ID or DNA. Her friend Jessica, who showed up at the Trust, didn't recognise me, and the only DNA of mine would have been on the mug of that dreadful coffee she served up, and I'll wager that was washed up within minutes of my leaving.'

Dryden's defensive but confident outburst reassured Harry that the resourceful archivist had things fairly well under control. Harry knew nothing of the secret file or its contents; just that something was of, "national significance", as John Fletcher had put it, and, "best not to ask any further questions." He knew from talking to Fletcher that something to do with Shakespeare was in the thick of things since he had as good as admitted that the 'Providential Discovery' was also in the mix. It made him wonder if it was indeed a very skilful forgery, and that, one day soon, the British Museum might come knocking on his door.

The Brethren filed into the main hall and the proceedings got under way. All their places for the opening ceremony were allocated and named. They would be forming a sort of 'guard of honour' for Her Majesty, and she would pass through their ranks to enter the Exhibition. The Trust members had their own seats on the dais closer to the Royal Party, and were to sit there, even if they were Masons. They were to follow the Queen and the dozens of national and international dignitaries into the huge marquees.

'God, what a bore,' thought Dryden, 'this is Bardology's finest hour; what a load of pretentious nonsense! If only they knew a quarter of what I know.' He found himself standing next to the Director of the Trust who was eager to thank him for all the unpaid time he had put in since the discovery of 'the page'. 'It was the least I could do,' he said. 'I do hope everything goes without a hitch on Saturday, and the weather holds out. Fickle April holds the door to May!'

When he had had enough, he slipped away unseen and walked briskly up the poorly-lit and silent street to get his car. As the police would be on the look-out for his Saab, he was still driving his classic Alfa Romeo which he hoped no-one would associate with him, and which he had secreted away in the terraced, urban grid to the north-east of the town centre.

Shortly after he left the Masonic Hall, Tony and Jessica drove up the street. Arriving later than he had hoped due to traffic delays, Tony was even more frustrated by finding a complete absence of parking places. As he drove round the block, neither of them recognised the man in black when he crossed the road ahead of them, striding purposefully along in the orange glow of the street lights to get his car.

By the time they had found a parking place, by the humpback bridge over the canal a couple of hundred metres from their goal, the road down by the Hall was filling with Freemasons. The meeting was over, and their chance of spotting Dryden with any of his close colleagues was gone. As they stood by the street-light, wondering whether it was wise or foolish to pursue their idea of identifying a suspect this way, a red Alfa Romeo Spyder drove past. Dryden recognised Tony and Jessica immediately.

'Not only have this irritating pair put two and two together,' he thought, 'but three and three as well!' He put his foot down and headed away from the town, and away from the prying eyes of the police or anyone else.

It wasn't only Tony and Jessica who had missed him. Lizzie Southwell, unaware that he was a Mason, had missed this golden opportunity to intercept her quarry too.

45

Tom Heywood parked the police car in the Emergency Services bay at Birmingham International Airport to await the arrival of Commissario Montano and his sergeant. Lizzie Southwell wanted to show the Italians that the British could do things in style and turned up in a classic Stella McCartney suit. She had her hair down and had chosen to wear restrained hand-made silver jewellery. She had no cause to check herself in the mirror-glass of the Airport entrance-hall as she knew she looked the business.

The flight was on time and the Venice Police officers, carrying only hand-luggage, were soon out through arrivals. They walked smartly up to the British detectives.

'Buon giorno, Signora, Signore. This is Sergeant Stefano.' He declared himself a man of urgent purpose, adding. 'Do you have him in custody?'

'Not yet, Commissario, we're still looking for him,' said Southwell.

'Not at home in his Cotswold farmhouse, then?'

'We're keeping an eye on it,' she said, 'but he hasn't shown up.'

'Credit cards?' added Montano, as they got into the car.

'He must be using cash. There have been no debit or credit transactions using his cards.'

They left the airport, swung round the island under the A45, and joined the M42. Tom engaged lights and sirens and moved quickly to the outside lane. He accelerated to over ninety miles per hour in a matter of moments. Southwell turned casually to the Commissario who was sitting behind her.

'Did you meet Tony Chapman and Jessica Marston at the Middletons' Palazzo?'

'Si. Why you ask?'

'They told me yesterday they were they coming across from Essex, and should be in the area now. You may find a talk with them very informative.'

'Why is that?'

'We have been investigating another mysterious death associated with Mark Dryden. Last Monday, before I was given clearance to reopen the enquiry, somebody sabotaged Chapman's car, and they ended-up in hospital.'

By the time their Indian-built, supercharged Jaguar XLH turbo was sweeping down the broad right-hand curve of the M40, Tom had it up to a hundred-and-forty-mph. 'They would have been doing about fifty or sixty kilometres per hour at the time of impact,' she said. 'They were lucky it wasn't worse. As far as I'm aware - no broken bones'

'I am pleased their injuries were not too serious,' added Montano. 'And Signor Dryden?'

'We don't know if he is directly involved; he doesn't appear to me like a man to get down on his hands and knees in a car-park and cut someone's brake-pipes.'

'They may have something "informative" for me to hear, you say?'

'Only last week, we had the most unusual event of a long-lost manuscript being discovered right here in Stratford. Miss Marston recognised it immediately as one of those….'

'Stolen from the Palazzo Magretti-Bellini?'

'Precisely. As I think you are already aware, she and Mr. Chapman were allowed custody of some of the pages by Mr. Middleton. I presume you met him, too?' she added, angling for a response.

'A celebrity with more screen-confidence than tact, Signora,' he said, adding: 'so, four centuries after they were taken to my country to be written upon, it appears that I follow their trail all of the way back to where they originated. To the home-town of the great dramatist himself.'

'I think you might find the jury is still out on that last point, Commissario,' she said.

In a little over six minutes, they had covered the eleven miles to the junction at Longbridge Island and left the motorway for the short drive into Warwick.

'I've sorted out a small family-run hotel in Leamington Spa for you, and we've put a car at your disposal.' said the D.I., as she got out. 'Tom will drop you off.'

'My *disposal?* Does this mean I have to get rid of it myself?' queried Montano.

'The free use of one of our police-cars, Commissario,' said Tom, 'just ring this number.'

As he was about to be driven away, the Commissario wound down the window. 'I know it's not *Armani,*' he said, 'but thank you. I see you again later this afternoon, and it would be most helpful to speak with Signorina Marston and Signor Chapman - if you could arrange it for me.'

'My pleasure,' she said.

2.00 pm. : WARWICK :

The Commissario greeted Tony and Jessica warmly as they entered the rather confined interview room at the Warwickshire Police Headquarters. Sergeant Stefano was present, as were D.I. Southwell and Sergeant Heywood. They all sat down and he addressed himself to Jessica.

'So, we meet again, Signorina. I see you still wear the bandages from your recent accident. The Detective Inspector, here, tells me you were lucky it wasn't more serious?' said Montano.

'It looks much worse than it is - and may I take this opportunity to thank you for being so understanding on the night Bianca was killed?' she said. 'I think I was very lucky last Monday. If it hadn't been for Tony's skill as a driver, it could have been much worse. Somebody tampered with the brakes on our car.'

'I am pleased for your good fortune - under the circumstances. Inspector Southwell informs me that you believe one of the manuscript pages stolen from Venezia is now to be found here in Stratford-upon-Avon? Is that true, Signorina?'

'As soon as I saw the photograph of it in the Sunday paper, I recognised it as one of those which 'B' and I had studied at Randy's Palazzo. She had taken three of the pages to Randy's study, because she wanted to take a closer look at them some time later. The thief obviously had no idea any of them were missing. One of the pages, which is now in our possession, is in sequence with the one in the Shakespeare Centre here in Stratford. You've only to see the two together to see the similarity. The handwriting is identical - everything. What's more, I'm certain that Mark Dryden, who works at the Shakespeare Centre is 'George Drummond'. Now that's hardly a coincidence, is it?'

'He's who?' demanded Southwell.

'George Drummond,' she replied, 'the man who said he was from the British Consulate, whom 'B' and I showed round the Palazzo, just before she was killed.'

'How can you be so certain?' asked Montano.

'Because we went up there and spoke to him, didn't we, Tony? He not only looks a lot like him, but he used an odd phrase - sort of formal and old-fashioned....'

'You never told me any of this, Mr. Chapman,' interrupted Southwell. 'This comes as a complete surprise.'

'We've been in a car-crash since then, Inspector, and Jess here has spent a night in hospital; so I think you can forgive me for it slipping my mind over the last three days; plus the fact that we've received a threatening e-mail - from an untraceable source unfortunately. I don't think you fully realise how courageous this young woman is, Inspector.'

'Point taken Mr. Chapman; and we can put one of our experts onto that e-mail for you.'

'Miss Marston,' continued Montano, 'what did Mark Dryden

say that betrayed his false identity to you?'

'He said: 'Would it not?' And he used it more than once when we were in Venice. It's far too affected for everyday English, Commissario. That's why I took notice of it.'

Montano felt more and more pleased that his trip to the UK had been worthwhile, as the case they were building against Dryden got stronger. His forensic team back in Venice hadn't collected any DNA from the Palazzo, and he thought it might be difficult to make Jessica's identification of him stand up in court. The clinching evidence, he felt, hinged on that piece of paper, securely locked away by the Shakespeare Trust. It was a long shot, but traces of a fingerprint, or possibly DNA, from Randy, Eddie, Bianca or even Jessica, might still be present. Even the slightest trace from any of them would establish the 'Providential Discovery' as a fake, and tie it conclusively to the Palazzo.

As he was intending to effect the extradition of Dryden to Italy, he had to construct a watertight case before he could put anything to the Home Office. At present, all the evidence he had against Dryden was circumstantial. Montano knew he was dealing with a clever and calculating man, so he couldn't rely on him to break down under questioning. It was therefore imperative to find him and to question him.

'How do you intend to catch him, Inspector?' asked Montano.

'He is to attend the Gala opening of the Quatercentenary celebrations tomorrow. His seat is reserved for him, and we shall be waiting. It would be a public snub to his employers, let alone the Queen, if he didn't attend. So, if we don't find him earlier, that's our moment.'

'Do you know if he attended the Masonic meeting last night, Inspector? We arrived a bit too late see if he was there,' said Tony.

'No, I don't,' she replied, and was unable to conceal her surprise at being caught out. Tony and Jessica had brought up the question of the Freemasons being involved a week earlier. Basic police-work was at fault and she'd been wrong-footed.

'How did you know he was a Freemason?' she asked.

'When he shook my hand last Monday,' he said, 'I found out about the meeting from the Internet. We were caught in traffic, and, by the time we arrived at the Masonic Hall, the meeting had finished.' Tony hadn't meant to deliberately upstage her and hoped no lasting damage had been done.

Pressing on, and trying hard to conceal her embarrassment, Southwell said, 'We're watching the lane that leads to his farmhouse, and there's an APB out for his car. One way or another, by this time tomorrow, he'll be right here, make no mistake.' She stood up. 'I've a very busy schedule for the next forty-eight hours, ladies and gentlemen, so you'll have to excuse me. Sergeant Heywood, here, will sort out all your security passes for the weekend. I've arranged a secure area on Waterside, at the bottom of Sheep Street, close to the arena for you all. So, I hope to see you there on Saturday morning.'

46

With every room in Stratford taken, Tony and Jessica had booked in at The White Bear in Shipston-on-Stour, eight miles to the south. The roads into Stratford were destined to be a nightmare, so they resolved to make an early start, hoping to jump the gun on other like-minded tourists. The day had opened warm and sunny and the temperature was rising steadily, but the forecast was that the bright start wasn't to last and there could be showers before the day was out.

Eddie had kept his promise to get his 'minidoc' onto TV before the weekend. He hadn't made the news channels but he had managed a perfect slot on *Newsnight*. They were amazed to see what he had managed to put together in so short a space of time, and it had been remarkably well received. Both of their acting debuts were surprisingly passable, probably because it had all been such a rush that morning that they had just got on with job and didn't have time to get self-conscious. Alex became an instant hero, and in the following interview there were one or two embarrassing silences on the occasions when his premature death was mentioned.

'If only Edward de bloody Vere knew what he'd started,' said Tony, as they pulled away from the Georgian inn and headed north. Half-an-hour later, they were sitting in a queue waiting for entry to the Bridgefoot Multi-storey car park, close to The Bancroft and the Theatres. Temporary fast-food outlets were already doing a brisk trade, serving to lines of colourful visitors of all ages and from every corner of the globe.

'Talk about the whole world being a stage!' observed Jessica, 'and there's still more than six hours before Her Majesty is due to show up.'

'It's not the "Old Dear" they're all coming to see, sweetheart.' said Tony, 'Princess Kate and her two little brats are going to be centre-stage, remember.'

The police were showing an uncomfortably high presence, and, while one of their teams was busying itself lifting manhole covers and peering under every other piece of movable ironwork in road or pavement, others with dog-handlers were prying into every conceivable corner above ground.

Huge TV screens already threw long shadows across Bancroft Gardens, the temporary seating and the central stage. By the time the day's events reached their climax, the vast sail-like awning they had watched being erected a week earlier would be casting its own shadow in their place. Rows of satellite-dish-bedecked TV vans edged all the nearby roads, but for a clear passage left over the nearby Clopton Bridge, the only road bridge over the river in this part of the town. This, and the road skirting the Gardens leading to Waterside, was the approach the Queen and the rest of the Royal party would be using when they arrived, around two-fifteen.

This was world-media heaven. By the afternoon, this extravaganza would be worth a million euros a minute, with the most bullish photographers, hundreds of them from all over the world, bagging the best viewpoints for their shots, not of the Queen, or the play excerpts to be acted out on the temporary stage, but of Princess Kate and the two little Princesses.

Tony and Jessica had to be sure of their places, too, so they decided to go and check them out. D.I. Southwell had arranged for them to have security passes and the use of the edge of an area reserved for the emergency services at the bottom of Sheep Street, near a shiny metal fountain. It would afford them an uninterrupted view of the royal seating area, but, more importantly, also the seats to be occupied by members of the Shakespeare Trust, including, they hoped, the elusive Mark Dryden.

'While we still want to talk to Dryden over the Alex Paris case, Tom, the 'Veteran Venetian' is never going to get to fly him out of the country - I'll see to that.'

'Yeah, but we've got so little on him, Ma'am,' replied Tom, 'and what we have got is circumstantial. It's going to be tough convincing our lords and masters we want to keep him here with no hard evidence, isn't it?'

'Ways and means, young man. Ways and means - that's how.' She upped her pace. 'Now, where are Essex girl and Essex boy?'

The D.I. and her sergeant were walking briskly along Waterside hoping to catch a glimpse of Tony and Jessica. Southwell was keen to deter Tony, in particular, from indulging in any heroics. She already had a strong feeling that Tony and Jessica fancied their chances at catching Dryden all by themselves; they had failed to conceal the emotional impetus driving their actions. Tony, rather naively, had made their intentions all too clear by admitting that they had gone after him on their own without informing her, on Thursday night. She now asked her trusty sergeant to keep a constant watch on the couple - just in case.

'That was not only arrogant behaviour, Tom,' she said, 'but verging on the reckless. Their actions could have jeopardised this whole operation. They might have alerted Dryden, and scared him off. We might never have seen him again!'

Tony was not flavour-of-the-month, and, as the officers walked up to them, Southwell's attitude and body-language made this abundantly clear. 'This is a police operation,' she said, addressing them both, 'and I shouldn't need to tell you that situations like today's are unpredictable. If we are dealing with a man who has killed, there is no knowing what he may do to escape arrest.'

'We are aware of that,' replied Tony, 'but if….'

'We're on the same side, aren't we, Mr. Chapman? Now, I would prefer it to remain that way - but, if I can't depend on the two of you to do as I ask and leave us to do the police work, then I will remove your passes and have you escorted a safe distance away from here, is that quite clear?'

'Inspector…' began Jessica.

'Miss Marston. I would like both of you to remain here, if that's possible, so that, if and when Mr. Dryden appears, I can be certain of a positive ID. Then, and only then, when I'm a hundred per cent sure, will I ask my officers to move in. I don't need to remind you, surely, of who will be up there.' She pointed to the principal seating area. 'The Chief Constable, the Lord Lieutenant of Warwickshire, ambassadors and civic dignitaries from around the world, and, last but not least, the 'Royals'. No heroics - is that understood?'

'Understood,' they replied.

Southwell and her sergeant moved away. She looked up at the recently refurbished theatre and its stark campanile-like tower; the black silhouettes of half-a-dozen police marksmen clear for all to see. She turned to Sgt. Heywood. 'If there weren't enough problems as it is, Tom, without the added worry of a couple of loose cannons!' she said.

'Shall I cuff 'em, Boss? To each other - and then the railings?'

'I wish,' she replied.

———

12.15 pm

Activity on Bancroft Gardens increased exponentially as the main event of the day approached. Tony and Jessica caught sight of Eddie three or four times as he and his sound-man scampered about inside the security zone, snapping at this and that. The mini-grandstands around the stage were still vacant; the honoured guests, soon to be stacked in them in neat rows, were off in town somewhere, enjoying a banquet.

The sun was now hidden under a duvet of cumulonimbus clouds, and as they discussed how the atmosphere was now far more bearable than at any time in the past three hours, they were alerted by a female voice from the other side of the security railings.

'You must be Jessica?' she said.

Jessica spun round with reflex-like reaction to find herself face to face with the unknown woman. Tony then turned around too, but more slowly having recognised the voice.

'Hello, Tony,' she said.

'Imogen! What on earth are you doing here? I mean, how did you know I - we - would be here?'

'Don't flatter yourself. I've come across you purely by chance.'

Tony looked around and saw that she appeared to be alone. 'Husband? Boyfriend?' he asked.

She looked directly at him and shrugged her shoulders. 'I saw *Newsnight* last night,' she said, 'and I thought I'd come down and be a witness to Stratford's greatest day for the last five-and-a-half years, not to mention yours.'

You could have filled the Olympic Stadium ten times over with the emotion that loaded her statement. He couldn't just let it go.

'There was no need for that,' he said quietly; but as he looked at her, he could see tears welling up in her eyes. She went quiet, looked away for a moment, and then looked back at him. He wondered if she had ever returned to Stratford in the intervening years - probably not. He was about to mention it, but she spoke first.

'I'm sorry, Tony, that was disingenuous of me. I guess you must have meant what you said about owing it to Alex,' she said. 'None of us can undo the past, but that film of him on holiday, looking so carefree and so alive, brought it all flooding back so vividly. Mum and Dad just sat and cried. I'm afraid you were something of a hero, even to Dad - believe that if you can.'

'Thank Eddie Gascoigne. All I did was to e-mail what I hoped might do the trick. Clever guy, our Eddie!'

'There's a Starbucks at the top of this road,' said Jessica.

'Good idea,' said Imogen, and the threesome walked away from all the excitement and up Sheep Street.

The van containing costumes to be used in the warm-up entertainment had to make a short journey across Stratford from the RST's props and costume warehouse to reach the main Theatre. It squeezed its way down Chapel Lane, a narrow street, now packed with the limousines that had brought the great and the good, which joined Waterside close to the service entrance of the RST. The van was reversed up to the props entrance and its rear roller-door opened. Mark Dryden, quite unseen, had stowed himself away amid the baskets of props to the front of the white van while it was being loaded at the warehouse. Dressed in jeans and T-shirt, nobody noticed as he slipped out, and cheerfully joined in. The rails of assorted historical costumes had to be carried across the Linking Foyer to the lift, and on up to the wardrobe department on the second floor. He was careful to remove his pack from the van, as it contained his change of clothes. He then went back up to the second floor, and, exiting the lift, turned right and then left, past the laundry, and so to the river side of the building, and a corridor full of dressing rooms. As the authorities had sealed off the entire RST and searched it the previous night, he felt free to choose any of the vacant rooms, and would take his chance with any patrolling security guards. His intention was to wait here in silent seclusion until he could venture outside to assume his seat.

He was just about to change into his suit when his phone rang. 'Who the bloody hell!' he said, and flicking open the cover, switched it to 'silent.' He saw that it was Steve Watson.

'What do you want, now, Watson?'

'I wouldn't even dream of coming to Stratford today if I were you,' he said, 'not if you could see who I'm looking at.'

'Surprise me.'

'Well, I spy a whole flock of twitchy vultures gathered outside the 'Palace of Thespis' ready and eager to peck your bones clean, Marky-boy - including a couple of particularly fine-looking Italian ones. So do us both a favour and stay off-limits, coz they'll have you collared before you can fart!'

'Mind your own business, and why don't you make sure *you* stay out of the way. I've already told you I'm not going to bring your name....'

'Who knows what you'll blab if you're dragged off to the land of Serenessima and banged up for a couple of months without your home comforts. If you know what's good for you, Dryden, you'll keep your distance from this fucking town.' Steve hung up.

Any remaining peace of mind Dryden had managed to salvage from the past few days was torched by Steve Watson's uncompromising words. He tossed his mobile onto the dressing table and continued to get changed. It would be more than an hour before the invited audience would be arriving. It was to be the longest and tensest hour of his life.

2.00 pm.

Mark Dryden had opened the window just a crack to get some fresh air. The loudspeakers outside were so loud it was easy to keep track of events. The Queen's helicopter would shortly touch down at Compton Verney, a few miles out of town, and she would then make the ten-minute journey to the Gala. Time enough, he thought, to get to his seat, and not to be exposed for too long. He checked his watch. It was time to make a move.

He made his way downstairs to the ground floor and came out by the Green Room, which, to his dismay, was being used. 'Guests', he thought. 'They could be my saving grace'. He hung his security pass round his neck, made his way quickly and quietly along the dark, narrow corridor that separated the two back-to-back theatres, cut through the main theatre's right wing-space, and made for the toilets. He waited in one of the cubicles until another toilet-user appeared. He flushed the pan, came out, made light conversation as he washed his hands, and strolled casually out through the main entrance to the outdoor arena's seating area.

Musicians and stilt-walkers, jesters and jugglers, were all doing their bit to entertain the crowds. He delayed taking his place and stood in the shade of the temporary grandstand unseen, and waited. The moment wasn't right, just yet. In the distance he heard a great cheer, rising to an almost hysterical crescendo. It got nearer and nearer, louder and louder; and, with the clapping and the commentary and the music it was almost deafening.

Princess Kate, Prince William and the two little princesses had arrived. This was his moment. While all eyes were on them, he slipped into his seat.

***

2.15 pm.

'I've briefed every gate allowing entry to the high-security zone, Mr. Chapman,' said Southwell, 'and no-one has seen hide nor hair of him. Looks like he's done the sensible thing and stayed away.' She had to shout to make herself heard as the world's photographers called to the Young Royals to get their attention. Their limousine moved away smartly, followed by another which disgorged its contents of attendants and personal security men, then it too made off.

The huge TV screens switched back and forth between live pictures of the Queen's journey into the town and close-ups of 'PK', as the Princess had become affectionately known, and her children. D.I. Southwell and Sgt. Heywood went off to join a group of heavily-armed policemen who were pointing this way and that.

The tension was drawing to a climax when suddenly, there was the piercing whistle of feedback over the PA system. It caught everyone's attention. The TV screens went blank for a moment and then Eddie's 'minidoc' came on. Tony and Jessica gasped in sheer disbelief as the short documentary about the authorship deception was relayed. The crowd was stunned. Many of those who hadn't seen it on television the previous night would have seen it reported in some of the morning's papers. How Eddie had got it onto the big screens was a mystery but its message was coming across loud and clear.

Tony looked along Waterside to his left. The Queen's deep-burgundy-coloured limousine with the Royal Standard fluttering over its roof, advanced towards them at a measured pace. Jessica grabbed his arm.

'Tony! Look!' she shouted above the din. But she wasn't pointing to the royal procession, she was pointing to the arena, and the tall figure of Mark Dryden, up on his feet, and staring open-mouthed at the screen. Tony called over to Southwell, but she was too far away to hear his voice above the cheering of the excited crowd.

As the royal car was about to draw up, Dryden left his seat and hurried towards the nearest marquee. He had already identified the temporary exposition as his primary escape route should anything go wrong. He glanced over to the welcoming party and the slowing royal cortege only to see Tony leap the barrier and head straight for him.

Tony swerved round the front of the now stationary limousine. The nearest security guard grabbed for him as he sprinted after the fleeing Dryden. In his eagerness to catch his friend's killer he stumbled and fell to the to the ground, crashing through the astonished dignitaries in the receiving line. Before any security men could apprehend him he was back on his feet, flashed his security pass at them and headed across the arena. He leapt onto the stage, scattering the alarmed actors. The Royal Protection Unit, guns drawn, were out of their seats in a flash targeting what they assumed was an attack by a crazed, lone assassin. By the time they had formed a wall to protect Prince William's family, Dryden had already left the arena and could be seen jumping the ticket barrier with Tony after him.

Suddenly, shots rang out.

47

As if in slow-motion, a rising cloud of smoke marked the spot, half-way up Sheep Street. There had been an explosion, and panic broke out immediately. The screaming crowd fled the scene as though blown by a bomb's pressure wave. The Queen was ushered back into her bullet-proof limousine, which sped her away past the RST, and along Southern Lane. The police, security and emergency services were, within moments, directing all their resources up the short, shopping street, which led directly away from the arena.

A police marksman, on the viewing platform at the top of the Theatre Tower, had followed the vehicle in his sights as it gathered speed down the street. He had been alerted by a colleague the moment the unmarked white van had careered through the police cordon at the top of the road. The marksman, training his gun on the driver fired several times, killing him instantly. But for the marksman's quick thinking, the van, on reaching the bottom of the road, would have crossed Waterside, entered the arena, and might possibly have exploded with enough force to kill everyone present - and bring down half of the RST at the same time.

The specialist Royal Protection Unit, initially alerted by Tony's dash across the stage, took up their places around the arena. The Royal party was then evacuated, with calm efficiently, to a waiting police launch which had been patrolling the river. It whisked them off to the Stratford Rowing Club Boat House, a hundred metres away on the opposite side of the river.

Southwell and her team, unaware of Tony's 'heroics', or even

313

that Mark Dryden had shown up, ran towards the scene of devastation. They crunched their way across a carpet of broken glass, and cautiously approached the blazing wreckage. Terrorist officers came running down, shouting orders to them to keep well away in case there was a secondary explosion. On their way back to the chaos at the site of the terminated celebrations, Southwell turned to her sergeant. 'What do you smell, Tom?'

He gave a huge sniff. 'Petrol, boss.'

'That's what I thought,' she replied. As they reached the bottom of the street they were greeted by Commissario Montano and Sergeant Stefano.

'Terrorists, si?' asked the Commissario.

'Not sure,' she said. 'It certainly has all the hallmarks.'

'But is bad, yes?'

'Difficult to say, but there's quite a lot of blood up there.'

'I'm sorry for you,' he said, 'this is a big shock for you whole country. It is almost impossible to stop a really determined person - one whose earthly life means nothing to him…'

'Excuse me, Commissario,' she said, looking at the empty medical station. 'Tom, where the hell are they?'

'Sorry, Ma'am. I took my eyes off 'em when I came up to help.'

She ran across to the arena where the invited audience was being ushered away by the police. There wasn't a sign of Tony or Jessica.

'Damn them, Tom! Where the bloody hell have they disappeared to?'

2.21 pm.

St. John's Ambulance teams, and other paramedics, mobilised themselves around where Jessica stood. She quickly got out of their way and soon found herself on the other side of the road, at the edge of the arena. She had watched as Tony disappeared into the tented exhibition just before the explosion. She now looked on in dazed bewilderment at the hi-jacked day. It wasn't Shakespeare's any more, but a dead fanatic's, who wasn't even here to see if what he'd done had achieved anything. She had no desire for the details and turned back to The Bancroft, and her worries for her missing man. She seized the moment, entered the arena and headed for the exposition entrance.

Inside, it was one of those layouts where the visitor has to journey through the entire exposition with no opportunity for short-cuts. She immediately feared for Tony's safety when, after turning the first bend, she saw a scattering of exhibits across the walkway. She clambered and jumped over an assortment of effigies of English kings and Italian dukes who were strewn about the floor, wondering for one irrational moment if one of their discarded swords might come in useful! She followed the noise of the disturbance up ahead; Tony, it seemed, must be having his work cut out to keep pace with the athletic Dryden.

The exhibition finished near the main theatre entrance and its shop. The final exhibit before the exit was a tall, clear-plastic display-case containing the 'Providential Discovery'. On approaching it, Dryden had little time to consider its significance, nor how his own highly skilled craftsmanship had become his undoing. He merely cast it to one side with a sweep of his arm, in his urgency to reach the foyer, and hide himself away in the vast purpose-built playhouse.

Tony leapt over the fallen exhibit, unaware that he nearly trod on Randy's manuscript in the process. He dashed up the steps, through a temporary gift shop outside the theatre's main entrance, and went in.

He found himself in the most surreal of surroundings. He had come through the theatre's original nineteen-twenties Art Deco Foyer to enter the black cavern of the main auditorium. Although it was, in itself, silent and tranquil, he could hear clearly all the goings-on resulting from the nearby explosion. It was like listening to the subdued soundtrack for a violent drama whose rehearsal was about to begin.

He mounted the stage and surveyed his situation. 'Where the hell do I start?' he thought. 'Where would *I* have gone to hide in here?' In the gloom, he felt his way through the left wing, and along a corridor which eventually brought him into the Swan Theatre, the smaller of the two theatres in the building. He walked out onto its stage. With only the dim emergency lights on, he could barely make out a thing. 'He could be hiding just about anywhere', he thought. He went into the wings, and, after fumbling about in vain for a light switch returned to the corridor and up a staircase to the first floor.

He still found no sign of Dryden, who by now had secreted himself away on the third floor, in the main theatre's control room in the gods, above the Upper Circle. In front of him, he had a state-of-the-art display panel showing him all the CCTV pictures from around the building. He got his breath back, watching Tony's uncertain progress and then saw Jessica's arrival as she appeared in the foyer.

'Tony,' she called, 'are you in here?' she too entered the main auditorium and mounted its thrust-stage. Ahead of her was the heart of this place, now a dark, forbidding interior beneath the Fly Tower. She shouted even louder 'Tony? Are you there?' She strained her ears for a sound of his response, but the only sound to interrupt the theatre's eerie silence was the continuous rumbling breath of its air-conditioning system. It was some time before her eyes adjusted to the darkness, and only slowly did the wings surrender their black infinity to reveal tangible walls and corners.

The soundproofing made any communication between them difficult. They might only have been a few metres apart, but, with a couple of walls and doors, or, maybe, a floor in-between, they would never know of the other's whereabouts. Dryden hoped to use this to his advantage when traversing the upper floors as he made his bid to reach the fire-escape at the far end of the building - and freedom. It was his only logical escape route.

'Tony. I'm going round the back of the main stage. Where are you?'

Dryden continued to observe them. Scanning the screens, he thought it was like playing a computer game in which the helpless humans had to find their way through a three-dimensional labyrinth while the worst monsters of their dreams lurked unseen round every corner. He had to fight his over-active imagination so as not to enjoy the unfolding drama too much; he needed to remain very alert indeed in order to avoid this persistent and determined pair.

As he studied alternative ways out from the detailed floor-plans on one of the monitors his phone rang. He looked to see who it was.

'John,' he said, 'how can I help?'

'I've been watching the TV, Mark. What's all this about an attempt on the Queen's life - and where the hell are you? I thought I saw you sitting near the Royals. Was that you?'

'I'm inside the RST, John - and, yes, it was me you saw.'

'Well you could help me, and yourself, by getting out of that building, and Stratford, as quick as you can - do it while there's still plenty of confusion outside.'

'I'll be on my way as soon as I know I can safely avoid the stubborn and increasingly troublesome pair from Essex.'

'Good God, man! Are they in there, too?'

While he spoke to John Fletcher, Jessica had made her way back to the main theatre. Her eyes were now well-adjusted to the dim interior and she became aware of the low-level green light emanating from the control room. To her disbelief, she could see Dryden clearly, still with his phone to his ear, and lit eerily from below by the soft glow of the monitors.

'Tony!' she called out.

'What is it, Jess?' answered Tony, who, to her shock and surprise, had entered the lower circle from her left and was only a few metres away.

'Oh! There you are! Look! Up there - in the control room,' she said, pointing up at the circle and the dimly lit figure.

Tony ran immediately to the main stairs that would take him to the upper floors. Jessica ran to the stairwell on the other side and climbed the flights as fast as she could. When they reached the third floor, they came out on opposite sides of an alien space. The underside of the theatre's roof was crowded with dozens of spotlights, hanging there like huge wingless bats not wishing to be wakened. They looked across the auditorium at each other, and then at the control room. It was empty.

'How did we miss him?' asked Jessica.

'Search me,' said Tony. 'Go back, and turn right as soon as you can. We should meet somewhere in the middle by the Fly Tower'.

Jessica took the same route Dryden had taken; past the top of the stairs and through the kitchen, where she turned right to rendezvous with Tony. Dryden, however, had gone straight on, but had found his route to freedom, via the fire-escape, barred by a locked door at the far end of the Company canteen. He had had to rush back to the stairs serving the kitchen and had gone down to the second floor. Emerging into yet another narrow and dimly-lit corridor, he became aware of nearby voices. It was the actors returning to get changed, their performances having been cut short unexpectedly. He fled back up the stairs; this time to the fourth floor, and, he prayed, his one remaining way out - by a spiral staircase down the corner of the Fly Tower.

Tony and Jessica were in a changing area on the third floor discussing whether or not to split up in order to continue their search, when Tony's phone rang. Checking the screen, he saw that it was D.I. Southwell.

'Would you mind telling me where you are, Mr. Chapman?' she asked.

'We're in The Royal Shakespeare Theatre, Inspector. Dryden is in here somewhere and we're trying to locate him.'

'You damned fools!' she said, 'I thought I told you not to go after him?' She turned to Sergeant Heywood. 'Get an officer to every exit of the RST five minutes ago, Tom, and I want six men to help me search that theatre - now!' She took off in the direction of the theatre, and returned to her phone. 'Get yourself and Miss

Marston out of that building immediately, Mr. Chapman - and no heroics! This time I *really* mean it.'

'OK! OK!' replied Tony. The couple thought it wise to comply with Southwell's demand straight away and set off for the ground floor. However, they made the mistake of taking the first door on their right, instead of the second, and found themselves on the balcony inside the Fly Tower. To their astonishment, barely twenty metres away in the gloom was the dark figure of Mark Dryden, only a few rungs from alighting on the walkway. Like a reflex reaction, Jessica shot off after him.

'No, Jess!' shouted Tony, 'leave him!' But she was gone.

As Dryden climbed the narrow spiral staircase pursued by Jessica, Tony looked for any other way to get after them. He saw that he was next to a service-lift, quickly realised that it was active, and pressed the ascend button. Whatever was up there, he hoped he would be able to intercept Dryden before he reached the roof and a possible getaway. It wasn't long before he was approaching level six. When he opened the cage door and stepped onto the balcony, he saw Dryden on the far balcony; having found the door to the roof locked, he was making his way back towards Jessica. To his chagrin, Tony found that the two balconies were not joined - there was a sixteen metre gap separating them. The void was filled with pulleys, ropes, block-and-tackle, and half-a-dozen background flats, all hanging there in the twenty-two metre drop to the solid floor below.

Jessica half-screamed Tony's name as Dryden grabbed hold of her. 'Don't make life any harder than it already is,' he yelled across at Tony. 'I just want to get out of here without anybody getting hurt.'

'Like Alex or Bianca, I suppose,' said Tony. 'I won't answer for what I'll do if you harm a single hair of her head.'

'None of us ever meant anyone to get hurt in all this business, Mr. Chapman, let alone die, believe me. The whole authorship issue ended up far bigger than we ever expected.'

'And now two innocent people are dead, and it's all your fault, you and your 'FCV'. How many of you are we dealing with,

Dryden - come on - how many of you are there?'

Jessica squealed as Dryden's grip tightened. 'We have survived for nearly four centuries, Mr. Chapman, and don't think for a moment that a Tintin and Snowy duo like you two is capable of stopping us in our work.'

Tony was now terrified as to what Dryden might do next as he was clearly hurting Jessica. He had to reach her soon - but how? There wasn't time to go down to the third floor and back up the spiral staircase to help her, as that would give Dryden plenty of time to push her over the balcony-rail, and make a run for it while he was gone. He weighed up the opportunity offered by the hardware that separated them. 'Those ropes look pretty strong,' he thought, 'and the pulleys made to last; and those screens and flats look solidly constructed. Surely they'll take my weight.' He looked again at the terrified and squirming Jessica. He reached over the rail, and pulled on a rope. It didn't give a fraction, but the flat suspended from it began to sway gently. He climbed over the rail, and gingerly stepped onto its timber frame.

'Don't, Tony!' screamed Jessica. 'It's not worth it. Let him take me.'

As Tony progressed cautiously towards half-way, Dryden took the opportunity to make off with his hostage; but, before he got very far, he became aware of a disturbance below. Suddenly the lights came on and he could see a group of actors looking up at them. They in turn were joined by the police, including DI Southwell, Sgt. Heywood, Commissario Montano and Sgt. Stefano. Two uniformed officers scrambled up the spiral staircase.

'The game's up, Dryden. Let's make it easy, shall we?' called Southwell.

He looked down at the gathering crowd. As they gaped up at him, like a nest-full of starving chicks, it looked very much as though he was expected to be their next meal. He loosened his grip on Jessica imperceptibly, and, in that moment, wondered what on earth had befallen him. 'What has it all been for?' he thought, 'What have I become?' He breathed a sigh and was quite motionless. But Jessica sensed the relaxation in him; 'This is my only chance', she thought.

Tony was now almost within reach. She broke free, and, in a second, was over the guard-rail. 'Grab me, Tony,' she called, and reaching for a rope, stepped across the narrow chasm to the gently swinging flat. She missed her footing and screamed. Dryden dashed to save her, and, stretching over the rail, caught hold of her arm. Jessica's weight in addition to Tony's, was too much for the suspension mechanism, and it gave way. As he hung onto her arm, the extra little tug that it gave Dryden caused him to overbalance, pulling him over the edge. While Tony and Jessica held onto each other, and onto the broken flat as it dangled by only one end, Mark Dryden plunged headlong to the floor.

'Get a doctor!' yelled Southwell.

Some quick-thinking actors rushed a stage-tower over to the stricken pair, as the unmistakable ripping and tearing sounds of the dying moments of the collapsing flat, pierced the air. Tony and Jessica were still a very precarious eight or nine metres above their would-be rescuers. One of the actors, with admirable agility, scaled the tower. Before anyone was fully aware of his actions, he had his arm round Jessica's waist and pulled her to safety. She descended the tower's ladder, with Tony following in similar fashion. As he stepped onto the floor, to the relief of all concerned, a mobile phone rang.

Everyone looked at one another. It was soon clear that the ringing was coming from the floor.

'Dryden,' called Tony. 'Someone's ringing him,' and he rushed forward.

'Keep back,' said Southwell, 'Officer!' She called to one of her men. The constable advanced quickly to protect the black-suited pile, oozing blood, that had so recently been the respected Archivist. She felt through Dryden's pockets for his mobile, took it out and opened it. The screen showed no name, just the caller's number. Still crouching by the body, she looked up at Tony, and then pressed connect and speaker. They heard a familiar voice.

'You're in that bloody theatre aren't you Dryden? Coz I've just seen Lizzie bloody Southwell swinging her tits into action, and the whole place is swarming with dark blue.....Dryden?... Dryden?' After a short delay he hung up.

'It's Steve Watson - and he's watching us from outside.' She rapidly handed out orders. 'You two stay here - Tom, you, and you, come with me.'

They made for the foyer and went out onto the terrace, closely followed by Tony and Jessica and the officers from Venice. The arena and its stands were now virtually empty and what remained of the crowd was being directed away by a phalanx of police and security guards. Several media helicopters and two pilotless drones whirred away overhead.

The inspector's phone rang. 'Southwell?' she said.

'God, you look sexy in that uniform!' he said.

'I'll have you, Watson. I'll have this town ring fenced in five minutes. You're not leaving Stratford without me!'

'Cut the crap, Lizzie. You'll never hold me and you know it. Oh! And give mine to Essex girl and Essex boy. Tell them I won't be seeing them!' He hung up.

She looked across the deserted arena and gardens. 'Damn you!' she said. 'Damn you to hell!' She addressed the whole group of officers, as they gazed out at both the disappearing crowds and the smouldering wreckage of the vehicle carnage in Sheep Street. 'He's watching us; but we're never going to find him amongst all that lot.'

She looked at Mark Dryden's mobile still in her hand and showing Steve's number. 'You insidious little man,' she thought, 'but I'll know precisely where you are from now on; because, now, I've got your mobile number.' She rang Traffic Division. 'I want road blocks...Yes all of them, minor and major.'

48

Tony and Jessica sat on the steps at the base of the Theatre Tower. Tony squinted up at the densely clouded sky. It was spitting with rain. They watched the ambulance carrying Dryden's body pull slowly away. Tony put his arm round the shivering Jessica's shoulder. She was in shock and a WPC was quick to wrap a blanket round her and give her a hot drink. Tears streamed down her cheeks and it took her all her strength to stop trembling all over.

The Commissario came over to them. 'That was very brave of you, Signorina. Foolish - and dangerous too - but, brave nonetheless. Perhaps if you had been fully recovered from your car accident you might not have slipped and lost your footing? But, that is now all in the past; you must look to your future. I trust we may meet again, in Venice, perhaps, and, in more pleasant circumstances; but, for now, arrivederci.' He took her hand and kissed the back. He then shook Tony's hand and bade him farewell, adding that, should he require statements from them, he was sure it could be arranged over the internet. Sergeant Stefano then came across to say good-bye, and after a few words with D.I. Southwell, they were gone.

The terrorist units and other special forces within the police had the whole area around what they believed was a failed suicide attack evacuated, and made it clear that they didn't want Tony and Jessica to remain inside 'Ground Zero' any longer than necessary, particularly as they still had a van to declare safe.

Southwell laid on a car to get them to a nearby hotel to recuperate. Whilst they were being driven there, Tony said to

Jessica, 'We never felt happy about Steve did we? I wonder how far he was involved?'

'I think he was delaying us all along,' she said. 'It wouldn't surprise me if it was him who sabotaged your car.'

'And sent that e-mail,' added Tony. 'Look, when everything has settled down, and we've seen Randy and Helena and told them how it's all worked out, I want to have a word with 'BJ'; because he's in for a big surprise when he hears what his friend Steve is really like.' With barely a break in his conversation, Tony said to the driver, 'Stop here, driver, please!'

They were going along High Street and passing the top of Sheep Street, where there was a gaggle of ambulances and police cars. Tony jumped out of the car. He had seen Imogen at the rear of an ambulance.

'Are you all right?' he called, as he ran across the road towards her.

'It's my son,' she said. 'We were up here when the white van sped past us. Little Toby was blown over by the blast and ended up with some bruises and a few cuts from the flying glass. He'll be OK.'

Tony looked into the back of the ambulance. There was a man sitting next to the boy. Tony gave her a hug and kissed her on each cheek 'Take care,' he said. As he spoke, sensed tears welling up in his eyes. He found her, with pink-rimmed eyes looking straight back at him, a tear losing itself in the light rain as it rolled down her cheek. 'You must be so relieved it wasn't worse?' he added.

'Thanks for all you've done, Tony; not just for Alex, but for Mum and Dad. I thought they'd never get closure, but, now, well, we'll see.'

'What really happened will be in the papers soon enough, I guess,' he said, 'but, with all this bomb business, I suppose it'll be buried away in the middle pages.'

'Can we get going, please,' said a paramedic, 'Sorry, but we've got a busy schedule.'

Imogen climbed quickly into the ambulance and it pulled

away without them having time to say good-bye. Its siren blared, ripping the air. Tony watched as it sped off along High Street for the short journey to Stratford General Hospital. He looked at Jessica, waiting in the back of the police car, and then back at the ambulance, as it disappeared left at the end of the road. 'Bloody hindsight!' he thought.

Back in the car, Jessica, still wrapped in the police blanket, turned to him. 'What was all that about?' she asked.

'Her son was slightly hurt in the explosion, but otherwise….'

'I don't mean that.'

'What?'

'You know very well!'

'I'm just pleased that I didn't mess up her life for her.'

'And…'

'Jess. She didn't bring her family here just to see those Princesses; she came to finish some history with me - to show me she'd moved on. As a result, her child was injured - and could easily have been killed. She attributed no blame. Saw it as pure chance and had her mind on her life, and her family. I'm genuinely pleased for her, can't you see that?'

'So she's gone?'

'Deleted; and I'm delighted,' he said with a smile.

The car took them to The White Swan Hotel in the Market Square, well away for the scene of the 'attack.' They sat in the intimate lounge inside the entrance and, as Tony was about to order them some drinks, Jessica turned to him and said, 'Mark Dryden said the strangest thing when he was holding me.'

'What was that?' asked Tony.

'He said, "You're quite safe with me; please don't be frightened."'

'Well he would, wouldn't he? He was trying to put you at ease by using some psychology. He didn't want you struggling and making his life difficult.'

'Maybe you're right; but that's not all. He also said, "I've never hurt a soul in my life". Now why should he say that - tell me?'

'Same thing, sweetheart. He was a calculating man and he was trying to get inside your head. It looks as though he's succeeded, too, by the look of it. I've heard that kidnappers often try to befriend their victims and vice versa. Perhaps, it's one of the ways guilt manifests itself, I don't know.' He held her knee, squeezed it and gave it a gentle shake. 'Come on,' he said, 'try to put it out of your mind.'

49

Tony's phone rang. It was D.I. Southwell and she didn't sound in a very good mood. 'Are you still at the 'White Swan', Mr. Chapman?'

'Yes, Inspector,' he replied.

'Stay there till I arrive please,' she said, curtly.

Tony was taken aback by the brusqueness of her tone so soon after what he and Jessica had been through; and after what, under the circumstances, they both thought had been a successful outcome.

Jessica was on her mobile to her mother who had rung to see if she was all right. 'Mummy says all the news channels are running the terrorist attack story,' she said, covering the microphone, 'and there are banners on all the live programmes. - Was that Southwell?'

He nodded. 'Not a happy bunny.'

'I'll ring you back, Mummy,' she said, and rang off.

As they awaited the Inspector's imminent arrival, they reflected on the day's tumultuous events.

'When you think about it from a police perspective, that wasn't a particularly good day, was it?' said Jessica. 'What with Dryden dying like that. She'll be annoyed that she didn't get a result; and the police don't like deaths on their watch, do they? What do you want to bet, she'll blame us?'

'Well she'd taken her eye off the ball hadn't she? - OK, so it was for pretty extraordinary reasons afterwards - but Dryden was legging it before 'white van man' blew himself up; what was I supposed to do; just stand there and watch him get away? - Bye

Mark, hope you enjoy the exhibition - Oh! and make sure you don't bump into anything!'

Their conversation was cut short as Southwell and Heywood entered reception. They walked briskly straight up to Tony and Jessica. 'May we?' asked the inspector.

'Please,' said Tony, gesturing to a vacant leather armchair.

'Are you feeling better?' she said, addressing Jessica.

'Yes, thanks,' she said, readjusting the bandage round her elbow.

'There will be an inquest, of course,' Southwell continued, 'and you two will need to make yourselves available. In the meantime, I have to face my lords and masters to explain where things went wrong.' She looked firstly at Tony, then at Jessica, and then back at Tony. 'Not where things went right - but where things went wrong.'

'Look, Inspector,' began Tony, 'neither of us expected....'

'Mr. Chapman, Miss Marston. I was charged by my superiors with the protection of our prime suspect until he was safely in custody. Then he would be somebody else's problem. I have to explain to them why I was unable to discharge that duty successfully.'

'We're so sorry he got killed, Inspector,' said Jessica. 'And if...'

'Your apology won't be reported in the *Police Gazette*, Miss Marston,' Southwell snapped back. 'And there are few ways open for me to mitigate things. However, anything you've got on Steve Watson would be appreciated. He's been a thorn in my side all week and anything I can pin on him, I will.'

'We haven't got much, I'm afraid,' replied Tony. 'He came across as something of a loner and a law unto himself. If we can help, we will.'

'Are you going to search Dryden's house to see if the pages are there? - The ones he stole from Venice?' asked Jessica.

'We're going over there tomorrow, and they are certainly one of the things we'll be looking for; but, even if he did take them to his home for safekeeping, there's no knowing where they are now. It would most satisfying if they were there, but I wouldn't hold out too much hope, if I were you.'

She looked at the couple long and hard. 'I think you are both very well-meaning and your hearts are in the right place,' she said, 'but you have proved yourselves to be impetuous and reckless. I am here to issue you with an official warning. If either of you should interfere, in any way whatsoever, with my investigations from now on, I will have you arrested for deliberately impeding the police in the exercise of their duty and I'll throw the book at you. Now, is that understood?'

'Understood,' they said in unison.

'Good,' said the Inspector.

She stopped for a moment to remove a small piece of folded paper from her top pocket. 'Do either of you know, or have come across, a 'JF' in all this business?'

They both shrugged their shoulders. 'No. Why do you ask?' said Tony.

'When I went through Dryden's pockets a few minutes ago, this slip of paper fell out of his wallet. Clearly, it is a reminder to meet someone. All it says is: "JF MON 1.00 pm? SOF." To me, that's a reminder to meet a 'JF', on Monday, at about one o'clock, at his farmhouse in Stretton-on-Fosse. If it was last Monday, then I would very much like to meet 'JF'. We'll have an officer keeping an eye this Monday anyway - just in case.'

'What's going to happen to the original inscription stone?' asked Tony.

'That will stay with us until the case is closed. In the meantime you might have a word with your solicitor; he should be able to help.'

'Thank you,' said Tony, and as the inspector made a move to take her leave, added, 'and I sincerely hope your bosses aren't too hard on you.'

'I'll manage,' she said. 'I'll manage. Oh! I nearly forgot. Those three pages of Randy Middleton's. They may prove vital in linking Dryden to the Palazzo robbery and Bianca Middleton's death after all. I want to tie up *all* the loose ends, so, if we do find the other stolen ones at his house, we're going to need them. I'll be wanting a short statement from Mr. Middleton, too, as it was he who found them.'

'I think Randy's in the States right now doing a show for NBC. I'll ring him to tell him what you've just said; and as soon as we can get back to Essex, I'll have a courier get the three pages to you.'

Southwell put on her professional smile and prepared to leave. As she stood up, Sergeant Heywood showed her a text that had just arrived on his BlackBerry. 'Well, well,' she said. 'It seems our 'bomber's' van was empty; and it also appears he may have been dead before he was shot.' She and her sergeant turned to leave. 'That's going to make some interesting front pages in the morning! Al Qa'eda - Not!' she added, and they left.

50

When their checks on Dryden's car had drawn a blank and, deducing that he had probably driven himself into Stratford the previous day, the police ran a second check with the DVLA and found he had two cars registered to him. It came as no surprise to find the car they had been looking for in his garage. Southwell and her team made a cursory check of the outbuildings of the modest farm before approaching the house.

Using the latch-key from the bunch of keys in Dryden's pocket, the officers entered the kitchen. The tabby-cats followed them in.

'In a word - fastidious, Ma'am,' said Sergeant Heywood, 'he even kept the dust clean!'

'Search thoroughly, team,' Southwell said to Tom Heywood and the three constables accompanying them, 'We're looking for a couple of dozen sixteenth-century manuscripts. You've seen the one in all the papers; well, our witness says the ones we're after are more or less identical. They could be in any card or plastic wallet or folder, a box file, anything. And there are two small leather-bound books of the same age.'

The search-team spread themselves throughout the house and its outbuildings; after only a few minutes, Tom Heywood called out to her.

'Better give the safecrackers a ring, Boss,' he said.

She rang her Headquarters.

'Get me a locksmith,' she said, 'one who can open a Chubb safe.'

When Mark's safe was eventually opened, the police were in for a surprise. Inside it were three A4 envelopes, labelled 'Tom', 'George', and 'Me'. They contained passports, driving licences, tax and insurance documents, and even household bills in all three names.

'Boss, take a look at this,' said Heywood.

'Well, well, Tom. Wouldn't 'Mister' Montano have loved to have seen this?' She started to go through the contents of Dryden's 'special' toilet bag. 'God knows how many identities you could create with this. Talk about a man of many parts!' There was also another mobile phone and, last but not least, his writing box. She opened it slowly and carefully, and noted the unusual collection of antique writing and drawing instruments. 'Now, tell me, Tom. Why on earth would anyone want keep their art materials in their safe?'

'Because they intend to be naughty, Ma'am?'

'Precisely, Tom which is why the Shakespeare Centre's 'magic page' and that old book in which it was found are going to spend a few days in our forensics lab.'

The contents of the safe were bagged and taken back to Warwick to be left with forensics. Southwell had Dryden's phone records checked, but it appeared that, as he had made extensive use of pay-as-you-go, they had no network provider to check the billing with. As a result, it was impossible to tell where he was when using his mobile. The only anomaly they found was that a number, which he had dialled several times using his land-line in late February and through April, was diverted to an offshore computer. As this number didn't connect subsequently with an active phone, they again drew a blank.

With no books or manuscripts to show for their troubles, Southwell switched her search to the Shakespeare Centre. She felt certain that Mark had an accomplice - was it the mysterious 'JF'? She concentrated on the Trust employees, even though no-one had the same initials.

Katie Lancaster's world was turned upside-down. No sooner was she grieving at the loss of her friend and colleague of many years standing, than all work in the Records Department was forced to a grinding halt. She felt violated as the police search-team robbed her workplace its of its peace and dignity.

APR. 26th: TUE: 10.45 am.

Lizzie Southwell was now desperate to build a cast-iron case against Dryden before she had to face the inquiry on Wednesday afternoon. Harry Gower called her into his office. Dryden's premature death had presented him with the ideal opportunity to sideline her and take control. He would also be perfectly positioned to govern how much interest would be shown in Steve Watson.

'I'm taking over the case, Lizzie,' he said, 'I think it's too big for you.'

'You can't do that! With absolutely no warning. I'm getting results.'

'Come on then, girl - tell me all about your "results".'

'I've got Dryden's belongings in forensics; I've got a team in the Shakespeare Centre; we've retrieved his car....'

'I said, 'results'. You're chasing your own arse, Lizzie, and you're getting nowhere. If you haven't got anything positive by six tonight, I'm taking you off the case. Last Wednesday I gave you a week, and that week's up in the morning. Oh! And by the way, the inquiry into Saturday's unfortunate events has been brought forward to tomorrow morning; so I'll see you in here at nine-thirty. Have your report on my desk by six tonight, OK?'

An incandescent Lizzie Southwell stormed out of the D.C.C.'s office. 'How dare he!' she thought. 'I'll show you, you chauvinist bastard!' Getting hold of Steve Watson was now her number one priority, for, without him, there was little to link Dryden directly with Alex's death. She had two officers in Essex tailing him with a warrant to have him detained, and they had informed her that his arrest was imminent.

With time rapidly running out, she found herself relying increasingly on the scanty evidence proving Dryden's complicity in the Bianca Middleton case. Montano's evidence, thanks to the pressure he had put on the British Consulate, put Dryden in the Palazzo, but no more than that. Without the stolen artefacts to tie him to the robbery, she was now depending almost entirely on what forensics might find. It was gone mid-day when there was finally a breakthrough.

'This is D. I. Southwell, who is that?'

'Forensics, Inspector. Tell me, did your suspect have a tabby cat by any chance?'

'Yes, you lovely man, he did!'

'It may not prove a thing, you realise, but I found a single hair caught in the bookbinder's webbing. If you can provide me with a match you can draw your own conclusions; if not, I've got a very good drawing board you can borrow!'

'I suppose you'll want a sample of fur for comparison?' she said. 'You'll have it before your lunch-bell rings.'

'One other thing you might be interested in before you dash off, Inspector. There was a stain on the suspect manuscript page.'

'And…'

'Well I thought it was just a water-stain when I first looked at it, but I ran a chromatograph test on it anyway, and guess what?'

'Don't keep me in suspense - come on, I'm working against the clock here.'

'It had minute traces of the Rondinella grape in it.'

'So?'

'It's a wine grape, and it grows almost exclusively in the Veneto. There were no modern additives of any kind present. If you want my opinion, whoever wrote that manuscript was probably in Venice about four hundred and fifty years ago, and was enjoying a nice glass of white wine at the time.'

'You're a star!' She said, 'and what about the writing on the back?'

'Too early to say. Written later of course; but by how much in years or centuries? - Too tricky to call at the moment.'

'I'm on my way,' she said. 'Give me an hour.'

She hung up and was off to track down Troilus and Cressida, hopefully before they abandoned the farmhouse belonging to the man who just had abandoned them.

51

Tony and Jessica drove down the leafy avenue of mature maples towards Richmond Park. The 'gentlemen's residences' that lined the road were built with a richness and generosity of detail that Jessica, in particular, found difficult to comprehend. These were houses that had the luxury of being able to sit back from the road in the comfort of their gardens, as confident reminders of a complacent age of Empire; a time when little was ever going seriously to disturb their quiet purpose.

'Isn't 'BJ' one of the luckiest people alive to be able to live amongst all this for more than twenty years?' said Tony.

'In one way, I suppose he is,' replied Jessica. 'Beautiful, but awfully insular. Have you been to his house before?'

'Two or three times; the last was with you-know-who, shortly before we got married. I've never forgotten my first impressions of it. You want to soak it all up while you've got the chance; but don't think of it as a time-capsule - think of it more as a work of art. I just hope he isn't too offended by our turning up so early.'

'Let me know a bit more about what I'm in for. You said he never married. Has he got a partner? - Is he gay?'

'No, he's not gay. He's as hetero as you and me. I remember him saying he thought his life was too full to expect any woman to share it, "and anyway, children, Tony," he said, "who wants them running all over your house? - Nothing but problems, puke and plastic!"'

'He sounds rather selfish.'

'I think he is. Bloody interesting though! - Hang on, I think it's this one here.'

They pulled into the drive, which swept in a perfect half ellipse across the front of the red-brick and stone, three-storey, house. It had many of the best features of Central European Art Nouveau, but was restrained by the unmistakable reserve of 'Arts and Crafts'. Tony rang the doorbell - they didn't have to wait long.

When the door opened, they were greeted by the smiling, enigmatic figure of Tony's uncle. A little over six feet, and in his late forties, he was Tony's mother's youngest brother. With his close-cut hair and greying temples, he looked disconcertingly like an older version of Tony, and, though he clearly knew how to look after himself, appeared a bit flustered.

'You're the Jessica I've been hearing about,' he said, 'call me 'BJ', everyone does.' He took her hand firmly and kissed her on both cheeks. 'Hi, Tony, lovely to see you. Come on in.' He walked off across the entrance hall ahead of them, and disappeared into a room on their left, leaving Tony to shut the front door. 'You'll have to excuse me for a moment while I do a quick bit of tidying up. You've caught me on the hop!'

'The roads weren't as busy as I thought they'd be,' said Tony, 'so we made good time - barely an hour and a half.'

Around the spacious entrance hall, and along a hallway ahead of them, was an enviable collection or original twentieth-century paintings, drawings and prints. Jessica recognised many of the signatures and couldn't avoid commenting on them, especially a Jim Dine watercolour, as Tony had an original by him too, which she really liked.

'Have you still got the large nude by Jim Dine, 'BJ'?' said Tony, as he followed his uncle into his study. 'The one like the wedding present you gave to Imogen and me.'

'I'd never get rid of it,' he said. 'It's here, look.' Jessica joined them.

'What a fabulous room!' she half-whispered, in an aside to Tony. She had the sense of entering the library of a gentlemen's club. The tranquil luxury of its self-indulgent ambience was a far cry from the commercial and media-driven world they had just left behind. A vast collection of books, both old and new, filled two of the walls almost three metres to the ceiling. From what Tony had told her, it came as no surprise that a large section was devoted to Shakespeare. The more she looked, the more she became aware that the room was almost entirely devoted to the Shakespeare authorship question. Not wanting to appear rude to her host, she returned quickly to the picture. 'My goodness! He can draw, can't he?'

'You're too right,' said 'BJ', 'but you haven't come all this way to talk art, and it's such a beautiful day. We should be in the garden - come on.' They followed him along the rear hall and through the kitchen to a terrace overlooking a large garden, dotted with sculptures. They sat under a natural-canvas sun-umbrella and 'BJ' went back to the kitchen to fix a large jug of Pimms.

'You were right - must be one of the forms heaven takes!' said Jessica.

'Now where have I heard that one before?' Tony replied.

'BJ' soon rejoined them. 'Well, who would have believed that you two would be feted as the champions of Oxfordianism? I bet you're not exactly flavour-of-the-month in Stratford these days though, are you?' He poured their drinks and handed them round.

'It's been more than three months and I can still hardly believe it all happened to us,' said Tony. 'If Bianca hadn't forgotten to take any cash with her that evening, Stratford would still be basking in 'WS's' reflected glory, its character unblemished. Instead, the narrow streets of Castle Hedingham are now packed with tourist coaches.'

'Yes, but that won't stop Stratford's cash registers ringing away merrily to the tunes of international tourism, will it?' asked 'BJ'.

'And it will for decades to come.' added Jessica. 'It's a town blessed with everything an inland resort craves: history, architecture, culture - and a river!'

'Talking of the river,' said 'BJ', 'What made the two of you embark on a harebrained scheme like searching the Avon for the Inscription Stone? It looked freezing on that TV programme.

You must have had second thoughts?'

'It looked colder than it was,' said Tony. 'And we found it quicker than we thought. Alex's last email to himself was on his computer. It was still in his wardrobe at his parents home; they hadn't the heart to throw it away. Two photos of "the slabbe", as he called it, were there for all to see. He did all the hard work - Jess and I only finished off what he'd started.'

'BJ' turned to Jessica. 'In the midst of what we all thought was a terrorist attack on the Royal Family, young lady, you get held hostage, almost getting killed, too, by the sound of it, and then hanging by your fingernails - the killer falls to his death right next to you. I take my hat off to you. You must have nerves of steel!'

'You make me sound very courageous, 'BJ', but I wasn't, really. I was scared witless, and just took my chance when it came.'

When Tony and 'BJ' started to talk more seriously about authorship issues and the Earl of Oxford, she excused herself to use the bathroom. Actually, it was just a pretext to have another look at the 'art gallery' she'd walked through and also to take another peek at his study, where the best artworks seemed to be.

'On your right, just past the kitchen,' said 'BJ'.

She was about to use the bathroom when she noticed that the study door was ajar. 'Dare I?' she thought, and, like a naughty schoolgirl, pushed it open, and went in. 'This is better than our library at uni,' she thought, running her fingers along a row of spines. The room, best described as 'literary baroque', seemed to have its contents arranged aesthetically rather than practically. However, the books themselves were arranged most precisely. Subjects included far more than just Shakespeare and the Earl of Oxford. Sir Francis Bacon, Christopher Marlowe, the Rosicrucians, Walsingham and the Secret Service; it was all here. Near to his desk and his computer, the shelves included many box files, entitled 'Early Quartos', 'Victorian Theatre Programmes', and so on. She noticed that one of them had its spine to the wall, and thought it was probably like that due to 'BJ's' hasty tidying up, caused by their unexpectedly early arrival.

She reached over and slid it out in order to turn it round. When she did, and read its spine, she got quite a surprise. 'Ca' Magretti-Bellini', it said. 'Heavens,' she thought. 'A whole file on Randy's palazzo - wouldn't he just love to see what's in here? She removed it, placed it carefully on the leather-topped desk, and opened it. When she saw its contents, she gasped audibly and turned round quickly to make sure she was still alone.

It contained the three dozen pages and two small volumes stolen from Randy's palazzo. She closed her eyes, took a deep breath and opened them; and looked again, in sheer disbelief, at the contents. As the sun streamed in through the tall, stained-glass windows, memories of the last time she had seen these objects came flooding back. Tears welled up in her eyes as she recalled Bianca sitting opposite her, cross-legged on the drawing room floor back in Venice, joking about Shakespeare's schooldays.

She quickly collected her thoughts. 'They could only be in front of me,' she thought, 'if he got them from Mark Dryden, or - stole them from the palazzo himself.' She was overwhelmed by a rush of fear. A cold tingling shot down her body and legs all the way to her feet. She had a hollow, sick feeling and sat down at 'BJ's' desk. 'Tony always said the sheets of paper would leave a trail leading to the killer - it can't be 'BJ', surely? All the circumstantial evidence pointed so conclusively to Dryden, but, the police never did find the stolen artefacts, or allow Southwell to pursue her 'JF', her, 'unknown man'. She felt so sure that Harry Gower had let him get away.'

Sitting at his desk, wondering what on earth to do, she glanced around at the busy clutter of his work, and at the eclectic mix of papers by the printer. On top, she noticed a sheet of Masonic headed-notepaper - a memo to some of the Brethren at his Lodge perhaps. But there was a second symbol and a second heading beneath the gilded Square and Compasses. The symbol was in the form of swan; beneath it were the Latin words: FRATERNITAS CYGNUS VERUS. It was signed: 'JF', and, underneath, was his name in print: Brian John Fletcher. 'Oh my God!' she thought, '*He* is the 'JF' Southwell was searching for. And that must be the name of their brotherhood, the 'FCV,' which translates to…. The Brotherhood of the True Swan. Of course, 'The Swan of Avon' - how Ben Jonson described Shakespeare.'

She put the file back just as she found it, went into the bathroom, took out her mobile and phoned D.I. Southwell. She got straight through. 'Inspector?…it's Jessica Marston…I'm fine, thanks…can you do something for me really quickly? …Find out if a 'Brian John Fletcher,' flew from the UK to Venice, or any other airport near Venice, around the last weekend in February, possibly on a return ticket …No, I'm sorry, I can't talk now; and please ring me back as soon as you can…Thanks.'

There was a knock on the bathroom door.

'Are you OK, Jess. You've been ages?' asked Tony.

'Sorry, sweetheart, women's troubles. Won't be long.' She waited for a minute, flushed the loo, and went back to the terrace.

'Are you all right, Jessica. Can I get you anything?' asked 'BJ'.

'I'll be fine, thank you,' she said.

'You look pretty washed out, love. Are you sure you're feeling OK?'

'Don't fuss, Tony - I'll be as right as rain in five minutes.' She may have passed her acting debut for Eddie and his mini-documentary, but disguising her sudden change of attitude was proving far more difficult.

Tony, however, was never more relaxed, and seemed to be in his element as their conversation continued. Jessica attempted to join in, but the overload of information pressing for dominance in her mind meant it was like trying to concentrate on subdued voices coming from a nearby, but far-off, place, like struggling to listen to a quiet radio, slightly out of tune. After a few minutes her mobile rang.

'I'm so sorry. I don't know what you must think of me,' She said, 'I should have switched it off.' She looked at the caller's name. It was Lizzie Southwell. 'Sorry, it's Mummy. Do excuse me, I won't be a minute.' She left the table, and walked out onto the lawn.

'Stanstead to Treviso,' said Southwell, 'that's just outside

Venice; on the Thursday. Verona to Stanstead, first thing on the Saturday morning. What's this all about, Jessica?'

'He's your 'JF', Inspector, and he's sipping Pimms not ten metres from where I'm standing. Tony and I know him as 'BJ', but when he communicates with his Masonic friends he's 'JF'. I've also just been looking at Randy's stolen books and manuscripts - they're here - in his house.'

'Where are you?'

'Richmond upon Thames, near the park.'

'Give me an hour and a half. Leave your mobile switched on and I'll locate you by GPS. Stay calm, and whatever you do, try not to rouse his suspicions. In the meantime, I'll get some local 'Surrey' units sent along.'

Jessica checked that her phone was fully charged, slipped it back in her bag and returned to the table. When 'BJ' went back to the kitchen to mix another jug of Pimms, she told Tony what she had discovered.

'Ask him about Steve Watson and find out if he knew Dryden.'

'What the hell are you talking about, sweetheart. Where has all this suddenly come from?'

'You always said there would be a paper trail leading us to the killer. Well, Randy's books and manuscripts are here - in your uncle's study - explain that, if you can; and you never told me his surname was Fletcher.'

'So?'

'B…J…F - 'BJ', and the 'JF' Southwell was always so interested in?'

'BJ' came back out onto the terrace with the replenished jug clinking with ice, and joined them at the table. Tony hardly knew where to begin. After some small-talk about the garden and the modern sculptures, the conversation died. Tony felt uneasy about Jessica's suggestion, but thought he would see what his uncle's reaction would be anyway. He came straight to the point.

'Why did you choose Watson to help us, Uncle?'

'He had a reputation for getting things done, Tony - you know, if you want to get something done, find a busy man.'

'But he was useless. We'd have been far better off without him. From quite early on we had to press him to get any information. In fact, he was more of a distraction than anything.'

'In fact,' added Jessica, 'he proved to be the ideal person to put us off the scent. I'm surprised you wouldn't have realised that, 'BJ'.'

'Merely a coincidence. I'd completely forgotten he had headed the original investigation into Alex's case…and I feel somewhat put out by the inference you're making, Jessica.'

'We had him on board for over a month,' she said. 'And he never gave us a clue as to his earlier involvement. That's suspicious in anyone's books, surely?'

'I must say I was most surprised when I heard that Warwickshire Police had had him in for questioning, but nothing was ever proved against him, was it? He was never charged with any offence.'

'D.I. Southwell, who headed the investigation, was certain that Dryden wasn't working alone,' said Tony. 'Her boss, Harry Gower, the D.C.C. for Warwickshire, was content with all the circumstantial evidence against Dryden, and pronounced him guilty at a news conference within a couple of days, closing the case barely a fortnight later. Southwell wasn't at all happy and confided in us that that was how she felt. Not just because she had some history with Watson, and was keen to see him put away, but because she was unable to uncover what was so important that Alex had to be got rid of. She knew it was about more than the 'slabbe'. She was also so starved of funds that she wasn't able to track down the stuff stolen from Venice, or to carry on searching for Dryden's accomplice. The whole Shakespeare-Oxford authorship business is out in the open now, 'BJ'. Be honest with me, is there something else that you know and we don't?'

Jessica could feel emotions building inside her and was terrified by what their portent might hold. She could feel her heart pounding faster and harder in her chest and hear it in her ears. She wrestled with her feelings as they battled for an outward expression. Tony found himself so confused, for a moment, it was hard for him to be fully conscious of the meaning in his words. He looked at her. She was staring at 'BJ'.

Before 'BJ' could answer, however, Jessica summoned up her courage, and said quite calmly. 'Do you know what I just found in your study?'

He looked at Tony, and back to Jessica. 'No, my dear, what?'

'A box file, that's what. And guess what was written on the spine?'

'Oh!' he said quietly.

'Oh! Is that all you've got to say? - Oh!'

'I can explain…'

'This is going to take some explaining, 'BJ',' said Tony. 'How did that file get here? And how many more are there?'

'It's a long story - about four centuries long to be precise. And it was fine until your friend, Alex, stumbled across that damned inscription stone lying in the grass. We had no idea it was there…'

Jessica interrupted him, sensing that he was about to intellectualise his way out of his guilt and out of trouble. She wasn't going to let him off the hook and quickly rounded on him. 'Every day for the past three months, I've had the same words enter my head, over and over again.' She looked 'BJ' straight in the eyes and continued. 'Just a few minutes before Mark Dryden reached out to save my life, and in so doing lost his balance and fell to his death, do you know what he said?'

'I think you're going to tell me anyway.'

She leaned towards him. 'He said, "I've never hurt a soul in my life." Now why should he say that, do you think? To me? - When he's holding me hostage - is in fear of arrest and trying hurriedly to escape? Why go to the trouble of saying that - hmm?'

'You tell me, Jessica.'

'You fucking bet I will. He said it because it was the truth. He never did kill anyone, did he?' She said, her voice rising to a crescendo. '*You* were in Venice on Carnival night, weren't you?

When 'B' and I came back without warning - It was *you* wasn't it?' she screamed and lunged across the table at him. 'It was *you* all along; *you bastard!*'

'Jess! For God's sake!' said Tony, grappling at her arms in an attempt to restrain her 'Well, 'BJ'? Were you there?' he asked.

'Of course not, Tony. Jessica here has put two and two together, and come up with five. I can imagine how upsetting this whole affair must have been for the two of you - and your emotions are running high. I know what this must look like, and I can explain.'

'Explain your way out of it to the police, if you can,' snapped Jessica.

'BJ' stood up and pushed back his chair. 'You haven't?…You have, haven't you?…That call just now?'

'That was Inspector Southwell ringing me back to confirm that you were in Venice the night 'B' died.' she said. 'Unlike Dryden, you chose to travel under your own name. You were backing him up because you were scared he couldn't go through with it if things started to go wrong. He was too nice to get really physical, wasn't he, and in the end you sacrificed him?'

'BJ' looked across the table to Tony. Jessica was now on her feet too, pacing up and down, sobbing, and with her hands to her head. He sighed. 'God, Tony, I'm so sorry.'

'You bastard! You bastard!' screamed Jessica. 'You killed my best friend and you say - sorry! You chased me half way across Venice…in fear of my life, and you…you've got the gall to just stand there…drinking your fucking Pimms, and you say - sorry! How dare you - How *dare* you?'

Tony jumped up, knocking over his chair. 'Sorry!' he shouted. 'Sorry! I can't believe what you've done!'

'Why the bloody hell couldn't you two leave well alone? Why did you have to go on snooping around? Tony - you of all people? Digging here, digging there. If you could have just left it to the police, none of this would have happened'

' 'BJ', please, tell me it isn't true?' said Tony.

'I wish I could. I never expected anyone to die. If only I could turn the clock back…'

'I wish I could turn it back far enough for you to *hang* for what you've done!' spat Jessica.

'You couldn't possibly understand,' he snapped back, 'This is far bigger and more far-reaching than either of you could ever imagine. So don't try lecturing me about the perspective of importance of things in this world. You might think Shakespeare is all about dressing yourself up for a night out at the theatre, little lady - well, you couldn't be more wrong; it's not only cultural and social, it's political. Things might have got out of proportion over the years, but huge issues were at stake.'

'So deceiving a gullible public is a *huge* issue,' said an enraged Tony, 'and the lives of our two friends isn't. That's one hell of an "out of proportion"!'

'It's the way thing are, Tony. Like it or not, those authorship files had to be protected. It must have dawned on you to question why nobody ever finds anything that proves Edward de Vere *was* behind the writing, and that William of Stratford *wasn't*. The 'Brotherhood' has been hoovering up the evidence for centuries. We've got the Royals, Tony, the Queen as Patron; and the respect of the whole nation - the whole world. Remember those huge tableaux at the Olympics with 'ideal Will' at the heart? What would you have had - Oxford? A philandering bisexual whose claims to fame are calling Phillip Sydney a puppy, and farting in front of his queen? I know he was the real author, Tony, but we're talking about a world-wide industry worth billions.'

'And if that industry moved from Stratford to Castle Hedingham, so what? If you'd had the guts, you would have done the transition years ago; and now look what you've done; and who gets hurt - a few Freemasons? Don't forget - one of your 'Brethren' died too. Wasn't *his* life a 'huge issue'? - Get real 'BJ'!'

Tony's comment about the death of his friend Mark really seemed to hit home. It left 'BJ' speechless.

'How many members are left in your 'Fraternitas Cygnus Verus' now?' said Jessica. 'BJ' didn't respond. 'It's just *you* isn't it? There isn't anybody else now Dryden's dead is there?' 'BJ' remained silent, staring blankly into his glass. 'I don't know how you can talk to him, Tony,' she continued. 'Leave him to the police. Lets just go.' She grabbed her bag, and made for the kitchen door. Tony followed her. At the doorway, he stopped and turned back to address his 'favourite' uncle.

'Either come with us and do the sensible thing by handing yourself in to the police, or stay and take your chance,' he said.

'BJ' forced his way past them and rushed through the house to his study. A few moments later he entered the entrance hall looking flustered and distressed. He had the look of a frightened child; he appeared lost in a world of his own creation, a man rudely stripped of his culture and sophistication. He walked nervously this way and that. It was only when he stopped to talk to them that Tony and Jessica noticed that he was holding a handgun. 'However did it get to this, Tony?' he said. 'I think I might need a little help here,' he added with a wry smile, holding the pistol as though waiting for someone to tell him what to do next.

'I would be properly frightened if I thought you were actually going to use that, Uncle,' said Tony, stepping in front of Jessica, 'but I know you're not.' Despite his Uncle's apparent helplessness, Tony was utterly terrified, but did his best to stay calm and keep Jessica safe. 'We're going to walk out of that door right now,' he said, taking Jessica by the hand and gingerly leading her across the hall. 'Please, don't try to stop us.'

'BJ' stepped in front of them. 'Don't go, Tony,' he said. 'Give me more time, please?'

'You've had more than enough time already,' said Jessica. 'You don't deserve another second. This whole house is probably surrounded by police by now. Just…give up, you stupid man - this whole 'FCV', and 'Secret File' business is all over; there *is* no 'authorship question' any more, can't you see? Just put that thing down and give yourself up.'

'She's right,' said Tony. 'This has all got way out of hand and it's you who's lost all perspective; and your waving that thing at us isn't going to achieve anything, is it? Why don't you do as Jess said and put it down? - better still - give it to me?' he held out his hand.

'BJ' considered his situation. He knew it was hopeless trying to reverse the circumstances created by Tony and Jessica. In the space of a few short hours his idyllic world had collapsed around him and he knew he was powerless to save himself from inevitable ruin. Facing public shame, particularly the ignominy of his peers, he found himself a shattered man. He fell still and silent slowly lowered the gun and gazed blankly across the hall.

Tony and Jessica moved cautiously to one side; without taking their eyes off him, inched their way towards the door. They opened it quietly and carefully and stepped outside into the porch.

Except for several police cars parked almost out of sight, they were greeted by a deserted road. The only sound - the air-thrashing throb of Lizzie Southwell's helicopter, touching down after its ninety mile flight from Warwick. The inspector ran from the landing-site, ducked under the cordon's blue and white tape and walked briskly across the road to greet them.

'I should warn you, Inspector,' said Tony, 'he's carrying a handgun of some kind.'

'There's no stopping you two is there?' she said. 'You pop up like magic wherever there's any trouble. Where did you park your Tardis - in the back garden! Just you keep well away, and leave any heroics to us. All right?'

Southwell took hold of a loudhailer and called out, not to 'BJ', but to the man she knew only as, 'JF'.

'Mr. Fletcher,' she said, 'I've been talking with your nephew and he is very concerned for your safety. It might be a good idea if you threw out your weapon onto the front drive and then came out yourself.'

John Fletcher went into his study still holding his handgun and sat at his desk. He scanned the shelves and their wealth of cultural and historical riches. More than twenty years of obsessive collecting and research surrounded him. For the three months since Mark's death, he had been struggling to find a way to release the information in the 'Secret Files', without heaping blame on either the Shakespeare Trust or himself and his fellow Masons. The 'Brotherhood' had garnered a string of prominent figures from British history since the middle of the seventeenth century and it was now his sole responsibility to protect their reputations. The realisation that he was, indeed, the 'last of the line' of four centuries of proud and dedicated men rested heavily and most uneasily upon him.

He was now truly alone, more alone than he could ever have dreamed. The strain on his mind was beginning to show dramatically. He surveyed the shelves of scholarship and learning once again - then, out of the corner of his eye, through the French-windows, he caught sight of a black-uniformed armed policeman scampering across his garden to hide behind an abstract sculpture. He smiled sadly. 'Poor old Barbara Hepworth,' he mused. 'She would turn in her grave.'

He looked down at the gun in his hand. 'I can't believe I just did that', he thought, 'and to Tony and his girlfriend, too - of all people'. A second armed-officer ran across the far edge of the lawn. 'How appallingly vulgar,' he thought, 'Sorry, Grandpapa, I never thought your beautiful house and garden would be treated like some inner-city housing estate.' The long-case clock in the hall chimed five. He looked up and cast his eyes one last time around his beloved study. 'Time to go, I think,' he said, and reached for his phone.

Tony and Jessica were on the far side of the road, talking to D.I. Southwell, when Tony's mobile rang.

'Will you tell whoever's in charge that I'm coming out, please Tony; and that I'm not going to be shooting at anyone?'

'Wise decision, Uncle. Just make sure you throw out your gun first.'

'OK, Tony. See you in a minute.'

As quick as lightning, 'BJ' was out of his study, through the rear hall and down the cellar stairs. At the bottom, he stopped, for a moment, to open and check the contents of a small travel bag which he kept ready in case of emergencies. He then doubled back to his right and entered a second room which he used as a wine cellar. He switched on his torch and hurried over to one of the wine-racks standing against the opposite wall. It was coupled to a concealed door. As he moved the rack out into the room the opening door revealed a narrow tunnel. He slipped through and closed the door; the wine-rack slid back into place. He bolted the door securely and moved swiftly down the passage's sewer-like vault.

The tunnel had been installed early in the second world war to connect the house to an air-raid shelter fifty metres away at the bottom of the garden. This in turn connected with the shelter in the garden next door. Less than two minutes after phoning Tony and concealed by the high dividing wall, he was out through his neighbour's garden door and strolling unnoticed, amongst the summer crowds, in Richmond Park. There would be no travelling under his own name this time. He wasn't going to let the 'momentary lapse of reason' that had nearly cost him everything, happen again.

'You know him, Mr. Chapman, He isn't likely to do anything stupid, is he?' asked Lizzie Southwell.

'He's not the suicidal type if that's what you mean.' said Tony. He paused for a moment. 'Are you worried that he's taking his time?'

Southwell used the loudhailer a couple more times to attract 'BJ's attention. Ten minutes - ten eternities - dragged by, but, still no response. Tony tried his mobile, but, it was switched off.

The inspector was getting increasingly fidgety. She had been in stand-off situations before and these were not the times for making hasty decisions. She considered her options and felt there was only one left. 'We have to approach the house,' she said, 'he's taking far too long.' She cast her eyes over the substantial property and then called over to a specialist unit. 'Heat-scan it,' she said. The rapidly mobilised technical support team went into action, but, were quick to come back to her with the worst possible news.

'Not even a mouse, ma'am,' said the officer in charge.

'Damn him!' she said. 'Damn him!'

Two hours had passed by the time the house and garden had been thoroughly searched and declared safe. It was not until the next day, when, after following up a complaint from the neighbouring houseowners that their garden door had been left unlocked, that the air-raid shelters and tunnels leading back to the houses were discovered.

Epilogue

Ford,

'…cry out thus upon no trail…'

Merry Wives of Windsor, 4, 2.

William Shakespeare.

52

'In answer to your question, Randy,' said Tony, 'you can't imagine what it was like for my mother. When I rang her to prepare her for what was coming, she said that everyone in the family knew 'BJ' was a loner and rather obsessive, but, to be able to kill somebody - never. She was in what amounted to shock.'

'And you hadn't an inkling either?' said Helena.

'The coincidence with Steve Watson was the only thing that made me wobble for a few moments, but it soon passed, because I knew him so well. Or thought I did.'

'And you've no idea where he could have disappeared to?'

'Not a clue. He had contacts all over the world from what I can gather. He'll have had his escape meticulously planned, knowing him.'

'Interpol? He is a double-murderer after all.'

'Southwell told me she'd handed things over to New Scotland Yard. So I guess that means Interpol will be taking a look - but, as for a result? I wouldn't bet too much of my hard-earned, if I were you.'

'Did the 'Cockney Colombo' cough once Southwell got hold of him?' asked Randy, 'I've only read a few things in the papers and Warwickshire Police have given us precious little feedback.'

'She was in seventh heaven when they brought him in, wasn't she, Tony,' said Jessica. 'You'd have thought she'd won a rollover! And it *was* him who sabotaged Tony's car. We always thought it probably was, but, it could just as easily have been Mark Dryden or one of his friends - even another bent police officer.'

'Lizzie Southwell was furious when she heard that we were almost killed because of Steve,' added Tony. 'The last time we spoke to her she was still purring like the fishmonger's cat! As soon as she gets any fresh shit on him - excuse my French - she piles it all over him! She'll push for a long custodial, if I know her.'

'Was it him who got into the police files, as well?' asked Randy.

'We don't think so. Suspicion points to someone still working in the Warwickshire Police. Southwell says she's pretty sure who, but - no names.'

Helena topped up everyone's drinks and raised a point much closer to home. 'Montano was such a nice guy but he was wrong right down the line. If he'd listened to you two from the start, do you think he might have been onto Dryden far more quickly?'

'I know what you mean, Helena,' said Tony. 'But if you looked at the hard evidence at the time, I mean, who would have dreamed that we were dealing with a conspiracy involving a secret sect calling themselves the Fraternitas Cygnus Verus and going back nearly four-hundred years? Arresting the 'Famous Five' for internet identity theft is more believable!'

'How did that uncle of yours do it, Tony?' asked Randy, 'because, when Dryden died, we, all of us, police included, thought that, that was it. Montano's been in touch and characteristically defensive and skimpy on the details, but, he too, was convinced, once he had the file from Bristol and Avon.'

'It seems that 'BJ' flew out to Treviso on the Thursday morning, Randy,' said Tony. 'There was a single call from his mobile, apparently, and it puts him in Venice around lunchtime. It was to Bill Harvey, at the Consulate, to arrange accommodation for himself. We think Dryden never knew 'BJ' was ever in Venice. The less he knew the better, I suppose. Loads of footprints were found on the balcony and the builders boards, and, although 'BJ's' would have been amongst them, Montano thought they all belonged to Zenobi's carpenters and tilers. As only one set of footprints was found inside the 'Magretti', he never expected there to be a second person involved, so, he never looked for one. 'BJ' must have been on the scaffolding before Dryden even arrived. Having secreted himself away, he probably left straight after the moment Dryden had locked-up and gone.

He must have had the shock of his life, when the girls walked right up to him, and he realised who they were. Having dealt with 'B' I guess he legged it out of Venice as fast as he could. Jess thought he'd chased *her* all the way to the Rialto, as you know, but it looks as though he went the opposite way and made straight for the station. Funny thing fear, isn't it? Sometimes it can give the imagination such an adrenalin fix! So, there it is, Saturday morning 'BJ' catches a cheap flight back from Verona to the UK - all done and dusted.'

'And our girl dies for thirty sheets of paper and a couple of books,' said Randy.

His words shocked them all into a realisation of their loss; the magnitude of their grief. Bianca's brilliant light might have been extinguished, but, the memory of her was still so vivid for them that they expected her to come skipping out onto the terrace at any moment, to regale them with the latest celebrity gossip. They sat in stunned silence. Jessica broke the ice.

'Have you been back?' she asked.

'Just to get the remainder of my things and to see the agents and stuff.'

'The fresco?' asked Tony.

'Zenobi is still fighting it out with his insurers. Could take years knowing the Venetians!'

'Are you still considering Italy?' he added.

'Yes. We're looking at 'The Lakes', at present,' he said. 'There are some villas with exquisite gardens up there. You've seen a couple you like, haven't you, darling?' he said, turning to Helena.

She looked at him with a tearful smile but said nothing.

Jessica helped her out by topping up everyone's glasses, and tried to lighten the load for them all. 'It was all quite a shock for the Italian stallion too, wasn't it?' she said. 'Is he still with you?'

'Living-in until we sell,' said Randy. 'Montano had him in

a second time, you know, and really made it sound as though he was convinced he had something to do with the robbery. I thought poor old Angelo was going to have a heart-attack at one point. He's all right about it now, but, he's a real softy and the stress really got to him. He was still seeing his doctor until a few weeks ago.'

'Did you get all the pages back - including the one from Stratford?'

'Jess, you've no idea how difficult it is to convince them to return it. That guy writes all over the back of one of our pages and the 'Trust' seems to think that, because, he was their employee that they have a claim to it! I'll tell you one thing - Dryden would have walked away with 'Fake Idol'!'

'Good idea for a show,' said Jessica, 'you should get hold of Eddie and ask him to do the filming for you - that 'minidoc' of his was brilliant - and it was going down like a dream until 'white van man' came along and stole his thunder! What a time to die of a heart attack. The poor guy ends up being world famous for fifteen minutes without even knowing it!'

'And talking of fame,' said Helena, 'You two have become pretty well known yourselves. How does it feel to have messed up everyone's cosy Shakespearean world?'

'We've had hate-mail, would you believe?' said Tony, 'and some of it very unpleasant I can tell you. As fully signed-up 'heretics', and very much the public face of what happened, only, what, five months ago, you would think it was all our doing. We've rocked the foundations, pretty thoroughly, for a huge number of Shakespeare lovers. Well, sorry about that, but, maybe they should have had the courage to listen more closely to what we were saying years ago and taken us more seriously. Fortunately, most of the reactions have been positive. One thing's for certain though, Helena; the world view of our cultural history won't be quite the same from now on.'

'Or the winding lanes of Castle Hedingham!' she said.

Notes

Sorting The Facts From The Fictions.

Although what you have just read was a novel, and, by definition, a fiction, it was stretched across a framework of truths. All of the characters portrayed in the story are a complete fiction, and bear no resemblance to any persons, living or dead. However, William Shakespeare, (or perhaps Shakspere, Shaxpere or Shagspere - there are many variations on the spelling of the name) of Stratford-upon-Avon, was a real man, as the documentary record of the time attests. This is also the case for Edward de Vere, the Seventeenth Earl of Oxford, who was a very high-ranking nobleman at the court of Queen Elizabeth I.

What follows is a short summary of that framework, enabling you to separate fact from fiction.

At times during the novel, and, especially, in these 'Notes for the Reader,' the following variation in spelling is used:

'William Shakespeare' refers to the dramatist and poet, active in London.

'William Shakspere' refers to the businessman from Stratford-upon-Avon.

The reason for this is because the spelling of the name when recorded in London is almost invariably Shakespeare or Shake-speare - pronounced with a long 'a'.

When the name is recorded in Stratford-upon-Avon it is almost invariably spelt to be pronounced with a short, hard 'a': Shackspere, Shaksberd, Shaxpere, Shakspere, etc.

WILLIAM SHAKESPEARE : 1564 - 1616.

When Tony takes Jessica on a short tour of Stratford-upon-Avon, in chapter 14, he explains many facts to her about the man commonly accepted as the great playwright and poet. The uncontested facts, listed below, are no secret, as they are all readily available to the public.

FACT: There is no documentary evidence that William Shakspere was born on 23rd April 1564. Nicholas Rowe, in the early eighteenth century, put together the first biography of Shakespeare, the dramatist, but could find no birth date. He invented a day to coincide with his (Shakspere's) death, which is recorded. (This also happily coincides with St. George's Day - that of England's patron saint). Edmond Malone (1741-1812) was the first biographer to attempt an accurate chronology of Shakespeare. (It is thanks to him that all subsequent orthodox biographers refer to the Strachey letter in order to affirmatively date *The Tempest.*).

FACT: There is no documentary evidence that the house in Henley Street, commonly called: 'Shakespeare's Birthplace', is the building in which John Shakespeare's son, William, was born. John Shakespeare acquired a house in Greenhill Street as part of the marriage settlement when he married Mary Arden. It is just as likely that William was born and raised there.

The property visited by millions today is a complete rebuild, based on an engraving of 1769, from a watercolour painting of about 1762, by a Richard Greene. Throughout the early part of the 19th Century, the property was half butcher's shop and half Inn (The Swan and Maidenhead), situated amongst a row of run-down terraced houses. The reusable timbers were saved for the reconstruction and all the surrounding properties demolished in order to create the feeling of a substantial detached house in a garden - something more fitting for a National Poet, perhaps.

FACT: There is no documentary evidence of any kind that Shakspere received an education at the King's Free School in Stratford-upon-Avon, or anywhere else, including Universities. In fact, there is no evidence that William Shakspere was able to write anything more than his name. The six extant signatures, all spelt differently, are written, or scrawled so badly in some cases, that many experts find it hard to believe that they are by the same hand.

FACT: The gravestone in the chancel of Holy Trinity

Church does not bear Shakspere's name. It is assumed to be his, because it lies between those of his wife and Thomas Nash, his granddaughter's husband. The monument on the north wall of the chancel is not the original. Documentary evidence shows that the first effigy was of a much slimmer man. He was of a very different appearance from the man we see today; his hands were on a wool-sack; there was no pen and no paper.

FACT: No 'paper trail' leads from the world of literary or dramatic endeavour in London to the world of William Shakspere, the businessman from Warwickshire.

'William Shakespeare' is on record in London as a shareholder in the Globe Theatre, a bit-part actor, tax delinquent, property dealer, and (in a court case of 1596), bound over to keep the peace, as he had threatened someone's life.

FACT: During his lifetime, the name Shakespeare or Shake-speare, appeared in print only on the title page of two narrative poems, a book of the Sonnets, some lists of players and playwrights, and several pirated copies of the plays. There is no documentary evidence that William Shakspere was ever in the company of dramatists, or that he was addressed as, or written to, as a dramatist or poet. No evidence exists that he ever received payment for any poetical or dramatic works, or authorised the printing and publishing of them.

There is no documentary evidence to indicate with complete certainty when any Shakespeare play or poem was written. However, there is documentary evidence to show when many of them were entered in the Stationer's Register, were printed, and were performed on stage.

FACT: There is no documentary evidence that either of his parents were literate, or that his wife, children or granddaughter were able to write.

FACT: In his highly detailed will, he bequeathed no books, or written or printed material of any kind, associated with literary matters.

FICTION: As far as I am aware, there is no 'original' inscription stone.

FICTION: As far as I am aware, there is no 'secret file' kept by anyone, anywhere.

EDWARD DE VERE, THE SEVENTEENTH EARL OF OXFORD : 1550 - 1604.

FACT: There is documentary evidence that he toured the continent in 1575/76, spending most of his time in Italy, visiting Venice, Verona, Padua, Milan, Genoa and Sicily on his travels. He lived in Venice for about nine months, in considerable style, 'building himself a house' (translating more accurately to 'made himself a home'), as one observer put it at the time. He ran up huge debts and had to leave the city in haste the day before Carnivale (Mon. 5th Mar. 1576) - and did, indeed, bring a Venetian choirboy with him back to England! (When Orazio Cuoco eventually returned home to Venice, all his immediate family had perished in the plague.)

FACT: Whilst in Venice he kept, for himself, a personal courtesan (prostitute). Her name was Virginia Padoana and she lived in or near the Campo San Geremia in the sestiere of Canneregio.

FACT: Many of his letters are extant and his handwriting is a very neat and regular italic. Besides his native English, he both wrote and spoke fluently in French, Italian and Latin. Some of his early poems were published under his own name and the verse form can be identified as 'Shakespearean'. He was hailed as one of the best courtier-playwrights in his lifetime.

FACT: There is documentary evidence that his father kept a company of players at Hedingham Castle (the place where Edward was born and his home until he was twelve). He was educated in the house of Sir Thomas Smith, who owned one of the largest libraries in the country, and received an MA from both Cambridge and Oxford Universities. He studied law at Gray's Inn.

FACT: On his father's death in 1562, he became the second premier Earl of England, (after his cousin the Earl of Norfolk). He was brought up as a royal ward, in Cecil House, on the

Strand, in London, by William Cecil, later Lord Burghley. When he achieved his majority Edward married Cecil's daughter Anne. His maternal uncle, Arthur Golding, who translated Ovid's *Metamorphoses* (hugely influential in a great number of Shakespeare's works), was resident there for a time as tutor and scholar when Edward was a ward. John Gerard, the country's leading expert on plants and flowers, was employed there for twenty years. He also befriended William Bird, one of the best Elizabethan musicians and composers, and John Dee, the astrologer and mystic, who was an adviser to the Queen.

FACT: There is documentary evidence that his daughters were educated and literate. His daughter Elizabeth was at one time betrothed to the 3rd Earl of Southampton, (to whom two of Shakespeare's major poetic works were dedicated), and Susan, his youngest daughter, married Phillip Herbert, 1st Earl of Montgomery. 'The Complete Works of Shakespeare', (or more correctly - MR, WILLIAM SHAKESPEARES COMEDIES, HISTORIES, & TRAGEDIES.), better known as the 'First Folio' of 1623, was dedicated to Phillip and his older brother William, the Third Earl of Pembroke, and, in it, they are referred to as "…the…Incomparable Paire of Brethren…". Their mother, Mary Sydney, the Countess of Pembroke, was, herself, a poet and patron of the arts; Shakespeare plays were performed at their home, Wilton House, near Salisbury, and the playwright Ben Jonson (widely believed to be the real editor of the First Folio), was a regular visitor.

FICTION: His precise address in Venice isn't known at the time of printing.

FICTION: The Rio di Magretti, and the Ca' Magretti-Bellini are inventions.

*For further information, the reader may wish to visit
the following websites:*

De Vere Society   www.deveresociety.co.uk

Shakespeare Oxford Society   www.shakespeare-oxford.com

Shakespeare Fellowship   www.shakespearefellowship.org

Further reading:

Anderson, Verily : *The de Veres of Castle Hedingham.*
Terence Dalton, 1993.

Bearman, Robert (Ed.): *The History of an English Borough.
Stratford-upon-Avon.* Sutton, 1997.

Bearman, Robert : *Shakespeare in the Stratford Records.*
Sutton, 1994.

Dugdale, Sir William : *Antiquities of Warwickshire,*
London, 1656.

Holmes, Edward : *Discovering Shakespeare.*
Mycroft Books, 2001.

Looney, J. Thomas : *'Shakespeare' Identified in Edward de Vere the
Seventeenth Earl of Oxford.* Cecil Palmer, London, 1920.

Malim, Richard, (Gen. Ed.): *Great Oxford.* Parapress,
Tunbridge Wells, 2004.

Mitchell, John : *Who Wrote Shakespeare?*
Thames & Hudson, 1996.

Nelson, Alan H. : *Monstrous Adversary*.
Liverpool University Press, 2003.

Ogburn, Charlton, Jr. : *The Mysterious William Shakespeare*.
New York, 1984.

Price, Diana : *Shakespeare's Unorthodox Biography*.
Greenwood Press, Westport, Connecticut, USA. 2001.

Strittmatter, Roger A. : *Edward de Vere's Geneva Bible*.
A Dissertation. University of Massachusetts, 2001.

Wraight, A. D. : *The Story the Sonnets Tell*. Adam Hart,
London, 1994.